PENDANT OF DRAGONS BOOK THREE

THE END OF ALL THINGS

K. ISABELLA FROST

Printed in Australia
First Printing, 2021
ISBN:978-0-6487529-1-2

White Light Publishing

*In memory of my good friend and mentor Charles Slucki,
who had so much faith in me and these stories.*

Acknowledgements

With this book, the third in the series, the story of Princess Leander Aldrich, Carden Highever, Amethyst and all their friends continues, heading now into a much darker time of their lives. But that's something we all face, hopefully with so many people backing us and helping us along the path through these shadows. And while we often feel like we walk alone, even in thoughts and love, and through the memories of those we've lost we are able to continue on.

I have had so much help as I've progressed through this book, the first of the darkest instalments of the Pendant of Dragons series, and I am so grateful for it. Of course, I've had help from my family, my friends, fellow authors who have helped me riddle out the plot, but also the darkest times of my life have helped me. There is no greater teacher than life itself.

I would like to thank Charles R. Slucki for his help in developing this book, for letting me read it to him and telling him the story as it was a work in progress. I hope this book makes him proud, wherever he is. And without him I would never have gotten into the head of my Princess, his mentoring of me as both an actress and a writer what has led me to the moment of releasing these books.

As always, thanks to my parents, Lynne and Kevin, my godparents, Sandy and Charlie, and to my siblings, Patrick, Jessie and David, for all their support and time spent together reading and telling stories. To those that have passed and that simply aren't present with me physically, like my grandparents, Fred and Betty Webster, my uncle and aunt, Allan and Liz Webster, and to fellow creatives Clarity Townsend, Liv Evans and Kade Everett. Those of you who have passed continue to inspire me in spirit, while those of you in other places of the world do so in many other ways. I hope we get to see each other in the flesh one day.

And to everyone at Mystical Dragon and White Light Publishing. Your continued support and inspiration will always be appreciated, and these books would not exist without you. Especially to Jennifer Valente, Amanda Godfrey, Karen McDermott, Julia Van Der Sluys and Lauren Kelly. Thank you so much.

Lastly, once more, thank you to the readers, both old and new, for turning these pages and giving this story life. I hope the third instalment of the story thrills you and brings you to the depths of all of your emotions. And maybe even inspire some new storytellers too. Thank you, and enjoy...

- K. Isabella Frost

Contents

Preface

Death had haunted me for *three* long, agonizing years, following me at every turn, prowling at my back like some great and terrible predator. Knowing what fate lay before me, I should have resigned myself to it, found the peace needed to face this horror and grief with the calm of a girl of my standing. But I couldn't.

Every fibre of my being fought to escape this terrible dark reality, to find a way to stop this from being truth. I had lost too many people I loved to Death's cold embrace, had prayed to Azmerath to guide them safely into the Beyond far too frequently of late.

But *this* promised death... *this* one I fought the hardest against, hoping that there was still time enough left to prevent another, worse tragedy.

I can't let this happen! I cried out in my tremulous and frantic thoughts. *I have to stop this! I have to stop Him! This can't become reality! It just can't!*

His dark smile beckoned to me, his cold, coarse, grey fingers curling to draw me forward. The gleam of those green eyes glowing beneath his shadowed cowl only strengthened my fear; his very presence trying to crush back my fighting spirit.

No! I decided as I met his cold, glowing gaze, my eyes darting to the sinister blade in his hand. *I will not let this happen! I will fight this! This will not be the end of all things!*

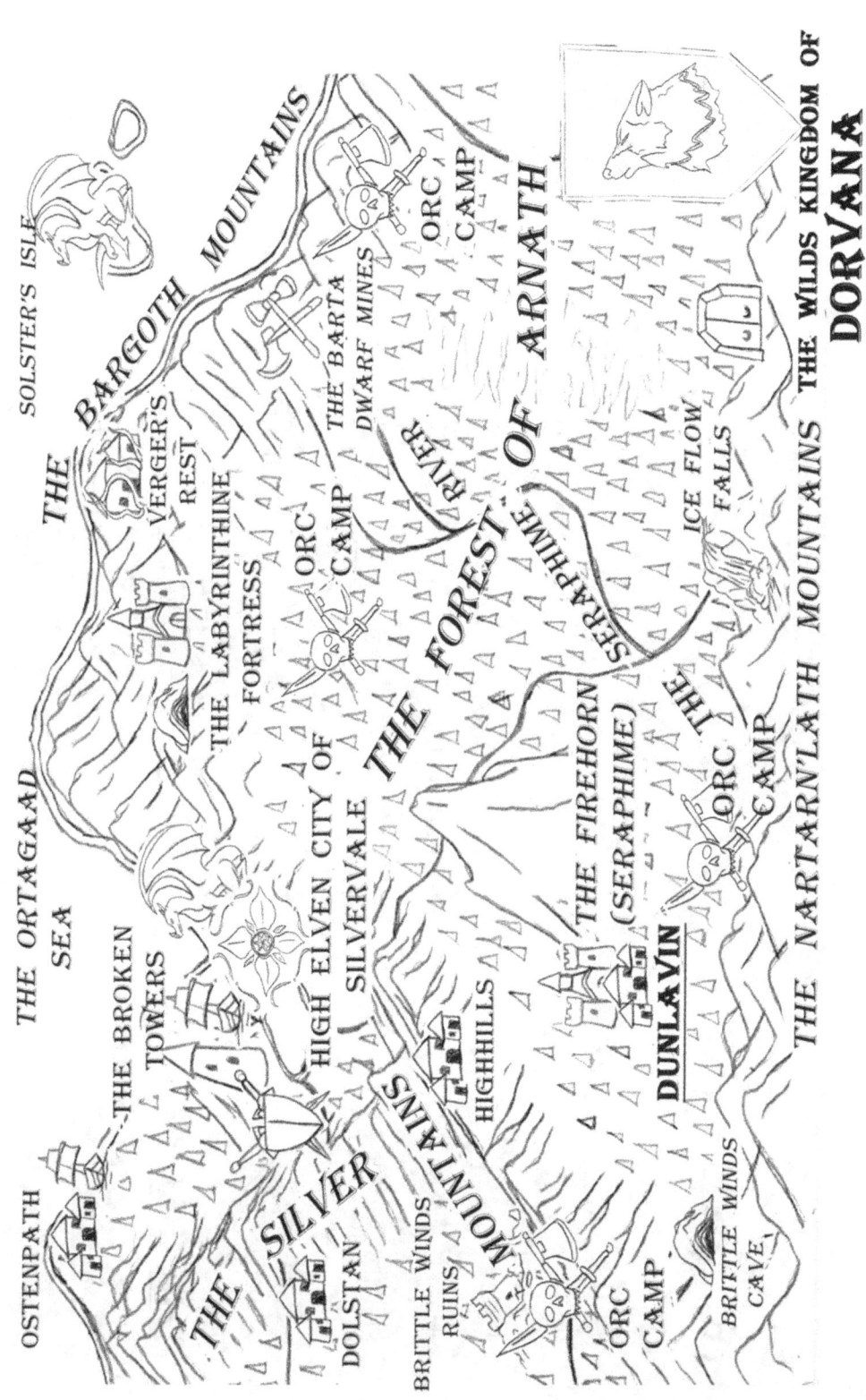

THE WILDS KINGDOM OF

DORVANA

THE BARGOTH MOUNTAINS

SOLSTER'S ISLE

THE ORTAGAAD SEA

THE BROKEN TOWERS

OSTENPATH

VERGER'S REST

THE BARTA DWARF MINES

ORC CAMP

THE LABYRINTHINE FORTRESS

ORC CAMP

THE FOREST OF ARNATH

ICE FLOW FALLS

SERAPHIME RIVER

HIGH ELVEN CITY OF SILVERVALE

THE FIREHORN (SERAPHIME)

ORC CAMP

DOLSTAN

THE SILVER MOUNTAINS

BRITTLE WINDS RUINS

HIGHHILLS

DUNLAVIN

THE NARTARN'LATH MOUNTAINS

ORC CAMP

BRITTLE WINDS CAVE

11

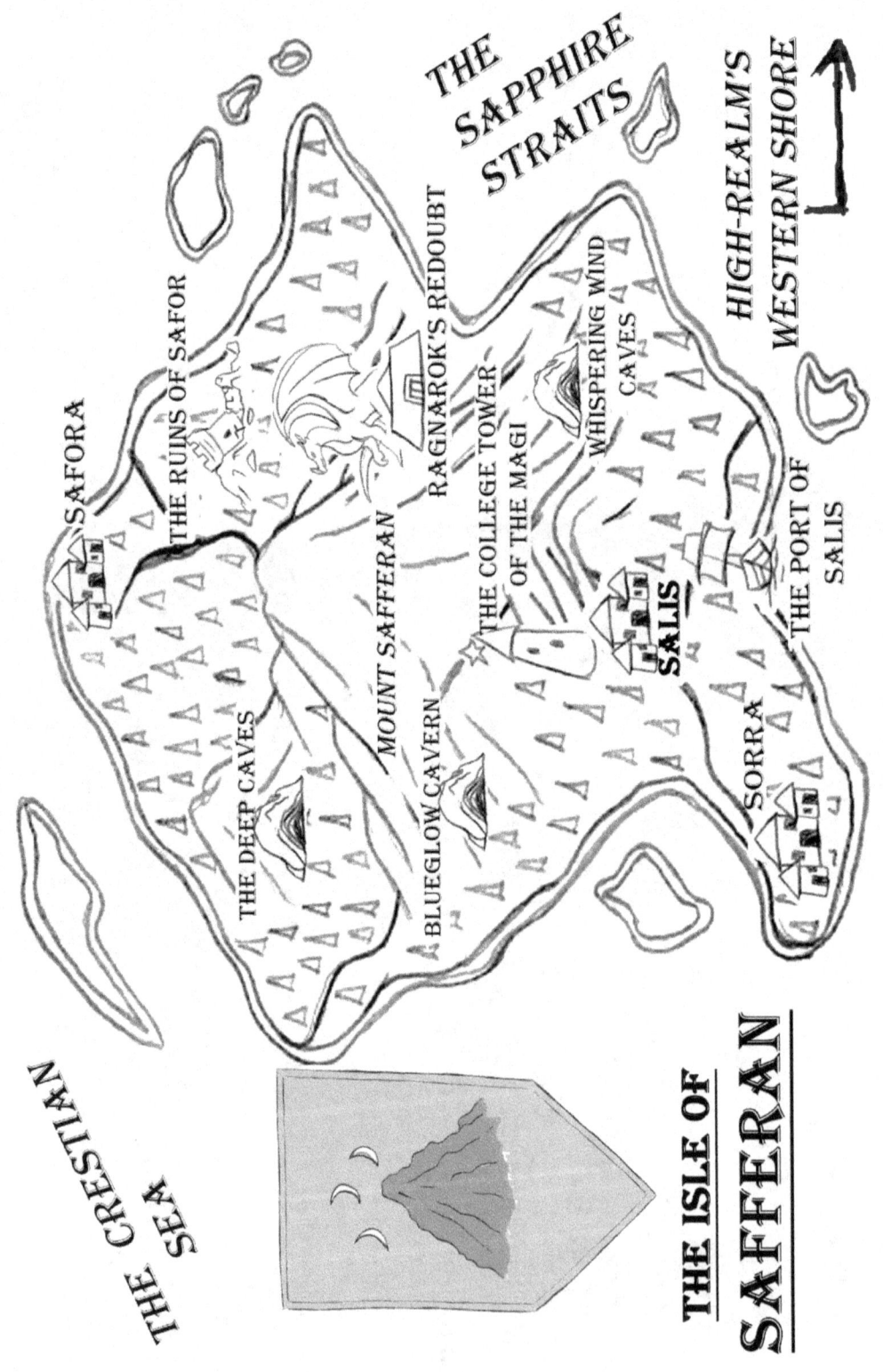

THE SAPPHIRE STRAITS

HIGH-REALM'S WESTERN SHORE

SAFORA

THE RUINS OF SAFOR

RAGNAROK'S REDOUBT

MOUNT SAFFERAN

THE COLLEGE TOWER OF THE MAGI

WHISPERING WIND CAVES

THE DEEP CAVES

A BLUEGLOW CAVERN

SALIS

THE PORT OF SALIS

SORRA

THE CRESTIAN SEA

THE ISLE OF SAFFERAN

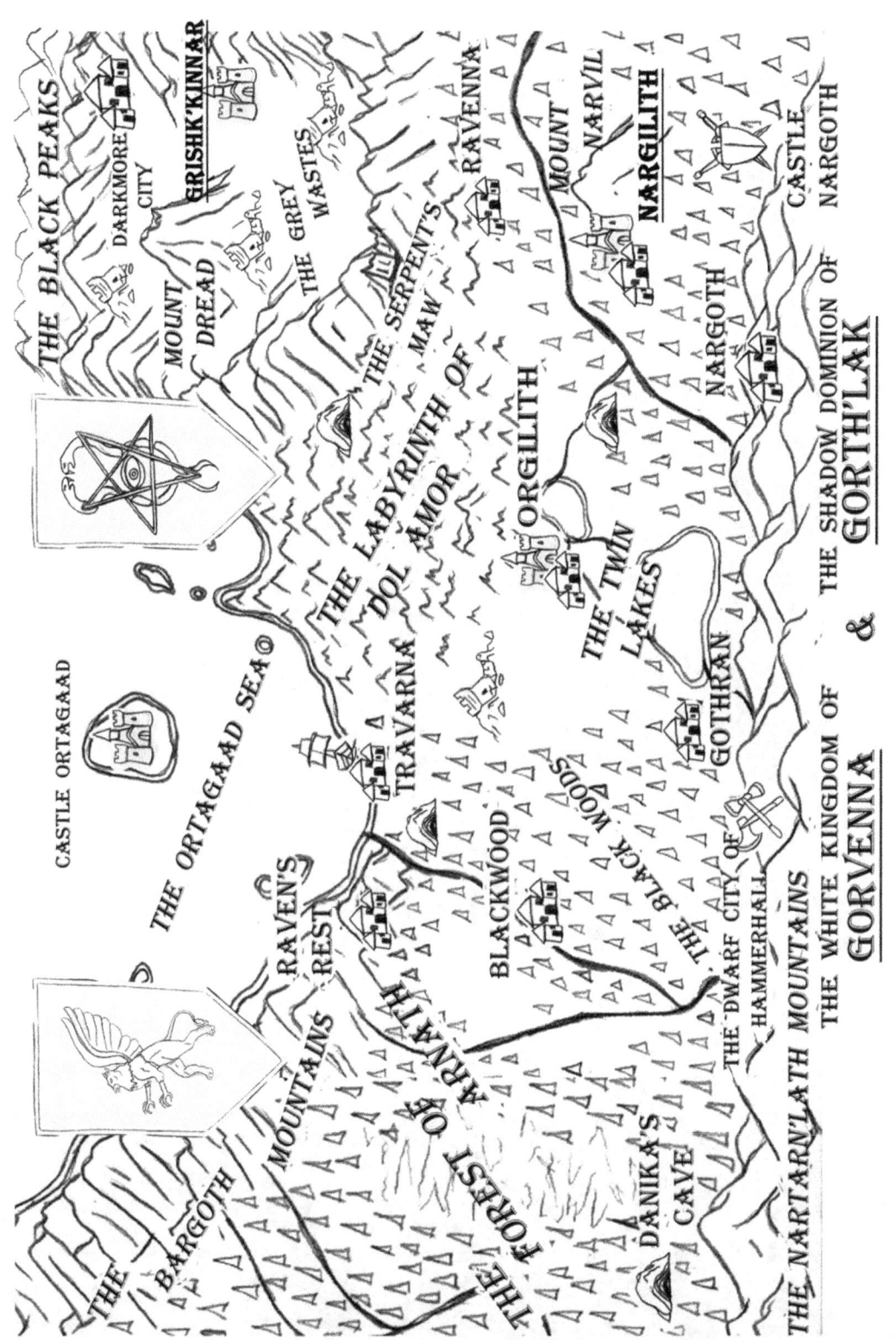

THE BLACK PEAKS

DARKMORE CITY

GRISHK'KINNAR

MOUNT DREAD

THE GREY WASTES

THE SERPENT'S MAW

THE LABYRINTH OF DOL AMOR

RAVENNA

MOUNT NARVIL

NARGILITH

ORGILITH

THE TWIN LAKES

NARGOTH

CASTLE NARGOTH

THE SHADOW DOMINION OF NARGOTH

CASTLE ORTAGAAD

THE ORTAGAAD SEA

TRAVARNA

GOTHRAN

THE DWARF CITY OF HAMMERHALL

GORTH'LAK

RAVEN'S REST

MOUNTAINS

THE BARGOTH MOUNTAINS

BLACKWOOD

THE BLACK WOODS

&

THE FOREST OF ARNATH

DANIKA'S CAVE

THE NARTARN'LATH MOUNTAINS

THE WHITE KINGDOM OF GORVENNA

Chapter One
The West Tower

T he warm sea-salted air and the call of white gulls was dulled by the panes of the large window; the gleam of the sun scintillating against the surface of the rolling waves far below dazzling as it accented the darker blue of the water beneath the brighter azure of the sky. Only a few white fluffy clouds made any kind of move to shield the brilliant hue, the sun allowed to shed its glow down over the white and grey stone city without hindrance.

It was one of those rare days where the rains didn't overtake the land with their cold drizzle and the clouds had no desire to take on their darker complexion. If I were to look out across the city to the north on a day like this, I would be able to clearly see the hazy shapes of the mountains without any trouble.

Leaning back against the wall where I sat perched on the softly padded ledge beneath the window, I let out a soft sigh, the slightly open pane of a smaller one nearby allowing the refreshingly warmed air to enter the room. It tickled my skin and made my auburn locks gust slightly at my neck, the clasp holding the strands at my nape doing its best to keep them from flowing wildly, though the breeze was too miniscule to have such an affect.

Relief filled my body after so long in a colder climate that I almost felt as if I couldn't remember being anywhere else, my right hand grazing my pendant's silvery shape where it dangled from my neck. Just being there was perfect, the sounds of Aneuran's streets below the palace only adding a new and further comfort to me while I relaxed myself. There were no aches now, though I felt certain that there should have been, but I couldn't recall why.

Letting my hand drop from my neck, I allowed my fingers to caress the inked words on the page I had the hardcover, leather bound book open to. Instinctively, I ran my fingers along each line as I read silently to myself, enjoying the story that lay within the smooth paper pages.

In the back of my mind, I had a minor thought reflect back to me as I read, somehow having the two separate mental focuses at once: *This is just what I needed. Some time to myself without people partitioning me for this and that. It's nice to have a break from my duties and stresses for a while...*

At that moment, I caught a strange sound warbling through the rooms around me, lifting my gaze from the page as a frown pulled at my smooth white brow. It seemed to be coming from the doorway I had my back to; the one whose archway stood only a few meters from the large window. Its tone was desperate, almost pained, like crying... a child crying.

That's a baby, I realised in surprise, closing my book and lowering my feet from where I had them resting on the cushioned ledge to the floor. *Why is there a baby crying in my rooms?*

Setting the book down, I got to my feet and started to slowly pad through the room, my slippers scraping the stone floor as I softly crossed the blue and gold carpet, passing by the lounge furniture of the space full of bookshelves. I barely took note of the fact that this was a royal apartment within the palace, that of a high-ranking member of the sovereign family. This was the sitting room that I had converted into a private library, the archway opposite the windows I had been sitting at opening to a small dining room where we took our meals.

It seemed odd to me that I had this knowledge when I also felt as if I should have been somewhere else, but I ignored it and continued through the open door to the next room.

With a flow of blue velvet around my ankles from my dress, I entered another room that looked like a bedroom, but minus a bed. Instead there was a white bassinette made of fine wood and dressed in the same blue as the rest of the palace's decor. The cry was coming from within its wicker walls and I found myself hesitating a little as I approached to look inside.

Nestled amongst soft white cushioning and warm white furs, there lay a tiny baby in swaddling clothes. It was no more than a month old, by my guess, it's eyes full of tears as it fussed and squirmed, its tiny hands shaking the way babies' hands do. I couldn't tell if it was hungry or needed changing, or perhaps just wanted to be held, finding myself overwhelmed by the sight of it.

Why is no one looking after this baby? I wondered, feeling a little distressed by its cries.

I stirred myself into action, gently reaching into the bassinette and lifting her into my arms. Now I realised that it was a girl, her whimpers and sobs so full of desperation that it made my heart ache.

"Shh... it's all right," I cooed gently, cradling her head in the crook of my right arm with my hand supporting her tiny shape, my left arm encircling her body with its palm to support her neck. "It's all right. I'm here. I've got you."

I started to slowly pace, my long blue dress trailing around me as I tried to soothe the baby, gently bouncing on the balls of my feet with each step I took. It was working because she started to calm down and her eyes opened wider to show me the gentle green of their irises. Her cries faded and she stared at me in silence, comfort in my arms the need that she had sought to have fulfilled.

A tear trickled down my cheek as my heart warmed at the sight of my beautiful newborn daughter, remembering that I had given birth to her less than five weeks ago. And with this revelation came so much happiness that I couldn't help but smile as I moved with her to the balcony to take in the warm sea air as we overlooked the city below.

"Leander?" a familiar male voice called as I stared into my baby's eyes, drawing my attention to the door.

"In here," I called.

Carden appeared there in only a moment, his expression warming at the sight of the two of us. He looked different to me somehow, the green of his eyes seeming brighter and his hair cut shorter, though still grazing his ears and forehead with its strands. He was no longer in Guardian attire but now wearing a dark blue doublet trimmed in gold that hung to his knees, all of his clothes now looking very regal.

"Carden," I smiled as I saw him, turning my attention back to our daughter as he crossed the room to join me by the doors.

"How is she?" he asked gently, placing his hands on my half-bared shoulders, pinning the blue of my dress to my snowy skin with his palms.

"She just wanted to be held," I replied softly, still rocking the baby gently. "That's all. She hardly ever cries except for when she wants me to hold her."

"And how about you?" he asked, leaning his face closer to mine. "How are you feeling, my love?"

I looked up at him, shrugging a little. "Tired, of course. But I'm getting better."

"I suppose a labour as hard as the one you just had would make you tired," he contemplated, still holding my shoulders. "I must say that I am amazed you are so active after it."

"I have no desire to lay in bed and let the servants tend to our child," I confessed, looking back down at her as she wrapped her tiny fingers into the velvet of my bodice. "I've waited too long to hold our baby in my own arms, and I won't allow someone else to raise her. That's our job."

"It is," he agreed with his own smile, lifting his finger and pressing it into her tiny hand. She immediately squeezed around his broad, long fingertip; her tiny digits barely able to enwrap it since she was so small.

I smiled as I watched him and her, my life feeling suddenly complete. This was the happiness I had longed for my whole life and I wanted nothing to prevent me from enjoying it. Yet, a cold chill that didn't belong in our warm world was casting against my back, and I felt myself beginning to slip from this place of bliss towards something darker... something that I longed to avoid. No matter how hard I tried to hold onto my baby and my husband, I felt my grip on this beautiful happiness fading away with the deepening of that relentlessly bitter chill that belonged in another world...

* * * * *

The cold wind woke me from the awkward, restless sleep I had spent so long trying to become accustomed to. It was like being pulled through a blizzard from the partial safety of my dreams and into a chill so cruel that escape would be impossible. Lying on my right side, I shivered against the frigid air, resisting my eyes' incredible urge to open, but this struggle was as unsuccessful as those that had brought me to my heartless imprisonment.

My eyes opened and the drab, grey confines of the tower cell flooded my waking vision. A small whimper of despair escaped my lips as I shut my eyes and dragged the worn, old blankets tightly around me.

As my cruel reality took the place of my truly blissful dreams, I felt my heart cry out and desperation clutch at me. Trying to recall the beautiful dream I'd had gave me nothing, every detail now lost to me along with the happiness it had filled me with, leaving only sadness in its place. I struggled against the tears threatening to wet my cheeks, their existence guaranteeing me a greater cold on my already vulnerable skin. My left hand buried its fingers into the faded pillows, clutching there as I wept beside them.

Once again, I found myself fearing the one who had put me here, expecting him to come and make good on his promised end. The last day I saw him replayed in my mind, and I heard his cold voice in my head.

"This little game of ours will one day come to an end, and only I shall stand as the victor. And as you know your last moments are approaching, you will look back fondly upon your time in this cold, dank tower cell and long to return, if only to forestall your end..."

My hand instantly reached for my pendant, my fingers only caressing the chilled skin of my chest and collarbones. Frantically, for a moment, I wondered where my treasured necklace and silent companion was, my thoughts soon clearing sleep away enough so that I remembered.

They took it from me, I reminded myself sadly. *Keilantra took the Pendant from me for herself, just as the Shadow Lord has taken everything else. Everything...*

The very thought of the monster whose dark desires dominated my life as it had become frightened me more than the cruelty I had suffered here. His nightmarish visage haunted me, leaving me fearing his sudden appearance in my cold prison.

I imagined him often, standing at the foot of the bed, wreathed in smoky darkness and shrouded in robes of deepest shadows. His supernatural eyes would flare their eerie green and his thin, grey lips would curl into that cruel smile. In that alone I would be made to dread my unknown fate and burst into a new flood of teary sorrow. But so far, he had never come back to me.

Slowly, as I had every day since coming to this frozen purgatory, I lifted myself painfully from the creaking bed and set my feet to the floor.

Undressing was decidedly unwise for me here, the cold of the cell such that it could only hurt me. My boots shielded my feet from the stone, my long sleeves and skirts protecting as much of my body from the chill as they could, though there was little comfort to be found. As for modesty's sake, it was easier to hide myself from the perverted guards who watched these cells and their base desires towards me if I stayed clothed.

Awkwardly, I stood, the icy air instantly hitting me as I did, my hand automatically snatching the blanket from the bed with the rattling of the chains on my wrists.

Pulling the blanket around my shoulders, I crossed the room to the narrow window. I had considered it many times, the space large enough to poke my head and one arm through, but definitely not a means of escape. From that window, I could see the north-western side of the castle, the ocean stretching far below towards distant shores I could barely see. Beyond the high walls of this place opposite my cell lay the northern shores of High-Realm somewhere to the south, the castle set on an icy island off the nation of Gorvenna.

I strained a little to my right to catch the only view available to me other than blank, empty seas. To the north-east I saw the jagged walls of the Black Peaks, the dark wastes of Gorth'lak lying behind them. Dirty ash clouds choked the shadowy skies above the peaks, green lightning flashing violently through the smoky black. I could even glimpse the fires of Dread Mountain glowing in the evil land's westernmost heart, burning relentlessly and strangling the air with its sulphur smoke plumes.

I shuddered hard, wrapping the blanket further around myself as I stared at the dark land. *He* was in there somewhere, set on Gorth'lak's Black Throne, reigning with malice and cruelty.

I knew he was thinking of me, my heart choking in my chest from his dread thoughts. He had bound me to him, trapped me so that I depended on him for my safety and survival - if it could even be called that. In every moment I felt him watching me, left to only imagine what twisted thoughts he entertained of me, his helpless and unwilling pet. He dominated me, keeping me afraid and alone as much as his sinister servants did, leaving me fearing the next torture he could devise to inflict upon me.

He's not here... Relax... He's not here...

Slowly, breathing deeply and evenly, but painfully, I sat in the corner near the window, hugging my knees to my chest and staring up at the cloudy grey sky. It was snowing, but that was common enough this far north. Yet even the ice couldn't halt the ebbing of the tides of the sea between the castle and the mainland, the crashing of the waves echoing far below the tower. I guess that was why Gorvennan prisoners were sent to Castle Ortagaad. It was truly inescapable.

I rested my head against the wall and sighed, my chest feeling tight.

Gods, please, what are they going to do to me today? What horrors will I be forced to endure? Or will I be left to my loneliness again?

I sucked in a shaky breath and closed my eyes against fresh tears.

Silently, knowing I couldn't escape, I prayed to Azmerath for a quick death, hoping the God would grant such a needed kindness. It would be better than this fate. Anything would be. Yet, my faith in the Gods was fading and had been for this time beyond all my counting spent in my silent, frozen limbo.

Do any of you even still hear me? I asked them silently, glancing up at the stone bricked ceiling as if to their divine realms beyond the heavens. *Does my life even matter to you?*

I slumped back against the wall and let fresh tears slip past my cheeks to my collarbones, hugging my knees tighter.

Maybe... maybe you aren't even there anymore, I said without my voice. *How many days beyond counting have I languished in this prison, only to be abandoned by your presence? How many cruel and humiliating tortures have the sisters inflicted upon me, only to find not even the smallest of protests from you? How many times have I screamed to you in desperate need, only to be ignored? Do you even care? Or is the life of one innocent girl suffering such terrible hurts and grievous losses insignificant to your eyes?*

I sighed and found myself sobbing anew, burying my face into my arms. *I don't care to have justice anymore, Thringar. Or for you to show sympathy and love for me, Isnari. Or for Maveria to bring the balance of the elements to gift me with even the slightest of chances to escape my terrible fate. You are the only one of all that I now call to, Azmerath. Please, let me lose myself in my sleep and find peace in the Beyond. Take me into Death and away from this torturous nightmare being forced on me. My faith and hope in escape is like my strength: wanning fast with each dreaded day I wake to find myself in this terrible place.*

I sat back against the wall and once again stared up at the ceiling through my fresh, rapidly chilling tears, imagining that the God could hear me: *Please, just grant me freedom from this life. Everything has been taken from me, so I might as well pass over.*

I waited in silence, measuring my senses and taking note of my body. But there were no changes, no call from my heart that it had decided to cease its constant beat. I still drew breath into my lungs and still felt the chill of the room around me, and the shackles' tightness on my wrists.

Fine, I soured mentally. *I guess I have my answer.*

I curled up again and stared aimlessly with silent tears at the bottom edge of the wall where it met the floor stones. There was no way for me to know how long I sat like this, no comprehension of any kind of time beyond the seemingly endless moments spent shivering. What felt like an hour could be ten minutes, and what seemed an eternity was nothing more than a few moments passing at a time. Even the seasons gave me nothing, only the icy cold of this wintry sea and wasteland lying beyond the castle's sinister walls existing. It was only when day became night, and returned once again to day, that I had any inkling at all of the passage of time. All else was static and unmoving.

I shivered hard, the cold seeming to deepen this high above the sea's swirling frozen skins. The blanket wrapped around me was losing its comfort and I knew that I needed more proactive attempts for warmth.

I stood and moved to the fireplace, setting myself down on the other, far more worn blanket that I used for cushioning against the hard floor. I let the blanket I wore hang from my shoulders and down my back over my dark teal dress, my slender hands scooping up what hay and kindling I could from the ground.

It's too cold. I need to light the fire again. I need to stay warm.

I had grown accustomed to the chains on my wrists, managing to turn my hands from them so as not to find them barring my fingers from my few menial tasks.

Meticulously, I made a small pile in the fireplace of twigs and hay, this was all that my captors would give me to aid in my quest for warmth. At least they worried enough to grant me this one kindness, though I was certain the Witches would be enraged if they had to face their Master and explain why I had frozen to death in their keeping.

I took up the flint and striking stone, slashing them together close to the kindling, sparks raining with brief flashes in the plain grey hearth with every hit.

Come on, I pleaded to the stone and flint. *Please, just light. Please...*

It took me four more tries, but finally a small flame began to burn atop the kindling. I leaned down, my palms to the floor, and gently blew through my lips. With each gentle breath I gave to the flames, they gained size and life until at last there was a small fire burning in the hearth. As the flames grew on their own, I sat back on my haunches and watched them, casting a few more pieces of kindling from the basket near the fireplace into their hungry golden-orange tongues. The warmth spreading over me was a small comfort, but the only one I had come to expect in this place.

Eagerly, I reached my trembling hands towards the heat of the fire, chasing away the bite of the deep cold. I rubbed the warmth from my hands up and down my arms and chest, placing my palms back to the flames as I edged a little closer, my eyes focused on my fingertips and my pink nails, watching the light dance beneath them.

I still hadn't managed to fix my right sleeve, the ribbon gone, whereas its twin still kept my left sleeve tied shut over my wrist. I let the split of pale blue fabric fall back in on itself as I turned the inside of my wrist up to study it, my fingers gently curling so that their tips aimed towards me. Though my pale white skin was perfect as I ran my left hand across the silkiness of my wrist, I remembered the scar that had once lingered there. That wound which my monstrous captor had healed after his overzealous loyalist had inflicted it on me was now long gone. But it was never forgotten.

My mind wandered back to that dark and terrible ceremony countless turnings of the world ago, the fear, humiliation and pain of it still fresh in my young mind.

This wound, I recalled, *was the true moment I was condemned. It was when they took the last thing I had left to me...*

I turned my eyes back to the fire, letting my hands fold together against my thighs. My tears hadn't ceased their terrible march the whole time I had been fighting to light the hearth, their heat pressuring behind my lower eyelids only to salt my skin further.

What am I? that single haunting question came back to me in the latest of an incalculable number of times. *Am I even still human? I can't age. I can't change. Gods, I can't live anymore. I don't even survive... I just... exist. I might as well be a ghost.*

I sniffed back my tears and sobs, trying to ease my aching heart as I once again tossed kindling into the flames.

And what existence do I have? Lying in this cell, fearful of the pains my abductors plan to force on me? It's no way to live or even exist.

I thought of my parents and of Mithras, of my sister still living somewhere south of where I now found myself.

Oh, how I wish I was home with you. That it wasn't just Aislinn and I living, but all of us, safe in Arvon. How I miss the Great River and the Nartarn'lath Mountains. What I wouldn't give to be held in your arms, Father, and to hear your sweet songs, Mother; the ones you sang to me when I was a child. A small smile tugged fondly at my lips. *Oh, Mithras, to see your face of amusement as I thrash your squires in the training room and hear your guidance regarding my skills with a sword. If only I could go back to those wonderful, happier days...*

Stop it! I scolded myself. *Thinking of home isn't helping me. Only Aislinn and I are left of our family - excluding Fane and his family, of course. I have to accept that. Mother, Father, Uncle Aric, Aunt Evangeline, Mithras... they can't come back. They were all stolen from me, just as my freedom and my humanity was. Stop. Thinking. About. Them.*

I sighed glumly.

There was so very little for me to occupy myself with in that cell and these thoughts easily slipped through to crack my already aching heart because of that. Finding a distraction had become impossible, my captors offering me next to nothing beyond the barest of necessities to keep me alive.

No books to read and lose myself in. No parchment or ink to write with. No one to even speak to. Maybe they're trying to drive me insane by forcing me to listen to only my own thoughts.

Even so, I had gotten used to sitting alone, though it had never stopped being hard or boring. Sleep had become my last salvation and I found myself napping more than I ever had, not from tiredness, but from lack of anything else.

A painful growl filled my midriff and I doubled over, clutching my slender hands to my stomach.

My gods, I am so hungry! I groaned loudly against the pain that rumbled within me. *Do they even plan to feed me at all today? Or am I to continue starving?*

I was agonizingly aware that I was thinner than I had been when I was last in Fawkner's house. The less than adequate food I was supplied barely kept me even nourished, let alone sated. Worse still, my captors saw to it that on certain days I would be left with little to nothing to eat. I was instantly worried that this would be another of those terrible foodless days.

I was grateful that my bodice was corded - given how much weight I had lost - able to tighten the black length crisscrossing the front of my dress together so that I was still firmly clothed. At least my body had seemed to have stopped thinning; very little fat remaining around my midriff, leaving me more lithe than I had already been.

It has been so long since last I had a decent hot meal or even eaten more than once in a day, I shuddered as another wave of hunger slapped me, closing my eyes as I felt sick. *Oh please, let me eat something...*

The sound of the doors from the room beyond my cell unlocking drew my swift gaze. They were coming in, though I couldn't tell who.

Like a frightened rabbit, I rushed into hiding by the wall nearest the bed, pressing myself into the shadowy corner just under the archway of my cell. I watched uneasily around the stone edge and through the iron bars, fearful of what travesties might come through the door. My breath hitched in my chest and I cringed back into the corner, only one eye surveying the chamber as the door opened.

The Witch Queen's Knight-Commander entered in his black and gold surcoat, his cloak swaying behind him and his armour clinking with his movements. The gryphon heraldry on his chest was like an insult to the great nation of Gorvenna, the sovereignty of my father's friend, King Thoralf the Greater, not of that foul woman and her wicked sister. As far as I was concerned, not *one* of the soldiers bearing that gryphon in this place was worthy of its honour.

Ulric didn't heed me any notice, his attentions on unlocking the cell across from mine as his men dragged in a struggling, thrashing figure. Between them was a girl, perhaps as old as I looked in my cursed unending youth, her clothes that of a commoner.

"Please!" she screamed frantically, tears rushing down her face like a rapid river. "I didn't do anything! Let me go! Please! Please!"

Her pleas were ignored as the men threw her to the floor inside the cell, Ulric slamming the door shut and sealing her in with only a small barred window to look through.

"Please!" she was at the window in moments, sobbing as her fingers grasped the bars. "Don't do this to me! Let me go! I've done nothing!"

Ulric regarded her coldly with his harsh emerald eyes. "I care not if you have committed a crime. Your fate is decided, and the Queen has condemned you."

"Please... help me..." she wept.

"You will find," he sneered at her cruelly, "that there are no friends to be found in this place."

She pulled away from the bars and I heard her hysterical cries of anguish from her cell.

Ulric had that same arrogantly leering smile as he stepped from her cell and gestured for the soldiers to leave. As he moved towards the door he paused, spotting me where I knelt fearfully in the shadows of my cell.

I feared what terrible words would ooze from his foul mouth, dreading the carnal fantasies and lustful remarks swirling in his depraved cesspool of a mind. Thankfully, all I received was that widening smirk, a light chuckle, and then he was gone with the slamming and locking of the outer door to the chamber.

I felt myself release the breath I had been holding in apprehension, all of my muscles relaxing.

Silence and the other girl's cries were all that remained, the guards leaving the chamber once more. Still, I didn't move, hesitant to even make a sound, remembering that any prisoner brought to this room may be one of the wicked sisters using an illusion to fool me. Too many times now Manth had used such tricks during my imprisonment to offer me false hope.

I can't just sit here though. I should take the chance to speak to her, even if it is just the Witch playing with me, I thought.

I hesitated, then slowly got to my feet, and moved further along the bars of my cell, trying to get a clear look at the other girl. From what I had seen of her she was definitely a Gorvennan, her hair like raven wings, her eyes like emeralds, her skin more olive than my fairer tone.

I wasn't sure that I could even speak, thirst clinging to my throat as I realised that it had been at least several days since I had actually used my voice. For the rest of that time I had been alone and silent.

I brushed my long dark hair over my right ear as I peered through the bars at the other cell, my efforts to see inside futile. My fingers grasped the bars between the squared off gaps and I composed myself.

It's better than sitting in silence, I thought. *And she could certainly use hearing a friendly voice.*

"Hello?" I croaked out softly, only half expecting an answer. "Hello? Are you all right?"

The girl appeared at the window and looked through at me with her tear soaked green eyes. I couldn't help but feel sorry for her. This was a pain I knew all too well.

"Who...? Are you a prisoner too?" she asked me through fading sobs.

I nodded, knowing she could see me with the window at my back. "Yes. What is your name?"

"My name is Virida," she whispered uneasily. "What's yours?"

"Leander," I murmured, the sound of my own name so foreign to me after so long without hearing it aloud. "Why did the soldiers bring you here? What were you accused of?"

"I don't know!" she moaned sadly. "They took me from my family's home outside of Travarna! I begged to know why they brought me here, but they wouldn't tell me! The men here are *so* cruel!"

I just nodded, not really sure how to respond. The truth of the guards' cruelty was beyond their unwillingness to explain a prisoner's crime. I was so certain that very few prisoners here were actually guilty of anything, especially the young women.

"Why are you here?" Virida asked me softly.

I glanced up and shrugged sadly. "I... I'm like you. They kidnapped me. I haven't committed any crime either."

"How can the King allow this?!" she exclaimed in terror and outrage. "How can he?!"

"The King is bewitched," I told her truthfully. "The Queen and her sister are witches and have poisoned his mind. It's them that keep us, not King Thoralf."

"How long have you been here?" she was studying me carefully, her expression that of vague familiarity.

I shrugged again and shook my head. "I don't know. A long time, I think. I've honestly lost track."

"That's terrible," she gasped.

I became very curious about the world beyond the castle walls. Virida had only just been brought here, meaning that she had more knowledge about current events than I did. There were questions I suddenly had, my mind urging me to ask them.

"Please, can you tell me what has happened in High-Realm recently?" I implored her gently, a little too hurriedly. "What has happened in Aldegaad?"

"Um... well," she thought about it uncertainly at first. "Just recently, Prince Fane Aldrich was crowned as King of Aldegaad..."

"What?!" I was horrified.

"There has been fighting throughout Aldegaad," she went on. "Some of the nobility have begun arguing against his rule, especially after the tensions between Aldegaad and Ivansten have started to worsen. Many of the Lords think the new King is a tyrant. They refuse to follow him. They still hold their loyalty to King Aric."

I felt a little reassured. "Then there are still those who would fight in my uncle's name..." I murmured to myself.

"Your uncle?" she frowned, having heard me, then her eyes went wide. "You're King Aric's niece?"

I nodded faintly but didn't speak.

"My Gods, your Highness, what are you doing here in Gorvenna?" she was very animated now as she spoke, though still afraid.

"Fane forced me to flee from Aldegaad," I confessed. "I was betrayed by someone..." my heart twinged at the thought,"...by someone I thought was a friend, and given to the Shadow Lord who rules Gorth'lak..."

"Then... the rumours are true?" she sounded terrified. "There truly is another Shadow Lord?"

"Yes. He had me imprisoned here in the keeping of the Witches of Raven's Rest, one of whom is Gorvenna's Queen," I explained quietly. "I don't know what he plans to do with me, but I know he never intends to let me go."

"Oh Gods," she was tearing up again. "A Shadow Lord... the Witches of Raven's Rest... These were all terrible stories I heard the boys in Travarna joke about. I didn't think them real."

"I know," I sighed. "Neither did I."

She looked up at me worriedly, trembling more at the knowledge of being imprisoned by the dreaded witches. If it were at all possible, her fear had more than tripled than when she had first entered the tower.

"W-what will they do with us?" her voice was shaking.

I shook my head uncertainly. "I'm... uh... I'm really not sure..."

"I've heard stories... of the Witches taking young girls from their homes," Virida murmured with terror tinting her words. "And with the Forests of Arnath on Gorvenna's border with Dorvana, people often speak of the necromancer taking victims to kill and make into a legion of undead."

"The Revenant of Arnath?" I frowned.

She nodded. "That is what the Dorvans call him. Here in Gorvenna we call him the Necromancer Wraith," she looked around at the walls surrounding us. "Knowing that this is where those terrible Witches are..." she was starting to cry again.

There was nothing I could say, no words of comfort I could offer her, for I had none to give myself.

"Have there been other girls brought here?" she asked me through her fresh tears.

I was hesitant to answer, but I knew there was no point in lying to her: "Yes."

"What became of them?"

"I don't know," I said honestly. "They... they never stay long before the guards come to take them from here. I don't know what happens to them, but they are never brought back."

"Never?" she looked horrified.

I shook my head. "I'm the only girl they bring back to this tower."

"What will they do with me?" she worried, staring at me hopelessly.

I shook my head, my gaze dropping from her face to the floor. I had no answers, not even any theories. I couldn't bring myself to lie to this poor girl. It felt wrong and offering false hope would be too cruel.

"I'm sorry, Virida," I murmured, studying my hands where they gripped the bars. "I wish I could tell you more and I wish I had comfort to offer."

"It's all right. Thank you, Princess," she seemed grateful all the same despite her fearfulness. "It is just nice to hear one friendly voice in this dark place."

I nodded, then turned away and moved to sit back down before the fire. I took up another few pieces of kindling, feeding the flames and helping them grow a little more, spreading the warmth further through my cell.

I hope they're merciful to her, I thought solemnly, though my heart doubted it. *How many innocent girls have these monsters tortured to death in this terrible place? Gods, it just isn't fair.*

I pulled the blanket up from where I had dropped it at the sound of the doors unlocking and shrugged it back over my shoulders. The chill was trying to invade my body again, pushing against the warmth of the hearth from the icy winds outside the window.

It's only a matter of time. They come for every girl they lock in this tower eventually, I thought, my heart shuddering with fear. *Even me.*

Chapter Two
Promised Pains

The day wore on, cold and empty, the deep silence broken only by the sounds of the winds and waves beyond the tower, then accented by the main door to the chamber unlocking once again. As before, I slipped into the cover of the wall beside the bars, desperate to stay hidden from the men entering. But there was no threat or cruelty in this short visit.

The guards brought food and water, my starving stomach aching ever harder now that I knew there was something to eat. All the same, I chose not to move from my exposed hiding spot, watching as the men put a bowl and jug through the slot under the door of the cell Virida was in before coming to mine. They set a bowl down with a jug of water and a cup on the floor just inside my cell, closing the barred hatch near the door and turning away. I waited for them to leave the chamber and close the door before emerging from my hiding place, feeling so much like a frightened animal shying away from larger beasts.

Pulling my chains with me, I slid across the floor to where the items had been left, picking up the bowl and distastefully studying the contents. It was a meagre amount of lukewarm gruel along with a little brown bread that was beginning to harden.

They give us so little, I thought as the very idea of trying to eat this food brought on a new nausea. *It seems like executing their prisoners would be kinder.*

Regardless of my lack of desire for this slowly staling food, my hunger drove me to take it. I walked with it back to the cot and sat down on the edge, balancing the bowl on my slender knees, the jug and cup by my ankle. At least I had been given a spoon to eat with, a luxury I didn't always find myself privileged to.

Dipping the spoon into the gruel, I took in a slow breath and braced myself for the taste, sliding it into my mouth quickly. It was bland and awful, whatever cooks there were providing this for the prisoners clearly not caring to add any real flavour.

It's better than starving, I reminded myself. *I need to eat and keep up my strength... what strength I have left at least.*

I took my time eating, not to savour the tasteless, tiny meal, but to ease it into my stomach and to fill up some of my infinitely empty time. All the same, the bowl was soon empty, and my stomach still gave protest despite me having eaten.

It was yet another of the constant pains I had been forced to live with in this dark cell.

At least the water was fresh, allowing me more motivation to drink than to eat. It washed away the foulness of the food and soothed my aching throat's dryness all at once. I had learned to be cautious with my supply of water, setting the jug somewhere I wouldn't trip on it by accident. They so rarely gave me more than a single jug in the day and I had learned to force myself to ignore much of my thirst, rationing what I had to last me until I fell asleep again in the night.

I didn't speak with Virida again, neither of us feeling like there was anything left to say. She had fallen silent some hours ago, by my guess, resigning herself to the loneliness of her closed off cell.

Once again, I tended the fire, poking it with some kindling to keep it burning. I couldn't cope with the idea of sitting there freezing, and this at least gave me a little to do, though not much.

I stood, the blanket wrapped like a shawl around me, and moved to the window with the clinking rattle of my chains. Getting up on the single step, I looked out at the world beyond the cell again, seeing that the sun had come out, though the grey clouds still dominated the air.

Trying to get some glimpse of the courtyards was nearly impossible. My view was more of the sea and the ice shelves than anything else, only a little of the castle visible below my window. I knew what I was looking for; the very same thing I had searched for since our escape attempt had been foiled days after our arrival.

Where have they got you, Amethyst? I longed to see my dragon, worrying that she was worse off than I was. *I wish I had never called to you with my pendant. If I hadn't... you would still be free.*

I spent a few more moments straining, then eased my body and simply watched the icy skies and seas for a time. It seemed so peaceful, though I knew in my heart the truth of this dreadful white and blue place. Its beauty was merely a mask for the darkness and ugliness it shielded beneath the surface.

Carden. My love's name came to me as I stood there, the feeling of tears threatening to break my defences rising to my eyes once more. *What are you going through, my handsome Guardian?*

His final words to me as he was dragged away from my sight to his imprisonment beyond this dire place echoed in my mind: *"It **will** be all right, Leander! I will come back and free you! I promise! I PROMISE!"*

My breath caught in my chest as his face in that terrible moment of desperation returned to me, my heart aching severely.

He said he'd come back for me, I remembered, hope kindling a new flame in my soul. *He and Tallinn surely escaped. They are Guardians after all. He's coming for me. He is... I know he is...*I felt a little more heartened by this, huddling for warmth beneath the blanket as I clung to my true love's words. *Carden has always come back* *for me. He'll save me... Then, we'll go far away together, somewhere the Shadow Lord can never find us. I know it.*

There was a loud unlocking and a bang, snapping me away from my ruminations about my true love. I spun around to the sound, the door into the tower chamber now open and a number of men entering, including the loathsome Ulric. He unlocked the door to Virida's cell, the girl instantly crying from within as the men entered the room. I dared not think of what horrors that poor girl was about to have inflicted on her.

I moved quickly to the bars of my cell, grasping them hard with both hands and watching on in terror.

"No! What do you want with me?!" Virida cried out in panic "Please! Please, what are you doing?!"

"Leave her alone!" I shouted at them, desperate to do something to help her. "Please, just leave her alone!"

Her pleas became inaudible as the men pulled the door behind them but didn't shut it fully. My heart sank as I knew what terrible thoughts lurked within their twisted minds, knowing exactly what they intended. I felt truly sickened to my core.

Ulric turned his green-eyed gaze to me, one hand on the pommel of his sword sheathed at his hip, the other at his side. That foul, smirking sneer spread across his face, his steps towards me deliberately casual.

I fought the repulsion building inside my throat, the bile rising to choke me. I had come to know too many men like this despicable lecher before me and had been forced to endure so many of their awful base desires being spoken to me.

"Well now," he was watching me through the bars, mentally undressing me, "how incredibly beautiful you look today, Princess."

His words may as well have been ice. I just hugged my arms tighter around my body, having dropped the blanket when I had run to the door, shivering more from the chill of his words than that of the room.

He leaned into the bars, his green eyes searching my body with lust.

"I wonder if the Queen and her sister will allow me the pleasure of your company again," his smile broadened. "I do so enjoy our time together."

I glared at him: "Why? Do you want to see how much harder you can hit me this time?"

He stared down at me coldly. "You should be grateful that I care for you, Princess. Anyone else would do worse to a girl like you."

A horrible, desperately shrill scream tore from the other cell and I instantly felt a stronger fear as tears ran down my cheeks. He smirked at me, slouching so that our eyes met.

"All that saves you from that same fate is my Mistresses' command," he took pleasure in his words. "Were it not for them and the Shadow Lord, I would already have broken your maidenhood and taken your virtue. How fortunate for you."

I cringed, fighting back my tears at his terrible descriptions. His desires for me were not something he hid well, though I doubted he made any real effort to do so at all.

Virida's screams and cries tore through the air and I cringed harder, closing my eyes. I tried to stop my mind imagining the terrible things being done to her at that moment, having feared the sensations of such tortures for so long myself.

"How I wish to hear you scream like that," Ulric sighed longingly as he watched the door to the other cell, turning his smile towards me again. "To see your young, virginal shape squirming in vain as I take you with your wrists in shackles..."

"You foul, wretched man!" I snarled, glaring at him through angry and frightened tears. "Does it really bring you so much joy to torture girls in such awful intimate ways?! Must you be so cruel?!"

"Cruel?" he snapped his hand through the bars, drawing a startled scream from me as he grabbed my dark hair at the nape of my neck and glared into my trembling face.

He twisted my hair, the strands pulling in my skin and jerking my head back, forcing my shoulders forward. I braced my hands into the iron bars, my wrists aching horribly at their sudden unnatural bend as my knees shook to stay standing. All I could do was meet his sinister gaze and try to stay on my feet, my breathing laboured and my chest heaving beneath my green bodice.

"You think what I've done to you thus far has been cruel?" he questioned me with a cold, low tone, glaring into my watering eyes. "Oh, Princess, how you know not what horrors yet wait for you."

His other large, grimy hand reached through the bars, slipping past my slapping hands to reach my body. I groaned and whimpered in panic, squeezing my eyes shut as he touched my smooth, delicate skin, his bulky fingers roving every crevice of my collarbones and throat. His smile broadened at my helplessness as he lowered his groping fingers down the edge of my dress's low collar, seeking their final dreaded purchase.

I felt tears slip from my eyes and a scream straining in my throat, but it wouldn't come out. All that came were weak, squeaking gasps of panic at his unwanted touch.

"Hm... so warm. So delicate," he mused, looking me in the eyes and forcing me to do the same in return. "You are truly a rare thing to behold, girl."

"P-p-please... s-stop," I gasped through sobs.

"Sadly, this is all I am permitted," he sighed, his grasping hand now rising again and closing around my throat.

"Please," I whispered, shuddering as his fingers coiled, "just leave me alone..."

"Have you not already spent enough time alone?" he chuckled, amused by my trembling and light squirming. "I would have thought my company would be welcomed in your solitude."

I forced myself to glare at him. *He wants me afraid and weak. He cares nothing for my wellbeing or my comfort. All he seeks is my virginity and my screams of pain. I won't give him any satisfaction. To the Void with him.*

The door to the other cell opened and the men stepped out, carrying Virida between them. She was sobbing softly, bruises forming on her cheek and neck, her clothes torn in places.

"Knight-Commander?" one of the four men turned to Ulric. "Your orders?"

"Take the prisoner to the Sanctum," Ulric authorised them. "The Mistresses have a use for her."

The guard who had spoken nodded and gestured for the others to follow. They dragged Virida from the chamber and down the stairs beyond the doorway. I knew I would never see her again, just as it had been with every other girl who had been brought to this terrible tower prison.

Ulric turned his attentions back to me, smiling coldly. He studied my features, his hand releasing my throat and stroking my cheek with his knuckles, brushing my hair from my eyes.

I shuddered in disgust.

"Do not fear, Princess," he smirked down at me. "You are not forgotten. The Mistresses have something in mind for you as well. Oh, I cannot wait to hear you beg."

I looked up numbly through my fading tears, bracing my hands against the bars to straighten my arms: "You won't."

"We shall see," he replied, casting me down onto the floor.

I grunted in pain as I landed on my back, my skull striking the stone and leaving it throbbing. I lay there, moving my legs shakily and raising my hands to my head as my eyes fell shut against the pain.

Ouch! Why must he be so rough with me?!

I heard two more sets of footfalls and the door to my cell was unlocked. I looked up as Ulric now entered the room and started towards me, two guards at his back.

Now?! They're taking me now?! Oh Gods!

He gestured and the two men were on me in moments, grasping my slender forearms and unshackling my wrists. I tried to slip free, but they were too fast and far stronger than me. I was then forced to my feet and made to face Ulric, looking up at his much taller frame despite my five feet almost eight inches. He smiled down at me and reached out to stroke my cheek.

I pulled away, yelping in pain a moment later as he struck me, the sound like a thud inside my head. The hot prickling covered my right cheek and the edge of my eye socket, my head swimming and my balance disrupted further. I then felt his hot, rough hand cup my chin and force my face towards his.

"I'd have thought you'd learned your lesson by now, girl," he hissed down at me, holding my chin in a way that hurt. "Whenever you resist, you shall be hurt."

"You're a coward!" I snapped, glaring up at him, my shoulders tensing against the guards' holds on my arms. "A vicious, disgusting coward!"

He glared at me and for a moment I feared a second reprisal. Instead, he simply nodded to the guards and said: "Bring her."

They forced me from the cell and down the spiralling stairs of the tower without question.

What horrors wait for me? I wondered, trying to remain strong, though I was terrified. *What terrors must I be made to endure this time? How I wish they would just leave me alone.*

We reached the bottom of the tower and stepped out onto the exterior walkway. I squinted hard in the afternoon light, the grey seeming harsher in some ways now that the sun had once again vanished behind the snowy clouds.

I shivered against the deeper chill as Ulric hooked my arm in his hand and started leading me forward with the guards following. His fingers crushed into my skin, causing the vapours of breath exiting my lips to flow more swiftly as my chest heaved at the pain in my limb.

As we passed through the walkways, I surveyed our surroundings. I saw the very same courtyard that my friends and I had attempted to make our escape from, the memories of that terrible day playing wildly through my mind. Now that same cold, grey stone yard was powdered with gentle dustings of snow, guards patrolling the walls under heavy cloaks and armour. I saw the shivering outlines of prisoners locked in tall, narrow, hanging gibbets, so few still alive. The thought of what they were enduring made my stomach churn.

In the yard at that moment a number of men were being led to a block and a burly, black hooded executioner. A man was forced to his knees, his head over the block and his hands bound behind him. He didn't fight, clearly resigned to his fate as the soldiers around him stood ready to strike down any who tried to run.

"Many a head has rolled from that block," Ulric commented, drawing my gaze briefly and smirking. "Can you imagine the pain of the axe cutting through your neck, the sound of your spine and sinews snapping loudly, or the horror of those final moments before your eyes go dark, Princess?"

I cringed at the very thought.

As the executioner raised his enormous axe, I closed my eyes, whimpering at the horrible chop that followed. *That's... oh my gods... I can't look...*

We entered the keep, the chill of the world beyond falling away as our boots scraped the stone floors beneath us. Only now did I feel safe enough to open my eyes, taking in the immense dark archways and stonework decorated with black and gold tapestries displaying the gryphon heraldry.

I knew where they were taking me, having been brought to that same dread place many times since my cruel imprisonment began countless days ago. At my best guess, I would have said that it was every nine to ten days I would find myself being taken to the only other place in the castle that gave me greater misery than the West Tower.

I won't show fear, I told myself, trying to be firm in my convictions. *They want me scared and crying, so I won't give them that. I'll be strong. I **must** be strong...*

I heard raised voices from the throne room to my left, glancing up through the large black doors. I got my first glimpse of Keilantra in so very long, the raven-haired Witch-Queen as severe and imposing as she ever was. Her hair was in a firm up-style beneath her sharply pointed crown, her jewelled hands at her sides. She wore a black and silver dress with trims of gold, the lining of her sleeves golden too.

She was talking with someone; a young Gorvennan man with black hair and a gently stubbled face. He was dressed in the shirt, trousers and jacket of a nobleman, the colours of black, grey and gold much like the Witch's own.

Anders? My heart swelled at seeing the Prince of Gorvenna standing there before me, one of the last good people I had expected to ever see again.

"My father is unwell," Anders was saying sternly, eyeing Keilantra with distaste. "This old castle is no place for a sick man whose mind is so confounded that he barely recognises his own son."

"Castle Ortagaad is the safest place for your father," Keilantra countered evenly, clasping her hands together against her stomach, her fingers intertwined. "Thoralf is ill, as you have said, Anders, and there are those who might take advantage of such sickness..."

"And *who* might these dread conspirators be?" the Prince demanded coldly. "I have not heard even the smallest of rumours of such plots against my father's life, yet you insist that he is safer here in this ancient relic fortress rather than the palace in Nargilith."

"Nargilith is not safe, son," she reached out her hand to stroke his cheek.

He pulled away. "I would have you keep your distance, Keilantra. I do not know what dire spell my father is under, but I will not allow you to bring me to the same fate."

Keilantra eyed him coldly, her false sweetness disappearing then as she stepped purposefully towards him: "That you are untouched by such afflictions should be an occasion of joy for you. And that I tolerate your baseless accusations is due *only* to my love for your father..."

"You love no one," Anders retorted. "I remain in possession of my wits *only* because it suits you and your sister to have me run the capital while you hide my father away from prying eyes."

"Your father needs his rest..."

"Our nation needs its King," he responded sternly. "Am I to continue to rule in his stead via those strangely scrawled letters he sends me? And what sense is there to make in them? They are the mumblings of a madman, not my father's intelligent mind."

I could no longer contain myself, the need to be heard overwhelming me.

"Anders!" I screamed, trying to pull away from Ulric, fighting as hard as I could to reach the doorway. "And- uhmph!"

Ulric slapped his hand over my mouth and swiftly pulled me around the wall out of sight as the Prince turned in response to his name. The cruel man squeezed me tight and snarled into my ear, his breath hot on my neck, his other hand now twisting my throat.

"Be silent, girl," he hissed lowly at me. "Lest you find yourself in greater pains than those already promised you."

I tried to struggle free, grasping at his hand and clawing his skin with my nails. He squeezed my throat harder and turned my face with the hand he held over my mouth, my neck aching at his twisting movement.

"Uh-ah-ah," he warned me, leaning over my shoulder, and pressing my back harder into his chest. "I would hate to have to snap your neck. Manth would be most displeased to have to restore it to full health if you should continue to push my patience."

I fell silent, tears bleeding from my frightened eyes. I choked back against a lump in my throat, moaning in terror as he edged my head a little further to illustrate his threat. I let my hands fall to my sides and he eased off the pressure as footsteps came from the throne room.

"Good girl," he sneered down into my ear.

Keilantra swept around the doors and glared straight at me, turning her fierce green eyes then to Ulric.

"*What* is the meaning of this?" she demanded.

Ulric forced a smile and answered: "The girl tried to step out of line, but I have silenced her."

"Keep her silenced, you fool!" she hissed in a whisper at him. "I cannot have Thoralf's son learning that we have her imprisoned here! Take her to the inquisition room *now*! I shall join you after I have settled this with the Prince!"

"I shall have her secured and prepared for you, my Queen," Ulric assured her.

"Just get her out of sight, you idiot!" she snapped, turning away swiftly and regaining her composure as she returned to the throne room, playing to Anders: "It was no one. One of the servants calling to you as a joke..."

Ulric heaved me away from the throne room, one of the guards leading us through a door down a dully lit corridor. Despair filled me as my gamble had left me with undoubtedly worse torture than that already promised to me. I feared the inquisition room, knowing immediately what terrors lay in wait for me.

I'm such a fool! Why did I call to him?! Now they will only force more pain upon me as revenge...

I was dragged by the cruel knight down the dark stairs into the lowest parts of the keep, his grasp around my throat and mouth never easing. He brought me down a corridor lit by only a few torches, passing by locked arched doors before coming at last to the one directly at the end of the hall. In mere moments we were inside, and I was surveying the horrors before me.

As Ulric dragged me towards the day's chosen device, I took in the horrible implements with my frantic eyes: the iron maiden, the rack, the pillory, the scavenger's daughter, the wheel, the thumb screws, the foot press, and the collar, just to name a few. I instantly felt sick. I trembled and closed my eyes, this chamber far darker and far worse than the one my uncle had hurt me in when I was in Aneuran. This one had the tortured and broken remains of prisoners still hanging in irons on the walls, most now only bones in tattered garb. And the smell... Gods... the smell!

Ulric and the guards lay me back on one of the racks, my struggles useless against the three very strong men. They seemed to enjoy making an innocent girl so desperately helpless. My wrists were forced over my head and secured by the restraints attached to the chains easily. I didn't plead though, determined to keep that satisfaction from these cruel monsters; even as they secured my ankles and stepped away, allowing me to squirm and writhe against my restraints.

With the raised angle the device stood at, I was able to take in all the terrors of the room, the pull of gravity only adding to my anguish as my body slid downwards, tugging on my wrists painfully. My back ached from the wooden frame pressing into my skin through my dress, my hips hurting already.

Ulric removed my boots to leave my feet bare, the chill of the room instantly attacking my toes and adding to my already relentless shivers.

"You look so attractive in bondage," he remarked, smirking at me as he reached out to stroke my face, grasping my chin and neck lightly to force my head back. "Perhaps today the Mistresses will grant me my most desired wish from you."

I blinked against tears, my lips pressed tightly into a line, my body shuddering painfully in his grasp. His breath on my neck made my skin crawl and already I yearned to be back in my tower cell. Somehow, though, I managed to find my bravery... or my stupidity.

"Wishful thinking," I uttered back at him, meeting his gaze. "You know they'll never let you have me like that."

I could tell I had irked him, yet he somehow kept his composure. "We will wait for them to come to us, Princess," he stepped away, running his hand along the steel torture tools hanging on one of the walls. "Then we shall have some fun."

It seemed like an eternity of waiting was crushing down upon me, my passive pain from the rack already taking its toll on me.

The waiting is a torture in itself, I thought, knowing the truth of why I was being kept like this for so long. *The anticipation of the promised pains only adds to its intensity. I have never known such cruelty. Even my uncle, foul as he is, has his limits. For him, torturing me was a means to get what he wanted from Mithras. But these witches... it is for the pleasure of causing harm and hearing screams...*

I tested the cuffs on my wrists, hoping against hope that I could slide free. It was a vain hope of course, especially with three armed men standing only a few feet from me. Even if I could get free of my restraints, I couldn't get past them.

What hope does a teenage girl have against three large, heavily armoured men? I thought dourly.

Closing my eyes helped, allowing me to at least block out the sights of that terribly hellish place. Though this small action didn't save my body from the aches and discomfort currently plaguing me, it gave me a reprieve from some small part of it and allowed me to think of something else.

Carden. My handsome Guardian entered my mind again, and my heart yearned for him. *If only I could be with you now. What I wouldn't give for you to make good on your vow and come for me. Gods, how I love you, Carden...*

The sound of the doors opening broke me from my respite, returning me to the harsh reality of my nightmarish existence.

"Mistresses," Ulric turned towards the Queen as she finally strode into the room, her dark clothed sister following silently like a wraith at her back.

With sudden violence, Keilantra struck Ulric hard, magic behind the blow she dealt him, the flash of a magenta glow illuminating her hand. The man hit the floor hard, stunned and cowering as he held his aching face.

"YOU FOOL!" Keilantra screamed in an inhuman rage so loud it hurt to hear it. "WHAT WERE YOU DOING BRINGING HER OUT WHILE THE PRINCE WAS PRESENT?! HAVE YOU LOST ALL SENSE?!"

She lashed out again, this time striking him with an electrical storm of magenta lightning, the Knight screaming and writhing on the floor in agony.

I cringed my face into my arm, trying to shield my eyes from the intensity of the strikes, fearful of feeling that attack again myself. In mere moments it was over, and the man lay breathless on the stone bricked floor, convulsing inside his armour.

"My step-son is already suspicious enough and, I am certain, aware that Manth and I have bewitched his father," she explained coldly through her teeth at him. "Convincing him of my *care* for his father's wellbeing is precarious at best, as it is proving my *goodness* to him. And what do you?" she erupted with rage then and screamed: "YOU ALMOST LET HIM SEE HER!"

She stomped down hard on his chest, the man grunting in pain as he gazed up at her fearfully.

"WHAT KIND OF FOOL ARE YOU?!" she continued to rant furiously. "I TOLD YOU TO WAIT UNTIL I CALLED FOR HER, YET YOU BROUGHT HER HERE ANYWAY! YOU ARE A PATHETIC WASTE OF A MAN, ULRIC! STOP DELIBERATELY PUSHING YOUR DESIRES TO BED HER AND DO AS I'VE COMMANDED YOU!"

Keilantra scared me when she screamed. Unlike the Shadow Lord, who remained calm and controlled, this wicked woman so easily lost her temper when she was slighted even the tiniest bit, violence assured to follow. The only mercy I had at that moment was that her rage was directed at Ulric instead of me.

"Forgive me, my Queen," Ulric begged, crawling to his knees and cowering beneath her hard, burning gaze. "I was careless and eager. I want only to serve you, Mistress..."

"Fine," she hissed. "Get up, you wretch."

He nodded and stood, surprised by the slap she delivered to his cheek and her heavy glare of green fire.

"Consider this a severe warning," she glowered, pointing at his face with one sharp finger. "Do *not* disappoint me again."

He nodded and stepped aside; his head bowed as he took up a position far behind her near the wall.

The Witches now turned their attention to me, their gazes cold and calculating as they swept slowly nearer where I was restrained. I froze as I stared at them, holding my breath in anticipation of the horrors to come.

"Princess," Keilantra threw me a false smile.

"What do you want with me?" I asked shakily, trembling from cold and fear, my limbs and back hurting so much already.

"How very direct," she nodded gently. "I can respect that. As you know, my dear sister and I are the Witches of Raven's Rest, a town in the Bargoth Mountains in High-Realm's far north. And there are *many* things we want..."

I watched her sweep to my right, pausing and smirking down at me as I tried not to whimper at the passive pain in my body.

"Yet, we shall continue with but *one* of my desires," she stated, producing something silvery and purple hanging from a glittering chain. "That which I have desired since first you entered my sights."

I stared at my Dragon Pendant, wanting nothing more than to take it back as my own again. It was so tantalisingly close to me, yet my bound hands could do nothing to reach it. The last thing left to me in this waking world and it dangled in the grasp of my cruel and vicious captor not two feet from me.

"I don't know what I can give you," I confessed, struggling to shift my body to find some measure of comfort against the rack. "You've taken my pendant from me and imprisoned my dragon. What more could you want?"

I know exactly what she wants, and every time she demands it of me my answer never changes. It can't. Oh Gods... I was truly afraid.

"You know what I want, girl," she said, hissing the words close to my face, my eyes locked with hers. "Control over both."

"But you have your own pendant and dragon," I pointed out, feeling like this was just a repeated dance of pain we had gone through so many times before.

She indicated the necklace she wore, identical to mine in everyway, except that the heart-stone in hers was topaz and the pendant and chain were gold, not silver.

"As you have reminded me before, child," she nodded, her voice even as she watched me. "Yet, I would also control yours and command your dragon to do my bidding, and that of our Master."

"How many times must we do this?" I asked, fighting back sobs and straining my arms against the restraints. "Every time you bring me to this dire place you demand this of me..."

"And every time you remain stubborn," Keilantra retorted in a low snarl, keeping my pendant in her hand.

"It doesn't matter what answer I give you," my words were rushed and breathy, my heart pounding as the thought of what would happen to me sped loudly through my mind. "You always torture me regardless..."

"If you wish to avoid such terrible pain as that which we have inflicted upon you before," she stated coldly, tilting my chin roughly to make me look at her, "then, you will have to offer me a reason to be merciful."

She let go of my chin and I felt tears start to slip free of my eyes despite my determination to be strong. *If stoicism had been my intention to give, then truly I have failed in that intent. Gods, why must I cry? Why can't I keep my tears dammed up and my sobs silent?*

The Witch arced around to stand before me as her sister was now eyeing the sinister tools resting on the nearby table. The darker eyed woman was already plotting which of these she would use to draw my screams and blood from my vulnerable body. I cringed at the thought.

"Now then," Keilantra flashed me a smile that only added to my unease, holding the Pendant out before me in her palm. "How do I take command of your pendant and your dragon?"

I remained silent, closing my eyes against my shuddering sobs, my rushing tears and my painful shivers of cold. *Is there any point in even answering her? "I don't know" never satisfies this vile, wicked witch. As if I would know how to do as she asks of me. I barely know how to use my pendant myself.*

"Will you remain silent then?" her words drew me to open my eyes again, surprised by her calm expression and tone. "Have you truly no desire to save yourself from the agonies we will inflict on you?"

I blinked against my tears, looking to my right and down at the floor, my heart aching with its thunderous beat and my breaths shaking inside my chest.

"Very well," the woman turned and nodded to Ulric, gesturing to the rack.

As he moved to the crank on the rack's side at my left, I whimpered and closed my eyes. All I could do was brace myself for the agony to come.

The mechanisms clicked loudly, and I felt the tension grow on my limbs, stretching my body tighter. I gasped at the sudden sensation and the gentle pain that was now plunging through me. Somehow, I managed to hide my anguish, gritting my teeth behind my lips and squeezing my eyes shut.

Don't scream. Don't scream. It hurts, but I can't scream. I won't...

The gears clicked into silence and no more movement pulled at my arms, the pain still present with my limbs tight on the rack. I opened my eyes and met the Queen's gaze as she studied me coldly.

"Feel as if you can pluck an answer from your wretched adolescent mind now?" she demanded lowly, her eyes like coals.

I sucked in a breath through my nose, whimpering a little through my closed lips. My tears were constant now as the pain was growing without the aid of the mechanisms. I doubted I could even give an answer, certain that there wasn't one I had that she would accept, even if I could bring myself to speak.

"Again," the woman glared at me and the mechanisms began clinking.

Oh Gods! My mind screamed where I kept my mouth tightly sealed, shaking and closing my eyes as the agony grew. *No! No, please, no! No! No, no, no! It hurts! IT HURTS SO MUCH!*

With a wave of her hand the tightening on my body stopped once again and I gasped an unintentionally loud breath. I fought to keep my eyes on hers now, her fingers pressing up under my chin painfully as my tears swept down my cheeks and I trembled helplessly.

"Do you know what this device does to the human body?" she asked me, revelling in my pain. "It tightens and tightens until you snap, your bones shattering and your limbs tearing from your body. I have seen it done before on men twice your size. What hope does a mere girl have against such mutilation?"

I whimpered and trembled, crying obviously now at the pain and her words.

"Save yourself from such a terrible fate, child," she urged me, "and give me that which I want."

"I... I... I don't know h-how..." I said with all the honesty I could manage, gasping in agony.

Keilantra snapped her hand up and I cried out as the wheels turned fast, pops filling my body and cracks sounding in my ears. Even thought eluded me now and all I wanted was to pass out from the agony tearing at my limbs as the ropes grew ever tighter.

"You are *not* the first Aldrich to deny me, Princess," Keilantra seethed as she stopped her onslaught again and I fell into a burning silence, tears tearing down my cheeks. "Ewan refused me too. Many years ago."

"My... my Father?" I was shocked, shaking with pain and struggling to breathe. "You... you knew my... my Father?"

"Yes," she acknowledged, grasping my hair at the nape of my neck to hold my face steady so she could stare into my eyes. "And he left me for Caralyn. He abandoned *me* so that he might give life to two wretched little daughters instead of being with me..."

"You and my Father?!" I couldn't believe it. "No! He would never love someone so... so cruel!"

She twisted my hair and jerked my head back, making me groan against this new pain in my neck. Her eyes were fierce, and her jaw set hard as she burned into me with that stare of fire.

"Your father made me what I now am," she hissed at me. "His rejection tore me apart and left me a ruined waste of a woman. My love for him became his weapon against me, and so all that I am I lay at his feet."

"My... my Father was a good man!" I argued, determined to fight the pain and defend his memory.

"Your father was a wretch and a liar!" she shouted back at me furiously. "If he yet lived, I would find him and take what he loves most, destroying it before his very eyes and driving him mad! In either case, you stupid, stubborn, wretched little girl, you would be right where you now are, only he would watch you suffer for his crimes against my heart!"

She slammed her hand around my throat now, pressing my head back against the frame of the rack, tightening her grasp so that I struggled to breathe.

"Instead," her voice was low and quiet as she sneered cruelly at me, "since he is passed and no longer living, I will gladly bring down *all* the torments I would wish on him upon his beloved little daughter. You *will* suffer agony upon agony, Princess. There is no escaping that truth," then she softened her expression mockingly. "Yet, I will be merciful to you if you simply do as I demand and give me control of your pendant and your dragon."

I took in another shuddering breath, looking up at her through my tears as the panic of my cruel situation only grew within me. I knew I would regret the words that slipped from my lips, but I couldn't hold back the hatred I held for this woman, especially now that she had dishonoured my father and mother.

"You are a vile, evil woman," I said quietly, glaring at her. "You will *never* be loved."

She snarled and glared at me fiercely. I waited for her reprisal, but it didn't come, instead meeting her blazing eyes in a moment of terrifying silence.

"Give me control of your pendant. Now," she seethed coldly.

"Even if I could... I wouldn't," I said through my teeth at her with all of my conviction. "I will *never* help you."

I yelped as my cheek burned with a sharp, prickling heat, the sound of the back of her hand hitting my skin almost deafening me. I breathed hard and turned my gaze to look back at her, seeing the rage exploding like a volcano inside her.

"Then you shall suffer, you insolent little brat," she glowered, turning on her heel and striding towards the door. "Manth, do as you will with her. I am wearied by her stubbornness."

As the door slammed and locked, I found my eyes falling onto the second woman dressed entirely in black. Manth was far more terrifying than Keilantra; her sister's rage and hatred explosively loud while she was silent and calculatingly vicious, much like her Master. But Manth was imaginative and violent, conceiving of greater horrors than any of the minds who devised the concept of torture ever did.

I couldn't even struggle as she stalked towards me slowly, the restraints too tight and my limbs nearing breaking point. Every trembling shake was agony to my cracking form, making me feel now that I was so fragile that a slight breeze could shatter me like fine crystal.

"You should not test my sister's patience, girl," the Witch spoke in her rasping, whispery voice, her black eyes so demonic it was frightening. "Your resistance only adds to the agonies you must endure."

"Please," I begged softly, my tears flooding anew in a heavy wash down my cheeks. "I'm not resisting her on purpose. I truly don't know how to give her what she wants."

The most terrible words then came from her dark lips and her pale, ghostly face, chilling me to my heart and shredding spikes of ice through my overtaxed spine: "I know."

I stared wide eyed at her. "You... you know?"

"The Dragon Pendants cannot be forcibly taken and controlled, nor can they be given away and still function," she leered at me cruelly. "They are not magical talismans to be conquered as my sister believes. *All* who command a Dragon Pendant do so because *it* has chosen them. You, girl, have no control over that and no command over changing its loyalties. Even the most powerful of magic cannot sway a Pendant from one to another."

"Then why are you letting her do this to me?" I asked, terrified to even know the answer.

"Because," she said, lifting my chin and staring deep into my fearful eyes, "I enjoy the suffering of young girls like you. *And* because Lord Morod has granted me permission to make you suffer, provided you remain in one piece without disfigurement, disability, or the destruction of your purity. He desires you to remain... *unspoiled.*"

"Please... please don't..." I couldn't help my sobs now that I knew after all the times they had tortured me, that she had done it for her own cruel amusement while knowing this hidden truth that might have spared me.

"Now," she stepped back and pointed her right hand towards me, "you will scream, Princess."

The flashing of magenta lightning struck from her fingertips and coursed through my whole body. I stifled the first scream fighting to break free, but my defences were fading fast. The pain was worse than that of the rack alone, but with both combined it was tenfold again. My shrilled scream broke past my lips and I cried in an agony so great that there are no words to describe it. My eyes stayed shut and I longed for this to end as my hysterical screams echoed throughout the chamber all around me amidst the crackling snap of her sinister magical lightning.

Chapter Three
Hope and Despair

Aside from the howling winds outside, only my broken, desperate sobs pierced the empty, lonely silence of the tower cells. The guards had brought me back what felt like hours ago, shackled my wrists and dumped me to the stone floor, which was where I still lay. My limbs ached from the stretching of the rack and my body shrieked with terrifying agony from all the sinister things Manth had done to me. I couldn't dare to recall any of it, the thought of such torments alone too much to bear.

True to her word, however, the wicked witch had kept her Master's decree in honour, leaving me without disfigurement and with my virginity still untouched. I knew that last part must have irked Ulric, but it was the only kindness I seemed to have been granted by the dark and terrible witch. I might have considered that protection of my maidenhood to have come from her also being a woman, but I knew it was born only of the Shadow Lord's commands. Had he not made such a condition I might have been violated thousands of times by now in this dark cell like every other girl they brought here, and she would have only ensured it happened.

My right side was in the least pain, though not free of it, and that was how I lay, my stomach partially against the floor. I had one knee bent towards my body, the other leg outstretched, the old worn blanket sprawled on the floor beneath me. I was only two feet from the fireplace, the embers struggling to stay alive now that I couldn't even move to feed them.

I shivered hard and cried out more sobs as the involuntary reaction aggravated my injured body. My eyes closed in the faint torch light and deep darkness as my tears continued their relentless march past my cheeks to salt my clothes and the stone floor. For hours upon hours I had been unable to stop the flood, both during the terrors of the torture I'd suffered and now as I lay helpless and broken in the West Tower.

Keilantra's a liar, I thought as my crying went on without faltering. *My Father was a good man. He didn't make her. She is just hateful and wicked.*

I rested my head on my right arm and felt my heart beating in my shuddering chest. Even breathing hurt now and I worried that I wouldn't heal, despite Manth casting spells to aid my recovery.

Why does she torture me, then heal me? It couldn't be regret, for she has no heart. It must be a further cruelty, her way of keeping me from breaking entirely so that she might devastate me anew with each time she torments me.

I sobbed harder at that thought, curling up tighter and feeling the folds of my dress slip free of my legs.

How have I survived so much agonizing torture? How is it that I still breathe? A dark thought crossed my mind as I continued to weep: *This isn't the last of it. They'll come for me again. They always do. Keilantra will never stop in her madness to claim my pendant and its powers, and Manth will never tell her it is a fruitless goal, just because she enjoys my suffering. Gods, they will never stop hurting me... And then the Shadow Lord will come to kill me...*

I sucked in another agonising breath, knowing that there was no hope in finding release from such pains while I remained in that evil castle. The Witches would never stop until I lay broken on the floor, and even then, they would continue with their vicious torments against my eternally adolescent body.

"Carden," I sobbed, my chest breaking with terrible pain beyond measure. "Carden... I want to be with you... Carden, please... I love you so much..."

But he was not there, not reaching his broad, long fingered hands to pull me into his warm embrace and keep me safe, not whispering sweet words of comfort to me.

"Carden..." I wept weakly, slumping to the floor with no strength left to even try to stay awake.

At first I thought that I was dreaming as I heard the door into the chamber beyond the bars open, but I soon realised I was awake as a figure entered alone. He wore black, was tall and broad shouldered, his hair the colour of a raven's wings. He was searching the cells, finally turning his green eyes towards my aching, pathetic shape lying limp on the floor.

Carden? Hope sprung up in my heart. *Oh, Carden, I knew you would find me...*

He moved towards my cell cautiously, looking over his shoulder in the weak light to check for anyone watching on. Satisfied that there was no one there, he came into my view and stared down at me from beyond the bars of my cell.

"Anders?" I stared up at the Gorvennan Prince in weak surprise as my vision cleared.

"Princess Leander?" he looked horrified as he studied me, taking in my broken, dishevelled appearance with quiet horror. "You look awful."

I struggled to push myself up onto my knees, crying out in pain with the effort against my stretched and nearly broken limbs. Awkwardly, I crawled to the bars, every movement agonisingly hard where once it would have been so simple. I slumped down onto the floor, sitting with my right shoulder to the bars, meeting his gaze as I grasped them, trying to keep myself sitting up.

I'm so weak. I could slip into unconsciousness so very easily.

I studied his handsome face as he crouched down to my level, the hurt at seeing me like this so evident in his emerald eyes.

"By the Gods, Leander," Anders gasped, "what have they done to you?"

The slightest touch of his hand to my cheek caused me great pain and I moaned against a hard flinch. My body was so ruined that I doubted in my heart I could manage to last the night, though I knew that the Witches would see to it that I did.

"How... how did you find me?" I croaked softly, battling my eyes' desire to close.

"Not all who reside in Castle Ortagaad are under the command of those devilish sisters," he replied earnestly, disgust in his voice at the mere thought of the Witches. "Those still loyal to my father told me of a girl, a princess, being kept in the West Tower. Since none have seen or heard of you in so very long, I dreaded the prisoner's identity. And here you are."

"I am so glad to see you, Anders," I managed a small, exhausted smile.

"As I am to see you, Leander," he tried to be reassuring, though I could see his distress as clearly as I could his face. "I wish this reunion were only under better circumstances, and you were not so injured. Gods, why are they keeping you here?"

"I am in the Witches' keeping for another," I started to explain.

"The Shadow Lord," he nodded.

I was surprised: "You know of him?"

"While his activities are kept secret there are those in High-Realm who know of him," he confessed evenly. "I was contacted some months ago and told of this monster's interest in you."

"And you didn't doubt it?" I asked.

He smiled at me faintly and stroked my cheek through the bars again: "It is you, most beautiful Princess, so many seek across all the lands; the namesake of the Heroine. If a Shadow Lord were to rise anew, then of course I would believe his interests would fall on you, as terrible and evil as that is."

"He... he has... done things," I started to cry again at the thought of all I had been through because of that terror in a black hood. "Because of him Arvon lies in ruins and my parents are dead..."

"I know," Anders looked saddened. "My father was heartbroken when he heard of Ewan and Caralyn. It was the last moment of clarity in his mind before Keilantra brought him here."

"I've seen him," I admitted, my heart aching at the memory of the poor King. "He doesn't look like himself. He knew me, but your step-mother wouldn't allow him time to remember and had him led away..."

"Keilantra is *not* my step-mother in anything other than name," he snarled with hatred. "She is a loathsome, vile and wicked woman born of the Void, as is her sister."

"Manth is the one who did this to me," I told him, cringing and wincing in pain. "She tortures me for her own amusement..."

"They are vile," he agreed severely. "To harm a young girl so beautiful and kind as you... it is beyond all the wickedness of the world. Even as a child you were such an innocent beauty," he looked nostalgic then, tears welling in his eyes, though they didn't flow."I remember my mother's passing when I was but nine winters old," he recalled softly. "It was autumn, and the leaves were falling in brown and orange hues in the palace courtyard. That was the first day I laid eyes upon you when your father and mother brought you and your sister to Nargilith."

"I... I didn't know I went to Nargilith," I tried in vain to remember.

"You wouldn't remember," he replied. "You had not yet reached your fifth winter. With your father explaining about my mother to you, you then took from his side and embraced me in a hug."

"And we were friends ever since," I nodded, knowing the rest. "We would write to each other so often once I was older."

"Until your correspondence ceased," he said gravely. "I worried that you had grown weary of me."

"Arvon had fallen," I explained sadly. "I had no moment when I could write to either you or to my sister while Mithras and the Guardians were trying to take me to safety."

"One of your last letters said that you were to be Aldegaad's next Queen," he reminded me of what I had written so very long ago now. "Yet, the news from Aldegaad is that Fane now rules from the throne."

"Fane set a conspiracy against my family," I explained, hating my last remaining uncle. "He was in league with the Shadow Lord and together they murdered my parents, Aunt Evangeline and Uncle Aric. I was to be his puppet on the throne when he captured me in Aneuran."

"Then the stories of you being abducted by renegades from your own wedding..."

"False," I hissed at the thought of that day. "My uncle sold me to Tibain Seward so that he might control me when I became Queen. The wedding was a farce for the people and a means to bind me to his cruel wishes, all to destroy Ivansten."

"And now Aldegaad and Ivansten both brace for war across the Nartarn'lath Mountains," he was piecing it all together, everything he knew now making complete sense to him.

"Uncle Aric's and my Father's fears have been realised," I murmured as I remembered how concerned they had been of a new war. "That is why it was me, not Fane, that Uncle Aric chose as heir to Aldegaad's throne."

"And now you languish in this wicked ancient prison, suffering horrific tortures at the hands of those despicable witches while you await the return of their dire Master," he shook his head with angry disgust.

"While my treasonous uncle is now free to enact his pointless war with Ivansten," I added, my chest hurting more now from the thoughts of these terrible events along with the previous tortures.

"This is wrong," Anders muttered, looking to the floor beneath me. "All of it."

There was but one thing in my mind now, one single request plaguing my thoughts. While I knew the chances were not good that my plea would be acted upon, I still felt that I needed to ask.

"Please, Anders," I begged quietly, drawing his eyes as I grasped his larger, warmer hands where he held the bars, "help me escape this terrible place. I can't endure the cruelty here forever, and I fear the Shadow Lord's return. He plans to kill me."

"Kill you?" he looked horrified. "Why?"

"I don't know, but he does," I felt my tears sliding down my cheeks. "I don't want to die. Please, Anders, help me."

"I wish I could, yet I have not been able to get my hands on the keys to the cells or to your shackles," his words broke my heart and made it sink into my chest. "Only my father can grant you your freedom, but with his mind so confounded I can't see how to convince him," he looked so pained as he held my cheek with one hand, studying my eyes with his own tears ready to flow.

There came a loud bang from the stairs and both of us snapped our gazes towards the open door into the chamber. Someone was coming and my heart began screaming inside my chest as my breaths heaved deep with panic.

"They're coming," I breathed frantically, my tears rushing again. "It isn't safe here."

Anders looked like a scared rabbit, his eyes flicking to the door uncertainly, then back to me rapidly.

"Don't let them see you," I urged him quickly. "If they should know that you have found me, they will do terrible things to us both. Please, my dear friend, hide."

He nodded and leaped to his feet, quickly slipping into the cover of a darkened section of the chamber where the guards never looked. He hid himself behind the stone bricks and stayed low.

Please, don't let them see him.

A pair of black and gold surcoat wearing guards entered and surveyed the room. They were on their nightly patrol of the tower, investigating the cells to ensure no prisoner tried to escape or had expired in the meantime. With only me at the very top of the tower their task was simple.

They stared at me where I sat curled up with a teary wet face, their expressions cold and careless at the sight of me. Then they turned and left, closing the door behind them. They were never very thorough in their searches.

Anders emerged from his hiding place, watching the door to be certain that they had left. Once he was sure of their departure, he knelt down with me and held my hands tightly again.

"I cannot stay, Leander," he told me in a hushed voice. "But I cannot leave you to rot in this cell."

"I understand. I couldn't bear the thought of you getting hurt because of me," I whispered, afraid that someone might be listening now.

"I must go, but I swear to you that you are no longer alone in this," he pulled my head gently towards the bars and kissed my forehead before looking into my eyes and caressing my cheek again. "Do not fear. Though I can't free you myself, know that help is coming to you."

"It is?" I felt hope burn in me anew.

He nodded. "As I said, I was contacted by a friend who knew of your plight. While you may be trapped here, know that you won't be forever. I promise."

With that, he stood and took one final look at me, then turned and left the chamber, disappearing through the door and down the stairs.

Knowing that the Gorvennan Prince and his mysterious friend were working to free me only added new courage to my heart. I instantly thought of Carden again, hoping that he had escaped the Revenant and had come for me as he promised.

I knew you wouldn't abandon me, my love, I thought, my heart so joyous though my chest felt as if it had been broken and pieced back together. *Please, don't leave me here for much longer, Carden. The sooner we are reunited and away from this dread place the better.*

* * * * *

My counting of the days since the night Anders came to me was blurred and - as with my total imprisonment - I had no recollection of how long it had been. He was the last person to come and speak with me for some time; my usual loneliness crushing back in on me like a haunting spirit whose voice was silence and whose presence was nothingness.

I was recovered now from Manth's and Keilantra's vicious assaults, no scars or marks remaining on my smooth white skin, and no pains yet lingering, save those within my soul. The Witches truly knew how to knit flesh and remedy pain as much as they could rend skin and cause agony.

Once again, I built the fire in a desperate effort to fight back the cold of Ortagaad's white storms, shivering beneath a blanket relentlessly. It had gotten colder in the West Tower of late and I wondered what time of year it now was.

The North is always frozen. How any humans can survive this blizzard choked land I'll never understand.

I went and lay on the cot with one arm over my midriff and the other resting in the pillows, my fingers curling through my hair in thought. My eyes were locked aimlessly on the ceiling above me, remaining like this for a long time.

...One hundred and nine, one hundred and ten, one hundred and eleven, one hundred and twelve, one hundred and thirteen, one hundred and fourteen... I was counting the individual stone bricks in the room, regularly losing count with the dullness that plagued me in this place. I let out a sigh and just stared at the ceiling. My thoughts were silent now, everything I could have conceived to think about already having entered my mind countless times.

All I had left to think of was all that had happened since my eighteenth name-day and I had no desire to revisit any of it for what I was certain would be the thousandth time. Then I started thinking on Anders' words to me that night, wondering what he and his friend were planning to do to help me.

It couldn't be easy. I doubt even an army could enter Castle Ortagaad; not with the frozen seas and the Culler Sharks surrounding it. How could anyone mount a rescue against this dreaded fortress? I sighed and closed my eyes, the light from the window hurting them in the cell's shadows. *But you know this place, don't you, Carden? You, Tallinn, Aldwyn and Fawkner will be studying all the possible ways to break me free. Perhaps the Dwarves plan on climbing through the sewer canals beneath the walls while Joran and Ellora cause some kind of distraction. Hm, I'd bet Holger would be incredibly unhappy about having to do something like that.*

I began imagining my friends gathered on the icy north shores of Gorvenna, clad in their cloaks and armour, their hoods drawn to shield their faces from the cold. They would be studying the black shape of Castle Ortagaad against the vast white laying over the blue of the sea, considering every possible way to breach the dark stone walls and rescue me.

The guards would never stand long against an angered Storvari. Joran would cut them down like reeds and Aldwyn would show the Witches the true power of white magic. Then, Carden will find me in this cell, break my chains and kiss me; and together we will leave this awful place to go somewhere quiet and safe where we can just be in each other's loving embrace forever.

Fantasizing helped me, it made me hope that with each day it would come true. My heart ached as I imagined him with me, his smile gentle and roguishly lopsided, making him so incredibly attractive. His eyes were full of life and his touch so delicate that it was surprising a man with such large, strong hands could have such a touch. I closed my eyes again, breathing in a slow, shaking breath as I began to really feel him with me, waiting for his lips to caress mine. I felt desire rise in me and want growing strong in my depths, telling me that it was him and him alone that I was meant for.

The bang of the chamber door startled me out of my imaginings, breaking the image of my handsome Guardian as if it were a mirror being struck by an iron bar. Reality flooded my eyes as I sat up and turned my gaze to the wall of bars that confined me, listening and watching for whoever had entered this place.

Ulric strode past my cell, his back to me as he unlocked the door across the way. Two guards dragged a figure into view, but not another girl of my age like I had expected. This figure was tall, a man of advanced age with long white hair and a white beard, though I didn't see his face. He wore long robes of green and brown, a brown hood swaying behind his shoulders. He must have stood at nearly six foot three, certainly of greater height than me.

Unlike every girl - including me - who had ever been brought here, the old man didn't struggle, seemingly resigned to his fate. No questioning words came from his lips, no pleas for his freedom, no demands to know what he had done to be so harshly imprisoned. Just silence.

He was thrown hard into the cell, a loud thud and a grunt sounding as the door was shut again. The guards were leaving, and Ulric turned, making me dread his lustful gaze.

Please, don't look at me. Please, just leave me alone. To my surprise, he walked past my cell and the chamber door closed, leaving me in silence. I felt myself relax. *Oh, thank the Gods...*

I was afraid to move from where I sat on the old mattress of the cot, shivering from the cold winds blowing through the glassless window behind me. Yet again, my curiosity was growing, and I felt that the opportunity for conversation was too great to ignore. I thought then of Eamnonn, the dragon in the Guardian Trials. Now I truly understood his thirst for speech with another.

Slipping from the bed, I walked quietly to the bars, trying to hold my chains silent as I went. I grasped the cold iron and tried to get a glimpse through the bars of the darker cell, barely managing to make out the shape of a figure.

"Hello?" I called so softly it may as well have been a thought in my head.

"Hello," the gentle voice responded from the darkness.

"Are... are you all right?" I asked in a murmur, straining to see him through the door.

"I am all right, child," he said, standing now and looking through the bars at me.

All I could see of him were two hazel eyes beneath greying eyebrows, the shadows of his cell and the door hiding him from me.

"Tell me, my dear, what terrible crime has a girl so young committed that she must be imprisoned in such a cold and lonely place?" the old man asked of me with a kindness I hadn't come to expect here.

"Nothing," I shook my head in all honesty. "I am here against my will for no reason beyond those of terrible and cruel people."

I didn't know if I should tell this man too much. It was strange to me that he was the first man I had ever seen imprisoned in the tower.

"I see," he considered me thoughtfully.

"Why are you here?" I wondered aloud, keeping my eyes locked on his. "What reason did they have for imprisoning you?"

"I crossed the Queen when I attempted to aid King Thoralf," he replied truthfully. "His mind has been poisoned by the spell of dark witches, and I sought to free him from such a nightmarish existence. The Queen had me imprisoned for my interference."

"You're a mage?" I asked.

"I am very well versed in the ways of magic, yes," he confessed. "Keilantra and Manth were quite surprised to find me tending to Lord Thoralf. I dare think that they thought none could undo their wicked conjuring."

"Then, you know that they're witches," I was surprised.

"The Sisters of Raven's Rest, yes," he nodded, his voice calm, though stern. "I am quite familiar with them. As a matter of fact, Manth and I have encountered each other quite a number of times in the past. I am fairly certain she will endeavour to conceive of a terrible fate for me."

"You must be a powerful mage if you could stand against that awful woman," I observed, shifting my hands and sitting down on the floor, my legs aching still.

"I am not one to brag upon my abilities, my dear girl," he responded quietly, watching me with gentle consideration. "Clearly I was no match for the sisters as my battle with them placed me in this tower."

"You fought them?" my voice was a little too loud as I said that, the very idea of someone being able to fight the Witches - beyond my imaginings of Aldwyn doing so - inconceivable to me.

"I did," the old man nodded again. "Though it was a bit of a task, I must admit, I did hold my own until I was overwhelmed by their combined powers."

I nodded, chewing my bottom lip in thought.

"It's strange," I said thoughtfully, "that they have chosen to imprison you here in this tower."

"How so?" he raised one bushy eyebrow at me.

I shrugged, pulling the sleeve of my dress over my exposed right shoulder to shield my skin from the cold a little better: "Until now I have only ever known them to bring girls to these cells."

"What became of the other girls, my dear?" he queried with a curiously dark frown.

I shrugged again, my breath catching and threatening to become sobs at the very thought of such terrible unknown fates: "I... I don't know. They never returned, though."

"And only *you* remain," he surmised, his voice low and soft. "Hardly a surprise."

"What do you mean?" I frowned at him.

"Historically speaking, Castle Ortagaad's West Tower has always been used to keep the important prisoners," he explained as if he were reading from a history book. "It is in these cells that prisoners deemed valuable enough to keep alive are kept by the wardens of this fortress. Prisoners such as... oh, say... the young Princess of Aldegaad..."

I stared wide eyed at him. "You know who I am?"

"My dear girl, I was aware of who you were the moment I was brought to this cell. Though, of course, I have also been very much aware of your imprisonment in this tower for some time."

Realisation struck me like a punch to the face and I stared harder at the man whose identity I couldn't see: "You're the one Prince Anders told me of. The one who told him I was here. He said you were working together to help me."

"Indeed," the old man confirmed with a gentle single nod, "though I must confess that things have gone awry, Princess."

I felt my heart sink deeper and I slumped my back against the wall, letting out a sigh of distress.

"If you've been captured," I said slowly, despair returning to me, "then your plans to help me have failed."

"Sadly true," he stated, his voice sympathetic as if he were trying to comfort me. "Though, I am not one to give up while there is still hope."

"What hope is there?" I murmured, staring at the floor dejectedly, my arms pulling my knees up to my chest.

Looking up at his face through the door I saw his cheeks stretch with a smile as he winked.

"Just a small hope," he replied. "And trust me, my girl, that's enough."

I just nodded and turned my gaze towards the rectangular narrow window in my cell. It was dusk, twilight setting in with the cold winds of the frozen tundra and seas beyond the tower walls. Splashes of orange and gold were trying to break the otherwise daunting grey of this lifeless place, spreading a gentle glow across the stone floor.

"How you must long to feel the sun on your skin and smell the wind as you taste freedom," he observed, watching me with those gentle, kind, hazel eyes. "Imprisonment is no easy thing to bear, especially for the innocent."

I sighed again, nodding at his words as I faced away from him. "I wish I could be free again."

"There is always a chance, dear girl," the old man told me wisely. "And yours is still yet to come. When it does, I pray that you are wise enough to recognise it and take it."

With that, he moved away from the door and I heard the springs of the cot in his cell strain under the pressure of him sitting down. I watched the door for a few long moments before turning my gaze back to the window and the slowly building twilight.

He's right of course. I can't just give up and resign myself to the fate the Shadow Lord has planned for me. Whatever happens, I must stay strong. If for no one else, then for myself.

I just sat there watching the sunlight fading away into the growing night after that, listening to the winds howling and rattling against the tower's stone facade. Sunset was the only beauty that seemed to be alive in this dreary place; the only time the stark greys and whites of Ortagaad were coloured with warmth and light.

With the last of the orange hues fading into darkness, I laid my forehead in my arms and closed my eyes, tiredness beginning to take me.

I hope I at least have pleasant dreams tonight. Everything else is just horrible and painful.

The distant bang of a door elsewhere in the tower drew my gaze back up to my surroundings, the sound of footsteps climbing the stairs growing louder.

Oh no...

I got to my feet and turned to look at the door into the chamber, straining my eyes in the faded torchlight. Terrifying apprehension filled me, my fingers crushing around the bars as I felt a heavy shudder hit me and become fearful trembling. I quickly tried to calculate how long it had been since I was last tortured.

Please let it be something else. Something good. Anything. Just not another interrogation. It's too soon.

The door to the chamber opened, five figures entering and looking around at the cells. They moved purposefully to mine, Ulric smirking as he saw me.

I pulled back and stood away from the bars, just far enough that he couldn't reach through and grab me again.

"Good evening, Princess," he spoke with a gleefully malicious tone as he took the keys from his belt.

"What do you want?" I managed to ask without stuttering, my body shaking hard as I edged away from the door.

"Your presence is requested," he stated as he unlocked my cell and entered, pausing as he handled the ring of keys in his large hands. "The Mistresses have instructed me to bring you to the inquisition room."

I instantly started to cry; no strength left in me to hold it back. My chest heaved and I sniffed against my sobs, backing away as he slowly and deliberately moved towards me.

"No... n-n-no, please," I sobbed quietly, my tears hot in my eyes. "Please, don't..."

"The Mistresses command it," he stated with mocking sympathy, closing in on me as two of the other men followed him. "I *must* bring you..."

"No..." I whimpered, hitting my back against the wall, nowhere left for me to go. "Please... no..."

"Oh, sweet Princess," he was right in front of me, looking down into my frightened eyes as he held my neck, jaw and cheek with one hand, the other stroking my hair out of my eyes, "do not fear. If you simply relent, you will not suffer so badly. Try to make this easier on yourself."

"That... that won't work," I shook my head fearfully up at him, my chest shuddering with my sobs. "They'll hurt me anyway..."

"Yes, Princess, they will," he smirked down at me, taking my right wrist in his hand and unlocking the shackle. "I suppose there really is no comfort for you."

He unlocked my other wrist and freed it, then brushed my hair away from my face and sniffed my neck, making me cringe back into the wall.

"You truly are fairest of all," he said with quiet lust. "Such a precious young beauty. And tonight, I once more get the pleasure... of hearing you *scream*."

I stared at him through my tears, my sobs now growing into full panic at his words.

He grasped me by the back of the neck and threw me forward towards the door, casting me down onto the hard floor. In moments, he was on me and my panicked screams tore through the stone chamber in shrilled echoes. I was on my feet as he lifted me up, the two men with him grabbing my arms tight enough to hurt me.

"Bring her," he turned and strode towards the door out of the tower chamber.

The two men dragged me after him, my struggles the hardest I had thrown for so long that I couldn't remember the last time I had fought so furiously. My boots scraped against the floor as I tried to plant my feet, my footing easily slipping as they roughly and carelessly forced me from the cell and down the stairs.

"NO! PLEASE, DON'T!" I screamed hysterically, struggling so hard my arms were hurting with the jerking of my body. "DON'T DO THIS TO ME! PLEASE! NO! NO!"

At the bottom of the stairs, my screams had frayed Ulric's tolerance and he spun around, backhanding me across my right cheek.

"Shut your mouth, girl," he snarled at me as I cried from fear and pain in his men's grasps. "While your screams may please me, truly you do irritate right at this moment."

I fell into desperate sobs, my tears induced blindness making it impossible for me to see where I was going now. My path was chosen by my cruel captors and all I could do was struggle, knowing that there was nothing I could do to free myself.

* * * * *

Once again, I found myself in the terrible torch lit dark of the inquisition room, the two Witches already waiting for me. At seeing them, I broke down and begged them not to hurt me, but their plans were set, and they would not relent to show me any kind of mercy.

For hours and hours, I was trapped in their painful company, at first trying to compose myself only then to give into my screams as they combined witchcraft with conventional torture. Of all the terrible days since I had been brought to this evil room I never suffered as greatly as I did that dark night.

Keilantra's fury was beyond all reckoning, her rage at my answers to her questions only increasing with each time I spoke or fell silent. I think I was subjected to almost every torture that didn't break the Shadow Lord's conditions for my treatment, every moment I was there spent screaming and crying at the cruel agony tearing me apart.

I felt sick as I sat there on the cold stone floor, my dress hanging down my arms to leave my shoulders bare, my breaths laboured and difficult in my chest. I could barely keep my eyes open, the exhaustion so heavy on me that I could feel the dizzying nausea that came with passing out swirling through my throbbing head.

Keilantra paced slowly, dressed in a totally black gown, her hand to her lips as she mused deeply. She kept glancing at me, studying my broken shape as I trembled and whimpered before her, as if she were designing her next vicious cruelty to inflict on me.

Why can't they stop hurting me?! This thing is so painful! Gods, I want it off me!

They had chosen to use a device which was the opposite of the rack, my body being crushed into itself painfully. It was a metal A-framed implement with iron cuffs at the ends with the most distance between them and a collar for the throat at its pinnacle point. It forced my body to be compressed so that my knees were bent, and my torso was curved forward with my neck being pulled towards my feet. My wrists were secured in the two remaining shackles a little more than midway to the point where my throat was held, pinning my elbows into my ribs and completely crushing me in place.

My back hurt so much that I feared my spine could snap if more pressure were to be added to my fragile body. My neck ached and I couldn't move my head properly as my hips and shoulders felt like they were separating.

This thing hurts so much, I thought as tears and sobs continued their fall from my eyes and lips. *I've been in it for so long it feels like I'll never stand up straight again. Oh, please, someone set me free from this monstrosity.*

A small glimmer of silver drew my gaze to Keilantra's hand as she paced, the woman still thumbing my pendant as she had been for as long as I had screamed that terrible night.

At last, she turned to me, her eyes hard, but her voice even: "How many hours of pain must you endure before you surrender to my will, child? Is it truly so hard to give me what I want?"

My eyes fell shut under my messy hair and I sobbed helplessly, even the shudder of my cries hurting my agonised body against the terrible device compacting me.

"I find her resistance invigorating, dear sister," Manth spoke from behind me, the place she had stood for so long now. "It is a pleasure to make her scream."

My screams ripped from my body once more as I felt the crushing pain of her dark magic working through me, my body trying to flail against it only to be hurt further by the torture device holding me. I could smell my own blood in my nose as vessels burst, my bones feeling as if they were shattering with the hard jerking against the iron confining me. I cried harder as my screams became more desperate and shrilled, every moment leaving me wishing that they would just kill me.

At last, Manth ceased her attack and I slumped against myself, still sitting up only due to the way my body was forced to be shaped. Keilantra was suddenly in front of me, my vision compromised by dots of green and black that danced in my sights.

"Manth will take any opportunity to torture young girls like you," she told me softly, though still coldly. "This need not continue, Princess."

I struggled to talk, my throat dry and raw from screaming, the iron collar not helping at all as it dug into my skin. I looked up at her face as my crying went on, desperate for her to stop.

"P-please... please stop," I begged through sobs, my voice tiny and weak.

"I will," she assured me, lifting my chin to keep me looking at her. "Once you tell me what I want to know."

Oh no! Please, no! How can I be spared this pain when telling the truth gives me nothing?! Oh, this will never end!

I started crying harder at hearing her words, wishing I knew the right answer to make her let me go.

She leaned closer to me, her other hand letting my pendant dangle from her fist right before my eyes. I looked to it briefly, then back to her, knowing the words she was about to speak and dreading the consequences of my only possible response.

"*How* do I take control of your dragon *and* your pendant?" she asked me for what was the latest in an infinite number of times at this point. "Tell me this and I shall free you from that cold device."

I closed my eyes and cried, my sobs all that I had left to give now. I was so tired and all I wanted was to sleep, to bury myself away from the tortures of this long night and never wake up again.

She grasped the bar holding me and jerked it, making me cry out and whimper, my eyes opening to look at her as she considered the thing binding me.

"It is a curious device, the Scavenger's Daughter," she mused, meeting my teary, pain filled gaze again. "An ironic counterpart to the stretching of the rack with how it crushes your body instead of stretching it. It is a slow, painfully agonising torture that does not require any outside influence to inflict its torments."

I closed my eyes, forcing the few tears left to slip free down my cheeks.

"It is strange that we so rarely use it," she said, smirking at the device. "I suppose it is one of those special little things to be saved for the right occasion."

"Please..." I let out a whimpering beg between weeping sobs, the pain only getting worse. "It hurts *so* much..."

"Then give me what I have asked of you," Keilantra dangled my pendant before my eyes again. "Tell me how to take control of this and your pain will end."

I gasped in a loud sobbing breath: "I... I don't know... Please..."

Rage filled her eyes and she backhanded me, the slap drawing a hysterical cry of pain that was intensified by the additional torment of the Scavenger's Daughter.

"Stop lying to me, girl!" she snarled at me, glaring into my eyes. "I *hate* being lied to!"

"I'm not lying! I don't know!" I screamed as she hit me again, then grabbed my hair and tilted my head back, the collar digging into the nape of my neck as my cries became more desperate: "Ugh! Stop! Please!"

"Tell me what I want to know!" she shouted into my face.

"I don't know! I don't know!" I pleaded in screams as tears came in a torrent from my eyes that was heavier than before.

"Manth!" Keilantra snapped to her sister.

"No, no, please! No! Argh!" the pain ripped through me again as the Witch behind me made my whole body convulse and I shrieked in agony, closing my eyes tight.

Keilantra didn't release my hair, keeping my neck craned back to make the pain worse. I kept screaming, losing my breath and getting so lightheaded that I felt I would collapse.

Make it stop! Someone, please make it stop! Please!

After a small eternity, the pain stopped with Manth withdrawing her power, the convulsing of my body falling still. I cried loudly and hopelessly as Keilantra let go of my hair and held my chin, forcing me to look at her, but I couldn't open my eyes.

"Look at me, girl," she hissed, then shouted: "LOOK AT ME!"

Afraid to incur more of her wrath, I did as I was told, forcing my weak eyes to open. I could barely breathe with my chest moving so quickly, my heartbeat so fast that it was painful.

"Your refusal to relent has gone beyond my tolerance," she grumbled harshly at me, her eyes like two fireballs of superheated emerald. "Tell me how to control your pendant and your dragon, and I will put an end to your suffering. Deny me *one more time* and I will make you scream and suffer beyond all knowing of such torments."

"Please... don't..." was all I could manage to choke out through my hard crying.

"Tell me, girl," she glowered and grasped my hair again.

"I wish... I wish I knew how to give you... want you want!" I cried out, desperate for this to end, my words broken up by sobbing, breathless gasps. "If it would save me... from this awful torment, I would... I would give you exactly what you want! I don't care anymore! Take it! Just take it! Please... Just... just don't hurt me anymore!"

I gave up. There was no more resistance left in me, the despair of these tortures outweighing my hope in rescue. And while guilt filled me at the thought of surrendering my treasured necklace, I would gladly give anything to save myself from anymore agony.

I looked to the Witch pleadingly through my tears and abused strands of hair, breathlessly whispering: "It's yours. The Pendant is yours. Just don't hurt me anymore... please..."

She scrutinised me as she knelt there, then turned her gaze to the Pendant. Her thoughts seemed to tick across her face as she considered my sobbing pleas and surrender, trying to decide what she would do next.

"Very well," she said at last, dread breaking through my ribs and spine at her severe gaze. "Ulric."

I cringed as he stepped up beside me, fearing what terrible torture would come next.

"My Queen," he bowed his head solemnly.

"Release her," Keilantra permitted, standing up and turning from me.

Release me? She's freeing me from this thing? Why? I didn't give her what she wanted.

Ulric didn't hesitate, moving to crouch beside me and first unlocking my wrists, taking my left hand and putting my palm to the floor behind me. I immediately put my right hand back too as he freed my ankles. He removed the collar from my neck, and I slumped to my left side, my legs and torso stretching out a little more to become comfortable again. My sobs fell more quietly now, though my tears were still high in their numbering, the agony of my body becoming lesser aches.

I rubbed my throat with both hands, trying to slow my breathing as I lay there with my eyes shut. Even they were beginning to hurt now from all my crying.

Slowly, I looked to Keilantra as she studied my pendant, her severe eyes taking in all of its facets and designs.

What will she do to me now? that was the only thought I could manage in the silent pain still breaking through me.

Keilantra turned back to me, her expression softer, though still harsh and cold: "Get her on her feet and bring her."

Ulric grabbed me and forced me up, my body so weak now that I had no choice but to hold onto his arm when my knees nearly gave way. I knew he was revelling in my necessary touch, but I couldn't stand on my own and had to push away the thoughts of his disgusting glee.

I looked back to Keilantra, wondering what plan she now had for me as I was taken from the room...

Chapter Four
The Secrets of Ortagaad

T hough they brought me out of the darkness of the inquisition room, I felt no
better than when I was inside it. My body burned with the exhausting pain
they had inflicted on me and I found that walking was now one of the
hardest things to do. Keilantra walked briskly, Manth and the guards surrounding
us, moving at speed to keep up. Ulric heaved me along behind the two women, my
own ability to move quickly entirely destroyed at that moment.

*They just made me spend hours with all of my limbs crushed in that awful device
and I've had no healing yet. How can they expect me to even try to keep up with them?*

Entering the keep's darkened expanse, I could see by the enormous
windows that it was still night outside, though I was certain it must have been
nearing dawn.

They've tortured me all night, I realised with a heavy, aching heart. *What
horrors wait for me now that can't be inflicted on me once I have healed? Maybe they
finally plan to kill me...*

I was taken through the keep and past the throne room, though we didn't
stop here. The Witches led us through darkened halls and along narrow corridors
of stone, much of the castle seeming as if it had been closed off from use.

Two large doors were opened, and I felt the chilly winter air of the tundra
topped seas on my skin. I looked up at the sky to finally see the stars between
sparse clouds in an otherwise clear night for the first time in I don't know how
long. The stars glimmered and shone brightly, thousands upon thousands of them
staring down at us where we stood on the dark stone walkway.

As we made our way across the walkway into the cold night I thought: *It's
as if the heavens are watching all that happens here. Maybe that's why that room is so deep
inside the castle. Maybe it's hidden to keep the stars from seeing such evils.*

There was a tower across from us, this one nowhere near as tall as the West
Tower. It was old, and like the tallest of its relations in the castle it had a pointed
roof with shingled tiles.

We made our way down a set of stairs into the courtyard outside the tower,
Keilantra striking out now with her heavy black, bear fur cloak pulled over her
shoulders, Manth beside her hidden beneath her own black hood. I shivered hard
against the cold with only my dress to shield me. The chill felt deeper than before
and I assumed it was because we had descended closer to the seas below the
castle's foundations.

Two guards waited by the enormous doors into the tower, torches lit on sconces behind them. They stood at attention as Keilantra moved into view, though whether they were fearful or reverent I couldn't tell.

"Open the doors," she commanded, and the two men immediately obeyed.

The room within was enormous, but it was as dark as a deep cave, no light at all filtering in to show me anything of where I now found myself. There was a sound within; a deep gusting, almost like someone was breathing, though whoever it was had to be enormous.

I felt a terrible knot tying up my stomach and I worried what ghastly visage I was about to be set before. I instantly recalled that gruesome experiment built by the Unseen in the Under Roads beneath the Nartarn'lath Mountains, my blood running cold at the mere thought of seeing something like it.

I heard the soldiers moving around us, Ulric not straying from my side, his hand tight on my arm. I had now managed to stand on my own, his grasp only ensuring I didn't try to run if I got the chance. In truth, my body hurt so much that I doubted I could walk on my own just yet, let alone try to run.

"Where are we?" I asked softly in the darkness. "What is this place?"

"Like the rest of this fortress," Keilantra explained, standing near to my left, "this tower is a prison, though not for humans."

Lanterns and torches came alight all around, spreading their flaming glow across all the stone and wood structures within. The space was enormous, the only stairs leading up to the walkways where the guards now took positions, more of them there than I had first thought. The ceiling was so high that even the tallest of ladders would not have reached the rafters above. There was another set of gigantic doors at the far end opposite the ones we had entered, but this wasn't the focus of my gaze.

The creature lay on the ground clad in chains, scaled in purple, blue and silver with great magenta wings. My heart shattered and I stifled a cry at seeing her.

"This chamber was built centuries ago for but one purpose," Keilantra sneered viciously at my side. "Imprisoning a dragon."

"Amethyst," I gasped as I beheld my beloved friend lying there completely helpless.

The sight was so incredibly heartbreaking. The Dragon was on her stomach with her front legs laid out before her like a human would lay their arms. Her rear legs were curled up, feet to the floor with her tail lying straight behind her. Her neck was outstretched towards where we stood, her head resting on the floor.

The restraints holding her were massive, a sort of two-part ring held in place around her body by heavy wooden beams and intricate mechanisms attached to the highest walls. Her wings were closed in and trapped beneath this against her sides, no way available for her to even try to stretch them. Gigantic shackles were closed around each of her wrists and ankles, chained to the floor beneath her body with barely any length to let her move at all. Custom shackles were also fitted to her tail, chains attached to a wooden crossbeam above her to keep it suspended. Her neck hung in much the same way with an enormous collar closed around it, a cruel looking steel muzzle clamped around her nose and jaws.

"Amethyst!" I cried louder, trying to run to her, but my legs gave out and Ulric pulled me back, holding both of my arms tightly behind me and crossing my wrists.

The Dragon opened her fire orange eyes and saw me. She made desperate growls and bleats, raising her head and trying to fight her chains to reach me.

"What have you done to her?!" I demanded as I glared at Keilantra and struggled in Ulric's grasp.

"The Dragon remains unharmed, I assure you, child," she told me, "I could not risk damage to such a fine specimen of her species."

I kept struggling against Ulric's hold as the Witch moved to study Amethyst up close. Instantly, the Dragon snapped and roared behind the muzzle, clearly hating this Witch as much as I had come to.

"You have to set her free!" I pleaded, my eyes darting back to my dragon's in worry. "You can't keep a dragon imprisoned like this!"

Keilantra spun around and glared at me, storming forward until she stood over me. "Set her free?! If I were to do so, the beast would turn around and wreak such powerful devastation upon this castle! With no way of controlling her, she is too great a risk to be freed from the confines of her cage!"

"And the Master," Manth spoke in that creepy voice of hers as she moved to stand in front of me, her coal-like eyes burning, "has commanded the Dragon be kept imprisoned, much as he has you, girl."

"Under *my* control, the Dragon will be shaped into a powerful weapon," Keilantra explained her dark designs. "Until then she remains in chains."

Amethyst snarled lowly, threatening the Witches in her own way. All she got was Keilantra's evil glare and sneer over her shoulder before I was given it again.

"That is why *you* are here, Princess," she said lightly, moving to stand to my left.

"What... what do you mean?" I stammered, looking to her uncertainly as I let my struggles fall still.

She smiled coldly at me: "If I cannot gain the control I seek from you, then perhaps I can gain it from the Dragon."

I frowned. "How?"

Suddenly, a guard was before me and my wrists were tied tightly together with coarse leather bindings. My weak struggles were useless and brief, the guard soon stepping away. Ulric hurled me down, my dragon instantly roaring a terrible sound of rage as I crashed to the stone floor.

"You don't like that, do you? Good," Keilantra laughed up at the Dragon. "Your loyalty to the girl is strong, and I can use it to mould you into the weapon I desire and make you my thrall."

Amethyst snarled and growled fiercely, smashing against her restraints as hard as she could manage. I could tell she was weaker than she should be, the poor creature looking as if she had suffered without proper feeding for so long.

"We can make this very simple, Dragon," the Witch glared up at Amethyst as I crawled to my knees. "Side with me or the girl suffers greater pains than those we have already spent this night inflicting upon her."

I screamed in terror as Manth crushed her talon-like fingers around my throat, the other hand holding my bound wrists. I squirmed to get away from her, but she was stronger than she looked. It was even easier for her to control me since I was so weak from the night of torture I had endured.

"No, Amethyst!" I screamed to my dragon. "Don't listen to them! They'll hurt me anyway!"

"Your courage is admirable, girl," Manth hissed into my ear, "but foolish."

She hurled me down and curled her sharp fingers above me like a claw. I started screaming and writhing on the stone floor as that same torturous magic ripped through my nerves, my blood feeling like it was boiling inside my veins.

I heard Amethyst roaring and howling in rage, her claws slamming hard into the floor and shaking the room all around us. She kept snapping behind the muzzle at the two Witches, desperate to rescue me from their cruelty.

No, Amethyst... That was the last thought I had that night, the strain from all of the hours of suffering they had inflicted on me finally taking its toll on my broken body. Darkness consumed me as the sounds of my dragon's roars began to dull, my own screams already silenced. I tried to stay awake, but it was now completely impossible.

The last thing I saw was Keilantra staring up at Amethyst in front of me, the Dragon still thrashing wildly to exact her retribution on our captors for my suffering. Then, all was dark and silent...

* * * * *

Pain shot through me like a hurled spear crushing my chest, drawing a hard, agonising breath from my lungs. I felt my body jerk against itself, my limbs still aching, my arms suddenly worse than my legs. A cough ripped from my heaving chest, leaving me temporarily breathless as the rush of the waking world returned to me. In a few moments my nerves had eased, and I slumped back against something hard.

Why do I have to keep waking up? I moaned as my head throbbed, my eyes staying shut with an ache behind them. *All this pain and suffering... it's too much for me. Why can't they just leave me alone? Why must they hurt me so terribly?*

I sat there as I was for a short time, my knees up and my toes braced against something. That was when I started to take stock of my body and realised that I could feel the biting cold of iron shackles around my wrists. The ache in my arms suddenly made sense and I opened my eyes to see that they were pulled up over my head.

Oh, Gods...

The horror that filled me was unspeakable as I came to find myself not in my tower cell as I had expected, but somewhere far worse. I was locked in one of the narrow gibbets that I had seen hanging over the walls of the castle, but this one was in a cavern. Chains kept my wrists shackled to the top of the cage, my long dress and sleeves slipping through the bars that surrounded me.

My fear of heights hit me hard as I looked down and saw the great drop below me in the dark of this cold place. I closed my eyes and whimpered, pulling my knees up closer to my body as I feared falling.

The cage was swaying on its mooring, which only made my fear worse. Even my own trembling made it move and I began to cry in growing terror of the thought of hitting the floor far below me.

"Calm yourself, child," a kindly male voice spoke from my right. "You are in no danger of falling. Just try to breathe."

I opened my eyes and looked to where the voice had come from. It was the old man from the tower, trapped in a cage identical to the one I was in, his wrists bound in the same way. Now I could see him clearly with the light of the torches surrounding us, gasping as I recognised him.

"You," I stared at him wide eyed. "I know you. You were at Eilath when the Revenant attacked me. You saved my life."

"Indeed, I did, Princess," the man nodded, forcing a weak smile. "And we have met before that."

When? When did I meet him before Eilath?

I thought about it hard as I studied his aged and lined face. His familiarity to me was so strong now, stronger than that which I had felt in the safety of Fawkner's home. Were it not for the blood and bruises that tainted his skin, my mind might have come to the conclusion much quicker than it did.

"Castle Arvon... That was you that day in my Father's study," I recalled, my heart rushing with quiet excitement. "The day my uncle named me as Aldegaad's next Queen."

"It was indeed, your Highness," he nodded, allowing me to unravel this myself, "though you and I did not speak on that day."

"You're the Green Wizard," I said, remembering that much from our meeting in Eilath. "You're one of the Custodians of the Past."

He conceded: "Perhaps so, though I am more accurately a member of the Elemental Brotherhood."

I frowned in thought. "But there's more than that..."

I thought back to when I had first seen his face, though I could scarcely remember now. It had been so long since last I had seen anyone who wasn't one of my vicious captors. In all the strange eternity I had spent here it had seemed like my life before was nothing more than a colourful dream.

I know I've seen him somewhere else... I know it... My parents were there...

"The Festival of Light," I remembered and met his hazel gaze again. "That was when we first spoke. You... you gave me the Dragon Egg."

"I am gladdened that your memory yet remains to you, dear girl," the Wizard smiled warmly, which was strange in this place.

"You knew about me," I surmised, at last understanding - at least in some part - my connection to this strange man. "You knew that the Pendant had chosen me."

"I had discussed it with your father and King Aric," the Wizard confirmed with a gentle nod. "Knowing that their intention was to give the Pendant to you, I read the signs and could see that the Dragon Stone was also destined to be yours," he smiled brighter with wonder in his eyes as he looked at me. "It is good to know that you truly are the one meant for both."

"Not that it's helped much," I sighed and tested my restraints. "Both my pendant and Amethyst were taken from me."

"The very reason the Raven's Rest Sisters have forced you to endure such tortures as you have," he said gravely, drawing my eyes back to him. "Regardless of their desires, it is well known that to keep a Pendant Holder helpless one must first take their pendant and their dragon. And while the Queen seeks to control both, the Shadow Lord seeks only your helplessness."

"You seem to know a lot about what has happened to me here," I observed, flexing my fingers against the pressure on my wrists.

His eyes grew dark and his expression serious: "I have made it my business to know what you have come to face. Especially after you identified our enemy."

I shuddered at the very thought of the Shadow Lord, still so fearful of his return.

The Wizard turned his gaze out to the darkness surrounding us, studying all that lay beyond our cages.

"Lord Morod's designs are yet a mystery, even to the Elemental Brotherhood," he said gravely, turning his hazel gaze back to me. "Yet, only one constant remains in his focus. You."

"I don't know what more he wants from me," I confessed, trembling from the sheer cold of the air around us.

"Indeed, he has already taken much from you to regain his powers and physical form," he considered, still very calm and even toned, "yet, I fear that there is more he yearns to take. Your very life itself is the prize left to be claimed, and it seems he is biding his time before doing so."

I shivered harder, not wanting to think of the horrors the sinister monster could be planning for me. I needed something to distract myself from such terrors, anything at all.

"Why are we in these cages?" it was the only question I could bring to mind.

"I am not certain," the Wizard was still surveying our surroundings. "However, we are most certainly not above the castle or the sea. This cavern lies beneath Castle Ortagaad..."

"You are so very right, old man," a harsh, raspy voice spoke from the shadows behind us.

I awkwardly craned my body around, twisting my arms with mild pain to see the speaker, blinking against my long dark hair. There was a stone archway behind us, our cages hanging from a wide semi-circle balcony built into the underground cliffs. The torches that flanked the archway gave a clear view of this small shelf and of the figures now before us. There were four of Keilantra's guards standing by the door in a line, stern and grim behind their helmets and black cloaks. Before them stood Ulric, as arrogant as ever, though his expression was severe.

Out from their lines like a black cloaked wraith, Manth strode towards us, seeming to glide with her feet hidden so perfectly beneath her dark dress. She smiled her deep purple lips, her hands hooked together in front of her lightly. Her completely black eyes didn't falter from our faces, her sneer only growing at my fearful gaze.

"This cavern does indeed lie beneath the fortress," the Witch explained as she gently moved towards us. "The sea crawls through gaps in the rocks to fill its lowest reaches and even allow the Culler Sharks to enter. A very useful occurrence should we wish to end someone in a truly gruesome way."

She turned her eyes to me as she said this, making me cringe away and whimper. The very thought of those black sharks swimming below us only added a greater fear to the vertigo that still crushed me.

The Witch turned her attention back to the Wizard, smirking at him: "To see you like this is only a greater victory for me."

"There will be no victory for you, Manth," the Wizard stated calmly and with great strength. "Nor will there be for your dark Master."

"You seem so certain, Wizard," Manth crooned at him as she craned her head unnaturally.

"Your defeat is inevitable," he said with conviction, "just as it was when you were defeated centuries ago..."

"You believe *this* girl," she jabbed one dagger-like finger at me, "even has any chance of standing against Lord Morod's might? We have all but destroyed her..."

"You have shown naught but cruelty and malice to her," he interrupted her sternly. "If your victory relies singularly on tormenting an adolescent girl, then you and your Master are to be sorely sorry when all comes to the promised end."

"Your prophecies mean nothing," she hissed at him lowly. "They are empty, broken, and have been proven false. *She* defeated the Master and passed into the Beyond of old age. Now, Lord Morod has returned, and your Champion is but bones and dust," she glared closer to his face, making sure to see the depths of his eyes: "Your prophecies...*lied*."

If their glares were swords, they would be locked in a death duel. The intensity of the hatred between them was like the brightness of the sun and I flinched at seeing it. The Wizard and the Witch didn't turn their gazes from one another for a time, almost as if they were battling in silence. But at last, their eerie staring contest came to its end when the question plaguing me slipped from my lips.

"Why have you brought us here?" I murmured so quietly that at first I thought I had imagined it.

Manth turned her eyes to me, moving to stand within closer range of my cage. I cringed as far from her as I could manage, but I knew there was nowhere to go.

"I have something to show you, child," she said in that hissy voice of hers, casting her hand to the depths below. "Behold."

I followed her gaze and, with a deep breath against my fear, looked down. This was when I noticed the torches below and the movement of many figures. The sounds of forges being tended, and of hammers hitting anvils echoed through the darkness as the growls and roars of beasts like a wretched choir singing bestially, guttural hymns rising from the depths.

My eyes adjusted and I gasped as I began to understand what lurked on the rocks below. There was a great and terrible horde of humanoid beasts, all of them I was able to recognise.

Towering Erks lumbered along with their large hands dragging across the ground, snapping and snarling like beasts if they crossed each other. Stumpy, squat Hurgarks squabbled viciously over food, looking like fattened little goblins in heavy armour that resembled the kind worn by dwarves, only ruined and aged. They shrieked and chirped in their bizarre way as they scurried among the larger beasts, easily being knocked down due to their short stature. Yet, they would just get up and go back to their scrambling as they fed and barked like mad things. The lanky, slender, leather wrapped Gymphs slunk through the shadows, their hideous faces snarling pointed teeth as they scampered out of sight of the other creatures. Their shrill shrieks were the highest and loudest of all the creatures, far less like something of any natural world than I had ever heard.

The two more human-like of the creatures were the naturally formed green skinned Orcs, and the by evil-forged dark skinned Gathlorks. Both were burly and brutish in appearance, but the Orcs had large tusks jutting up from their bottom lips while the Gathlorks had evenly jagged teeth on both jaws. The Orcs were also much neater in their appearance, rough as it was, the Gathlorks much more frightening and savage.

Both species worked the forges and the anvils, building weapons and armour in great volumes, their bodies as black silhouettes against the molten glow of the metal fires.

In the midst of it all, there were ghoulish feminine forms that looked like they had been corrupted by terrible magic. They were tending to great cocoons which opened to produce the terrible beasts, but only the Hurgarks and Gymphs, the Erks seeming to be the corruption of some kind of animal.

They're breeding the Scourge here! I stared in horror at the monsters below, trembling with shuddering breaths at the sight of them. *It's an army of those terrible beasts!*

Screams echoed in another area as I saw a human girl being dragged into a cave-like opening by a number of Gathlorks, their torsos unclothed. I shuddered, repulsed by the thought of what they were doing.

That's how Gathlorks are bred?! Oh Gods!

"Is it not glorious?" Manth was staring down into the depths of the horde.

"It is an atrocity!" the Wizard declared, turning his angered gaze to her. "Never mind the horrors the young women forced to breed Gathlorks must endure, you are allowing a terrible plague to fester beneath Castle Ortagaad! If it were to spread across High-Realm..."

"Precisely the plan, old man," the Witch replied darkly, her smile and words sending a death chill through my spine.

She turned her gaze upon me, then looked back across the sea of monsters as if she were an artist admiring her grand work.

"This breeding ground is but one of many," she stated evenly. "The Master wishes us to prepare for what is to come."

"What is to come?" the words were out of my mouth before I could stop them, and I cowered under her evil black gaze.

"War, Princess," the Witch sneered, insane bloodlust in her eyes. "The last war of this world. The Dominion will spread over all of High-Realm, then Therras, and finally the world. Then, Lord Morod will rule all..."

"You would spread like a plague across this world," the Wizard shook his head furiously. "You would destroy all the innocents who live so that your kind might lay waste to all the lands and cover it in an evil darkness."

"Why are you telling us all of this?" I asked, regaining the woman's stare.

"Because" she replied, "there is nothing you can do to prevent it, Wizard. As for you, Princess, the Master would have you know the scale of his designs before you meet your end."

I stared wide eyed at her, my heart skipping a beat from her terrible words. *They'll destroy High-Realm and kill everyone... How can anyone stand against such evil?*

"Now, however, you are required elsewhere, child," she gestured, and Ulric opened my cage and began freeing me from my shackles.

I was lifted from the cage and my wrists were chained in front of me, the man roughly squeezing my arm to hold me steady once he was done.

"Take her to the Sanctum," Manth ordered him briskly. "I shall join her soon, as will my sister. I would speak further with the Wizard."

The Sanctum?! my heart began to race wildly. *That's where they take all the other girls that never return! Why would they want me taken there?!*

Ulric heaved me by my shoulder, lifting my arm hard as he forced me quickly away from the cages and towards the stone archway. I easily lost track of where I was being taken, the close corridors and narrow stairs all looking the same in the barely broken darkness, and I was soon being brought into the keep once again.

Ulric took me up the grand staircase that led to the floors above, not caring that I struggled to keep up with him. He led me down a long corridor with windows on all sides, one view showing me the courtyards below, the other displaying the far distant spread of the sea. It was sunset, the golden orange hues of the sky choked dark by the heavy clouds that cast deep snows over everything surrounding the castle.

We turned right and passed by closed doors on all sides, virtually no guards stationed here. He brought me to the very last door at the end of the hall and opened it.

I was shoved through, losing my footing and hitting the hard floor with a grunt of pain. I turned over with the rattling of the chains on my wrists to face the crude knight and the two guards standing at his back.

"Now, you be a good girl and wait here for the Mistresses," he told me in the mocking way someone would speak to a child. "They shan't be too long."

With a chuckle he closed the door behind him, the locks sealing with loud booming clicks.

Hesitant and uncertain, I turned my gaze from the door, already knowing it was pointless to even try to fight it open.

I took in the room, ill at ease by its decor and floor plan. It was a cold black stone place with an almost rounded design. To my right and before me were two enormous windows with cruel looking black frames holding the glass in place. To my left was an old desk and a couple of chairs, a collection of shelves set behind the desk. And lastly, in the centre of the room - as I had expected from all the fairy tales I had ever read - there was a large cauldron set over an unlit fire pit built into the floor.

Slowly, grasping my teal velvet and blue linen skirts so as not to trip, I got to my feet and started to carefully explore. There were at least a dozen black bookshelves that stood tall against the walls, many more set behind the desk. They were all stocked with books and various other less friendly things. Set around the room were also display cases, though I was too uneasy to dare to go near them.

This really isn't somewhere I expected to end up, I worried as I looked at all the witchcraft artefacts that surrounded me. *I don't think me being here is a good thing.*

There was a mirror set to the wall between the two windows, a full six feet in height and framed with ebony. *I haven't seen my reflection in so long. I wonder how bad off I am.*

I moved to the mirror and was shocked by my reflection. The girl in the glass looked like me, but she was more frail, though not dangerously underweight. My collarbones were a little more defined and my frame was slimmer, but I could tell by my shoulders that I didn't have bones poking through with a complete loss of my health. My face and much of my skin was smudged with grime and dirt, my hair hanging dark and lifeless over my right shoulder and down to my breast. My hips looked more obvious now beneath the tightened bodice of my dress, the fabric easily sliding from my shoulders as the weight of the over-sleeves dragged them down my arms. But it was my expression that worried me the most. I looked drained of all vitality, like some terrible thing had been drinking all the life from me. I still appeared to be eighteen, but tired and weak, barely the same girl I had been in Arvon however long ago.

I look awful. How can I have remained so youthful and yet become so haggard? Is this what loneliness, starvation, torture and imprisonment can do to a human being?

I pulled my gaze from the mirror and turned my attention back to the room. Falling on my old tendencies, I found myself very quickly studying the books on the shelves. There wasn't a single one I would have considered reading, many - if not all - written on subjects of witchcraft for the use of evil.

Fitting, of course, considering the women whose Sanctum this is.

My eyes travelled then across one of the shelves directly behind the desk and I felt sickened to my stomach. There were dozens of glass jars set there, each one containing a human heart within its transparent confines. Worst of all, the hearts were still beating.

I was horror-struck by the sight. *What of the people these hearts belonged to? They aren't alive, are they? This really is a dark and evil place.*

Turning my gaze from the jarred hearts, I looked to the desk, desperate to find something to take the haunting image from my mind. There were parchments, scrolls and a couple of old books laid out there, most of the scribbling in languages or runes that I couldn't understand. But there was one that drew my gaze, marked with drawings of four black dragons surrounding a creature of black flame and shadow.

I studied the designs, then turned my gaze to the book beside it and began reading the last page left open.

Chief and most atrocious of all ancient evils are the Beasts of Ragnarok, the heralds of the End of All Things. With them the world was plunged into the terrors of the World Ender and plagued with Famine, Pestilence, War and Death on a scale beyond all reckoning.

I frowned. "Ragnarok?"

I read on: *These princely evils were defeated long ago by the Blood of Innocence so that they would never again threaten the world. Yet, should the Seals of Ankorect ever be broken, the evil shall spread into the world once more and the World Ender shall rise again with the Lunar Joining and the Dragon's Key...*

My frown only deepened as I read the words scrawled over the page.

What does any of that mean? Blood of Innocence? The Seals of Ankorect? Lunar Joining? Dragon's Key? The ancient scholars were very cryptic in their writings. Why did they never make these things clear?

I turned the page and found myself staring at a drawing of some terrible, sweeping form with great wings of smoke and shadow, blue flames glowing from beneath deepest darkness. The eyes of the hidden monster glared up at me and I felt a terrible chill fill my chest as a new fear crushed around my heart.

I jumped as the door unlocked, quickly backing away from the desk with the clattering of my chains and the rustling of my dress. My breath caught in my chest and my heart skipped a few beats as my eyes set on the opening door and the figures that traversed its threshold.

The Witches stared at me coldly as they entered the room, Manth remaining solemn while Keilantra immediately smirked at me.

"Ah, Princess..." the Witch-Queen hissed.

Chapter Five
Desperate Opportunity

I backed further away, my heart racing wildly in my chest at the sight of the two women. I slipped swiftly from their reach, letting out a startled yelp as my back hit the cold, black stone wall, my eyes locked squarely on them.

The two Witches almost seemed to slither into the room, Manth closing the door behind her and locking it so that I couldn't escape. They moved towards me, their hands suddenly seeming like claws. It was as if I could see the dark and terrible creatures that lurked beneath their human skins.

What are they going to do to me now? I trembled, too afraid to move from where I stood. *More cruel tortures? Something worse? Oh, please, just let me get out of this place...*

Keilantra now stood over me and I closed my eyes as I buried my chin into my right shoulder. I felt her long, pointed fingers pry my chin up and turn my face towards her, my eyes opening instinctively to meet her gaze. She studied me as I shook so hard the chains on my wrists rattled, her expression one of deep, calm consideration.

I braced myself for the inevitable explosion that I knew would come, silently fearing all the unknown pains I could suffer through.

"Such a pretty girl," the woman mewed as she analysed every flaw and nuance of my young face. "Truly the fairest of her kind... and the most innocent."

"She is, Keilantra," Manth agreed, standing over my left shoulder now. "And that is her greatest value to the Master."

"Indeed," Keilantra never took her eyes from mine, her fingers hurting my chin as they applied more pressure. "And so strong to hold out for so long against the tortures we had devised for her. How utterly intriguing..."

She let go of me and, with a sweep of her black and gold queenly robes, she moved to the desk. She took up three silver goblets and began filling them with water from a silver pitcher.

I glanced at her, then at Manth, frowning at the sister Witches and their calm, casual manners. *They aren't threatening me, and they offer me compliments? Something is terribly wrong here.*

Keilantra turned with one goblet and handed it to Manth, then offered the second to me. I didn't move, too afraid to make any sound or take a single step. Though I had seen her pour the water, I couldn't help but worry that she had done something to it.

"Come now, girl," she urged me, "you've been in that cage for nearly two days. You *must* be thirsty."

*I **am** so very thirsty*, I admitted to myself. *But can I trust that there is no vile or dangerous catch to taking this drink from her?*

"Please," she urged me again, unnaturally gentle. "Drink."

Slowly, I moved from the wall, trying to keep both Witches in my line of sight, which was difficult with their different positions in the room. I reached the table and carefully took the goblet from Keilantra with both hands.

Experimentally, I held it to my nose and sniffed the water, checking for any foul scents, but found none. Hesitantly, I edged it to my lips and started to drink, tasting the freshness, but also a flavour of sweet fruits. I thirstily drank down the contents, taking three breaths, though I managed to remain quiet and sedate as I did so. After a couple of minutes, I had finished the goblet and stood holding it in my hands, so grateful to have had something to drink.

"There," she smiled and took the goblet from me, "that's much better. Is it not, child?"

I took a few moments to gather myself and chose the first question to ask. There was only one after all.

"Why have you brought me here?" my voice sounded so small in my own hearing, my hands twisting and fidgeting together nervously.

"Simply to talk," Keilantra said after swallowing a mouthful of her own drink and sitting down at her desk, gazing up at me.

"You want to talk?" I was surprised, though I kept my voice quiet and even. She nodded. "Yes."

"Not to torture or interrogate me?" I raised a curious eyebrow at her.

"There is nothing left to be gained from that," she concluded, swallowing more of her drink and locking her gaze with mine. "It is clear to me now that there is no parting you from control of your pendant or your dragon. Such things are indeed impossible."

I huffed a small breath as I frowned incredulously at her. *Now she decides this? After all the countless hours, days, weeks and gods know how long I have screamed from the tortures she has inflicted upon me? What am I supposed to say to that?*

"You made your case," she stood and came to stand over me as I rested my palms against the desk. "No one would proclaim such things as you have under the tortures you have suffered without it being truth."

"So... what do you intend to do with me now?" I tried to sound steadfast as I spoke, though my knees shook beneath my skirts.

"Ah, *that* we shall discuss in a moment," she decreed as she turned and placed her hand on my arm to lead me. "First I would show you something."

What horror will this be?

Obediently, I followed her across the room to the window opposite the desk where a display case stood. It was gold and silver, framed with perfectly polished glass and a black velvet cushioning within.

"There are many things I collect, you see," she explained to me as we stopped before it, my eyes focused on her out of mistrust. "Some things are darker and more gruesome than others..."

I cringed at the thought of the jars of living hearts. I didn't dare to even try to consider what other things she would collect.

She went on: "But the rest are so rare and beautiful that they can never be compared to anything, for their worth is beyond imagining. Such as these."

I looked down at the display case and gasped: "Pendants?"

"Yes," Keilantra prided beside me as she ran one hand over the glass. "These are but a few of the Dragon Pendants. With yours added to the collection I now possess six of the thirteen."

I stared in wonder at the intricate and different designs of each one, mine set central with its silver flowery coiling and purple heart-stone standing out. There was one with a deep blue heart-stone and forged of gold, another with a turquoise-coloured heart and sculpted in a white metal next to it. The last two were both silver like mine, their stones a dark silvery grey and a gentle yellowish green. Each design was unique and as detailed in its intricacies as the others, so fine despite being such small things.

"I have been tracking the Pendants down for quite some time and I have only ever known of seven to exist," she explained. "I carry the Topazian Pendant, the Master possesses the Obsidian Pendant, and you, child, held the Amethian Pendant."

"I worry how you ever managed to gain possession of the other four," I looked to her uneasily.

"Various ways," she shrugged nonchalantly. "Some more violent than others. Though, I bartered the Sappherian Pendant from a Dwarf-merchant who thought it only to be a worthless trinket. That was perhaps the easiest of my acquisitions."

All I felt that I could do was nod. The thought of how she acquired the rest of the Pendants in that case left me feeling uneasy. I couldn't take my eyes from the necklaces, but it was *my* pendant that kept my gaze as I let my fingers intertwine before my hips, only dimly aware of the chains binding my wrists now.

"It has taken centuries to gather these few," the woman went on in a soft, whispering breath, caressing her hand over the case, "yet, I will search centuries longer if I must to find the other six that still remain."

"Why do you desire them so greatly?" I looked at her curiously. "You can't control them or the dragons that are bound to their heart-stones. Why go to so much effort?"

"Because, girl," she said slowly, almost like she was talking to a small child, "many are without owners and are scattered and lost throughout High-Realm. They *must* be discovered and secured somewhere safe."

"Somewhere no one else can find them," Manth added from behind us. "Only in this way can we prevent the return of the Dragons."

"So that's it," I looked between the two Witches, fully understanding now. "You want to ensure that there are no Pendant Holders beyond you and the Shadow Lord."

"The Pendant Holders are the ones who possess the greatest power in all the world," Manth stated coldly, drawing nearer and staring down at me with those harsh coal-like eyes. "Without them and the Dragons who defend them, the world is easily controlled..."

"And that only helps you to conquer High-Realm with your armies," I realised, horrified by this seemingly simple thing.

"Beyond the Master and myself," Keilantra reached out her long hand and caressed my cheek with her knuckles, "only *you* exist as a Pendant Holder in this time."

"Then I'm a threat to you," I said softly, my heart beginning to spawn a whole new kind of dread.

"Without your pendant and your dragon, you are powerless, girl," Manth told me with harshness in her voice. "Regardless of that fact, you will not be a threat for very much longer."

I frowned uneasily at her. "What does that mean?"

Keilantra swept past me and returned to her seat behind the desk. Manth took me by my arm and led me to stand before her sister again, slithering up beside her like a liquid shadow in the fading evening light a moment later.

"Your time is up," Keilantra smiled coldly.

I frowned deeper, dreading what that meant. "I don't understand..."

"On this day," she explained, "you have come of age. Your twenty-first year would have seen you take the throne as Queen of Aldegaad; however, this age is also what *we* have waited for in the years that you have been here."

*I've been here years?! Oh my gods! How could I not have known that, even without any measurements of time?!*I flinched at the sound of those words and swallowed back against my unease. I needed to find something to say, to know why my age was so important.

"Morod made me immortal and ageless when he put me through that dark ceremony," I told her quickly, urgency in my voice. "I am still eighteen winters old..."

"It is not your physical age that matters, but your time existing in this world," she clarified. "After all, there is no change between the ages of eighteen and twenty-one in any real physical sense."

"Why does it even matter that I am twenty-one?" I was struggling to keep my composure now.

"Because," Manth explained darkly, "it is the age when you can be used in the ritual yet to come."

"What ritual?" with each question my fear only grew, and my heart beat faster, though I tried so desperately to hide it.

"Come, child, do not be so coy," Keilantra sat back and smirked at me cruelly, "you were reading the writings I left on this table for you..."

"You... you intended for me to see those?" I was shocked.

"Indeed, though I doubt you fully understand," she nodded, enjoying my worried expression. "A little taste of what the Master plans after your demise."

I gulped hard, my breathing halting for a moment as I remembered his sinister promise of my death two years ago.

"Ulric," Keilantra called gently and the door opened as the Knight entered.

"You called, my Queen?" he bowed to her and sneered at me.

"Take the Princess back to the West Tower," she stated as she rose from her seat and came to stand before me, drawing my frightened gaze into her snarling eyes. "She has very little time left in our company and must rest before she departs."

"Yes, my Queen," Ulric sounded a little disappointed, but moved and took me by both arms from behind.

"What do you mean by any of this?!" I demanded frantically, keeping my eyes on Keilantra. "What's going to happen to me?!"

She lifted my chin with two fingers and glared into my eyes, still sneering evilly.

"You are to leave Castle Ortagaad in only a few days," she explained, enjoying every critically agonising moment she made me endure with her words. "Prepare yourself. Lord Morod comes for you soon."

"But he's... he's going to kill me!" I panicked, shaking in Ulric's grasp.

She nodded mockingly, still smiling. "Yes, girl, he is. Take her away."

With heaving breaths and frantic tears, I fought as Ulric dragged me from the room, my eyes falling on the sneering, cruel faces of the sisters until I could see them no more.

Ulric soon had me back in the tower and was shackling my wrists into the chains bolted to the wall. He didn't speak to me, simply slamming the door shut and leaving me to ponder my coming fate. I stood still, my body shaking uncontrollably as silent tears rolled down my face.

I'm going to die... He's coming to take me and I'm going to die...

I couldn't get my thoughts around that knowledge, couldn't bring myself to say the words aloud. A truly evil end had been promised to me and now I could see it approaching with every vicious second that passed me in my cold prison.

I crawled onto the bed and hugged my knees tight to my chest, quiet sobs heaving my breasts and slipping from my lips. The fear that had plagued me in all the horrible, icy cold days I had spent here was now about to be realised and all I could do was cry.

He's going to kill me... No... I don't want to die! Please, Gods, I don't want to die!

"Princess?" the gentle, kindly voice called from across the way beyond the bars of my cell.

I looked up to see the Wizard's gnarled hands coiling their fingers around the bars in the door of the other cell, his hazel eyes watching me with gentle concern and deep care.

"My dear girl, why are you crying?" the Wizard asked softly. "Did they hurt you again?"

I shook my head, sat up and hugged my legs tight with my fingers curled around my ankles, my chin to my knees. I kept crying, struggling to breathe, let alone speak a single word of what I had learned.

"Come now," he urged me kindly, "tell me what dread thoughts make you cry so."

I managed to calm my sobs enough that they didn't hurt my chest and throat, trying to keep my eyes on where he stood. It was so hard to focus on this man when all I could see was the wooden door.

"They're... they're going to kill me," I whispered.

"Why?" he frowned as I looked up at him.

"Today I have reached my twenty-first year and come of age," I explained what I could manage while my sobs had withdrawn a little. "For whatever reason, this is the time Morod has waited for, and why he has kept me here for the last two years. I have only a short time before he comes to take me... before he..."

I couldn't go on, my heart cracking in two at the thoughts swirling in my mind. So many horrible ways he could kill me filled my head and all I wanted was to feel and think nothing so that I had at least some reprieve from it.

"Leander," his use of my name surprised me, and I immediately looked up to see his sympathetic eyes behind those iron bars. "Oh, Leander... What words can I offer to ease your young heart? What kindness is there that can grant you relief from this terrible knowledge?"

I shrugged and shook my head. "I don't know."

"Do not give up hope, child," he urged with all his conviction, keeping his hazel eyes locked with my blue ones. "There is yet time to save you from him."

"How?" I asked with sniffing sobs of fearful panic. "How can anyone save me now?"

"There is *yet* time," he repeated firmly.

"How can you be so sure?" I frowned at him.

"I am a wizard, my dear," he responded and winked at me. "I am certain of many things. Now, please, try to get some rest and take what you can to eat. You will need your strength."

"For what?"

"For what is yet to come."

As he turned away, I chewed on his words, trying to figure out what he meant.

Does he have some secret plan for escaping this place? What is it that has him so certain that I can still be saved?

I sighed and lay down on the bed, curling up to rest away all the stress I had felt in the last two days.

He knows something that I don't.

My mind began to wander, and I once again longed for the quiet grove I had laid in on that summer day two years ago. I saw my handsome Guardian's eyes and smiled in my mind though my lips stayed saddened.

Oh, Carden... Where are you? Help me...

* * * * *

His green eyes glared at me from beneath his black cowl as I instantly felt a very real and choking terror close over me. I struggled against the restraints binding my wrists, screaming as he moved towards me, his long, bony fingers stretching over my throat.

"Don't! No!" I cried, staring up at him through my sobs.

"It is your time to die, Princess," he spoke as he held a sinister dagger in his right hand.

"Please... don't..." I sobbed frantically.

He swiftly hurled the dagger above his head as he pinned my throat to the stone altar with his left hand, his expression severe as he glared down at me.

Movement caught my gaze and I looked up to see Carden standing there, his sword in hand and his eyes terrified.

"Leander!" he cried in pure and furious panic, moving to run towards me.

"Carden!" I screamed back desperately.

The Shadow Lord plunged the dagger down hard and I screamed as relentless, agonising pain shot through my chest...

"Carden!" I cried out, my eyes flying open and my surroundings leaving me disoriented.

Once again, I found myself faced with the cold, dully lit tower cell I had spent two years trapped in, my eyes locked on the ceiling above where I lay on the old bed. I sighed deeply, feeling my body yearn to let fresh tears flow once again.

I ran my hands through my grimy hair and closed my eyes, thinking about the dream. The dagger was only the latest method of death I met at the Shadow

Lord's hands in my nightmares. Death had shown a myriad of itself to me now, my end coming in so many different and agonising ways. The only constant was Carden.

He keeps trying to save me, but failing, I thought as I opened my eyes and lay staring at the ceiling. *I hope this is only a dream and not some vision of things to come.*

I sat up and swung my legs over the side of the mattress, setting my boots to the floor, my chains rattling with the movement. I stared blankly at the stone blocks beneath my feet as I curled my fingers into my hair and rested my elbows on my thighs, trying to clear my mind of the images by watching the blank stones.

Can I really escape this fate? Is it even possible for me to run from him and go somewhere he will never find me? I inhaled my next breath slowly to stop myself crying again, so tired of sobbing and weeping in hopelessness. *I'm out of time. I can feel it.*

"You're awake," the Wizard noted as he once again stood at the window in his cell door. "It seems that your nightmares grow more terrible."

"They keep haunting me," I closed my tired eyes and held my face in my hands. "Every one of them shows me a different death, a different means for him to kill me."

"And Carden?"

I looked up at him in shock. "How did you...?"

"You cry out to him in your sleep," he replied with a gentle nod. "That is the young Guardian you were with in Eilath. Am I right?"

I nodded. "Yes. He was captured with me, along with Tallinn, the female Guardian who protected me. They were taken away from here. Morod wanted me isolated and alone."

"Do you know where they were taken?" the Wizard enquired.

"Arnath," I murmured with dread from only the place's reputation, not firsthand knowledge. "They were taken to Arnath by the Revenant."

"A dark fate indeed," the Wizard stated gravely as I continued to stare at the floor.

"I'll never see them again," I sniffed against the threat of more tears and sobs.

"There is still a chance," he uttered the words he had been saying to me for the last few days. "All is not lost."

"You keep saying that," I muttered and turned my eyes to him, "but you don't offer a way to escape this place or my fate."

"Is that what you expect of me?"

"You're a wizard," I reasoned, standing and moving to the bars to get a better look at him. "You must have some kind of magic, or knowledge of some spell that can free us from these cells."

"I'm afraid that my powers are greatly diminished without my staff," he told me regretfully.

"Your staff?" I frowned.

He nodded. "A wizard's staff is what allows him to channel and use his powers. Though I have some healing abilities and a few smaller skills with my hands, it is the powers I use through my staff that can truly help us in such a situation as this. Without it, I am as helpless as any other prisoner."

"Oh," was all I could say as I sat down with my back against the bars, sighing in defeat. "Is there no power that can help us?"

"There is," he confirmed.

I turned over my shoulder to him: "Then use it. Please."

"It is not I who possess this power," he stated knowingly, "but you."

"Me?" I frowned. "But... but I'm no mage..."

"You do not need to be," he told me. "Your power comes from your heart, and it is the very same which allows you to command your Pendant."

"What is it?"

"Love," he said with all honesty and belief. "Hold onto the love you share with your soul mate, think of seeing him again and returning to his embrace. With that held firm in your heart, you can succeed at any challenge you face."

He turned his gaze towards the stairs, and I jumped as I heard the distant bang of a door.

"The time to use such power is now upon you," he directed me calmly, but with urgency. "I will help you if I can, but it is *you*, Leander, who must take the actions necessary to survive now."

"I'm scared," I confessed, looking up at him as I now grasped the bars with both hands.

"I know, my dear girl," he tried to offer me a comforting gaze as the bangs grew louder and the sounds of footsteps drew closer. "Hold firm to your faith in your love and do what you must to avoid this dire fate. Be brave and know that you will succeed."

He stepped back into the shadows of his cell and I stood as I heard the door from the stairs unlock. I decided to lay back on the bed and pretend to be asleep, not certain about how I was going to overpower whoever came to get me.

*My love will save me? Okay, I believe in love more than anything else. I **will** be reunited with Carden, and these bastards aren't taking me from him ever again.*

I closed my eyes, just barely getting a glimpse of a black cloaked figure entering my cell with the squeak of the door. I had to force my breath to be slow and as even as possible, but I had no control over the racing of my heart any more than the thudding of my pulse in my neck.

The figure was standing over me, his presence strong and close. I felt him sit on the bed, instantly certain of who it was as his warm fingers caressed my cheek and chin in an attempt to wake me.

All right. I'll play along.

I let my eyes flutter open as I stirred very slightly, turning my steel blue gaze up to the dark-haired man leaning over me.

"I am sorry to wake you," Ulric was trying to hide his hideous smirk as he studied my smaller, more delicate feminine form.

"You didn't," I said softly, meeting his gaze. "I was just resting."

"A wise decision," he said, his hand uncomfortably touching my midriff, his fingers caressing the cords of my bodice. "You will need all the strength you can muster for the journey which lies before you."

I stared at him, unable to help the tears in my eyes or the short, soft breaths hitching behind my lips.

"I'm afraid," I whispered, letting my left hand rest against my sternum and my right hand lie in the pillows.

"Of course you are," he reached his hand further up my body, his fingers grazing over my knuckles and making me suppress a shudder of disgust. "Your fate has been decided and you will die in some terrible way beyond your adolescent imagining."

I closed my eyes and tried not to whimper as his hand found its way to my cleavage, his fingers caressing my warm skin roughly, but slowly.

"It is such a shame to waste such a perfect young body," he mused, drawing my gaze again.

I let out a startled yell as he abruptly lifted me from the bed and hurled me to the floor without any warning. I tried to scramble back, but he was on me, grabbing me by my hair and forcing me onto my knees.

"What are you... doing?!" I cried out, gritting my teeth and grabbing his wrist with both of my hands.

"I will not go wanting for the knowledge of you, girl," he said hurriedly, forcing me to where he wanted me. "I may not be able to feel you as I so desire, but there *are* ways I can have you without breaking your virtue."

He's not... He wouldn't! My mind flew with panic and I felt my heart scream against the new assault he had planned for me.

"LET ME GO! GET OFF ME!" I screamed, a blow to my right cheek silencing me and dropping me to the floor.

"Do not fight me, Princess," he dragged me to my knees again and held me by the throat with both hands, making me meet his gaze. "It will only make things harder on you and I do not wish to leave too many unexplained marks on your flesh."

"Please, don't..." I whispered, my chest heaving as I looked up at him, his right hand holding my hair.

I closed my eyes and cringed away as his left hand began to unbuckle his belt, the knowledge of his plan for me fouling my throat.

"I would have you show me how well you use that pretty mouth of yours," he stated, smirking crudely. "At least before you depart to the Shadow Lord's keeping."

I let my eyes open as I worried about the assault I was mere seconds from enduring. That was when I noticed the chains on my wrists and where they lay. A glance to my left showed me that the door to the cell was still open and he had set his keys down on the bed where he had sat.

This is my only chance. I have to take it.

I coiled the chains in my hands below my waist, hoping that I could keep him from noticing what I was doing as I let my quiet sobs slip free. His hand was now gently smoothing my dark hair down my cheek as he continued to work at his filthy task.

"Just be a good girl," he told me with his foul smile, "and you might even enjoy it..."

I met his gaze and kept it, preparing myself with a last breath. *Now!*

I jerked both my arms back as hard as I could, the chains going taut between his legs and stunning him. He cried out and I threw my leg beneath his, tripping him backwards. He landed hard with a loud cough of pain, hitting his head on the stones.

The keys!

I grabbed at the keys and fumbled for the one to my chains. In seconds, I had my right wrist free and was working to release my left. My eyes darted to him, seeing him recovering from his shock and panicking that I was running out of time. I freed my left wrist and lunged forward, securing his right in the shackle and locking it.

"What the...?" he stared at me in surprise.

I threw myself away from him, crying out as he grabbed my hips and tried to pull me back.

"Give me those keys, you little bitch!" he screamed at me in rage, digging his fingers into my hips and making me yell.

I tossed the keys for the door, knowing that this way he couldn't snatch them from me. Now I was free to focus on escaping him.

"You wretched little girl!" he howled at me, trying to drag me closer towards him, his strength giving him the advantage.

"Get off me!" I screamed and slashed with my fingernails at his face, tearing four red marks over his eye.

His screams echoed through the cell as he grasped at his face, his distraction giving me the chance I needed. He tried to snatch my ankle as I jumped to my feet, missing by an inch as I sprinted through the door and slammed it shut.

Where are they?

I searched for the keys in panic, soon finding them by the central pillar of the chamber. Snatching them up, I quickly slid the cell key into the lock and started turning it as fast as I could, struggling at the length of time it took to lock one of these doors.

I screamed and jumped back as Ulric lunged, his hand reaching through the bars at me and nearly catching my hair. I backed into the pillar, staring at his grasping fingers breathlessly, clutching the keys to my side.

"Open this door, girl, and *maybe* I'll be kind!" he shouted, his eyes like those of some wild madman.

I turned and rushed towards the Wizard's cell, quickly seeking the key I needed.

"What are you doing?" the old man asked with surprise and urgency.

"We're both getting out of here," I had decided, finding the key I needed and working it in the lock. "I can't escape this tower on my own and I would never leave someone to suffer here."

"Very well," he nodded, and I tore open the door, then freed him from his shackles.

"COME BACK YOU WRETCHED GIRL!" Ulric screamed as we turned and ran for the stairs. "YOU CAN NEVER ESCAPE ME! *NEVER*!"

The Wizard and I ran down the stairs as fast as we could manage safely, my panic at the idea of getting caught leading me to stumble only for him to steady me. I flashed a thankful gaze to him and continued on, the two of us spiralling until at last we reached the bottom. Here the Wizard recovered his staff; a tall oaken limb with root-like growths at the top that held a green crystal in place.

I edged open the door of the tower with my knee, my hands gripping the hems of my skirts so that I could run easier. I peered out into the cold air, shivering as my breath appeared as vapour before my lips, my eyes stunned by the brightness of the noon sunlight.

The Wizard kept his hand on my shoulder, his hazel eyes watchful for the guards as much as mine were. Once we saw a clear path we hurried along the walkway, taking refuge in the cover of a guard tower just before the keep.

I stared down at the courtyard and across at the keep, the number of guards so incredibly overwhelming.

"How can we ever get past so many guards?" I wondered in a whisper as I hid behind the wall, peeking over my shoulder around the corner.

"I will draw their attention," the Wizard offered as he knelt below a partition, his white hair and beard windswept now. "Do you know where your pendant is being kept?"

"Yes, but how is that important right now?" I asked.

"You *must* retrieve it," he replied sternly.

"I *have* to help Amethyst," I said with certainty.

"You retrieve your pendant," he directed me firmly, "I will see to freeing your dragon."

I wanted to protest but I could see the logic in his words. I just nodded and pressed myself back into cover, narrowly avoiding the attention of two passing guards.

"Do not move until I have drawn their gaze," he instructed me. "Do you understand?"

I nodded swiftly, breathing hard.

The Wizard flashed me a smile, then got to his feet and rushed down the stairs into the courtyard. There was a green flash from the top of his staff and a number of guards cried out as they were hurled against one of the walls.

"Prisoner escape!" a guard shouted, raising the alarm. "Capture the old man!"

The guards were pouring out of the buildings, the Wizard spinning his staff and casting them down with ease. Now my way was clear, and I started to run as I heard the continued cries to recapture my mysterious ally echoing through the courtyard.

"Forget the old man!" Ulric's voice bellowed and I paused at the doors of the keep seeing him storming from the West Tower with two guards. "Find the girl! She's the one of importance! Find her now!"

A green shot hit Ulric and he fell to the ground, the Wizard shouting to gain the soldiers' attentions away from their search for me.

I slipped through the doors into the keep and carefully, but quickly made my way up the grand staircase. I recalled the path to the Sanctum as clearly as I could remember, taking cover behind a pillar as four guards ran past me with their weapons ready.

I waited until they had gone, then continued to carefully make my way along the corridors, at last finding the one that led to the Sanctum. I paused at the corner and looked to see if there was anyone outside the doors. The way was clear.

Quickly, I walked down the hallway, reaching the door and seeing that it was unlocked. I shoved it open, struggling under its weight.

How do Keilantra and Manth ever open this?

Cautiously, I surveyed the room within, relieved to find that it was empty. Immediately I moved to the display case, my eyes locking on my pendant where it lay against the black velvet cushion. I was so close, and I only needed to open it. I tried the latch, but it was locked.

There must be a key here somewhere.

I started searching the desk, opening the drawers to see if there was any sign of the key to the display case. I sifted through papers anxiously, worrying that I was running out of time.

A shout from the hallway drew my attention and I ran to the door, grasping its edge with both hands as I leaned out to look.

"There she is!" a guard shouted, jabbing one hand at me.

Five of them started running towards me from the end of the hallway, their weapons sheathed at their hips. They would be on me in seconds.

I shoved the door shut and searched for a way to lock it.

"No! No!" I cried in panic at the lack of a key, looking around the room and settling my eyes on the bookcases flanking the door.

I ran around to the side of the bookcase and braced my back against it, pressing one of my feet to the wall to gain some kind of leverage. I pushed and grunted, struggling against the sheer weight of it.

"Come on! Please!" I groaned, closing my eyes tight and using all of my muscles to push.

The bookcase toppled over, slamming against its twin and blocking the door as the guards tried to open it, spilling all of its shelved contents across the floor. I backed away breathlessly, studying the door uneasily.

That's only bought me a little time.

"She's blocked the door!" I heard one of the men shout, the sound of them fighting to break it down echoing from the hallway.

I returned to the desk and continued my search, but it was useless. Then my eyes fell on a silver candlestick. *Why not?*

I snatched it from the table and ran back to the display case. Shielding my eyes with my left arm, I swung the candlestick, a loud shattering tearing through the air. Dropping the candlestick, I looked down at the display case's ruined glass, the five pendants within now easily accessible. I recovered my pendant and held it in my hand for the first time in two years, feeling a sense of warmth and safety instantly fold around me like my mother's embrace. It felt so good to have it back, but it was a short-lived relief.

"She's in there, your Majesty," a guard was saying, snapping my gaze from my pendant.

"Get out of the way!" Keilantra's voice ordered viciously from behind the door. "I'll do this myself!"

Panic filled me as I looked around at the room, no other doors available to me apart from the one the Witch and her soldiers were now trying to tear down.

I'm trapped! What do I do?!

My eyes flicked to the windows and I felt a terrible sick feeling at the thought of my only option.

I can't be recaptured. I have no choice...

I rushed to the window, clutching my pendant tight in my hand, deathly determined not to lose it again. The window was unlocked, and I pulled it open with ease, stepping up onto the ledge. I sucked in a sharp breath as I was faced with the drop before me, the waves crashing hard on the jagged black rocks below. To fall from here would be certain death.

I have no choice! I groaned in exasperation and fear, climbing out the window.

The winds were gusting, tugging at my hair and clothes with icy grasps, already trying to pull me from the ledge and into the seas below. I braced my feet to the ledge and my back to the wall, turning my eyes to the way ahead to my left. My eyes surveyed the walls, catching sight of an open window on the opposite side of the keep with the courtyard below it.

If I can get there, I can find a way out.

Suddenly, a powerful explosion rocked the walls and I realised that it had come from the Sanctum.

There's no choice, Leander! Move!

I started edging along the ledge, my back hard up against the wall and my eyes focused on the stone beneath my feet. If I looked down, I knew for certain I would lose my balance and fall.

"Get back here, girl!" Keilantra screamed, drawing my gaze back to the window she and Manth now leaned out of with a number of soldiers. "Stop her! STOP HER NOW!"

An arrow splintered against the wall only inches from my face, drawing a scream from my lips and making me shield my eyes with one arm. The guards on the wall of the courtyard were firing up at me, the clattering of the arrows' steel heads hitting stone cracking all around me.

"STOP SHOOTING YOU IDIOTS!" Keilantra screamed viciously. "WE NEED HER ALIVE!"

The arrow storm stopped, and I resumed my perilous shuffle along the ledge. There was a curved wall before me and it was going to be very difficult to get around easily, but I was determined to escape. I took in a deep breath and reached out my right hand, pressing my stomach to the wall as I stepped over the gap in the ledge. All else had to be ignored, my single focus now needing to be making it around this narrow path without falling.

"Come here, girl!" a voice shouted, and my wrist was seized by a guard.

"Let go of me!" I screamed, trying to fight the man off as he reached through the nearby window at me, a second guard behind him.

I managed to slip my hand free, pulling away further along the wall. The two guards stepped out of the window after me, much larger and finding it more difficult to traverse the narrow ledge than I was. They kept reaching for me, relentlessly pursuing me at a staggered pace while also fearing falling as much as I did.

A golden glow caught my eyes and I looked to see Keilantra grasping her pendant.

She's summoning her dragon!

Almost in response to my terrified thought, there came a great roar and a sweeping shadow fell across the castle. Kuldar flew above us as if he had materialised from nowhere, his great golden wings gusting against the castle.

I fell against the wall, crying out as the power of his wings nearly threw me from the ledge. The guards struggled to keep after me in the sudden gale, one of them managing to snatch my wrist tightly again.

Oh no! How am I going to escape them? I panicked as I looked up at him, trying to pull away.

A second roar echoed from above and I briefly caught view of a tremendous green dragon with four long horns sprouting from his head. He roared again and ploughed straight into Kuldar, the two dragons now fighting in mid-flight as they snapped and roared at each other.

I pulled away from the guards and tried to continue forward, but they were closing in on me quickly. It was becoming clear that I wouldn't be able to escape the way I wanted to.

Suddenly, there was a great crashing and the breaking of stone, the two dragons slamming into the wall with us. I cried out and tried to recover my balance as the impact destabilised the ledge I stood on, but it was no use. With a panicked scream, I slipped from the wall, debris and dust falling with me. I had only seconds, the ocean coming towards me as I drew in a deep breath, closing my eyes tight and bracing myself for the inevitable impact...

Chapter Six
Wandering the White

T he first seconds were the worst by far; the sounds, the feeling, the taste, all of it violent and sudden, rushing over me beyond all of my senses' ability to endure. I felt like I was spinning, deafened by the rushing of the water, my limbs strangled by my own clothing as I tasted the saltiness of the tides. It was like being buried in ice, the sudden chill agonising and making me want to scream out, but I held my lips tight, fearing I would drown.

Floating and bewildered, I opened my eyes, the sting of the water as bad against them as the impact had been on my body. I blinked and squinted, trying to clear my vision and get it used to the feeling of the water invading my sight. The rush of the bubbles from my impact was still loud around me, my hearing slowly clearing to take in the gentle murmur of the seas.

I turned my gaze around, taking in all that surrounded me. Broken stones from the castle walls sank through the clear dark blue, disappearing into the deep blackness below my feet. They fell with trails of bubbles and foam in their wakes, slow and graceful despite their bulky shapes.

I turned and covered my mouth to prevent a scream escaping and casting my air from my lungs. One of the two guards who had been on the wall with me drifted before my eyes, his body broken from the fall, blood tainting the water around him a dull red. He had been killed as soon as he'd hit the waves, probably struck by a falling block of debris.

I looked above me, seeing the shimmer of the sun shining through the sea's scintillating surface. That was where I needed to go, my only hope of surviving this deep watery cold.

Swimming wasn't easy fully clothed, especially not in a dress, my mind instantly flashing back to the night we escaped Castle Arvon. I had at least had the Guardians to help me there, now relying only on myself.

Swim! Swim, Leander! I urged myself on, digging my hands through the waters above me and trying to pull myself up through it.

There was suddenly a pressure around my right ankle, and I let out a gurgled cry, turning my eyes towards my feet. The other guard from the wall had survived, trying to swim after me, squeezing my ankle tightly now as he grasped at me.

No! I won't let him overpower me!

I started thrashing and fighting to free myself, the man clawing at my legs and grasping the floating hems of my dress. I kept trying to reach the surface as I kicked at him, my arms tiring quickly with his added weight holding me down.

Let go of me! I lashed out at him, kicking his face, which only made him angrier. *Let go of me! I can't breathe!*

My eyes widened as I saw it then, hidden in the dark depths beneath us. At first, I had thought it was just the currents, but now I could see the black sheen on its skin as its twin fins cut through the water.

I pointed frantically at the thing, trying to get the guard to look. He frowned at me, then turned his gaze and let out a gurgling scream as the great jaws closed in around his waist.

As blood filled the water, I pushed myself away, afraid of becoming the next target on the beast's menu. I saw only the swishing of its tail amongst the deepening darkness of blood in the water, my heart pounding heavily in my chest like a great hammer.

The dead guard was suddenly snapped up by a second of the great black sharks, the creature not seeming to care that he wasn't alive. It just plunged back into the depths, dragging the corpse along with it.

If I don't move, I'm fish bait! And it's getting too hard to hold my breath! I need air!

I pushed all the strength I had left into my arms and legs, kicking as hard and fast as I could, my body starving for oxygen. Suddenly, it swept past me, the terrible black shape missing me by a foot, then turning around to charge me again. I swam backwards, now lined up directly with its enormous teeth filled jaws.

Get it away from me!

I instinctively held my hands forward and closed my eyes, knowing that it would do nothing to save me.

A bright flash of purple light shone through my eyelids and illuminated the seas around me. I opened my eyes to see the stone in my pendant's heart glowing brightly and projecting a magical shield around me. The shark hit the shield with a purple flash and a resounding bang, then turned and swam away swiftly into the dark. More bangs and flashes followed, three more sharks turning away from me to disappear into the deep black.

As it had many times before, my pendant had saved my life.

I can't breathe!

I made for the surface, clutching the Pendant tight in my palm, the chain catching on my wrist with my rapid ascent. The light of the sky above grew brighter and at last I broke through. The pain of the wind on my wet skin was instant, sharp and bitter, a scream tearing from my burning lungs as I bobbed amongst the flowing waves. Screams and gasps were the only sounds I could produce at that moment as I felt the worst iciness I had ever known, blinded for a few moments by the water in my eyes.

I gasped in all the breaths I could, my chest feeling crushed by the lack of air that came from being as long as I had been beneath the surface. I shivered hard, my eyes searching for which way to go.

The castle lay before me, so far away already. I knew it had to have been the tide which had pulled me from the cursed place and out into the open seas. In the skies above were flashes of fire as the two great dragons continued their battle over the fortress; a shimmer of green and a second of gold slamming into each other all that identified them to me from where I floated. Their roars echoed amongst the clouds, the collision of their gigantic bodies like thunder.

I knew I couldn't stay floating like that and turned around, brushing my soaked hair from my eyes awkwardly. My gaze fell on the distant deep grey that I knew was certainly the Gorvennan mainland, the mountains of Gorth'lak standing tall to my left.

I don't know how long I swam towards the mainland, my arms exhausted, my legs falling into the worst frozen aches and my body sick from cold. *I don't think I can keep going. But I have to. I have to keep swimming, or I'll drown. I can do this! I can!*

I forced myself to keep moving, my eyes now locking on a white body of ice that stretched out far before me. It was an ice shelf and perhaps my best chance to escape the freezing waters.

Swimming as hard as I could, I was soon grasping onto the ice, slipping with the tides as they tried to pull me beneath it. I clenched my arms and held myself firm, every bit of effort seeming to take that much more than normal. Finally, with a cry of frozen agony, I dragged myself up onto the ice and collapsed in a heap. I lay there shivering so violently that I was getting nauseous and struggling to breathe again, my head in my arms.

It doesn't matter that I'm free of the castle, I realised grimly. *With my clothes soaked, I won't last long in this cold.*

I coughed up water and felt my eyes swell with tears as I breathed shards of ice in the air. The pain in my chest was excruciating and I knew that I would die here like this.

Why aren't I dead yet? I should have frozen and drowned already. How am I still breathing?

I became acutely aware of the Pendant in my hand, turning my shaking palm over to look at it. The heart-stone held a deep inner glow, a gentle warmth flowing from the Pendant onto my skin.

"It's... it's... k-k-keeping m-m-me alive," I stammered as I trembled hard. "Ugh... I have to... k-keep... moving."

I pulled myself awkwardly to my feet, my body wavering as I now held the Pendant between both hands. I knew it would be better around my neck, but my fingers wouldn't work well enough with the cold to allow me to open the clasp.

"Ugh!" I gasped as I felt the chill of the wind biting my skin as it picked up, my hair and clothes flowing wetly around my slender body.

Gods, it would be nice if my pendant could dry me off and warm me up.

I had only one plan in mind at that moment: make it across the frozen ice shelves and reach a town or house somewhere to ask for help. The thought of a warm fire and shelter outweighed everything else, including my captors, who were certain to be enraged by my escape.

As I walked, I turned my eyes up to see a dark shape sitting across from where I was standing on the ice. The flicker of the Gorvennan flag caught my attention as I saw the ship resting at the edge of the ice shelf. A group of small black shapes caught my attention beside the ship, moving swiftly across the ice. My eyes widened and I realised what they were as the ice vibrated with the pounding gallop of hooves.

I grasped my skirts and held them tight as I turned to run, my body aching worse now that I was half frozen.

I have to run! I have to keep going, no matter how badly my body hurts!

My boots pounded against the ice and snow with every long step I took, my chest hurting as my breathing grew harder with each passing second. I turned over my shoulder, terrified to see the black and gold clad riders and their mounts closing in fast. They were not far behind me now, the thundering of hooves like a storm in my aching ears.

Two of the riders got ahead of me, trying to cut me off. I desperately searched for a way to slip through the lines, but there was no way to get by the aggressively stamping horses that now neighed loudly and circled around me.

I darted back and forth helplessly, trying to find something I could do to escape them, but it was no use. I came to stand still as the horses slowed around me, gently halting under their riders' commands.

Shivering hard, I turned my gaze to their leader and felt instantly sick to see Ulric's glaring eyes and harsh smile. He had four red scratches over his right eye and cheek from my fight with him in the tower, that alone allowing me some small satisfaction, but also presented me with fear of his reprisal.

"Princess," he shook his head as he dismounted and strode towards me, his cloak flowing behind him. "Now really, you have been a bad little girl."

"S-s-stay a-away from m-me," I fought the cold as I tried so hard to talk.

"Oh, now look at you," he smirked mockingly, hands out towards me. "You're frozen half to death. Was it really worth running from us when this is the result?"

"B-b-better than w-what you were g-g-going to... to do to me," I retorted, wishing I wasn't stammering.

He snatched me by my now brittle hair, making me cry out in pain as he forced my face up towards his. He glared down at me with vicious intent in his green eyes, his teeth clenched behind his lips.

"I should do worse," he hissed at me. "Now, stop resisting and come with us back to the castle. At least there you will be warm."

He snagged my arm and started dragging me towards his horse, his grip hurting me so much with my half-frozen skin. I dug my heels into the snow and struggled as hard as I could manage in my heavily weakened state.

"Stop making a fuss, girl!" he snapped and pulled me harder.

"Let go of me!" I shouted, punching his arm, though it hurt my knuckles to do so. "Help me! Please!"

I felt the heat rise from the Pendant in my right hand, the purple glow shimmering through my fingers in response to my plea. Instantly, there came a very familiar roar as a great purple and blue scaled dragon appeared above me.

Amethyst swept in towards us and landed hard, shaking the ice shelf and startling the horses, even knocking a couple of their riders from the saddles.

"The Dragon is free!" Ulric was horrified as he released me and drew his sword.

With fire in her orange eyes and rage in her heart, Amethyst bellowed a terrifying howl straight into the Knight's face, showing him all of her long sharp teeth. She closed her jaws, then roared again and began fighting the riders.

She stomped and threw them from their mounts, the horses rushing around in panic as the Dragon snarled and roared in rage. She whipped her tail around and flung a number of men from the frozen shelf into the nearest section of water, some of them slamming into the ice again with a painful crushing thud.

"Bring it down!" Ulric shouted, then turned to me. "Come here, girl!"

"No!" I kicked him as hard as I could and shoved against his chest.

He stumbled and slipped on the ice, landing hard on his back.

I ducked away from the soldiers, managing to keep myself free from them as they tried to evade my dragon's strikes. Her snapping jaws carried another hapless soldier into the air, only for him to then crush headfirst into the ice.

"Amethyst!" I cried out, trying to reach her in the confusion.

She turned her gaze to me and barked out a sound of concern, moving to safeguard me.

At that moment, another great roar tore the skies and the golden form of Kuldar was suddenly crushing down on top of her, his claws at her throat. Amethyst howled in pain as he buried his teeth into her back.

"AMETHYST!" I screamed in panic.

"Lay down, whelp!" Kuldar snarled at her, keeping her pinned. "You will not keep my Mistress from the girl!"

A third roar echoed, and I looked up as the great dragon covered in scales of varying green swept from the sky. He opened his jaws and fire erupted across Kuldar's face and back, causing him to bellow and stagger backwards with a pained roar.

Taking her chance, Amethyst swung her barbed tail and caught Kuldar across the eyes, the gold dragon roaring in agony and clutching at his face with his massive, clawed hands.

"My eyes! Argh! Cowards! I will burn you!" he bellowed, thrashing as he struggled to see.

Kuldar hit the ground hard as the green dragon slammed into him with all four feet, the two beasts then flipping from where they had fallen and facing off, their massive claws cracking the ice where they landed.

"Amethyst!" I ran towards her, reaching out to her with my right hand. "Come on! We have to go!"

She turned and roared at me, the sound one I recognised as telling me to run.

"No! Not without you!" I protested.

She roared again and nudged me with her nose, slapping more soldiers away from me with her right front claws and her tail. She urged me with her orange eyes, pleading with me.

I nodded and turned as I gathered my dress hems, sprinting away across the ice. I didn't look behind me now, the roars of the Dragons battling too much for me to bear.

Oh, Amethyst! Why couldn't you just come with me?!

I kept running as the winds blew the snow and ice into the air, the great white starting to blind me and shield the vicious battle from my view. In minutes, all I could hear was the roaring of the Dragons' voices along with the crashing of their bodies colliding with each other and the solid ice sheets. But soon even those sounds were gone, taken over by the howl of the winds.

Though my legs ached and burned, I just kept running, too afraid to stop. I had no thoughts now, acting on impulse to keep moving and get away from the dangers that lurked somewhere behind me in the sweeping snowy winds.

Is anyone following me? this thought entered my mind what felt like ages later and I stopped, breathing hard with a jabbing pain in my chest.

I turned over my right shoulder, my damp hair flicking into my face only for my left hand to brush it away. There was no sign of any living person or creature behind me, no shadowy shapes moving through the frosty white air to follow my path. All I could see was the far stretching white of the snows and ice shelf, the foggy looking air choked with white snow fragments and my own footprints, which were slowly fading with the winds.

There's no one. I'm alone. That thought didn't comfort me, despite the gladness I had at not being pursued by my abductors. *I'm all alone...*

I shivered hard, my clothes still wet and not feeling as if they were drying in the icy winds. I struggled to pull the sleeves of my dress back up over my exposed shoulders to shield my skin, but the water had made the fabrics so much heavier.

Clutching my pendant in both hands to my chest, I staggered forward, my eyes struggling against the ice in the winds. It was getting so hard to see as the blizzard increased its ferocity and I came to know a new understanding of what it was to be cold.

I wish I had a cloak, gloves, something to keep me warm. I'm freezing...

Soon all thought had frosted away from my mind and all I could do was focus on my breathing and my path. I listened to the whistling howls of the wind, my shaking breaths and the crunch of my boots in the snow, all in an effort to keep my mind aware of something at least as I found myself wandering the white of the tundra.

It began to feel like I was trapped again, but this prison was more surreal than my physical cell in the West Tower.

I wonder if the Wizard made it out, I thought, trying to force some words into my mind to keep me moving. *Did he escape the fortress as I did, or was he recaptured? One thing for sure, he definitely freed Amethyst. Oh... Amethyst...*

"Am...Am...Amethyst," I stammered through my chattering teeth, squeezing the Pendant close to me. "A-Amethyst, please... F-find me..."

I turned my steel blue eyes to the white whipping skies, searching for some glimmer of mauve and violet, or the flap of magenta wings, but there was nothing.

I willed harder as I tightened my frozen hold on the Pendant and closed my eyes: "Amethyst... please come to me... Please..."

Another look to the sky and to the white lands around me showed no sign of the Dragon. As before there was only the blinding white snows driving across the ice shelves. My heart sank and I turned back towards the way I had been heading.

Where are you, Amethyst? Are you still fighting Kuldar with that other dragon? Gods, he hurt you. Are you even all right?

The fear I felt for my beloved dragon grew in my heart, and I would have started to cry but for the worry that my tears might freeze in my eyes. The memory of her roaring cry of pain was still powering through my mind and with it came so many terrible imaginings of what had become of her.

Keep moving. She told me I had to run, and I can't stop now until I'm safe.

Convicted in my decision, I kept walking on through the blinding snows, clutching my pendant between both hands as I felt a warmth grow from within it to help me stay alive. It wasn't enough to make me comfortable, but it would stave off death and frostbite at least.

So, the Pendants can keep you alive even in the harshest of weather conditions. Maybe there is some truth in that old story about my ancestor being blasted with Dragon Fire and surviving untouched. I wonder what else my pendant can protect me from.

It seemed like I had walked for hours and hours, the deepening white starting to darken and the cold growing more bitter. My shivering had gotten worse and my mind was losing its strength now as my eyes struggled to stay open.

It's getting so much colder. How can I survive? I doubt even my pendant can keep me going in this.

I staggered and fell to my knees in the snow, my eyes shutting and my body slouching forward to try and find some sort of warmth. The wind was tearing at my hair and tugging at my clothes, the strength of it like a giant trying to pick me up off the ground and hurl me backwards as if I were a ragdoll.

I can't keep going like this. I need shelter or I'll freeze, Pendant or not.

There came a growing warmth in my hands, and I looked down at my pendant. The heart-stone started to glow and fade in a slow pulse, almost like it was responding to my thoughts. I raised an eyebrow at it curiously, not certain what to do as I watched its gentle flash of light.

"F-f-find me shelter n-n-nearby," I murmured to it and the Pendant started to shine more.

It couldn't be as simple as that old childhood game. Could it? I turned to my right, watching the stone slow its pace even further, then turned left to watch it increase. *It is that simple.*

I struggled to my feet, that simple movement alone seeming to take so much effort with my aching, stiff legs. I kept my eyes on the heart-stone, adjusting my path as it pulsed more rapidly, finally finding the way to go when it stayed lit completely. I felt relief in my heart and walked the path, keeping to the guidance of my strange, enchanted necklace.

With the delicate silver chain curled through my fingers, I watched both the Pendant and the way ahead, making certain to avoid any obstacles or hazards that may have laid before me. I fought through the snowstorm for what felt like another hour, the sky darkened deeply now and the way seeming so much harder to make out. Only the glow of the Pendant gave me any light, the purple illumination allowing me to see my body and the way around me for about six feet in all directions.

It's so dark. How will I ever make it through these icy lands without falling into trouble?

Out of the darkness and the blizzard there loomed a large black shape, ominous and mysterious.

I stood still and caught a breath in my chest, holding it as I watched the shape. It didn't move, remaining as it was. It was certainly too big to be a person.

Cautiously, I continued forward, the Pendant guiding me directly towards the shape in the storm.

I just have to trust the Pendant.

My feet touched rocks, which surprised me, the ground feeling more solid and less slippery, despite still being dressed in snow. There was a rise, and I could smell sea water around me, the sound of waves somewhere to my left. I caught sight of the small shore of rocks some many feet from where I stood, the dark waters washing over them and up against the edge of the ice shelf.

An island? Then I've walked over the sea itself all this way.

I turned my attentions to the massive shape before me, the same one I had seen in the distance. It was an old ship, wrecked on the rocks of the island. Its masts had collapsed and a hole was ripped through the side of its wooden hull right where I stood.

Well, I asked for shelter, I reasoned with a shivering shrug. *I just hope it doesn't slip into the sea with me inside.*

Carefully, stepping with my toes experimentally onto the wood, I made my way through the gap in the hull. Instantly, I felt relief as I was shielded from the battering ice storm outside, the light from my pendant giving me sight of the interior of the old wreck. Rocks had broken up through the floor, allowing sand and snow to dust the boards where they had sunk into the earth. The chilled air pushed through the gaps just as the weak light of night time tried to barter for a way inside the ship through the storm.

I need to find somewhere safe to rest for the night. There's no way I can go back into that blizzard. Not unprotected as I am. Gods, I was lucky to make it this far.

The floorboards creaked as I moved, letting my pendant light the way in my held-out hands. The place was definitely deserted, not even the bones of some poor sailor left there to rot.

Maybe they all made it off before the ship ran aground.

I made it up the unsteady stairs and to the next level, finding that the floor here was sturdy and the shelter stronger against the winds and chills. It was only a small ship, barely the size of a brig, this room I had entered filled with stores of barrels and crates.

I searched the crates and barrels thoroughly, hoping to find warm clothing, blankets and food. There was no food to be seen, though I did find some water still safe within its flask. As for blankets I found a good many of them and made myself a little place to sleep for the night.

I fought for my body to warm up, desperate to build a fire. I quickly pulled an old cast iron pot from the floor and filled it with kindling from one of the broken barrels. I searched for a flint, but there were none to be found.

I need to light this somehow.

A tremendous heat spread in my hand and I gasped, opening my palm to see the Pendant trying to flash purple energy up from its core. I frowned, then turned the stone towards the pot, a bright flash of purple fire and electricity briefly lancing towards it. In only a few moments the wood was alight with gentle flames, the purple hue soon turning to orange.

"It's a Dragon's heart," I murmured to myself, looking down at the Pendant again. "Of course it could light a fire. I had never even thought of that," I half laughed and shook my head."Listen to me, talking to myself."

I sat back on my haunches and watched the fire.

I suppose I may as well talk to myself. Maybe it will help in my loneliness, I thought.

I looked at the Pendant in my hand once again, studying the facets of the purple heart-stone as they danced with firelight. It seemed that what had first been a strange little trinket my uncle had given me had now become my only lifeline to surviving this ordeal.

I brushed my drying hair over my shoulder and fastened the chain around my neck, feeling that easing comfort at having it back where it belonged.

Quenching my thirst with the water I had found; I then lay down and wrapped myself in about five blankets with another few bundled under me for comfort against the hard floor. I shivered relentlessly, my fingers grasping the folded blankets I had placed under my head tightly.

This is still more comfortable than the bed I had in the tower. I'll warm up soon. I'm sure I will.

The small fire helped to chase away the cold and soon enough my clothes had dried, which made me feel much more comfortable. At last, my shivering stopped and I breathed a sigh of relief, lingering in my thoughts as I watched the fire flicker in the pot.

I have to decide what I'm going to do next. I can't stay here in this old wreck forever. I doubt the Pendant, as incredible and versatile as it seems to be, can conjure me something to eat.

I sighed and lay my head against the bundled blankets and my left arm, my right hand gently running its fingertips across the Pendant at my neck.

Eventually, Keilantra's soldiers could find me. So could the Shadow Lord. Regardless of whichever threat I face, the fact is that I can't stay here.

I closed my eyes and took in a soothing breath, feeling the warmth of the blankets and fire now completely chasing away the cold that had invaded my body.

I wonder what Carden would suggest if he were with me now. Hm. He'd probably lay with me here and hold me close to keep us both warm. Oh, how I miss him...

Thinking of my love, I let myself mentally wander away from the cold and the wreck surrounding me, slipping into a deep, restful sleep for what felt like the first time in these past two long and agonizing years.

Chapter Seven
The Way Through Travarna

I woke to the sound of a gentle wind outside my temporary shelter, the relentless howling and thrashing of the storms now faded. I blinked as sunlight shone through a crack in the wall, blinding me for a moment as it brought me from my sleep.

I yawned and pulled myself up to sit, still wrapped in the heavy blankets and furs, my hair hanging around my face unkemptly. It took a few moments for my mind to clear and return me fully to wakeful reality.

I took in my surroundings, seeing the inside of the ship so much clearer now in the morning light that was piercing the gaps in the walls. The fire had died hours ago, though I'd not noticed as I was fast asleep without as much worry as I had thought I would have.

I'm still free. I'm not in the tower or being taken to Morod. It wasn't a dream. Relief flooded me at the prospect of my freedom but was quickly quashed under the recall of my reality. *I may be free, but I'm not safe yet. I need food, water, a warm cloak and somewhere safe to go. I need to somehow find the others, maybe get a message to Aldwyn or Fawkner. Surely they could find a way to help me now. But is it even wise to try to contact them? The soldiers will be looking for me and I'm certainly in no position right now to be sending off letters. No. I need to focus on getting to the mainland alive. That has to be my priority right now.*

I got up and once again searched through the crates and barrels, the chill of the air hitting me hard and immediately making me shiver. I wouldn't dare brave the wintry frozen sea again without some form of protection other than my pendant. It would be too easy to get lost out there and freeze where I fell or slip beneath the waters to drown under the ice.

At last, I came to an old footlocker and pried it open awkwardly, the latches rusted by the salt air. It groaned open and I rustled through what lay inside, finally pulling out an old heavy cloak made of dark brown hide. The cloak smelled funny, but I wasn't about to reject it because of that. I pulled it across my shoulders and fastened the clasp at my neck. It was too big for me, definitely having belonged to a large man rather than a teenage girl, even a tall one like me.

I finished the last of the water I had found, then made my way back down the stairs to the lower hold and the hull breach leading outside.

Beyond the ship's walls, I got a look at the seas, my eyes squinting in the midmorning sun. There was nothing but rocky rises jutting from the surf and frozen sheets of white drifting across the dark blue expanse. I couldn't even see Castle Ortagaad anymore.

I must have run a long way yesterday. I wonder how I should get to the mainland.

I explored the small island I was on, the rocks and uneven ground hidden by snow making my feet slip and forcing me to hurt myself to regain my balance.

A twisted ankle. Wonderful.

I had fully circled the ship now, noticing that I was much farther away from the Black Peaks than I had been the day before.

I must have run south-west. All right, but how far am I from the coast, and which coast?

I surveyed the way before me so that the distant black of those dreaded mountains were to my left. Immediately, my eyes locked on the stretch of dark grey in the distance, which looked bigger than it had the day before.

"The mainland," I murmured, pulling the hood over my hair to shield my face from the cold.

I have to get there by sunset. I may not find another shelter like this one if I stay on the frozen sea.

I perilously stepped back onto the ice shelf and began walking towards the mainland. The snow on the ice gave me enough grip for my boots so that I didn't fall, but it was equally hazardous to trap me.

I slipped once, my foot sinking into a deep well of snow. Awkwardly I pulled my leg free and noted the little bit of water that stained the end of my boot.

"Right. I have to watch where I step," I murmured to myself, getting to my feet and continuing on.

My day was spent crossing the ice in silence, more or less, though I tried to hum tunes from my childhood to help pass the time. That, however, only lasted me a short while until I grew weary of the sound of my own humming and fell back into silence.

Growls came up from my stomach and I felt hunger gnawing at me.

Gods, I haven't eaten since... I'm not sure. It's been at least a couple of days. I don't think they fed me before my escape... not including Ulric's disgusting plans for my mouth.

I shuddered at the thought of what that man had planned for me, pushing it quickly from my mind and continuing on.

I had no choice but to ignore my ravenous hunger, a difficult task with the growing intensity of the growls and pains in my stomach.

The only sounds not coming from me were those of the winds and the tides, no life seeming to exist on the ice besides myself. The loneliness truly began to creep over me and crush hard then, and I let my right hand grasp my pendant.

Amethyst. Please come to me.

I turned my steel blue eyes to the sky, but once again there was no beat of magenta wings and shimmering of purple scales.

Am I not doing this right? Is there some other way I'm supposed to call to her? Out loud, maybe?

"Amethyst," I called, closing my eyes and wishing to see her as I tightened my grip around the Pendant. "I need you. Please, come find me. Please."

My call was met with only silence, my eyes opening once again to a still empty sky. My dragon hadn't come to me like I thought she was meant to, leaving me then with a terrible worry in my heart.

*What if she's hurt? Oh, please don't let her have...*I didn't finish that thought, choosing instead to focus on what I had to do to help myself. *I'm no good to anyone if I drown or freeze out here. I have to keep moving.*

The day whiled away as I walked, the dark line in the distance growing with each mile I travelled towards it. As the sun was sinking behind the horizon, I at last came within clear sight of the shore, working my way awkwardly across the broken pieces of floating ice. Much of the ice here was less solid than what I had walked over, the shore separated from me now by a ten-meter gap of open water.

How am I going to cross this without getting wet? I can't go through that again. Not without shelter.

I studied my surroundings, noticing the various rocks and rises sticking up from the water. I began trying to figure the distance between them to see if it were possible for me to climb along them to the shore without falling in.

I can do it.

Taking a small running jump, I cleared the gap between the ice and the nearest large rocky rise, my feet hitting the black ground and my hands bracing against the tall rocks. I steadied myself from making the jump, then turned my attention to the rest of the way.

With some floating pieces of ice between them, the rocks and small banks became like steppingstones and I was able to very carefully traverse them. Within a half hour, I was across and setting my boots to the damp sand and pebbles of the beach.

I can't believe I just walked across a sea, I looked over my shoulder back at the way I had come. *It's like something out of a fairytale, or an adventure story...*

Baffled by my crossing, I turned to the land and started walking along the shore. There were high grey cliffs all around me, dusted with snow and too slick to be climbed. I was losing the light and I needed to find a way off the shores before night came, lest I come under attack by creatures other than my pursuers.

After ages of walking to the west, I came across a path up through the cliffs, not well travelled, but clearly defined enough to see. I started up, my boots crunching stones under them with each step, the steepness instantly requiring more of my effort. The cold had deepened, and I tightened the old cloak around my body to try and keep what warmth I had. At last, I reached the top of the path and stood there within the crags of some great stretch of jagged rocks.

Where am I? I thought I was walking towards Gorvenna.

Slowly, I made my way down the only paths available to me and started working my way to my right, which I guessed was west. Going west was my only clear thought and I couldn't figure out why, except that Eilath was south-west somewhere.

The sun was setting now, and the shadows of the jagged rocks were growing longer. It felt so easy to become disorientated in that strange, barren place, the only plant life in the area being these strange, thorny, yellowish coloured weeds.

I kept moving, feeling more and more lost as I went, not so certain that I could make my way out of the strange labyrinth of rises, ditches and towering rocks. And when I found that I had passed the same rock structure four times I let out a groan of distress.

"I'm going around in circles," I realised, trying to pick up my bearings again by looking around me, then up at the sky. "It's night time. Gods, how am I going to make it out of here?"

There was no clear way to choose, no obvious path leading me out of the stark, cold place. My situation was only getting worse with each step I took and I began to see that there was no way to navigate the frightening labyrinth.

This seems familiar. I've read about a labyrinth of rocks like this when I was being tutored in Arvon...

Realisation hit me and I looked around at the rocks in terror.

"Oh no!" I shook my head, a cold shudder breaking through my back. "I'm in the Labyrinth of Dol Amor!"

Now I could remember the geography lesson my tutor had been teaching me of foreign places in High-Realm. The Labyrinth of Dol Amor was in the far north-east of Gorvenna and was also the way leading into the Maw of Gorth'lak. Dol Amor was literally a naturally formed maze of razor-sharp rocks and towering monoliths which were nearly impossible to navigate. Only the path through to the Maw was known clearly, the rest of the Labyrinth left unexplored for fear that trying to map it would cost far too many people their lives. And here I was, standing lost inside the most notoriously disorientating rock expanse in all the nations of High-Realm.

"Dol Amor," I repeated hopelessly, gazing around the deep shadows and jagged rocks. "This is a really bad place to be. How am I ever going to get out of here?"

Then a thought occurred to me: *My pendant led me to the shelter of the wreck. Maybe it can guide me out of this gods-forsaken place.*

I lifted my pendant from my chest and held it in my hand, looking down into its stone.

"Help me get out of the Labyrinth," I pleaded to it gently, hoping this would work.

Just as it had when I had asked to find shelter, the Pendant began to feel warm against my skin and the heart-stone started to glow. At first it barely flashed, but with me turning where I stood it started to grow more rapid in its flickering until it at last stayed fully lit.

I looked from the Pendant and up at the way it was directing me, seeing the path winding through the rocks and crags.

"All right," I nodded to myself. "Now I'm getting somewhere."

I walked the paths my pendant led me through, pausing only when there was no further way to go and the stone started flickering again. Playing hot and cold with the purple glow of the heart-stone made my seemingly impossible task that much easier, and I started to feel more at ease.

I'll be out of the Labyrinth in no time. This is really working.

I came to a large open space and frowned as the Pendant started to flicker wildly. I turned in all directions, but it wouldn't show me the way I needed to go.

"What's wrong?" I asked it quietly. "Can't you show me the way to safety?"

That was when I heard it.

There was a hissing from behind me, a sort of wheezing, cackling breath and the sound of something moving across the rocks. Out of the corner of my eye I saw a grotesque, skinny figure crouched on its hands and feet, its bald head hanging low from its slouching shoulders.

Oh no... No... What is that thing?

I gasped a small breath, freezing where I stood, sensing the creature as it started to circle me. All the while my pendant kept flickering wildly and I realised what this now meant.

That flashing is a warning...

The creature was making a strange clicking noise in its throat as it skulked in the darkness, the flashing of my pendant only giving me brief glimpses of it.

It was repulsive, with sunken white eyes and jagged, pointed teeth in a scowling mouth. It was bony and lanky, what little hair it had on its head stringy and greasy. Its hands were clawed, and its spine was spiked, the thing resembling a deformed human, but only just.

It was then that I noticed how it was searching, feeling along the ground with its hands.

It's blind. I know what this thing is. It's a Yirlla.

Like the Labyrinth, I had learned of the Yirlla from my tutors once I was old enough to know such things, though it was Mithras who was brave enough to tell me of them. They were wretched, broken humanoids that had lost the ability to see after living in the dark caverns beneath the Labyrinth for so long. They were carnivorous and were known to kill and devour humans that wandered into the rocks of Dol Amor.

I swallowed hard and started to back away from it, pausing to the sound of more sniffing and scraping behind me. Another Yirlla had appeared, more feminine than the first, their lack of any sort of clothing making their genders easy to determine.

There were about five or six of the hunched creatures lurking around where I stood, sniffing the ground, picking up the rocks to smell, and making that strange clicking noise.

I couldn't fight them, completely unarmed and lacking the strength and skills necessary to take on the creatures. I had to somehow get past them without drawing their attention and get as far away as I could. Their advantage, however, was that despite their blindness they knew the Labyrinth better than any human ever could.

Trying to be *very* careful and quiet, I moved towards the only opening in the rocks that I could see. My breath hitched and I covered my mouth as I gasped, two of the creatures snapping their heads up in my direction.

Don't let them hear me...

My foot crunched loudly on some of the hard grass and snapped it in half. The creatures let out horrible bloodcurdling screeches, their jagged-toothed jaws opening wide as they threw their heads back.

I swore under my breath and turned on my heels, sprinting as fast as I could. The creatures were clambering after me on all fours, screaming and howling as they ran, my footfalls, heartbeat and frantic breaths leading them after me.

I let out a startled scream as one of them tackled me from behind, knocking my hood from my head as it slammed me to the ground. I kicked hard, the creature rolling off me then turning and rushing at me again as I crawled backwards.

The Yirlla grasped at me, my hands slamming up against its forearms and wrists to hold it back. I squirmed against its naked shape, crying out as I tried to keep my face away from its grasping teeth, its claws trying to slash at me in the darkness that was perfect except for the flashing of my pendant.

"GET OFF ME!" I screamed, closing my eyes and pulling my face away.

The Pendant grew warm across my chest and I felt the heat intensify. Suddenly, there was the flash of purple energy and the creature was hurled away from me, slamming hard into the ground several meters away.

I crawled to sit up, looking at it as it recovered, the others closing in around me now.

I need something! Something that could make them leave me alone! Think, Leander, think!

"GIVE ME LIGHT!" I cried out and the Pendant exploded a bright purple glow from its stone.

The Yirlla screeched and held their hands up to fend off the illumination that only seemed to brighten from my pendant and shield me with its glow.

Light hurts their eyes! They're not used to it!

The Yirlla tried to rush me, but the light only made them scream and howl as they covered their eyes, backing away as I got to my feet. I edged a few steps towards them and all six of the monsters turned away, cowering behind their bony white arms. They cried out and howled, scurrying back into the darkness, their screams echoing through the shadows of the rocks until they faded away.

I stood there, breathing heavily from the desperate sprint I had made, trying to fight back the dizziness that was heavy in my head.

It worked. Oh, Gods...

I was relieved, easing my frantic breaths and slowing my heart's panicked pace. I turned my eyes to the Pendant and held it in my right hand, squinting at the blinding light it was emitting.

"Okay. Thank you," I said gratefully, though I knew it wasn't truly a living thing. "Now, please get me out of this place and to the nearest town."

The glow remained bright, but returned to its finder flash, easily directing me along the path I would need.

I spent the entire night wandering through the Labyrinth of Dol Amor following the Pendant's guidance, finally reaching the open lands beyond just before dawn. From here the Pendant led me through thin clusters of trees and shrub land until I finally found a road.

The glow of the stone fell dark as I stepped onto the road and turned my gaze up from under the hood to the snow powdered sign standing there. The arrow directing me south-east had the word *Orgilith* carved and inked black above it, while the one pointing westward had the word *Travarna*.

Weighing up the difference in the miles marked beneath the names, I decided that Travarna was where I would go. I knew it to be a port town that sat on the Ortagaad Sea and so the closest to where I now stood.

*The only problem with Travarna is that that's where we were taken from by boat to Castle Ortagaad. The guards there will be watching out for me by now, but I don't have any choice. I'm exhausted and starving. I **have** to go there.*

I trudged along the side of the road in the mud and snow, pulling the old cloak further around me and making certain to hide my face. By the treads in the dirt, I could tell that carts and carriages frequented this road a lot, as did mounted riders and people on foot.

There was no surprise then when a merchant drove his carriage past me, heading the same way I was. I thought to ask him for a ride, but decided against it, feeling that it was too risky to talk to anyone I didn't know. Besides, my parents had always told me never to accept rides from strangers.

An hour later, two more carriages passed me by, these ones closed in and more like those of nobility. They were heading the other way and I had no desire to draw their attention as I kept my eyes down.

Maybe this cloak will disguise me. After all, it isn't the sort of thing a young girl would wear. Maybe they'll think I'm a sailor, though it is far too big for me.

I glanced up and quickly hid beneath my long hair and the hood as I saw the riders on horseback following behind the carriages. There were four of them, all wearing black and gold surcoats branded with the Gorvennan Gryphon over their steel armour. Holding my breath, I kept moving as they trotted by, worrying that they would turn after me, but they didn't.

Sometime after midday, I came upon the walled town, stopping several meters back beside the sign with the town's name branded over it. It looked like a miserable, cold place with black rooves and dark grey buildings, almost everything made of stone, and very little greenery to be seen apart from the few trees that still held leaves.

I sucked in a hard, sharp breath as my eyes fell on the guards at the entrance to the town, all of them dressed as Keilantra's men were. There were five of them there; two guarding the open portcullis, the other three talking in a gathering off to my right near a stable. I noticed another two patrolling the perimeter of the walls, passing each other at the gate and continuing on their paths.

"I can do this," I whispered to myself, trying to find my courage. "I've come this far."

A carriage came past filled with supplies, surrounded by merchants and their escorts.

Okay. That works.

I slipped in at the back of the merchants, keeping my dress hems lifted in my hands as I walked. They weren't even paying attention to me, the guards seeming indifferent as I glanced up at them.

I was stunned as I passed through the gates behind the group of merchants, glancing back over my shoulder at the guards.

They didn't even question any of us. Perhaps entering the town is the easy part. Maybe the heavier security is around the docks. Fortunately, I'm not going there.

I turned my gaze to the town and started walking forward, separating from the merchants. I pulled the hood closer around my face and surveyed all the black haired, olive skinned people that surrounded me.

If I keep my hood up and stay quiet for the most part, maybe no one will realise that I'm an Aldegaadian, not a Gorvennan. I mean, from a distance my dark hair could be seen as black... I guess.

I made my way through the dank, cold streets, the ground paved in grey dirt and snow dusted cobblestones. There were people everywhere, yet the town seemed scarcely populated.

It is cold. Maybe people are staying indoors.

The town centre was also the marketplace and where the tavern was located. Here was where there was the most activity and I found it very easy to blend in with the near total lack of colour that the people wore. The cloak covering my dress from sight matched the rest of the grey, brown and black clothing easily, many of the people looking like they were unhappy and grizzly.

The tavern has to be my best bet. Maybe they can help me or give me somewhere to rest.

Finding the tavern wasn't hard, its doors open to the street and a sign hanging above reading: **The Northern Winds Tavern**.

I steeled myself and stepped through the doorway into the smoke choked air. It was a grim place, the voices of the patrons low and sullen as they huddled over their mugs and plates, looking like they were expecting their meals to be stolen.

I noticed a hooded figure sitting by the fire with his back against the wall, his face hidden by his cowl. He was alone and heavily armed, giving me a clear idea of what the people here were like.

All right... avoid men like him if I want to stay alive... and a virgin.

I found my way to the counter, staring up at the tavern keeper uneasily. He was a large, burly man with a little too much weight around his belly, his head bald and one eye white with blindness, a red scar over the lids. He was wiping down a plate with a cloth that didn't look very clean, which only made me cringe in disgust.

"Excuse me," I spoke so softly that it was barely more than a whisper.

"What do you want?" he demanded harshly with a gruff, angry glare, pausing his washing.

"Um... I... I was wondering if you could..."

"Get out of here!" he snapped fiercely at me. "We don't serve children in this tavern!"

"I'm not a child," I murmured uneasily.

"We don't serve teenagers neither!" he growled loudly. "Now, piss off, you stupid little bitch!"

I nodded quickly, too scared to argue with him.

As I rushed towards the doorway, I noticed that many of the rough men had turned their attention to me, curious to see what the tavern keeper was yelling about. The man in the hood was eyeing me too, his dark brown eyes watching me over his black face scarf.

In moments, I was back in the cold street, holding the cloak tightly around me as I searched for the next place I could try to go for help. My stomach was so painfully aching now, and I needed to eat something; an apple or a crust of bread, just something to take the edge off my starving hunger.

I wandered amongst the small crowd in the marketplace, glad to be shielded from their gazes by my hood. While the people looked merely miserable, the guards across the way gave me a deep feeling of dread. It occurred to me then that there were far too many guards in the area.

I'm not safe here. I need to leave soon or else I'm finished. How many more soldiers could rush out of the unseen places in this town at the raising of an alarm?

My eyes focused on the stalls and the merchants huddling under the shelter of their structures. There were quite a few stalls stocking armour and weapons, clearly competing with the blacksmith across the way. Still, if I were to choose, despite how burly and aggressive the man looked, the blacksmith would be my choice to buy armour and weapons from, not these half rate merchants.

There were a number of jewellery and clothing stores too, though the snow and the damp air were certainly playing havoc with the hanging fabrics. Like everything the townspeople wore, the clothing was colourless and drab, mostly furs to shield against the cold.

I guess it makes sense this far north that function would be chosen over fashion.

At last, I came to the stalls stocked with varying foods, a butcher who was also a hunter selling meats of all kinds the first I came past. That did nothing for my appetite, and I moved on to the baker and a grocer.

I browsed the foods thoughtfully, my hands rubbing together to keep my fingers warm from the cold. The very sight of the food made my stomach growl all the more and I wanted so badly to taste something that would sate this intense hunger. I had never felt so hopelessly in need for something as basic as food in my life. My royal upbringing suddenly seemed all the richer to me.

The storeowner I came across was a kindly looking, though gnarled, old woman, her face lined, and her grey hair hidden beneath a bonnet.

"Can I help you with something, dear?" her gentle, frail voice caught me by surprise.

"I... I was just looking at your stores," I confessed, trying to be as gentle and sweet as I could manage, somehow thinking I sounded pathetic.

"You poor girl," the old woman frowned sympathetically and touched my arm across the counter. "You look like you haven't eaten in months."

"Days at least, I think," I couldn't exactly remember the last meal I'd had.

She smiled with gentle green eyes: "Well, dear, what can I get for you?"

I stared at her in shock.

Oh no! I can't pay her for anything! I have nothing at all! What am I going to do?! I would never steal from anyone!

"I... uh... I don't have any money," I murmured my admission, feeling ashamed. "Maybe I could work for..."

It was frightening how quickly her demeanour changed, her kindness blasted away by hatred. She lashed out and threw me back from the stall with a hard palm to my chest, startling and bruising me.

"No money, no food! I'm not a charity for penniless wretches like you!" she snapped at me. "Scram, street rat!"

"I'm sorry," I turned and started to walk away, keeping my head down as I pulled my hood back up.

Street rat? I've never been called that before. Is everyone in this town so cruel to those in need?

I was so distracted by my wonderings that I didn't notice the figures in front of me until I collided with them. They were taller and stronger than me, the impact knocking me backwards and nearly to the ground, but for the grasp of one of the men. As I went to thank him, I looked up and froze in terror. The men were Gorvennan soldiers, both eyeing me with distaste.

"What do we have here?" the one holding me up asked with a cold smirk. "A young street urchin causing trouble? We've had complaints about you."

"Complaints?" I was stunned into numbness.

How could there have been complaints about me?! I've done nothing wrong! I've barely been in this town an hour!

"Yeah," the second guard said, his voice rough and his attitude very cold. "You caused a bit of a show at the Northern Winds. Didn't you, little girl?"

"I only..."

The first guard cut me off: "You don't get to say nothing yet. Come on, urchin."

"Let go of me!" I cried out as I was dragged through the crowd by my left wrist, the man's hold crushing so hard I feared my bones would break. "I haven't done anything!"

They took me to a side street, and I was hurled hard against the wall. Before I could move to recover, the first guard had his hand around my throat, pinning me back against the hard stone and wood. I cried out a small whimper, squeezing my eyes shut at the impact of his grasp.

"Right then," the man said as his companion watched on with a disgusting glee. "Let's get a look at that pretty little face of yours, girly."

He ripped the hood back from my face and they sneered as I watched them fearfully.

Why does this keep happening to me?

"She's pretty," the second guard chuckled, reaching out his hand and smirking as I tried to pull away from his grimy fingers. "I like the pretty ones."

"Let's just see what contraband you have on you," the first said with a gleam of lust in his eyes, spinning me around so that my face was to the wall.

I closed my eyes and drew in a few panicky, shaking breaths as his large hands roughly probed my body. His palms fell on my lower back and slid down, the sensation making me flinch hard.

"Don't!" I cried out, trying to grab at him only to have my wrists pinned to the wall above my head by the other guard.

"Shut your mouth, girl," he hissed viciously at me. "Another outburst like that gets your pretty little mouth slapped."

I fell silent and let out several hard, shuddering breaths, fighting back tears at the first man's groping as the second released my arms.

"This isn't a girl's cloak," the first guard observed and ripped it from my shoulders. "Too manly."

I felt the clasp tear as it choked me briefly and the chilled air hit me bitterly.

"Look at this," the second man chuckled again. "She's finely dressed for a street rat. Teal velvet and purple silk? Very fine."

The first guard's hand was firm as it crushed on my right shoulder, spinning me towards him again, my back slamming heavily against the wall a moment later.

"Very, very fine," the second grinned as he studied my slender, feminine shape, and how the teal and blue of my dress fitted closely to my torso and hips.

"Where does a penniless little whelp get such fancy clothes?" the first man questioned me, leaning over me.

I couldn't help my heaving, loud breaths or my teary gaze, afraid of what they were going to do to me.

His eyes fell to my pendant and he tapped it with his finger."And this? This is a very fancy bauble for a street rat to have."

"She must have stolen the clothes and the necklace," the second guard decided, both men standing so close that I felt very small.

"A pretty little thief as well as a disturbance to the peace," the first guard nodded with mock thoughtfulness. "Isn't that interesting?"

"I'm not a thief!" I defended earnestly, frightened of what they would do to me. "I would never steal anything! I swear!"

"She couldn't be a noble," the second man looked to the first with a serious frown. "Could she?"

"A noble who travels without sovereigns to spend? Especially a girl? I doubt it," the first scoffed.

"But she's not from around here," the second guard observed. "Just look at her; greyish blue eyes, auburn hair, fair skin, and that accent..."

"Very Aldegaadian," the first guard agreed with greater seriousness.

I held my breath and pushed myself harder against the wall, half wishing it would open up and pull me away from them.

"Hey, wasn't there a call to be on the lookout for a girl like her?" the second man recalled, looking to the first curiously.

"I remember hearing about a prisoner escaping Castle Ortagaad three days ago but wasn't that a man?" the first frowned with deep thought.

"Nah, nah, remember how the Knight-Commander came through yesterday and said we were to look for a girl of Aldegaadian birth," the second turned his hard gaze to me and smirked. "I think we just found her."

"Well then," the first's face widened with a devious smirk, "we'd better lock her in the jails until we can send word to Knight-Commander Ulric. And while we wait..."

I whimpered and pulled my face to my left shoulder, closing my eyes as he touched my cheek and neck with one hand and the exposed skin of my décolletage with his other.

"...we can have some fun with her," his eyes flashed with lust and all the promises of violation as he said this.

No! No, don't let them! Please! Stop them! NOW!

That familiar heat spread over my chest and I opened my eyes as the Pendant glowed bright purple. The two men had only a second to express their surprise before the Pendant let loose its repulsing blast of energy and slammed both of them into the wall opposite me.

For a moment, I stared at the two men where they slumped, breathing hard, my chest heaving fast beneath my bodice. The light from the Pendant faded into the stone and I pulled myself out of my shock, doing the only thing left to me.

I didn't wait to see if they recovered, scooping up my dress hems and running from the side street back to the market. I knew there was no way that the sound of the Pendant's blast would go unheard, my only option left now to run as far and as fast as I could before the town's guardsmen could capture me.

I skidded straight into view of the dull, bland place, my revealed attire now drawing dozens of gazes.

"Stop her! She's the prisoner from Ortagaad!" I heard the first guard shout as he and the second staggered to their feet.

"You, girl! Halt!" another soldier shouted from the way to the main gates as he ran towards me with four others, their swords drawn.

I let my distress and exhaustion at these pursuits show on my face, taking to run away from them with all the energy I had left.

"Stop that girl!" the shout was louder, the people around me gasping and crying out as they leaped from the soldiers' path.

I sprinted hard through the streets and the market, ducking and dodging between stalls as I heard the thundering of the soldiers' heavily armoured footfalls behind me. A quick glance over my shoulder and through my hair showed that they were not caring how much damage they caused, throwing people out of the way and knocking over stalls to gain ground.

"Grab her!" a voice shouted.

I spun around and let out a startled yelp, barely managing to duck away as two soldiers lunged at me. I managed to slip by them, though it was awkward, rushing past a number of commoners that watched on with stunned expressions.

I have to reach the gates out of town! I have to get out of here now! Let me escape, please!

Turning right and skidding in the mucky, snowy slosh, I steadied myself to keep running, jerking away from a few men by weaving to the right, left, then right and right once more so I didn't hit them. I heard a heavy crash and two thuds, knowing without looking that one of my pursuers had run into the men and hit the ground.

I was struggling to keep my pace now, my legs tiring and my breath burning inside me.

The western gates out of the town came into view, three soldiers visible with them, their swords at the ready. I noticed that the third was running for the winch to lower the portcullis and trap me as the other two moved to close me in.

Before he could reach the winch, there was a whistling in the air and an arrow shot past me, making me skid to a dead halt. The arrow buried its steel head into the soldier's back, a cry issuing from his lips before he fell to the right and hit the snow dusted street, dead.

What the...?

The two soldiers running towards me turned their gazes to their right and cried out, trying to move out of the way as a cart hurtled towards them. They were hit hard, thrown with the cart as it smashed to pieces against a brazier, knocking it over and scattering burning coals to the street in the collision.

I looked up to see the hooded and masked man from the tavern with a bow in hand. He regarded me with strong, stern eyes and nodded once hard towards the gate out of the city before turning to the soldiers behind me.

He's helping me? But why would he...?

The heavy footfalls of the soldiers drew my quick gaze over my shoulder, and I ran swiftly towards the gates as I was reminded of their intentions. Another heavy smash and more yells rose from behind me, but I didn't dare to stop and look back, desperately trying to make it out of Travarna.

In several agonising moments I was through the open gates and sprinting from the city walls, my eyes searching wildly for any sign of the guards that were patrolling the outside.

Another arrow whistled and there came a fast clacking of gears followed by a heavy bang. I spun around to see that the portcullis had slammed shut, the masked and hooded stranger standing before the wreckage of a large collapsed stall. He stared at me, then looked up to the soldiers recovering from his distraction, before turning and running as fast as he could down a street, disappearing from my view.

"Someone get that girl!" the first of the guards who had grabbed me ran to the gate as others started struggling to open the portcullis.

A couple of the soldiers ran after the masked and hooded man, but the rest kept their focus on me, their anger at my running from them so clear that it burned in their furious green eyes. There was a click and they started manually forcing the portcullis to rise, using pry bars and their hands to lift it. In mere moments, they would be through and closing on me again.

Run, Leander! Just go! I screamed mentally at myself as I saw two flickers of black and gold surcoats rush from outside the walls to my left.

Spinning around and holding my dress hems tight so I didn't trip, I threw myself back into my run, my feet pounding the wet, snowy road hard as my long dark hair trailed behind my shoulders with a flicking flow. I rushed past a caravan of very shocked traders and kept sprinting down the road, ignoring their stunned comments of disbelief.

The heavy pounding of armoured feet was behind me now and I had no other thought in my mind but to keep running, no matter how hard it was to breathe or how much my legs were hurting. I just *had* to *keep* running...

Chapter Eight
The Kindness of Strangers

I t was hard to breathe with the air rushing into my labouring, burning lungs so fast that it was like a hurricane filling my chest. Running into the wind was not helping this feeling, but with the turning of the paved roads I had little choice.

I looked over my shoulder, seeing the men sprinting after me. There were nine now, their black and gold surcoats flapping around their bodies, their black hair flashing around their necks and faces. If their eyes had been arrows, I would already have been slain and dropped to the hard, wet, dirty, snow covered stones of the road over two dozen times.

Flashing my eyes forward to the way ahead, I forced myself to keep moving, my imprisonment seeming to have weakened my stamina greatly. I felt that this run was drawing all the life from me, a choking pain crushing my throat and chest to try and slow me down. It was like my own body was battling against me, trying to surrender me to the villainous coterie rushing behind me with their blades drawn. That was my only advantage, their swords slowing them and the weight of their armour draining their strength faster than mine.

"Get back here, girl!" one man bellowed roughly at me, a sound that was a throat ripping scream to my ears.

I can't stop! I won't! If I do, I'm dead! My mind's voice was all I had, my physical one strangled into silence with my unending breathlessness. *Oh Gods! I really can't breathe!*

My side felt like it was tearing open with my efforts, my shoulders hurting with my chest and making me feel as if my heart was dying inside me. Still, I kept running. I had to.

There was a fork in the road ahead and I rushed for it, ignoring the signs posted there as I sped to the right. It didn't matter at that moment where the road led, as long as it led away from Travarna and the soldiers chasing me.

I risked another glance over my shoulder, this revealing to me that they were starting to lose ground. It was a small advantage, but it was better than nothing.

Keep going! Just keep going or your dead!

I had never felt more desperate in my life than I had since my chance first came in Castle Ortagaad to escape my dark fate. Even the pounding headache and the awful, dryly drowning breathlessness couldn't quench my desire to survive.

If I stop, they'll take me back to the Witches and to Him! Then he'll kill me! I can't let him kill me! I can't!

Reminding myself over and over was the only way I could find the strength now to keep myself moving as fast and as hard as I was. I had never pushed myself so relentlessly before, never exerted my body to the point where I was doing nothing but causing myself harm.

I tried to grasp my pendant in my violently shaking hand, nearly crying from the pain tearing through my heaving chest.

Amethyst! Help me! Please! Amethyst, I need you! Help! Help! Please, Amethyst, please! AMETHYST!

As before, there was no roar of a dragon's voice, no beating of great wings and no appearance of my enormous defender. I felt forsaken, tears slipping free at last as the pain of my exertion and fear overwhelmed me to breaking.

Why aren't you helping me?! Where are you, Amethyst?! Please, I'm in trouble and I need you! Help me!

Still nothing and I threw my hand from the Pendant, grabbing the velvet and linen of my dress once again.

Then I heard a terrible sound that only spiked my fear more strongly in my breaking chest, looking over my shoulder in panic. Black horses charged around the corner of the fork past the rocks and the leafless trees, their riders pushing them hard. The horses grunted and snorted with rage filled determination as they were forced to gallop at full speed after me, the seven of them closing fast.

I cried out a choked sound and pushed myself well past my limit, staggering and fearing I would fall.

*I can't outrun horses! There's no way! What am I supposed to do?!*I noticed a deep ditch and hill to my right, the snow there thick and easily able to cushion me. *I have to!*

As the horses closed on me and the men prepared to launch their attack, I threw myself right with a shrilled cry, my feet leaving the road. I felt a man's hand graze my shoulder blades as the horses suddenly tried to halt fast, but he missed his hold and I fell.

For a few painful moments, everything was a blurring rush of colour and sound, my cries mixing with the crashing of my body against the snowy slope. I closed my eyes to spare myself the dizziness and covered my face, hoping to protect what I could.

I hit the bottom of the ditch hard, coughing out loudly in pain as I rolled onto my back. The freezing touch of the snow on my back and neck snapped me from my shock, and I scrambled to my knees quickly, turning my gaze up through the trees to the road again.

"She's just a young girl! Get after her!" a man who must have been a captain bellowed. "Don't let some wretched teenager make you look foolish!"

I struggled to my feet, my ankles sinking into the snow as I turned away from the road and started trudging into the dead woods. The pain from my breathlessness was at its highest and I felt the sickest I ever had in my life. Even trying to move now was becoming too hard and I knew it was only a matter of time.

Choking and coughing, I threw my gaze back through the woods, the black and gold all that I could see of the soldiers as they dismounted and began trudging after me.

I can't keep this up! My body isn't going to last much longer! I can't breathe! Oh, it hurts!

I managed to pull myself onto more solid ground, stumbling forward now as one hand clasped my throat against my discordant, choking breaths, the other holding my chest. My eyes were failing and my legs wobbling from exhaustion.

There were only minutes left before I would collapse without being able to rest, the blackness of unconsciousness pushing in on me. But I resisted, fighting with all my lasting strength to keep moving.

My foot suddenly broke part of the ground and I fell with a strangled scream. I don't remember the fall, only the landing, the pain of it making me arch my back and cough out several terrible, agonised cries.

It took me a few moments to recover my sight in my air starved haze, my eyes flickering open to see the light of the grey day staring at me through a cave opening above. In my struggling exhausted consciousness, I had missed it and fallen in, but that wasn't the worst part.

There was a low growl that echoed from the cave and I painfully made myself sit, turning my gaze to the white mass that towered before me. The snow bear glared down at me with black eyes, its mouth opening to reveal its sharp teeth as it roared.

I couldn't even cry out, my rattling, frantic breathlessness leaving me silent but for my heavily wheezing gasps. There was nothing for me to do, no way to defend myself from the enormous white furred animal as it now stood and lumbered towards me.

A snow bear... I'd rather have it kill me than the Shadow Lord... Still, it is such a beautiful creature...

I met its gaze, feeling a strange wonder take over my panic, my heart beginning to slow its frantic pace and my breathing becoming easier.

The snow bear quieted its voice and settled itself, watching me with a gentle quality I had never thought to see from such a creature up close. It moved near enough that I had only to reach out and touch it, its demeanour so strangely calm. It let out a gentle growl and bowed its head before me.

I was stunned.

It's not trying to rip me apart! I thought snow bears defended their dens fiercely.

Carefully, I reached out my right hand as my left held against my deeply cooled cleavage and collarbones to help ease my breaths, my eyes staying locked with the animal's. My palm caressed its furred head, and I felt a weak smile pull at my lips as the creature let out a contented sound.

I have never in my life thought that I would one day be petting a wild snow bear safely. Why is it being so gentle with me?

At that moment, there came the crunching of boots and the clanking of armour from above.

"She came this way!" a soldier was calling as they searched for me.

"Spread out and find her!" the commanding soldier ordered. "She couldn't have gotten far!"

Panic filled me again and I knew there was no way I could make my legs move to try and escape. They would need only to turn their gaze down into the cave to see me sitting helplessly at the bottom. I was trapped.

I'm done for. There's no way out of this.

As if it knew what was happening to me, the snow bear reached out its large white paws, pressing its black pads to my body and started trying to move me deeper into the cave. Again, I was shocked, but I forced myself to move with it with my hands, finally slumping down onto the ground within the cave's shadows. The bear moved to position itself between me and the entrance, keeping its face close to mine and one of its great furry arms draped softly over my lithe waist.

It's trying to hide me from them. This is... so incredible!

I lay there for a while, comforted by the warmth of the animal cuddling me into its side with its arm, grateful for this furry shielding from the icy cold. I listened intently to the sounds outside the cave, silently worrying that the soldiers would think to come down and look in the bear's den.

At last, there came the sound of feet crunching the snow above and the clink of armour drew closer.

"Well?" the commanding voice demanded.

"Nothing, Captain," a soldier reported. "We've been searching for over an hour and there is no sign of the girl."

"How can an adolescent girl escape seven heavily armed, well trained soldiers?" the Captain glowered.

"We found her footprints some way back before the rocks, yet there is no trail we can discern hence."

"Could she have been picked up by someone?"

"Doubtful, sir."

"Very well," the Captain sighed. "We'll return to Travarna and send word to the surrounding garrisons to be on the lookout for her. The Queen will not be pleased that we let her missing prisoner slip through our fingers."

The crunching of their feet grew distant and soon fell into silence. I breathed out a sigh of relief as the snow bear got to its feet and moved to the mouth of the cave. The animal seemed to be checking if the way was clear, turning to me after a short time and growling an affirming sound.

Aching all over, I got to my feet and unsteadily walked to stand by the bear, the animal so large that its back was nearly at my shoulder on all fours.

"Thank you for helping me," I stroked its white furred head and offered it a kind smile.

The bear uttered a welcoming sound and I climbed up from the cave with it nudging my back to help me. As I walked from the cave, I turned back to see the bear watching me, standing up on its back legs and raising one paw at me. It was almost like it was waving goodbye.

I struggled back through the woods, following my trail as far as I could manage. I had wandered away from where I had fallen from the road, but I soon came upon a different part of the paved thoroughfare.

There was no plan in my mind as I walked the road, my chest and limbs still hurting so badly. All I could do was follow the trail and hope I could find a place kinder than Travarna had turned out to be.

The day was waning and with it the last of my strength. The cold was heavily biting me like the teeth of dozens of angry, ravenous creatures lashing at my skin. Without the cloak I'd found, I had no protection from either the cold or from the gazes of the Gorvennan soldiers. They would recognise me with ease now that I was dressed only in my velvet and linen dress.

I lost all thought, staring tiredly with sore eyes at the road as it began to bend and wobble in my perceptions. My hunger and exhaustion had finally overwhelmed me after two days without satisfying either need, and my feet slipped from under me as there came the champing of hooves behind me.

I felt myself fall to my left, slumping to the ground and dropping backwards to lay there, coughing loudly with a chilled, sickening, heaving wheeze. A cart was pulling up, old and wooden with a single large brown Clydesdale horse pulling it.

My mind couldn't form words and I couldn't see the faces of the figures as they climbed down to stand over me. Everything was blurring as my eyes drifted shut, too heavy now to hold themselves open as I continued to cough sickly.

"Son?" a man's voice came to my ears as footsteps crunched the snow and dirt. "What is it?"

"I saw someone fall from the road," a younger man's voice spoke with genuine concern.

There were a few moments of movement and I felt someone leaning over me, a leather gloved hand brushing my hair from my face.

"Well?" the older man called, further back from where I lay.

"It's a girl," the younger responded with urgency. "I think she's hurt."

"Is she breathing?"

A pressure was laid on my chest and I dimly realised he was listening to my heart and my breathing.

"Aye," the younger responded. "Though poorly."

"Get her in the cart," the older instructed.

I felt the younger man's large arms hook under me, my body completely limp and useless. He held me close to his chest and started carrying me, my awareness slipping from me now. There wasn't even enough strength in me to worry about the strangers taking me to some unknown place. I hadn't the energy left to even try to feel such concerns.

As I felt my body being taken from the snows, I slipped away from the world and into the release of unconsciousness.

* * * * *

A hard cough tore from my lips and I felt my body wrench at the roughness like sand inside my chest. I didn't open my eyes, my fingers crushing the softness of bedclothes against my palms at my hips, a dampness covering my skin. I had no idea where I was or how I had gotten there. I felt so sick, sicker than I had been in some time. I couldn't even begin to form words within my turbulent, darkened mind, my head hurting as I coughed again, this time harder and a little more violently.

Weakly, my eyelids flickered open and I squinted hard against the candlelight of the otherwise dully lit room. It took me a few moments to get my eyes used to the light again after being shut for however long, but I at last opened them to see around me.

The room was small, its walls made of stone pieces held together with thick mortar, wooden beams and framework reaching all around to hold the roof above. There was a door to my right, left open, the warm glow of a hearth coming from the next room.

Two figures were in the room with me, both watching me with green eyes and heavy expressions. They were men - actually, more boys - the elder of the two perhaps my age or a little more, the younger only in his fifteenth winter. They were both tall, with black hair of differing shades, their skin a gentle olive tone. They were dressed like simple country men, their clothes coloured in greens, browns and off-white hues.

"She's awake!" the younger of the two exclaimed, his eyes wide. "Brother, look, she's awake!"

"I see that," the elder brother turned from where he stood with his arms crossed, moving to crouch between where I lay, and his brother sat."Relax," he advised me, "don't try to move. You are not yet strong enough."

I recognised his voice; the same one that had belonged to the younger of the two men who had taken me from the snowy ground by the road.

I squeezed my eyes shut against the terrible burning headache breaking through my forehead, groaning a little, then turning my eyes back to him.

"Where am I?" I managed weakly, my voice sounding so small and faint in my own ears.

"My father and I found you on the road some miles past Travarna," he explained gently. "We took you into our cart and brought you here to our home."

I suddenly became aware of my body, feeling nothing but the sheets and blankets against my skin. I felt a thrill of panic and pulled the sheets closer over my chest with my right arm, desperate to shield my modesty.

"Where are my clothes?!" I asked a little too frantically.

"Mother took them to wash and mend," said the younger of the brothers. "She said she'd leave them for you once she was done."

"I... I need to go!" I tried to sit up, the world spinning around me. "I have to leave!"

"Calm yourself," the elder brother held my bare arms to steady me, looking into my eyes. "You need rest and food. Please, just try to calm yourself and lay back down."

"No! I..."

"Please!" he urged me, pushing me back down onto the bed, my shoulders slumping into the pillows. "You're very sick and cannot leave until you are well."

"But..." I tried to think of something to say, yet nothing came to my mind.

"Leif, Kell," a woman called as she stepped through the doorway, drawing our gazes.

She was raven haired like the two boys, though with tints of grey forming near the roots of the strands. She wore a plain dress with long sleeves and an apron, her hair tied back neatly into a simple, yet elegant braid from her beautiful, gracefully aged face.

"What is all this noise, boys?" she demanded with her arms crossed.

"The girl's awake, Mother!" the younger boy explained with excitement.

"She wishes to leave before she is well," the elder boy added, standing and turning to the woman.

"Does she then?" the woman asked and looked to me. "Kell, fetch me the bowl with the remedy I have been preparing."

"Of course, Mother," the elder son turned and left the room as the woman came to my side.

"Leif, go and find your father," she instructed her younger son. "Tell him our guest has awakened."

"But I want to stay and talk to her!" he whined.

"Leif," she gave him a stern gaze.

"I'm going, I'm going," he stood and stomped from the room.

There was the groan of a door opening and then slamming with the brief glow of grey daylight as he left.

"I *really* need to leave," I coughed as the woman took a bowl of water and a cloth from a bureau, setting it down on the table by the bed as she sat. "I can't... I can't stay here..."

"You cannot yet stand, let alone go anywhere, my girl," she told me, soaking the cloth and wringing it out before gently dabbing and wiping my bare skin. "You have contracted an illness called Frost Lung whilst laying unconscious in the snows, and a fever has come upon you. You need rest and to have a decent meal once you are able."

I closed my eyes, my breath heaving my chest with the deep pulling of air into my lungs, my body shuddering as I felt the coolness of the water on my skin.

"How... how long have I slept?" I wondered, turning my blue gaze back to her.

"Since my husband and son brought you here; three days, two ere your arrival here," she answered.

"F-five days?!" I was horrified. "I really have to leave!"

She pushed my shoulders down and met my eyes with sternness and calmness, just as my own mother would have.

"You are in no danger from the guardsmen here, child," she told me honestly. "Fugitive or not, you are in need of aid and *we* do not believe you are being pursued fairly."

I frowned at her in bewilderment. "How do you know any of that?"

"You have spoken aloud in your delirium," she explained, dampening the cloth and placing it to my forehead again. "Such words of dragons and snow bears I must admit were a little too fanciful for my mind. However, that the soldiers pursue you unfairly for the desires of the Queen... *That*, child, I can certainly believe."

I didn't remember telling her or her sons any of the events that had led me to find myself in their care, though I knew that if I had been speaking in a fever fuelled unconsciousness that it was definitely possible that I had.

"I'm sure my sons have told you," the woman said, "but I have taken your clothes to clean them. I will return them to you; however, your fever would only worsen if you were clothed. I have spent much of the last three days trying to cool your body to bring the heat from your fever down, just as I have attempted to warm your lungs and melt the ice lying within them."

"Mother," the elder son, Kell, was in the doorway again, a wooden bowl in his hands along with a few herbs. "Here are the things you wanted."

"Bring them here, Kell," the woman beckoned.

He brought them to her, and she took the bowl, setting it on the table beside the bed. She then started pulling apart herbs and plants, mashing them in her palms and putting them into the bowl.

"What is that?" I asked, feeling so exhausted that I wasn't certain I could stay awake much longer.

"Kell, dear, go and fill a cup with water," she directed him, watching him leave before answering me as she worked. "It is a remedy my grandmother taught me when I was a girl no older than you are now. I have resisted giving it to you before your eyes opened from fear that you might not be able to swallow in your sleep."

I just nodded, not really certain what to say as I lay there watching her work.

"It does not taste sweet," she confessed, "and its texture is most unkind. Yet, to restore you to health I do not think such pleasantries as taste should be the highest of our concerns."

"No, of course not," I agreed, coughing into my hand and laying my head back as bile fouled my throat. "I feel I can scarcely stay awake, let alone move or complain of such things."

Kell returned with a cup filled with water, standing silent in the doorway holding it in both large, callused hands. I could tell he was no stranger to hard work.

His mother completed her task, taking the bowl and presenting it before me. I could see a watery green liquid swirling in its wooden confines, the scent seeming pleasant, though the taste would not be.

"Here, girl," she lifted my shoulders with her other hand, helping me to keep my head up. "Your body is so very weak and needs time to heal. Drink. It will help and it will soothe the pain in your throat."

Hesitant as I was, I let her put the bowl to my lips and swallowed down the vile tasting remedy, forcing myself not to cough.

I've been made to drink worse things before. I reminded myself cringingly.

Swallowing the last of the remedy, I couldn't help my expression of distaste, the woman quickly taking the cup of water from her son.

"Here," she offered it to me. "The water will cleanse the taste from your throat. Such is the way of my grandmother's remedy."

I let her feed me the water, my hands too weak now to do more than grasp at the sheets like a newborn child's. In moments, I had completely finished the water and breathed in a refreshed sigh, my lips feeling cooled and easing from their previous dryness.

"There we are," she smiled at me kindly, pulling the blankets further up my chest. "The remedy will allow you to sleep more peacefully."

I nodded, closing my eyes and breathing in a slow breath.

Wait... She took my clothes, right? What about...?

"My pendant!" I gasped, trying to sit up. "Where...?!"

"Around your neck, dear," the woman assured me, easing my shoulders back. "I dared not remove it, fearing you should wake and worry for it. It seems to be such a preciously sentimental thing for you."

I reached my right hand to my neck, feeling my smooth, cooling skin with my fingertips until I touched the gentle shape of my silver companion. I immediately relaxed as I took stock of it, feeling the heart-stone with my hand and hearing the tiny clinks of the slender chain.

"It is," I agreed as I lay my head back into the pillows. "I can't bear to lose it. It's all I have left..."

"You can speak of your tale once you have recovered," she stood from her seat and handed off the bowl and cup to her son. "For now, rest and fear not. You are safe in this house."

I reached out and took her hand, gaining her gaze with a curious frown of her black eyebrows.

"Thank you," I murmured, trying to smile, but certain that what I gave was nothing close to one. "For your kindness."

"You are welcome, dear," she smiled and set my hand back on the covers. "Now, close your eyes and take your rest. I will be right outside should you need anything."

I watched her and her son leave, the woman closing the door over and leaving it ajar as she left me to my oneness.

Her remedy was definitely working, my cough having eased and the scratching in my chest lessened. With it, though, I also had a tiredness unlike anything I had felt before.

I let my eyes drift shut and all thoughts fade from my aching mind. My right hand touched its fingers to the Pendant, a warmth filling it and spreading through my body. It was comforting and made me feel much better as I slowly drifted back into a fitful sleep.

Chapter Nine
Blackwood

I woke to a gentle comfort filling my body, surprised that I had so little pain now. Every inch of me felt at peace and so free of all the grumbling hurts that I had gathered since escaping Castle Ortagaad. My eyes blinked on their own, my vision clearing away sleep to allow me to see the very same room I had found myself in before. I stared up at the ceiling's rafters, trying to decide whether this was real or yet another dream in my confused existence.

I feel so much better. So rested. Was it the remedy that woman gave me? Gods, how long have I been asleep this time?

Experimentally testing my body, I sat up, holding the sheets around my naked form to maintain some measure of modesty should one of those boys enter.

The last thing I need is one of them seeing me naked. Where are my clothes?

I let my eyes rove the room, studying every detail in depth now that I was fully awake. It was simple and bare in many ways, with only the bed I lay in, the table beside me, a dresser across from me and two chairs to furnish it. The only light came from a small lantern with a candle burning within its glass confines set on the bedside table. The door to the room was shut, granting me added privacy. That was almost a relief.

The sheen of teal velvet caught my eye, and I recognised my clothes sitting there on the dresser, folded neatly, my boots set on the floor by the door. Keeping the sheet around me, I slipped from the bed, setting my feet to the rug covering the floorboards. I wobbled and grabbed onto the nearest column in the wall.

I'm really unsteady on my feet. I need to take my time and not rush things yet.

Recovering my stance, I turned and walked delicately to the dresser, glancing over my shoulder at the door curiously. I could hear voices outside the room and smell food cooking over the fire. My stomach immediately growled at the scent and I remembered that I hadn't eaten since Ortagaad.

I checked my clothes, finding everything there and quickly started dressing, underwear, then leggings, my slip, my blue dress, then my teal and purple overdress. I laced up the bodice of my dress in the usual intricate crossing of its black cord, then picked up my boots. Once I had them on, I moved to the door and, with both hands, opened it a little to peer out.

I saw four people out in the larger room of the house, a dining table set in the centre and a stove against a wall opposite the door I stood behind. Herbs and fish hung from the ceiling near the stove and the counter with it, this area where they prepared their food. There was a set of stairs leading up to a sleeping space on a loft above, two more doors set into the wall behind the dining area. There was also a number of chairs and a pair of loveseats placed in a semi-circle facing the hearth.

I recognised the two boys, though at that moment their names did elude me, their mother - whose name I hadn't known yet at all - working over the stove. The last figure with them was an older man with a greying beard and long hair tied back behind his neck. He wore off-white shirt and dark trousers, the stains of sap telling me that he was most likely a woodcutter.

They seem nice so far. But I can't help wondering why they would bring a girl they don't know into their home like this. Maybe... maybe I should be careful, but show my gratitude all the same...

Carefully, quietly, I pushed open the door and stepped into the room, the two boys immediately looking up.

"Mother! Father! She's awake!" the younger of the two exclaimed excitedly, interrupting his parents' conversation.

I looked down at my toes and ran my hand through my hair nervously as I felt all eyes lock on me.

"Praise the Gods!" the man boomed brightly, standing and moving to my side, his arms out wide. "We were beginning to fear that you might never open your eyes again, girl!"

I just nodded, looking up and meeting his gaze, not certain what to say. It had been so long since I had been in a place as inviting as this, or with people as welcoming and kind.

"You must be starving, dear," the woman was on me in only a moment, directing me towards the table as her husband pulled out a chair. "Here, sit. You must eat."

"Thank you very much, but I'm really fine," I said as I was made to sit.

"Nonsense," she said, turning back to the stove and her cooking. "You haven't eaten, at least since you arrived, and I'd say perhaps not since before even that."

I conceded: "Um... well... that's... that's true."

"Then we'll hear no more about that," she chimed as she was filling bowls and handing them to her sons. "A home cooked meal is precisely what you need."

I felt so incredibly awkward as they moved around me, preparing for their meal. It was like I was an invader in their family's normal routines, and I wasn't so sure that any of this felt right.

I'm not feeling right because of what the Witches did to me, I explained to myself. *They used so many wicked illusions to torment me that now I'm questioning what is real and what isn't. Just don't over think it.*

"Here you are, dear," the woman set a bowl of food in front of me, then a large plate of cut up bread in the middle of the table.

"Thank you," that was all that I felt I could say.

"Eat up," she directed me as she sat beside her husband to my right, their sons to my left. "You need to recover your strength."

There was no doubt about that, my hunger maddening and my body feeling so drained of all the energy I might have had. I picked up the spoon and dipped it into the brown coloured stew, then took a mouthful. The warmth and the taste of it was amazing after so long without anything like it. I was so bewitched by the flavour and comfort that I had to force myself to slow down or risk making a mess of myself.

"You must be hungry, then," the man noted as I ate. "Hardly a surprise given how long you've slept."

"How long have I slept?" I asked, looking up at him.

He scratched his beard in thought: "Let me see... uh... we found you on the fourteenth, so that would be... nine days."

"Nine days?" I nearly choked.

"Including the two it took to bring you here," he added, seeing my concern and trying to be comforting. "You were truly in a very sorry state when we found you by the side of the road, and soon after, a terrible fever set in."

"I remember. Your wife told me about it when I woke and gave me medicine," then I looked to the woman, frowning. "I'm so sorry, but I didn't get your name."

"I am called Hulda, dear," she answered me, then introduced the others. "My husband is named Storr. He owns the town's mill. And our sons are Kell and Leif."

"I'm the youngest," Leif patted his chest and smiled at me.

"What should we call you?" Kell turned his gaze to me, sitting right at my side.

I probably shouldn't use my first name. I think I'm the only girl in all of High-Realm named Leander. I've always heard Mother and Father say it was a name reserved only for our bloodline. But my middle name is common enough...

"My name is Idona," I replied, convinced that my middle name was the wiser choice. "It's so nice to meet you and thank you so much for all of your kindness."

"You are welcome, dear," Hulda smiled warmly. "Idona is such a nice name too. What does it mean?"

"Youthful, I think," I replied, not too certain of the truth of my words.

"You hail from Aldegaad, am I right?" Storr asked, swallowing down some of his stein filled with mead.

"Uh... yes... I do," I felt like I was being interrogated again.

"What would a girl from Aldegaad be doing so far north-east from her homeland?" he asked of me.

"That... is a *long* story," I confessed, eating more of my meal so as not to have to go into it. "So, you own the mill?"

Storr nodded. "Aye, that I do. Lumber is my trade and believe me that this far north lumber is in high demand."

"Because it's so cold here," Leif added in excitedly, trying to keep my attention.

"Where are we exactly?" I felt bewildered at not knowing the answer.

"A small town called Blackwood," Storr answered with pride in his voice. "I was born and raised here just like my Da and his Da before him. It is so called because of the black wood of the trees that grow in this area."

"Are there many people here?" I was trying not to worry, but I could feel dread growing as the image of a Gorvennan garrison or barracks entered my mind.

"Only about four or five families," Storr replied with a shrug. "We are a small town, barely more than a homestead in truth. And before you ask, no, there are no soldiers here."

I frowned at him. "Huh?"

"That is why you were so far outside Travarna with neither supplies nor horse, is it not?" he was so incredibly perceptive, and it worried me. "Not to mention that we had passed through Travarna earlier that day where I had learned from a friend of mine that the soldiers had been chasing a young girl through the streets."

I swallowed hard, gripping the seat of the chair with both hands.

Oh no... They'll think I'm a criminal...

"Perhaps you do not remember," Hulda drew my gaze with a kind smile, "but I heard you murmuring while you slept. You are in no danger here and we will not hand you to the guardsmen."

"You... you won't?" I was surprised.

Storr shook his head. "Never will I stand in idle while those bastards hound the innocent, like yourself!"

"But, don't you owe allegiance to the Queen?" I asked uncertainly.

"The Queen?! Ha!" Storr snorted loudly. "That Witch should be garrotted and burned at the stake, along with her blighter sister and all their perverted guardsmen!"

"Then you have no love for her?"

"Let me tell you something, girl," he pointed his finger at me as he leaned across the table. "I am a true Gorven. You Southerners call us Gorvennans, but it is Gorvens. And we Gorvens are a proud and loyal people."

"Damn right, Da!" Kell and Leif both shouted together.

"I know a man from Gorvenna," I said, thinking of Carden once again. "It's strange, but your accent is different from his."

"He must be from the cities," Hulda spoke up from where she sat, drinking from her cup. "Or perhaps he was raised elsewhere. We are of the Northern

Gorvens and while the city folks' tongue might sound similar, ours is stronger in the old ways that we share with the Dorvans."

"We are honourable warriors!" Storr slammed his hand hard on the table, startling me. "Even those of us who work as labourers, miners, woodcutters and hunters! We are all Sons and Daughters of Gorvenna! That Hag who sits on the throne is nothing more than a usurper of our rightful King! And that king is Thoralf the Greater, not some Witch with her evil magic! And in time, his son, Anders, Prince of the White, shall too be our King! And him I would follow, just as I follow his father!"

Hearing such loyalty and love for Thoralf and Anders only made me feel so much warmer inside.

It is so good to see that there are yet those who hold their loyalty for their beloved country and their true rulers close to their hearts.

"And let me tell you this, girl," Storr went on. "There are so few that align themselves to Keilantra's reign of evil, for far too many have lost beloved daughters to the towers and dungeons of that cursed fortress out on the icy seas. So, believe us when we tell you that you are safe here."

"I believe you," I said, nodding quickly. "I am glad to know that you don't think I'm a criminal."

Storr spat hard and snorted: "Criminal?! Bah! As soon as Kell and I found you in the snows I knew you were anything but a criminal. Your innocence lies upon you like a cloak, and so we would never believe anyone as good or pure could be such."

"But you were being hunted by the soldiers," Kell noted, his voice gentler than his father's. "That is why you were on that road."

I nodded. "Yes, I..."

I had to think about what words to use for a moment. I still didn't feel entirely at ease, not now that I had noticed the weapons stowed on the walls, but then that was likely typical of their culture. I had to admit that my imaginings of what the Gorvens were truly like was far lacking the truth, my only contact having ever been King Thoralf, Prince Anders and eventually Carden.

At last, I decided that I could tell some of the truth without telling all of it.

"I... was a prisoner in Castle Ortagaad," I confessed honestly, "held there by the Queen and her sister."

"Without crime too, I am certain," Storr grumbled, sitting back and finishing his mead. "Come then, girl. Tell us your story."

I nodded and did as I was asked, careful not to mention who I am or anything about my pendant, Amethyst or the Shadow Lord. I had decided that such things need not be discussed in newly met company.

We all moved to the seats in front of the hearth as I told my story, Kell and I seated on one of the long loveseats, Leif and Storr both in chairs as Hulda was tidying up. It seemed more her own compulsion to do so than anything else.

I shrugged as I finished my telling: "And that is when you found me."

"You saw real dragons fighting above Castle Ortagaad?" Leif was so full of excitement and wonder that I couldn't help recalling how I had been when I had first met the Guardians.

I nodded solemnly: "Yes. Two great dragons; one the colour of gold, the other green as an emerald."

"It is such a hard story to be believed," Hulda commented, now clearing the table as we sat. "Dragons fighting over the most infamous Gorven controlled fortress, Culler Sharks nearly devouring you, Yirlla chasing you towards Travarna, and a snow bear hiding you from the Queen's guards? It sounds like fantasy."

"I know," I agreed as I set down my cup of water, "I can scarcely believe any of it myself, but that *is* what happened to me."

"It just feels as if there is something missing," she shrugged, fussing with the plates at the counter now. "Some miracle or magic must certainly have been at work to save you from such trials, for you cannot have done so on your very own. No one could."

I nodded, touching my pendant thoughtfully. "It must have been something like that. Don't you believe me, though?"

"In my forty-seven winters, I have seen many a strange thing living in this town," Storr responded as he smoked a pipe, sitting back with his ankles crossed. "And I have heard rumours of dragons for decades, so I am not so surprised that you saw such a thing as a battle between the great beasts so far north. After all, that is where our people believe they went when they left High-Realm. As for the Yirlla in Dol Amor, it is well known that many a traveller has met a gruesome end at the mercy of their claws and teeth."

"And the snow bear?" Hulda glanced over her shoulder at him.

"I have heard a few times of snow bears being accommodating to humans in need," he shrugged, explaining my case easily. "Though much of that is legend, yet I know that there are those who possess an affinity with the beasts enough to gain their loyalty through simply being present."

"Nonsense," Hulda snorted, going back to her work.

"Ignore Hulda's incredulousness," Storr urged me with a nod. "She does not believe in the magic of the natural world any more than she does in the magic wielded by mages, witches and wizards. Yet, both exist."

"And dragons?" she threw him a hard gaze.

"You worship Ankorect, do you not?" he responded sternly. "Is she not a dragon?"

"Don't worry, Idona," Kell spoke gently to me, sitting back into the cushions beside me. "My parents often argue about such theological things."

"Not that they ever settle their arguments," Leif chuckled, lounging his legs over one arm of the chair.

"I merely state fact," Storr said in all earnest, "that the dragons were first before us humans, and as such powerful beings descended from Ankorect, they would not simply have vanished."

"It could be another two hours before the debate comes to a stalemate," Kell smirked at me, drawing a smile and a giggle from my lips. "I'd bet your parents are much the same."

Those words were like a knife of ice into my heart. I hadn't been prepared for someone to mention my parents, even in such a vague way. In two years, nearly three, I still hadn't fully recovered from my grief and now I doubted that I ever would.

"My... my parents are dead," I murmured, sitting back and staring at my hands in my lap.

"Oh... uh... I am so sorry," Kell looked like he had just left devastation by his words and felt only regret. "I didn't mean..."

"It's... it's all right," I assured him, meeting his gaze. "It happened a few years ago now. I... I'm not really comfortable talking about it."

"We will not pry, Idona," Storr assured me, reaching forward and placing one large hand on my knee in comfort. "We all know such pains, and I am certain your parents would be enraged at the treatment you endured within Castle Ortagaad."

"I know they would be," I agreed sadly, fighting the urge to cry.

I will not cry again! I've done enough of that!

"Do you have no family left at all?" Leif asked quietly, the most subdue I think I had seen him in all the time I was there.

I nodded. "My elder sister is in Daamenhall in Balganis. I suppose it is only the two of us now."

"Then who's Carden?" Leif's question was another shock to my mind, drawing my gaze at a snap to him.

"How do you know about...?"

"You talked while you slept," Hulda called from the kitchen as she washed dishes. "You said many things. Amongst them was that name. You must have called to him many times."

"I didn't realise," I felt so strange, thinking of my beloved and once again longing for him to be with me.

"So?" Leif pushed. "Who is he?"

"The man I love," I answered, smiling softly. "He is... my soul mate."

They were all gentle in their expressions, the two boys listening intently as their father nodded while holding his pipe to his lips. Hulda smiled brightly at me where she stood, her eyes warm and aglow with all the joy she had.

"He must be a truly good man for you to call for him so much," she said, romance clearly one of her loves.

I nodded, feeling sadder than I wanted to: "Yes. He is. But I haven't seen him since I was imprisoned in Castle Ortagaad."

"When did you last see him?" Leif asked gently.

"We were taken with a friend of ours from Eilath in Lorveren," I explained, once again careful to avoid such details as Gathlorks and the Shadow Lord. "Our abductors took us to Castle Ortagaad and my friend, Tallinn, and I freed ourselves, then found Carden. We tried to escape," I shook my head, feeling tears trying to push past my eyes, "but they overwhelmed us. Carden and Tallinn were taken from Castle Ortagaad and the Witches had me imprisoned in the West Tower. And that is where I stayed for two years."

"Do you know where he is?" Kell was close to me at that moment and I couldn't help feeling his attraction for me, which made me a little uneasy.

"Yes, I do," I answered, taking in a deep breath to brace myself for what I was to say next. "He and Tallinn... were taken to Arnath."

Plates clattered and smashed to the floor, all of us throwing our gazes quickly to Hulda. She stood trembling with terror in her eyes, her hands shaking.

I turned my gaze across the faces of the other three. Leif and Kell looked pale, glancing to each other uneasily, while Storr coughed on his pipe and batted his chest with his fist to clear his lungs.

"Arnath?" Hulda looked to me with a pale, petrified stare. "That is not a good place."

"No, it is not," Storr agreed, putting his pipe out and looking to me hard. "Do you know what horrors lie within that dread place?"

I shook my head. "Not really. I've only heard a few things."

"The Forest of Arnath," he said gravely, "is a dark and terrible place, which Blackwood has the misfortune of lying not but a mile from the borders of. Only the Rangers of Dorvana and the High Elves of Silvervale dare to tread within its dread boughs, and few ever return."

He leaned towards me, making me pull back into the cushions uneasily. His face was so severe, his eyes darker now as the shadow of fear flowed over him.

"My grandfather heard stories of that place as a boy, stories he told to my father and to me," Storr explained darkly. "There is tell of a necromancer who rules the forest as if he were a king ruling all the terrible beasts and curses that hide within. And it is at the heart of the forest where he resides in a labyrinthine castle, where the dead rise and walk in unholy damnation."

He grasped my wrists and pulled me close, startling me. I could only stare into his eyes and pay close attention to all he said.

"You must *never* enter that forest, girl," he warned me fiercely, though his voice was calm, "for if the beasts do not get you, the Necromancer Wraith will."

I just nodded and pulled my hands back. He had frightened me, there was no denying that.

"I... I should go," I got to my feet and started quickly for the door. "I've taken so much from you already and... I should be leaving..."

Storr snatched my upper arm in his large hand as he stood and turned me to face him with a gentler gaze: "You are still too weak, and it is far too dangerous at night to travel the roads. Besides, where would you go?"

"To my sister," I said, knowing it was the only logical place left to me. "Balganis isn't too far."

"Far enough that you cannot safely walk across all of Gorvenna to reach its borders alone," Kell stood and came to my side. "My father is right. You still need to rest, and you should not walk beyond Blackwood at night. Not so close to the Forest."

"And not with the Queen's soldiers looking for you," Hulda added, now having cleaned up the broken plates. "Stay here with us and we will help you reach Daamenhall and your sister."

I sighed reluctantly. *They're right. Of course they're right.*

"All right," I nodded reluctantly as Storr released my arm. "I'll stay."

* * * * *

For several days I rested inside the woodcutter's home, his wife caring for me and ushering me to eat what I could, when I could. It was strange to me, being allowed to eat anything I desired again. So long in that dark tower with only what little the guards had deemed fit to feed me had left me lost to such luxuries.

When I wasn't in bed, I sat by the fire, a blanket wrapped around me at Hulda's urgings. She seemed certain I would catch a new sickness if I didn't stay bundled up. I would sit there and watch the flames, allowed to read any of the books they had on the shelves. This was another luxury I had sorely missed in my imprisonment, so glad that despite my lack of practice my ability to read had not diminished.

So many times, I fell asleep as I read, even this simple act to amuse myself taking so much out of me. Storr would often lift me in my half wakeful state and carry me to the bed they had put me in. I began to know what it was like to be someone's daughter again, though Storr was certainly larger than my father.

Leif and Kell were always spending time with me when not working with their father at the mill or studying, as was Leif's case more often. I began to feel a definite affection for the two boys, though Kell was certainly more a man in age than his brother.

Being with him only made my heart ache and I yearned to be with Carden all the more desperately. I often lay by the window watching the trees and mountains beyond with a heavy heart as I imagined my raven haired, green eyed love walking up the cobblestone road to find me there.

I sighed, resting my head there against the glass as I watched the gentle rain begin to fall amidst the patches of snow, tears sliding down my cheeks.

I miss you so much, Carden. Gods... it's as if you never existed. But you must have, because your absence leaves me with only heartache.

I closed my eyes and rested my head as I slipped away into sleep again, the blankets keeping me warm in addition to the fire in the hearth.

Hulda never seemed to bother me when I felt like this, and quite often she was outside tending to their garden where she grew her own vegetables. Only once did she see me crying like this and asked me what was making me so sad. Her response to my answer of missing my beloved was like any mother's, and I was so grateful for her care.

At last, I had strength enough to do more than just lie or sit, offering to help Hulda where I could around the house. She didn't give me much to do, but I gladly did what little I was allowed, mostly putting away a few things or doing a little sweeping. Hulda was a proud woman, and her home was her domain, as if she were Queen of her own little piece of High-Realm. I understood her desire to do things her own certain way as I would wish to do for myself.

I quite often then fantasised about Carden and I having a place like this as our own, wondering what it would be like for the two of us to have a peaceful life such as this. Yet, when my mind wandered to old age and to children, my heart broke and I remembered what the Shadow Lord had taken from me.

I had been there for more than two weeks when at last I felt that I was strong enough to enter the town itself. Hulda fussed over me and gave me a dark grey woollen shawl so that I would stay warm.

"Are you certain you wish to go outside, Idona?" she asked me as she pulled it across my shoulders.

"I can't stay inside for the rest of my life," I replied, grasping it with both hands to keep it close around my chest. "I just wish to breathe the air and feel it on my skin for a little while."

"All right," she nodded. "But you be careful and do not leave the town. Go to the mill if you wish. That way at least Storr can keep watch over you."

I nodded and for the first time in more than a fortnight, I opened the door of the house to the cold air and the beauty of the foothill forests surrounding Blackwood.

Standing there on the wood board porch was like stepping into a fresh world. To my left stood great mountains that towered high to the sky, some way off, though close enough that I would crane my neck to look to their snow-capped peaks. To my right were rolling hills dotted with tall black bark pines stretching to another far distant set of mountains.

I wonder which way is north. It has been so long since I set foot outside that I can't even begin to guess which direction is which.

I started walking along the cobblestone road, taking stock of the thatched roofed, pine wood framed, stone walled houses that surrounded me. There were only a half dozen there, not all of them along the same path, the woodcutter's house set off the main road. The Blackwood Trader and the Inn were the most obvious and largest of the buildings in the town, standing out above all the houses with their similar, yet different designs.

I paused at the small stable beside the house, smiling as the brown Clydesdale clopped to the fence where I stood. I reached out and stroked his nose and mane, the sensation of the coarse hair seeming brand new after so long isolated.

Turning from the horse, I made my way along the paths to the main road through the small town. There were only a couple dozen people living here, including a number of children. Though I was a stranger amongst them, they didn't treat me as such.

I smiled as the children ran and played in the street, a dog barking and chasing them happily.

I am so glad that there are still places like this in the world. It's good to know that not everything is darkness and despair.

I found the mill without trouble, the single largest structure at the edge of the town just before the stone and wood wall above the archway that served as a gate. It stood on the banks of a blue flowing river, its waterwheel turning as logs were sawn in half up on its highest level. Storr acknowledged me with a nod as I moved to sit over the edge between the columns that held the roof.

As I watched the river flow and took in the cold scent of the mountain air, I began to feel like I had at home. Though the atmosphere was much colder, so much of Blackwood reminded me of Arvon and I longed to return to my childhood home.

If only Arvon still stood by the Great River's edge. How much I wish I was back there before any of this had happened...

"Hey!" Leif grabbed my shoulders and startled me, Kell shaking his head as he joined us.

"Gods, Leif!" I cried out, smiling at him. "You scared the wits out of me!"

"Just keeping you on your toes!" he grinned, dropping down hard beside me. "So, out of bed at last, huh?"

I shrugged as Kell sat down to my right. "I've been here more than a fortnight, including the time I was unconscious. I decided I wanted to take in some air."

"It is just good to see you up and about, Idona," Kell smiled and went to touch my shoulder, but rethought it as he withdrew his hand. "Staying in bed is never a good thing."

I nodded, turning my eyes back to the water. "It truly is beautiful here. It reminds me of home."

"Where is home for you?" he asked me gently.

"Arvon," I answered, the sound of my home's name suddenly like an icy dagger to my heart and I felt my expression drop. "I... I was born in Arvon."

"Ah..." Kell nodded and coughed. "Yes... uh... we... we heard of what happened there."

"Did you see it burn?" Leif asked a little too excitedly, taking a punch to the shoulder behind me from his brother. "Hey! Kell!"

"Do not be so unkind, Leif," he turned to me with sympathetic eyes. "I am sorry for my brother's thoughtlessness."

"It's all right," I assured them with a sigh. "I haven't been home for so long now that I doubt there is much left of the town... or the castle."

"Did you ever go up to the castle?" Leif asked, a question that made me smile.

"Yeah, absolutely, all the time," I turned to him with a fondness in my heart. "In truth... I lived in Castle Arvon. That was where I was born."

"I figured as much," Kell smirked and patted my back gently, whispering then: "Your secret is safe with us, your Highness."

I stared at him in disbelief. "You knew?"

"Mother and Father knew," he answered me with a shrug. "They were in Arvon five years ago during the Festival of Light. As Father said while you slept 'it is a hard thing to forget the face of Aldegaad's most beautiful princess'," he chuckled at his imitation of his father, smiling at me gently.

"Hm," I looked back out to the waters in thought and disappointment. "I had hoped no one here recognised me. And I'm not *that* beautiful."

"Most people in Blackwood wouldn't know who you are," he confessed with a light shrug. "This is a small town far from the places where such things would be known. Only our family know who you are."

"Where did you get the name Idona from?" Leif shifted where he sat, turning his back to the column nearest him and resting his feet on the floor as he leaned against it.

"It's my second name," I admitted. "I'm sorry I didn't tell you who I am from the start. I just... I wasn't sure I was safe."

"I think you have reason enough to be cautious," Kell replied, leaning back on his palms.

I nodded, watching the river for a moment before turning my eyes to the mountains. "What mountains are those?"

"Those are the Nartarn'lath Mountains," Leif answered, looking over his shoulder at the great peaks. "I want to climb them one day."

"I've never seen them from this side before," I mused as I studied the crags and ice. "In my home we saw them every day as we were settled in their foothills along the Great River Arvon."

"That's on the southern side. This is the northern side at the far eastern end," Kell explained, breathing in the air deeply. "I suppose you're a long way from home, Princess."

"Don't... don't call me that," I looked to him with a gently pleading gaze. "Please, don't."

"All right," he nodded. "It makes sense... Idona," and he winked.

"Thank you," I smiled.

I turned my gaze in front of me and frowned thoughtfully at the far-reaching stretch of forest that lay beyond the mill.

"Is that the Forest of Arnath?" I asked without thinking.

"Eh-hem," Kell coughed lightly. "Yes. That's the Forest. It makes everything dark, which is probably why we have all these black barked trees in the area."

"It can't be easy living so close to such a frightening place," I said as I studied the overgrown trees in the distance. "I mean, the stories alone..."

"I'm not sure about *all* of the stories," Kell confessed as he crossed his arms. "While my father always speaks the truth, I am not convinced that everything he tells us about the Forest is real."

"What sort of things are in there?" I turned to him curiously, pulling the shawl tighter across my shoulders as I felt the bitter wind blow colder.

He shrugged. "Wolves, of course. Bats. I have even heard of groundmerks skulking in the shadows of that place."

"They're large vermin, right?" I tried to recall what little I remembered about such things. "Like rats?"

"They're not rats," Leif shook his head, taking this as another chance to play up. "They're half the size of a full-grown man with huge, jagged teeth and six legs, their faces like a cross between rats and wolves."

He knelt over me and imitated being one with his fingers posed by his mouth like fangs.

"And if they bite you, their poison will kill you!" he went on, pretending to maul my shoulder playfully before sitting back normally, making me smile. "Mother said that as skilled a healer as she is, she can't cure groundmerk venom. Only the High Elves can do that."

"The High Elves?" I frowned.

"Aye," Kell nodded and pointed way out at the forests. "Beyond the Forest lies their city called Silvervale, where all the High Elves of High-Realm reside. That is also where lies the Broken Towers, home of the Wizards of the Elemental Brotherhood."

"I've heard of them," I recalled my time in Eilath when Ellora had spoken of both Silvervale and the Wizards. "Have either of you ever seen any of them?"

"We sometimes see the High Elves travelling on the main road and over the bridge," Leif affirmed with a nod. "They pass through the Forest without fear. Da says it's because the High Elves have powers of light strong enough to fend off the darkness of Arnath, so they are safe while no human can ever pass through. That, and they use the Elven Road."

"Have you ever seen Elves?" Kell asked, turning his gaze to me.

I nodded. "I travelled to Galvenin with my friends and met the Snowleaf Wood Elves. I am even friends with one of them."

"You're friends with an Elf?" Leif was excited again. "What's he like?"

"*She* is very wise and very beautiful," I answered as I thought of Ellora. "I trust her with my life, as I do all of my friends," then I added softly: "Especially Carden."

"You must truly miss him," Kell noted with a gentle voice.

I nodded, hoping I didn't start to cry again: "With all the love in my heart. I worry for him, wondering where he is and what he is enduring."

"Is he a very capable warrior?" the young man asked quietly, almost jealously, though he tried to hide it well enough.

"Very," I smiled as I thought of him. "He is a Guardian after all."

"A Guardian?!" Leif's excitement returned yet again, and his eyes lit up as they widened. "As in *the* Guardians?!"

"Yes," I nodded, smiling at him. "I know four Guardians, including him."

"Do you think he yet lives?" Kell was quiet, cautious as he asked this.

I nodded slowly as I thought hard about it. "He and Tallinn are alive. I know it, and they must have escaped the fortress by now. If I could escape Ortagaad, then they would have no trouble escaping Arnath. The Guardians are the greatest warriors in High-Realm. I'm certain they would easily have made it through those forests to safety. Even with wolves, bats, groundmerks and whatever else lies within."

"Trolls, giant spiders, orcs," Leif added without thought, then tapped my shoulder to gain my attention. "There was even something with giant wings out there."

"Really?" I was surprised and fascinated.

"Oh, not this again," Kell rolled his eyes and stared at his brother. "Leif, I keep telling you that what you saw was some kind of bird or a bat."

"It wasn't anything like that!" Leif insisted, looking to me with an expression that told me he hoped I'd believe him. "I saw it one night about three days before Da and Kell brought you here. It was big, bigger than big even! It flew with wings like a bat and went down into the trees!"

"You saw a bird, Leif," Kell shrugged nonchalantly.

"Shut up, Kell!" Leif snapped. "It looked like a dragon, just like what Da always says! You believe me, right, Idona?! I mean, you actually *saw* real dragons fighting!"

I shrugged. "It could be a dragon. They are very big with enormous wings like that."

"Now you're encouraging him," Kell shook his head, getting to his feet as we heard footsteps.

"Are you three enjoying the mountain air and song of the river?" Storr smiled as he approached us, the mill now silent as it had stopped for the night.

"Idona thinks I saw a dragon, Da!" Leif exclaimed like he was trying to prove a point.

I felt myself blush as I looked down at my hands, then up at Storr.

"Perhaps you did, my son, but it is not something we can see for ourselves," Storr replied, patting the boy on the shoulder. "And we will not go looking for such a magnificent being. Dragons deserve our respect, not our ogling. They are creatures with wild hearts that may never be tamed, and such should be the way of it."

"What of the Dragon Pendants?" the boy raced his words with enthusiasm. "Don't they tame dragons?"

"No, Leif. The Dragon Pendants were gifts from the Dragons to humankind long ago," Storr explained with gentle humility. "But none yet exist to be found now. They are lost to the ages."

"It's too bad your necklace isn't like that," Leif turned to me with a sigh. "Imagine if you could call a dragon with it."

"I'll bet it would be amazing," I humoured him, glad that secret was still mine to keep.

"All right, enough talk of lost legends," Storr ushered us, helping me to my feet by lifting me by my arm with one large hand. "Let us get indoors before the cold deepens and we all catch the sickness. I'm sure your mother will have evening meal prepared by now."

I walked with the three from the mill and along the paved paths back to their house. I watched Leif as he continued talking about dragons, allowing myself a small smile at his enthusiasm.

I see so much of me in him when I was only fifteen winters old. And my father was just as encouraging to me about these things as Storr is to him.

That night we ate a hearty venison stew, then rested by the fire. I helped Hulda clean up, giving her more time to sit with the rest of us as Storr sang old Gorven songs of warriors from ages past, and even of the dragons and their eternal greatness. Like Leif, those songs were the ones I loved best.

I went to bed that night dressed in all of my clothes for extra warmth, but also out of a lazy lack of energy. I had no desire to bother untying my bodice and found it easier just to rest as I was.

I dreamed of Carden and of the home we could have like this, for once letting my thoughts extend to us with children. There had not been so much happiness in my heart for so long, but it was soon shattered.

A hard hand suddenly pressed to my mouth and I woke with a muffled yell. I froze where I lay, looking up at the green-eyed man standing over me, my heart racing in my chest.

"Stay quiet, girl," Storr urged me with concern in his grave voice. "They have come."

Chapter Ten
The Black Woods Burn

I couldn't take my eyes off the sword in his large hand, my heart pounding up into my throat at the sound of his dire words and the sheen on his cold blade. *Who? Who has come? Who is he talking about?*

Slowly, Storr withdrew his hand as I lay still, my fingers grasping the pillows uneasily on either side of my head, my eyes wide with terror.

"Remain silent or else the soldiers might hear you," he ordered me as there came shouts and clattering from the roads outside.

I nodded frantically, obeying him without question, my heart racing inside my chest, my breaths labouring with fear.

He took me from the bed, ushering me out into the main living area. Hulda was armed with a large war axe, Leif and Kell both with swords as they stood in their trousers and nightshirts, bleary eyed from sleep.

"There are a couple dozen of them outside," Hulda said as Storr led me into the room. "One of *them* is here too."

"Curse them!" Storr snarled viciously, moving to look out the window as Kell took my arm and brought me close to him and Leif. "Those Witches are nothing if not persistent!"

"Witches?!" I felt my heart sink. "One of the Witches is here?!"

"The other one," Hulda nodded as she was now loading a crossbow, "not the Queen, but her sister. I heard it said that she is the worse of the two."

"Oh, Gods..." I gasped, backing up against a column beneath the loft, trembling in terror.

Manth is here? If she's come for me, then how can I ever escape her gaze? How can anyone hide me from her?

"It is all right, child," Hulda assured me, patting my shoulder as she handed the crossbow to Leif. "We will not let her, or her men find you."

"They come this way," Storr warned, turning to us and moving to a back room. "Kell, Leif, Idona, follow me."

I obediently followed behind Leif as Kell kept his hand to my back protectively. We entered the storeroom where they kept barrels of food and supplies stowed, Storr crouching down and opening a hidden trap door.

He turned his hard eyes up to us and nodded: "Kell, you first."

"Right, Da," Kell nodded and jumped down into the darkness beneath the house.

Storr reached out his hand to me. "Idona."

I moved forward, taking his hand and letting him help me down. There was no ladder or stairs, the strong man having to lower me to his son's waiting arms. He let go and I slumped against Kell's chest, looking up at him gratefully for catching me.

There was a thump and I turned to see Leif as he jumped down into the hiding place. The three of us then turned to look up at Storr where he crouched over the hatchway.

"Whatever you hear, do not make a sound," he advised us as the noises from outside grew louder. "Do not let them find you. Boys, protect her."

"We will, Da," Leif responded, clutching the crossbow to his chest.

"I will come for you once they have gone," Storr assured us, then added: "Kell, Leif, your mother and I love you, no matter what happens."

"And we you," Kell replied, still holding me close to his broad chest.

As Storr closed the trap door, I could feel that same sense of worry that had filled the air the night we had abandoned Castle Arvon. I closed my eyes and tried to slow my breathing, wanting to remain as calm as I could be.

Ankorect... please... protect us all.

There was a loud bang and the sound of heavy boots on the floor above us.

"Shh," Kell whispered to me. "Come with me."

I followed Kell as he led me to stand under the floor of the main living area, Leif right at our sides. I managed to get a glimpse of what was happening through the floorboards, seeing Hulda and Storr as they faced the soldiers in their black and gold surcoats. I felt terror grip my heart as two more figures entered, one dressed in the knight's armour of Gorvenna, the other in black with her hood drawn.

"What is the meaning of this?!" Storr demanded with strength as he faced them. "You have no business bursting into our home in the middle of the night!"

"Our business is that of the Queen's," Ulric replied with a curt casualness as he surveyed the house, "and that means we may do as we wish."

"You have no reason to come this far out from the cities," Storr pointed out, holding his sword ready. "What reason could there be for people such as you to come to Blackwood?"

"As I said, the reasons are the Queen's," Ulric glanced at the blade in the woodcutter's hand. "You should drop that sword, Woodcutter. Unless it is death you seek."

"I have a right to defend my home!"

"And we shall not cause you or your home harm, as long as you cooperate," Ulric said, then gestured to the soldiers. "Search every room."

The soldiers started moving through the house, only a few remaining by the door. Storr and Hulda just stood their ground, glancing at each other as they allowed the search. Clearly, they were confident that we wouldn't be discovered.

Please don't let them find us. Oh, please...

"What is it that you search for, soldier?" Hulda asked in a quieter, yet still stern tone. "Why do you think you'll find it here?"

At that moment, Manth drew back her hood and let it hang past her shoulders. Her black eyes looked so much darker now and I could feel the waves of evil coming off her like the swell of the sea. She regarded the man and woman harshly, though her calm was unbreakable as she stepped in front of Ulric to get a better view of them.

"A fugitive is what we seek," she answered in that tiny, raspy little voice that sent painful shivers down my spine as soon it issued from her dark lips.

"A fugitive?" Hulda raised an eyebrow at her, not seeming even the slightest bit unsettled by the Witch.

"One of the prisoners kept in Castle Ortagaad escaped," Manth explained darkly, "and was seen heading this way two weeks ago from Travarna. Perhaps towards the forest?"

"Then he is dead," Hulda commented with certainty.

"The prisoner is a girl," Manth clarified.

Hulda laughed lightly. "Then *she* is most certainly dead if she went in there."

Manth eyed her coldly, her gaze like that of someone trying to find some hidden truths. She turned the same stare to Storr, but both he and his wife were too hardened to fall to such a gaze, even knowing the Witch's powers.

There were footsteps and the soldiers returned from their searches, drawing Ulric's gaze while Manth kept hers locked on the man and woman.

"Well?" Ulric demanded.

"Nothing, Knight-Commander," one of the soldiers reported briskly. "All we found were empty beds that were still warm from persons sleeping in them."

"There are others here?" Ulric turned his gaze back to Hulda and Storr.

"My sons," Storr responded sternly. "They went to alert the neighbours of your arrival."

"Indeed?" Ulric didn't sound convinced and I felt a strong ill in my stomach growing. "You are not unknown to us, Storr of Blackwood. You have no love for our Queen and no loyalty to Gorvenna."

"*All* of my loyalty is to Gorvenna!" Storr declared strongly. "I am like any other Gorven Son of this land!"

"You are buried in the old ways," Ulric shook his head and drew his sword, "allied to a King who is too enfeebled to rule without aid."

"Thoralf the Greater is the true King of Gorvenna!" Storr snapped and swung his sword at Ulric as Hulda attacked with her axe.

There was a scuffle, and I could barely see more than colours and flashes before there were thuds. I heard Hulda cry out and Storr growl in pain to the sound of a sword cutting flesh. I covered my mouth to keep from crying out, looking to the two boys. Kell was fighting to remain calm, holding his hand over Leif's mouth as the younger boy struggled against him.

Oh Gods! I should never have stayed!

"You are as weak and foolish as your brethren who choose to stand against us," Manth hissed in her sinister little way as she stood over the two, who were now forced to their knees by the soldiers. "This uprising of yours threatens all of Gorvenna, and only offers pain and death to our people."

"*You* and your *sister* are *not* of the Gorven People, Hag!" Storr roared, then grunted as he was struck hard.

"*We* rule Gorvenna," Manth leaned down to him, tilting his chin with two pointed fingers to make him meet her gaze. "The Sons of Gorven only damn themselves with their resistance against us. I know both of you stand as warriors of their malicious little sect, that you would see my sister lose her throne to Prince Anders. That will *not* come to pass."

"If you know who we are," Hulda growled, glaring up at her, "then why not just kill us as you have so many others of our brothers and sisters in resistance?"

"I will offer you a chance," the Witch responded, straightening up and staring down at them. "The prisoner we seek is infinitely more valuable to me than a pair of freedom fighters. Tell me where she is and I will spare your worthless lives, as well as this pointless little town."

"And if we refuse you will kill us," Storr determined with a hard glare, his jaw set firm behind his beard. "You will slaughter all those within Blackwood for our resistance."

"I will do this and more," the Witch promised darkly. "I will hunt down every last member of the Sons of Gorven and I will exterminate them, then present their heads on the walls of Nargilith itself. But *only* if you *don't* tell me where the girl is."

Storr refused to answer and was struck across the face with the pommel of Ulric's sword.

I gasped behind my hands as I held them over my mouth, fighting back worried tears as I watched on helplessly. The two boys were fighting with all that they had to remain silent, the fear of being found so strong a reminder.

"You bastards!" Hulda screamed, struggling as she was held firmly by the soldiers. "You wretched bastards!"

"Answer me, Woodcutter," Manth snarled at Storr, glaring at him with her charcoal eyes burning. "Where is the girl?"

"I will never tell you, Witch," Storr stated simply in a low, calm tone.

Manth was not one to suffer continued insult, unlike her sister. Where Keilantra had persisted for hours upon hours with the same question, Manth could only tolerate so much. I couldn't see the gesture she made, but the sound of a sword breaking flesh and bone, and Hulda's gagging cry told me what order she had given.

I looked away, closing my eyes and tightening my grasp on my mouth to stifle my fearful sobs. I heard scraping behind me, knowing that Leif had tried to shout out and move to his parents' aid, only for Kell to subdue him.

"Hulda! My beloved!" Storr cried out in rage and grief. "No! No, you killed her! YOU KILLED HER!"

"Last chance," Manth whispered eerily without even acknowledging the fresh murder. "Where is the girl?"

"Burn in the Void, Witch!" Storr shouted angrily, jumping up and throwing aside the soldier holding him.

There were more strikes of blades going through flesh, cries and a struggle flashing above us. All I could see through the floorboards were shadows and the soles of boots as they fought. Two thuds landed before I heard Storr shouting.

"FOR GORVENNA!" he bellowed and howled a fierce battle cry, the sound of fighting continuing until he cried out: "Argh! Ah!"

I braced my back to the wall, tears burning my eyes as fear gripped my heart. I couldn't take my gaze from the shapes above us, only just seeing the boys in my periphery. They were on their knees, Kell holding Leif to his chest, tears in his eyes, though he made no sound.

*They're dead! They're dead because of me...*I dropped to the ground and curled my knees to my chest, closing my eyes as the guilt hit me hard. *I never should have been here!*

"Blasted rebels," Ulric hissed above us, stepping over the bodies. "What now, Mistress?"

"The girl is here somewhere in this town," Manth determined as she sniffed the air. "Tear *every* building apart until you find her. Then, when you do, bring her to me, bound and alive."

"And the town?" he asked with a hint of cruel eagerness.

"Cast it to the flames," the Witch commanded and strode from the room.

"Shh," Kell held his finger up, looking to me. "Stay quiet. Wait."

There was a lot of movement above us then, the banging and dragging of heavy things suddenly loud. Glass shattered and an unnatural heat began to grow. The soldiers left and the glow of flames shone down from above us as smoke started to penetrate our hiding place. We waited for as long as we could manage, but the heat and stifling air was becoming too much. In only two minutes, the three of us were coughing and choking, Leif jumping up and rushing to the trap door. He braced against it as Kell and I followed him, covering our mouths with what we could - him using his hand while I held one of my long sleeves to my face.

"It won't open!" Leif shouted, looking to his brother worriedly. "Something's blocking the way!"

"Move!" Kell ordered and began slamming his shoulder against the door.

Still, it wouldn't budge, and I moved to press my hands up against the wood to help him. I felt my body straining against the door, gritting my teeth and using all the strength I had to push.

"Leif!" Kell shouted. "Use your sword to pry this open! Hurry!"

Leif rushed between us and wedged the blade of his sword into the small gap we had managed to open. He worked the weapon like a lever as we continued to push, the heavy thing on top of the door finally falling away and the hatch opening, spilling us to the floor.

Firelight shone brightly through the opening and smoke poured in, the three of us coughing harder still as Kell jumped and pulled himself up to the main floor.

"Idona!" he reached for me. "Take my hand!"

I jumped and grabbed his wrist with both hands, bracing my feet to the wall to help get myself up. In moments, I was out of that small space and back in the storeroom as Kell aided Leif to do the same.

The house was alight, the soldiers having set fire to all the straw and wood of the roof and floors. The inferno was great for such a small space and it didn't seem that there could be any way to break free.

My eyes fell to Storr where he lay on his back, blood covering his white tunic shirt, a war axe at his right hand. Hulda lay to his left, face down, her blood staining the floor red.

"No!" Leif was past me and on his knees as the fire consumed the house around us.

I shielded my face with my hands, following as Kell came up behind me, the two of us reaching Leif and Storr where they lay.

"Da! Da!" Leif was shouting, shaking Storr.

Storr's eyes fluttered open and he looked up at us as we knelt beside him. My heart ached at the sight of all of this and I saw my father's face as the night of his death returned to me, tears flowing down my cheeks.

"Run... my sons," Storr ushered in a weakening voice. "Go..."

"We won't leave you!" Leif insisted as Kell took his shoulders and held him tight.

"J-Join the resistance..." Storr said as blood tainted his lips and his breathing wheezed. "Take the... the fight to the Queen... Help the Sons of Gorven defeat her..."

"We will, Da," Kell promised, fighting his own tears.

"Princess," Storr grasped my arm and looked deep into my eyes. "Run. Find... find your Guardians and... and help them to save High-Realm. It is what you are... what you are meant for, girl. Now... go... All of you... Go..."

And he died.

I covered my mouth and pulled back on my haunches, horrified by this terrible disaster before me. His words stuck themselves in my mind and I felt sick as I closed my eyes against the guilt of what I had brought down upon this kind family.

"Da..." Leif was crying as Kell got him to his feet, then grasped my shoulder.

"We have to go," he snapped me from my thoughts with a rough shake. "Princess! We have to go, or we'll burn here!"

I got to my feet and we ran for the door with them, Leif slamming into it hard and Kell shunting it with all the strength he had a moment later.

"They've sealed it!" Kell growled and rushed for the nearest window as he took a chair.

With a tremendous bang, he obliterated both the chair and the window, jumping through and turning to me. I followed next, cautiously pulling my dress hems close so as not to get stuck, stumbling into his arms and nearly knocking us to the ground. Leif leaped after us and the three of us turned to the town. I felt my breath catch in my chest as I stared in horror at Blackwood burning bright in the darkness of the night.

"Where do we go?!" Leif cried out as we started moving.

"The river!" Kell decided, drawing his sword and taking my right hand in his left. "Come, before they see us!"

I hitched my skirt hems in my free hand and ran beside him with his brother at our backs, the three of us running down the cobblestone paths through the burning houses and towards the main road. Screams of panic ripped through the cold air as the townspeople fought to survive, Blackwood's streets now having become a battlefield. The men and women struck with swords, axes and pitchforks as they joined battle with the black and gold clad soldiers, refusing to relent to this destruction. Children ran with their mothers as they were slaughtered, bodies of both innocents and soldiers now cast all over the ground.

Oh Gods! Is this what it was like when Arvon fell?! How can they do this to so many innocent people?! To children?!

Suddenly, I was grabbed from behind and pulled from Kell's grasp, screaming in panic and thrashing violently. The soldier held me tight around my waist, pulling me back from the two boys.

"LET ME GO!" I screamed, kicking back and hitting him, but he wouldn't release me. "LET GO!"

"RELEASE HER!" Kell was rushing after us with his sword as Leif aimed the crossbow, struggling to find a shot.

"LET ME GO! PLEASE! LET ME GO! GET OFF ME!" I struggled, then there was a hard strike and the man cried out to the sound of a blade cutting flesh.

I was spilled to the ground, catching myself on my hands and knees as he fell dead behind me. I looked up over my shoulder to see that same masked man from Travarna that had save me from the guardsmen, his sword gleaming red with blood in the firelight, his movements swift as he engaged the soldiers.

I don't care if he seems like he's helping me! He followed me here and that can't be good!

Kell grabbed my arm and helped me to my feet as I gathered my skirt hems in my hands and turned with him to run.

"There she is!" a voice shouted, and I looked back over my shoulder, skidding to a stop in the road with the two boys.

Ulric was pointing at me as Manth glared from beneath her hood at his side, so much shorter, yet more frightening than him.

"Get her!" Ulric ordered loudly. "Get the girl!"

"Run!" Leif shoved me after Kell as we turned from the scene.

In only a couple minutes, we were near the mill and sprinting towards the gates out of town. I could hear the hammering of heavy feet and the clanking of chainmail behind us, knowing without looking that a number of soldiers were closing in on us.

As we reached the way out of town, there came a loud cry and two soldiers surprised us as they leaped from behind the walls flanking the road. I skidded my heels against the flagstones and jumped back, staggering as I avoided one man's grasping hands.

Leif fired his crossbow, the bolt lodging in that man's side and stunning him as the boy drew his own sword. Kell was shouting the same war cry his father had bellowed and was cutting the air at the second soldier, his blade meeting the man's as they began fighting.

"Go!" he shouted at me, forcing the soldier away from the gates as Leif slew the first and turned towards the other soldiers closing in.

"No!" I returned loudly, desperate not to watch them fall too. "We go together!"

"Princess, run!" Kell ordered me as he ran his sword through the soldier. "We'll be fine! Just go! Please!"

"Go!" Leif agreed, taking the knee out from under another soldier and engaging the one behind him with ease. "We'll buy you what time we can!"

I watched the boys fight so ferociously, squeezing the fabric of my dress tight as I agitatedly moved on the spot. I wanted to help them, but I knew that my presence would only get them killed.

If I run, the soldiers will chase me and leave them. I have to...

I turned and started running along the road, the sounds of battle growing more violent behind me. I couldn't bear to look back, fighting new tears as all kinds of imaginings of death and horror plagued my mind, my heart burning with guilt's relentless flame.

"Princess!" a voice shouted and I looked back to see the masked man rushing after me.

Just run! Run! Don't let him get close! Run, Leander, run! I turned back and started pushing more strength into my legs to gain speed.

Yells behind me caused me to flick my gaze around and I saw the masked man fighting the soldiers. I decided not to debate whether it was good or bad that they had stopped him and focused instead on escaping.

The soldiers had come by horseback and I found the two dozen horses waiting just outside the town. No one was guarding them, and I knew there was no way I could outrun them on foot.

Horse thieving is hardly the worst thing I'll have to do to survive this! I reasoned mentally.

I mounted the nearest horse, a beautiful white stallion who had a much kinder demeanour than the other horses. He didn't stomp or snort at me, simply allowing me to mount his saddle and take his reigns.

Turning the reigns, I guided the horse away from Blackwood, looking back at the burning glow of the fires with a heavy heart.

I don't have time to feel guilty or to grieve. I have to keep moving.

I urged the horse forward and led him at a gallop away from the town into the dark night. The air was so chilled on my skin, the wind biting me with bitterness as it cast my long dark hair back past my shoulders and drew ripples in my dress. I felt tears threatening to break my defences again as I thought of Storr, Hulda and the boys, my heart tearing at itself because of what had just happened.

I couldn't rest, needing to keep moving, needing to go somewhere I was unlikely to be followed. *But where should I go? Balganis is in the other direction, and without Storr's help I can't make it on my own. It will be more than a week to the border and further still to Daamenhall.*

I looked up at the mountains rising to my left, their majesty hidden now as darkened shapes in the shadows of night. Without any first-hand knowledge or a guide to help me, there was no way I could search for another safe place there.

I'll have to make for Dorvana. That border is so much closer, but it means the Forest. The boys said the High Elves travel through the Forest by way of the bridge up here. If I follow that path, then maybe I can find the safe way they take through.

I nodded to myself as I urged the horse to move a little faster, but not so fast as he would grow tired beneath me.

All right. I'll try to make it to Silvervale. At least there the Gorven Soldiers can't follow, and maybe the Elves will protect me... I hope...

* * * * *

I rode for what felt like hours, the night slowly thinning as I reached the bridge and continued in the direction of the Forest. I knew that if I kept the Nartarn'lath Mountains to my left that I was heading in the right direction, though my heart was heavy at the prospect of entering such a dark place as the Forest of Arnath.

As day broke the hills, I became aware of the thundering of hooves around me, looking through the trees to see the fluttering of black and gold surcoats and the shapes of horses moving at speed. Dread filled me at the sight of them and I felt a new panic arise.

Oh, Gods! They must have sped through the night to catch up to me!

I influenced the horse to move quicker, hoping my touch to his mane would serve me as well as my touch to the snow bear's brow had. In response, he sped up, his hooves now hammering the flagstones of the road and driving us ahead of our pursuers.

I threw a quick glance over my shoulder, my breath catching and my heart sinking as I saw them. There were a dozen riders closing in from all sides, moving up the road behind me. Ulric was at their lead, his eyes locked on my shape in the white horse's saddle, his jaw set hard as his hands squeezed the reigns of his dark brown steed.

Then, there came the most horrifying shrieks from the back of their pack as five black horses with terrifying coal-like eyes hounded their way after me. They cleared the group and I stared in horror as four black armoured and cloaked Shadow Knights appeared, Manth taking their lead with fire in her black eyes.

I turned to my horse and urged him: "Please, go faster! Please!"

My horse called out in reply huskily and forced a deeper run into his long legs, barrelling along the road now as the Shadow Knights screeched and followed faster than the soldiers. One Shadow Knight closed in to my right as Manth directed him, my horse turning left swiftly to avoid his outstretched metal grasp. We then weaved right again as we avoided a second monster's reach and kept charging out through the fields as the Black Woods opened up into the rocky foothills they rested on.

I ducked as one of the Shadow Knights snatched at my neck, my horse galloping faster again to get ahead of the supernatural midnight-coloured steeds. Like their dread riders, the beasts howled monstrously and kept pace with my horse, the soldiers farther back, but staying with us.

I have to reach the Forest! Gorvens fear that place! Perhaps the soldiers will too!

I screamed as an arrow shot past my face, throwing my gaze over my shoulder and through my whipping hair. Two of the soldiers were riding with bows at the ready, firing to try and throw me from my mount in an attempt to avoid the arrows. Manth snarled and threw them an enraged stare as Ulric ordered them to cease firing and continue pursuit.

They truly are desperate to stop me now, I thought as I turned my attention back to the way ahead. *Gods, they'll stop at nothing to capture me again.*

I could see the Forest looming before me, a great monstrous mass of tangled trees that seemed to stretch on endlessly to both mountain ranges on either side of me. A deep dread filled me as the details of its overgrown, old boughs cleared to my eyes, but there was no turning back. Not now. Not with the soldiers and the Shadow Knights closing in.

They've driven me from the road! I can't follow the Elven paths now! I have no choice!

The trees were closing fast, and I urged my horse to coax what speed he could manage to add to our flight, gaining distance between us and our pursuers. I took a deep breath as if to prepare to plunge into the sea, watching the dark trees suddenly rush up around me...

Chapter Eleven
The Haunted Depths

The cries of the horses behind me was terrifyingly loud and sudden, their hooves stamping hard against the ground. I didn't dare to look back but knew as my horse charged on through the thick boughs of the Forest that they had come to a halt.

I allowed myself a small smile, my heart filling with a mild sense of victory. *I knew it! I knew they wouldn't follow me in here! No Gorven would dare enter the Forest! That's what Storr said!*

While I was right that the soldiers wouldn't pursue me, the crashing of large shapes through the underbrush behind me told me that others would. I looked up again and saw the four Shadow Knights still in pursuit, their eyes glowing viciously beneath their terrifying helmets, their heavily gauntleted hands crushing the reigns of their steeds tightly.

Of course! Shadow Knights know no fear!

I ducked closer to my horse, pinning my body against his back to avoid the closeness of the trees, their branches snapping at me as if they were arms reaching to snatch me up. I had no means to guide the horse now, relying on him to get me away from the Shadow Knights safely.

We weaved through the immense maze of dark boughs and broken trunks; the rising sun now hidden as nothing more than a faint grey light struggling to pierce the thick canopy above. I couldn't turn to look back, holding on too tightly to the horse now to allow myself such a movement. I could certainly hear my pursuers.

The monster horses grunted and howled as they broke the woods around them, the Shadow Knights on their backs lashing out with their swords, the clang of metal cleaving wood unmistakable to my ears. They shrieked out in their awful language, directing each other as I felt them drawing closer to my mount.

Judging the way was impossible, the sheer number of shadows that lingered passing nearly for darkness, the thickness of the vegetation and trees obscuring all sight I could possibly have had. Rises and dips were abundant and there was no way of seeing hazards before they appeared.

We burst through the thickest part of the woods around us, the horse maintaining his gallop, though I could feel his strength fading. All that saved us was that the Shadow Knights and their horses had slowed to hack their way through the trees, though not by much.

Suddenly, the horse reared and screeched hard, kicking his front legs in panic. I held tight, fearing that I would easily fall from his back to the ground. He settled and I looked to see what had startled him. There was a chasm before us, overgrown with vines as it was, but wide and with mists hiding its true depths from sight.

How are we supposed to make that? I wondered as the cold fear of heights that plagued me crushed in around my heart.

The howls of the Shadow Knights drew my panicked gaze, and I watched the woods for them, seeing only the black shapes of them fighting through the trees.

I turned my eyes back to the chasm, closed them and took a deep breath. *I really hope this horse has a long jump...*

Turning the reigns, I guided the white horse back a short way, then brought him to face the chasm once more. He seemed to understand my intentions and at my urging, threw all that he could into his forward charge. The edge came upon us so fast that I barely had time to realise it, holding on tight and closing my eyes as the horse leaped hard. I heard the snapping and breaking of trees behind us as we jumped, the Shadow Knights not even slowing their pace as they continued the chase.

In seconds that seemed to pass in an eternity, my horse landed and broke into a new run, continuing his charge away from the chasm. I opened my eyes and looked back to see the Shadow Knights making the jump, *all* four of their black steeds leaping the gap and charging as soon as they made the ground.

There is just no stopping them!

I knew without thought that there was no escape for me if I couldn't somehow slip away from the supernatural knights like I had the soldiers. I also knew that my horse wouldn't be able to keep this pace forever.

We entered the depths of the forest once more, ploughing through the deep overgrowth and along unbeaten trails amongst the boughs. Still, the Shadow Knights kept their pace with me.

As my horse made a jump over a downed tree, there came a loud whistling, and I was suddenly jolted hard. The horse neighed violently as he fell forwards, my own scream shrill as the world spun around me. Everything was a blur and in only a few moments I lay on my back, crying out in pain from the rough impact.

After a few moments spent recovering from the fall, I rolled onto my side and gasped as I saw the horse laying a few feet from me. I scurried to him and pressed my hands to his neck and mane, seeing the black arrow that had lodged itself into his throat.

"No," I felt as if I could cry as I stroked the poor beast's mane, looking into his eyes. "I'm so sorry..."

The horse grunted and shook his head, then lay still, no breath drawing from his body. I closed my eyes and let my head hang as I placed my hands to the ground, feeling hot tears burning their way down my cheeks. My guilt grew greater with this animal's end and I wanted nothing more than to lie there and cry, but I knew I couldn't.

I could hear them charging towards me and got to my feet, immediately breaking into a desperate run through the black forest depths. *Just keep moving! I have to keep moving! They're so close! Keep going!*

I was maybe only ten meters from the dead horse when the Shadow Knights and their mounts erupted from the forest depths to surround me. I skidded in the dirt and looked around as they circled me and dropped from their horses with heavy, clanking thuds to the ground, their red eyes locking on my trembling shape.

I whimpered, turning to each Shadow Knight as they began a slow, deliberate march towards me, the space closing and my options down to nothing. My only defence now was my pendant, and I knew that I couldn't use it to defeat the Shadow Knights like I had the Yirlla or the soldiers in Travarna.

I took a deep breath and held still as I faced one of the towering black armoured knights, looking up at his great intimidating size in fear. There was nothing I could do now but close my eyes and accept that I was going back to the Shadow Lord in chains.

Suddenly, there were shrieks and my eyes snapped open to see what was happening. The Shadow Knights had all drawn their swords and were now slashing at what I first thought to be an invisible enemy. My horrors only exploded as they reached a new level of intensity at the sight before me. The Forest was attacking them, lashing with vine tendrils and branches to close in on them. It even attacked their horses, the beasts stomping and screaming as they tried to fight their way free, only to be strangled and dragged down.

I let out a scream as I felt something grasp my ankle, looking down to see a coarse vine groping to get a hold on me. I managed to slip my foot free and started looking for an escape as a Shadow Knight was dragged away shrieking into the haunted depths of the forest.

The last three Shadow Knights were struggling to keep their ground, one caught by his ankles and flying upside down into the trees' canopy above with a terrifying shriek. He disappeared and was soon silenced by the foliage and twisted limbs.

As vines overwhelmed the last two knights, I managed to slip past them and sprint into the woods, running from the trees as fast as I could. I ducked and jerked myself sideways as viny tendrils snatched at me, trying to grab hold of my limbs, but only flicking at my clothes.

Quickly, I took note of the trees these vines linked to, easily recognising them and managing to break away from where they were. The mere concept of them was bewildering, leaving me both fascinated and terrified. *Trees that lash with vines to kill?! Gods, just when I think I've seen everything I find another surprise in this world! I guess the stories about the Forest of Arnath are true!*

I kept running as long as my strength would hold out, slowing as I entered a part of the forest where the canopy was thinner and there were none of those man-eating trees to face. At last, I could take in air and rest my burning limbs.

Finding a quiet place beside a tree, I dropped to my knees with my hands to my thighs and my head tilted back. My eyes fell shut and I breathed in deeply, the air close in that old, bitter and angry forest.

I am so exhausted. I need rest. But I can't sleep... Not here... It isn't... It isn't safe...

I sat back against the tree and rested my head on its trunk, feeling as though my mind was swirling within my skull as if it had now formed into a tremulous sea of anxiety. My focus became easing the ache in my chest and the shortness of breath plaguing my lungs, nothing else seeming to matter right at that moment.

As it became easier to breathe, my mind wandered back to Blackwood and I started to cry, closing my eyes and burying my face into my hands.

"I should never have been there!" I sobbed, my chest shuddering with my cries. "Because of me... they're all dead. A whole town... Oh, Gods..."

I let my pent-up grief and guilt spill out onto the forest floor with my tears, laying down to rest amongst the soft fallen leaves and moss that covered the ground beneath the tree. My exhaustion was too great to allow me to get to my feet again and I closed my eyes, wanting to just rest as I sobbed.

* * * * *

I woke with a start, some terrible nightmare that I now couldn't remember having woken me from my exhausted sleep, leaving me to look around frantically. I breathed in the air of the forest, my sights showing me only the trees and their black boughs as I recalled where I was with dread.

I sat up, looking at the place where I had laid and turning my eyes towards the sky above me. The clouds were darker, and the cold air was deepening with a new chill that I was certain was not of the weather, but the forest itself.

I fell asleep under a tree - here? Gods... I must be tired. Well, I did ride all night from Blackwood, and walked a long way since those grasping trees took the Shadow Knights.

I got to my feet, brushing off my hands on my teal dress to cleanse them of moss and dirt as I took in my surroundings. No matter which way I looked, it was all the same; thick, black trees with coiling vines and heavy overgrown bushes amidst grey mists.

I need to find safety. I can't stay here.

Turning slowly around, I chose a direction and began to follow the small path I had seen. I pushed branches and vines away with my palms, carefully stepping over low obstacles so as not to trip and fall. The forest depths seemed to grab at my clothes as if trying to slow me down, but I would just pull myself free of the brambles and continue on, I added more than a few cuts, scratches and bruises to my current collection.

I couldn't tell how far I walked or even where I was going, and time here was beginning to seem like it did in the West Tower as it eluded me. All I could do was keep moving and hope that I came across safety soon enough.

After what I counted in my head to be about an hour, I stepped through the underbrush and into a small area where the trees weren't quite as thick. There was a rustling sound that made me pause and listen carefully. I could hear my quiet, labouring breaths and feel the solid beat of my heart in my chest, all else in the dark forest silent. I searched with my eyes, taking in the misty boughs and depths in the fading light. Dread choked me and I felt certain that there was something else watching me beyond the trees themselves.

The rustling came again, this time to my left. I snapped around to see a group of bushes moving, then falling still as the sound ceased. Another rushing of leaves drew my gaze right, once again watching the bushes fall silent before another set of shrubs rustled behind me.

What's out there?! What is it?! Oh no! I... I have to get moving! It could be anything! Wolves, maybe?! Something worse than wolves?!

I started moving farther through the area, my focus on the trees ahead of me while I kept watching for whatever was out there. I just had to be careful or else face some new threat that yet lurked unseen around me.

A loud snap startled me, and I looked down to see that a large twig had broken under my foot. I froze and held my breath, waiting for what I felt was to come. Then a heat filled my chest and I reached for my pendant. It was flickering with purple light just as it had in Dol Amor. I immediately knew it was warning me.

"Oh no," was all I managed to say.

A horrible, howling shriek filled the forest and I looked around frantically for its source. Before I could even find where it was coming from, there were suddenly more shrieks and the rustling in the bushes grew more intense.

Without thinking, I reached down and took up the thickest branch I could find, preparing to defend myself from whatever was about to strike at me. I tried to slow my breathing, recalling my duelling lessons with Mithras and focusing on my footwork.

Mithras always reminded me of my footwork needing attention. I hope I can best whatever is about to come at me.

My eyes locked on a single spot that was shaking in the bushes, my hands tightening their grasp on my makeshift weapon. I drew in a breath and readied myself.

The attack came from my left, the creature hurling itself at me with gnashing teeth and a screech so monstrous I couldn't begin to describe it. I cried out and managed to sidestep it, the thing hitting the ground on its six pink claw-like feet and skidding in the dirt.

It turned towards me, its eyes blood red, all four of them, its face like a twisted rat-like thing with a hooked snout. There seemed to be spiny ridges running along its hunched back, its body covered in shaggy brown fur as a whip-like tail snapped wildly behind it.

"A groundmerk..." I gasped in terror.

The groundmerk shrieked and rushed at me, foaming at the mouth with its madness. It leaped with its front claws outstretched and its howling jaws snapping.

I swung the branch hard and smashed it across the face, hurling it down against a tree with a resounding thud. It was stunned, but not defeated, more rustling surrounding me as it recovered.

Horror gripped my heart as more groundmerks swarmed out of the forest depths and the deepening mists, too many to count with their rapid leaping and scurrying. I had never seen rats as big as these mutated cousin-rodents, each one half my height when they stood on their larger back legs.

They charged me and I swung my weapon, striking them and trying to force my way backwards. I screamed as one jumped against my back and threw me to the ground. Rolling quickly as the creature struck again, I pushed the branch forward as it lunged straight at my face. Its teeth locked around the wood, drooling viciously as venom dripped from the nasty jaws crushing the bark.

Using all of my strength, I strained, fighting to keep it from latching onto me. It tried to snap its jaws along the branch towards my hands, forcing me to move my fingers further out of its reach. Its six feet were scratching and clawing at my midriff as it struggled with me, its crimson eyes flashing wildly with predatory bloodlust.

I screamed and threw it to my left, casting it into some of its circling kind and scattering them in a pile. It sat up as I got to my feet and backed away, closing its jaws hard to shatter the branch to splinters.

They're impossibly strong! How am I getting out of this?! I'm dead!

I backed away, my shoulders hitting a tree as I had felt the incline of the ground under my feet. I gripped my hands behind me against the bark, staring fearfully at the creatures as they closed in towards me, their teeth at the ready and their gazes blazing with a hungry need.

There's no one who can save me now. This time I really am going to die...

I closed my eyes and turned my face into my left shoulder, bracing myself for the agony of the dozens of groundmerks eating me alive. I took in one last breath and let my fearful tears flow as I accepted my gruesome fate.

A roar broke the forest air and I looked up as the groundmerks began chattering in a terrified manner. The roar was familiar and there came the smashing of underbrush and wood as heavy feet pounded the ground. Then something appeared out of the forest and mists. It was large and fierce, far worse than the dozens of groundmerks.

They shrieked and scattered as the creature broke into the small clearing, roaring and snapping its large jaws. Purple scales gleamed in the mists as magenta wings beat the ground, a great purple and silver tail whipping through the air as its orange eyes blazed.

Amethyst! My heart soared as I saw my beloved dragon charging to my rescue.

Amethyst snapped and roared loudly, her shout so powerful that the ground and the trees quaked around me. She started swatting the groundmerks with her mighty claws as they lunged at her. She buried her horns low and hurled a group of them high into the air, sending them crashing far into the trees behind her. The Dragon turned and stomped on one of the beasts as it rushed for me again, crushing it under foot as she killed three more with a sweep of her great tail. She snatched one in her jaws and lashed it away off to my right, dropping it hard to the rocks and underbrush with a heavy crash.

The groundmerks were trying to climb up on her, clearly determined to take on the much larger creature. Amethyst merely shook them off and proceeded to crush and hurl them as she roared and snarled viciously.

In less than two minutes, she had greatly thinned their numbers and the remaining groundmerks were screeching as they ran away from her. She killed two more as she chased them at a gallop, watching the rest retreat through the woods. She let loose one final bellowing roar, warning them never to come near us again.

Slowly, I pulled myself away from the tree I had clung my back to, stepping down the incline and turning my gaze up to her.

"Amethyst," I said softly, the Dragon turning to look at me with those beautiful orange eyes.

She suddenly became very soft and friendly, nudging her snout towards me and pressing her nose against my chest. I smiled and laughed softly, hugging her snout and rubbing her scales with my palms.

"I'm so happy to see you too," I told her, smiling more than I had in so long now. "I am so glad you found me. Those things would have killed me if you didn't come when you did."

She growled, nodding as she withdrew her head from my grasp to look me in the eyes.

She's really here. She's real and she's with me again. I'm not alone in this ordeal anymore. Those thoughts were enough to draw my lips to smile and encourage my aching heart.

"So, Leif was right when he said he saw a dragon fly over Blackwood," I commented, reaching up and patting her silver scaled chest. "He saw you."

She gave me a gentle gaze and I could feel her bond with me even stronger than before.

"I was worried I'd never see you again, Amethyst," I said softly, looking up into her eyes solemnly. "I tried calling for you when I was in trouble... but you didn't come..."

Amethyst growled lowly and turned her head towards her left side as she stretched out her wing. I followed her gaze and gasped.

Her wing was twisted and had slashes through her skin and scales. The softer skin that formed the sail of her wing had rips through it that were healing but had a long way still to go. There were also old wounds closing now across her back below the thicker dark blue and deep purple plate scales running from her neck to her tail.

"Your wing!" I moved to stand at her left side, studying the damage. "Oh, Amethyst, you're hurt!"

She growled and hissed as I gingerly touched her side, pulling her lips back to show her gritted, pointed teeth as I touched her.

"I'm sorry," I looked up to her, trying to be gentle. "It must hurt so badly. Did... did Kuldar do this to you?"

She nodded gently, letting out a quiet growl.

"No wonder you didn't come at my call," I sighed, hating how badly she was injured. "You can't even fly with your wing like this."

She groaned sadly, lowering her face to mine and looking deep into my eyes. I reached up and stroked her firm round cheek, completely understanding her even without her using human words.

"It's not your fault, Amethyst," I tried to reassure her. "You're hurt. You couldn't have even tried to come to defend me. And I'm all right."

She snorted and eyed me harshly.

I raised an incredulous eyebrow at her comment: "What do you mean I'm not?"

She growled and huffed her response.

I crossed my arms in front of my chest and furrowed my brow at her: "I'm alive, aren't I?"

She snorted at me again.

"All right," I nodded and shrugged with a sigh, "so it hasn't been easy... and...and people are dead... because of me..."

She snapped and growled loudly, shaking her head lowly at me.

"I know I shouldn't blame myself," I sighed, feeling so much sadness all the same. "But I'm the one the soldiers came for and..."

Amethyst cut me off with a low sound, keeping her eyes locked with mine. When I tried to look away, she pressed the smooth end of one long claw under my chin and made me look up at her. She let out another soft growl, her eyes so gentle and kind despite her fierceness.

"All right," I forced a weak smile and nodded at her. "You're right. I have to stop finding reasons to blame myself for everything that goes wrong."

A rumble drew our eyes to the sky as the clouds grew darker and the wind began to pick up.

"A storm's coming," I murmured, then turned my gaze back to her. "We need to find someplace where we can take shelter from the rain."

Amethyst nodded and turned, beckoning with a jerk of her head for me to follow her. I didn't even hesitate.

Following the Dragon was easy, her larger purple shape standing out better to my eyes than any human would have in the thick mists of the forest. Even as darkness descended on us, I knew she would keep me close as we made our way through the thick boughs and underbrush.

Amethyst led me to a place where the trees had grown so thick together that they had formed a natural roof over a small section of ground. It was now raining and growing heavier as I hurried into the shelter with her, breathing quickly where I stood with my hair and clothes soaking wet.

"We need a fire," I said, looking up at her, my arms around me as I shivered hard.

Amethyst gave me a worried gaze.

"It's all right," I assured her. "I know you can't breathe fire yet. I'll handle it. Can you get wood?"

She growled in the affirmative and quickly set about grasping what we needed with her front claws. In less than a few minutes, she had piled up some branches and kindling that had taken her only seconds to break up, leaving me to set rocks around them to keep the fire in one place.

As the cold worsened and the rain grew heavier, I knelt before the fire, taking my pendant from my neck and unclasping the chain. I stared at it in thought, trying to remember what I had done to make it light the fire in the shipwreck.

"How did it work?" I mumbled with a hard frown of concentration. "Um... right. Please, I need to light this fire."

Heat rose from the Pendant in response to my plea and I watched as a purple flame looped and flickered up out of the heart-stone with a gentle crackling of electricity around it. I glanced up at Amethyst where she lay within our shelter, her wise orange eyes watching the flame and miniature lightning dance across the stone's smooth surface.

I turned the Pendant towards the sticks and branches, and just like before the flame stretched out like an arm, casting purple fire into the wood. As the flame retreated back into the Pendant's darkening stone, the fire changed to an orange glow, the sudden warmth so welcome.

Refastening the chain around my neck, I sat back on the soft mossy ground and hugged my knees to my chest, brushing my soaked hair away from my face with one hand.

"See that?" I turned my gaze to Amethyst, smiling softly. "The Pendant will light our fires for us. Now we won't freeze."

She nodded, seeming impressed.

I turned my eyes to the rains pouring outside the shelter, shivering at the wind chill that slipped through the boughs to reach us. My mind began to wander and I thought again of Carden for the latest of the countless times since he was taken from me.

I just wish you were here. I miss you more than I can say, and I want to hear your voice. If you were here now what would you say? What would you do? Gods, I just want you to hold me, Carden. I love you so much...

Amethyst nudged my left shoulder with her nose, drawing me from my silent thoughts so that I would look up at her. She spoke in her gentle voice, softening her scaled features as she asked me what was wrong.

"I keep thinking about Carden," I confessed as I felt new tears slip down my cheeks. "Gods... I... I can't stop thinking about him."

She uttered gently, her eyes showing all the understanding that she had.

"I do love him," I agreed sadly. "With all my heart. That's... that's why not knowing where he is and not being with him hurts so, so much..."

Her front claw came forward and she pressed it gently to my back, a gesture she had clearly begun to imitate from watching us humans comfort one another. It was strange having such a large hand touch my shoulder blades, but it was still a great comfort.

"I keep thinking about when we were in Eilath, about how hard it had been for us to speak the truths in our hearts," I murmured, sniffing against my tears and tightening my hug on my knees. "You saw what lay inside our hearts, Amethyst, and you urged me to speak my true feelings for him. That afternoon in the grove has been all that I have had to keep me warm these past two years in my dark prison..."

I started to cry now, my heart feeling so broken that the pieces stabbed the insides of my chest.

"I just want him back," I sobbed, burying my face into my forearms. "I want us safe and together, somewhere we can just be happy."

She softly spoke and rubbed my back.

I looked up to the fire, trying to quiet my sobs a little: "Whatever life I could have had with him is gone now... Morod destroyed it."

She growled quizzically.

"I didn't tell anyone," I confessed sadly, "but the ceremony he forced on me stole my changing. He took my aging, my adulthood, my motherhood, my mortality... He made me immortal... and forever young."

I closed my eyes, trying not to cry as I finally confessed the dark secrets I had carried for two years to the caring ears of my dragon.

"What life can Carden and I ever have now that I'm not human anymore?" I wept into my arms again, my chest shuddering and heaving. "The Shadow Lord took everything from me... Everything..."

I felt Amethyst's claw move from my back and once again it was gently under my chin. She made me look up at her as she lowered her face towards mine, her gaze sympathetic and the fires within her eyes glowing duller with her own feelings of sadness.

I knew she was trying to reassure me in her own way without words, and I was so grateful.

"Do you think...do you think he can still love me?" I asked her in a tiny, shaking voice. "Even with this curse I've been left with?"

She brushed a tear from my cheek with her claw and simply nodded.

"I'm glad we found each other again, Amethyst," I said, crawling closer and hugging her neck tightly. "I missed you so much."

She closed her uninjured wing around me, urging me to lie down against her for warmth.

With her wing serving as a blanket, I lay with my head against her arm and edged my fingers to my lips as I watched the fire burn, my eyes heavy with sleep. I was far from safe and my ordeal was long from ending, but at least at that moment I could rest easy...

Chapter Twelve
Guidance Unsought

I woke to the chilled mists and grey surrounds of the forest, letting out a small groan at seeing it all again. I had hoped it had just been another terrible nightmare, just like I wished everything I had gone through since Arvon fell to be. But it was real and harsh, my reality still the same grave, stark coldness that I had been forced into over the last three years.

My eyes turned to the fire, which was now no more than smouldering embers and smoky heat from a blackened circle of stones, finding myself just staring for a short while. So many thoughts raced through my mind as I snuggled beneath Amethyst's wing, listening to her rhythmic breathing. I didn't even know where to start trying to figure them all out, yet over all the chattering memories and thoughts, only those concerning Carden truly stayed clear.

A small sigh slipped from my lips and I closed my eyes, envisioning his handsome features and his roguish smile. For a moment, I felt as if he was with me and I yearned to kiss him as we embraced. But that was just a daydream, nothing more, and I very quickly felt the absence of him in my life once more.

Amethyst stirred, opening her orange eyes and yawning a great growling sound with her jaws spread wide. She then clicked her tongue against the roof of her mouth as she raised her head from the ground and gazed around the murky grey forest once more.

I looked up at her, watching her survey our surroundings with the quiet diligence I had come to expect from her. Slowly, Amethyst turned her gaze back from the forest and down towards me, her eyes brightening and her features softening. She nudged my cheek lightly, making me smile and laugh a little.

"Amethyst!" I looked up at her, sitting on my knees as I grasped her nose gently in both hands. "That tickles!"

She grunted out a few short sounds as she locked her gaze with mine and I knew exactly what she meant.

"Of course I'm really here," I assured her, stroking her long, scaly snout. "I wasn't a dream. See?"

The Dragon was much more at ease as I said this, pulling me closer with her right wing and snuggling her snout to me in a dragon hug. It was amazing that a creature so great and strong could be so delicately gentle in her touch.

I am so glad that I found her out here. Never mind anything else that happened, having Amethyst with me makes things feel so much better.

After a few minutes more, I sat back on my haunches and lifted her jaw with both hands so that we were eye-to-eye.

"We can't lay around here all day," I told her quietly, studying every facet of her purple scaled face and her living flame eyes. "We need to keep moving and find a way out of this forest."

She responded with an affirming bark, getting to her feet and moving slowly towards the world beyond our tree formed shelter.

I picked myself up and followed as the Dragon kicked dirt over the fire with her front claw. She was dismantling the campfire stones as well to keep our trail hidden from any who might follow us.

After what I saw this forest do to four Shadow Knights yesterday, I don't think for even a second that we'll be followed. Who in their right mind would even try?

* * * * *

By the time the sun had risen behind the thick black clouds above, we had already been walking for several hours. Travelling with a dragon at my side made me feel so much more secure, her heavy footfalls and her gentle breathing welcome sounds in the otherwise complete silence.

This would feel so much worse if I were still alone trying to find my way through these trees. I considered quietly.

We made our way down an embankment, passing by large rocks and grizzly old trees with no leaves amidst the twisted trees whose tops were covered in foliage. I was very careful to watch where I stepped, the ground littered with vines, broken branches, roots and rocks, all very capable of tripping me to the dirt covered ground.

I was hyperaware of my surroundings, my eyes scanning for any sign of the groundmerks making another attempt at me. With a dragon watching over me, however, any that were nearby would surely have turned and run back into the deep mists for fear of being crushed by her powerful jaws and claws.

After a long while, I looked around as I came to a stop, frowning at the forest. Amethyst halted behind me, watching me with those fiery glowing eyes curiously.

"Which way?" I wondered aloud, looking at all the trees and winding gaps through the mists. "Gods... It all looks the same."

Amethyst grunted her agreement, moving to my right side and looking around with her piercing gaze, clearly able to see more than I could.

"Do you hear that?" I turned to her, gaining her attention.

The Dragon listened carefully, her eyes flicking as she searched the air and the forests for what I meant. Then she looked back to me and growled her response with confusion.

I nodded uneasily. "Exactly. It's so quiet here."

She sniffed the air and commented in her grunts and growls, watching the sky above us with a frown.

"You're right," I looked to the sky as well, holding my arms tight around my body as I shivered in the cold mists. "There are no birds. No animals. Nothing living here except the trees. How can a forest be so empty?"

Amethyst snorted and groaned out a series of gentle growls, her eyes locked on my face, her neck coiling to aim her snout towards me.

I nodded again, shuddering at the thought of what she had said. "I don't even want to think about what kind of evil lurks in these trees."

She growled warningly at me with great seriousness.

"Yes, we have to be careful," I agreed, meeting her gaze again from studying our surroundings.

She gave me an intense stare and growled.

"What do you mean by that?" I frowned at her, turning my body to face her fully, my arms still held around my torso.

The Dragon snorted and growled her reply.

I shook my head. "Come on, Amethyst. I'm not *that* danger prone."

She snorted and rolled her eyes, something I didn't know a dragon could do.

I frowned deeper at her, getting a little annoyed. "That's not fair."

She shrugged her shoulders at me.

I shook my head, breaking away from her comments: "It doesn't matter. Right now, we need a way out of this forest to safety. Any ideas?"

She sniffed and growled.

"Aren't dragons supposed to be able to find their way through any place they find themselves?"

Her response was simple, and she edged her wing towards me.

"Oh... of course... You can't fly," I felt like a fool for my assumptions. "I'm sorry, Amethyst."

She apologised for picking on me and rubbed her scaly cheek against my arm.

"It's all right. I know you just worry for me," I said, patting her nose with my other hand. "But we still need a way to get out of this place. And I don't know about you, but I'm getting pretty hungry and thirsty."

Amethyst simply nodded, remaining silent as she returned her gaze to surveying our surroundings.

Hm... How do we find our way out of here?

I looked up above me to all sides, but I couldn't see any sign of the mountains, nothing else showing me which way we should be going. With the thick rain clouds that still rang with thunder, but didn't yet release their storm, it was impossible to use the sun to gauge our direction.

*So, we can't use landmarks or the sun to find our way. There has to be some way to... Wait...*I lifted the Pendant in my hand and studied the purple stone again.

Amethyst looked to me and growled curiously.

"The Pendant could help us find our way," I said simply, turning my attention back to the necklace: "Show me the safest way for us to leave this forest."

The Pendant's stone began to glow as it answered my request, flickering on and off like before. Again, I turned on the spot until it began to glow brighter and speed up its pulsing, finally holding its glow solidly.

Amethyst clucked out an impressed sound that was really like saying "Hm."

I smiled up at her. "See? The Pendant will show us the way out."

She asked me a question.

"Yes. It is," I replied with a small nod. "This is also how I got through the Labyrinth of Dol Amor and escaped the Yirlla. Don't worry, it works. Trust me."

I started walking forward, making sure the stone continued to glow, then adjusted my path as I needed to.

"Follow me, Amethyst," I directed her softly with a gentle call over my shoulder, my eyes flicking from the stone to the way ahead.

The two of us made our way along the winding paths of the forest, carefully ducking and sidestepping the low, twisted, reaching branches of the black trees, the mists making it very hard to see where we were going. I just kept watching the stone in my pendant, ensuring that I stayed on its directed paths.

It hasn't failed me yet. We'll be out of here soon enough, I thought hopefully.

After about an hour of walking, we came to a clearing and Amethyst became very agitated.

"Amethyst?" I looked up at her and frowned. "What's wrong?"

She told me instantly without further urging on my part what it was that bothered her.

"No. No, we couldn't be," I looked around and felt my heart sink in my chest.

Oh, no... She's right!

I groaned with annoyance and tiredness: "It's just taking us back towards where I entered the forest! No, this isn't what we wanted!"

Amethyst shook her head and snorted out a low, annoyed growl.

I turned the Pendant in my hands and looked down at it, the stone still glowing brightly.

"This isn't what I meant!" I told it sternly. "We *don't* want to go this way! The soldiers will still be waiting out there for me! This isn't right!"

The Pendant's stone flickered and suddenly the light went out. I stared at it and shook it in my fingers, feeling a deep, terrifying dread clutching my heart.

"No! No, don't! Don't do that!" I cried, trying to make the light come back. "Gods damn it!"

Amethyst watched me as I sat down with my back to a tree, my knees up and my face buried in my hands. I couldn't figure out why the Pendant was suddenly acting up, every explanation that ran through my head making no sense.

*It can't be magical interference because the Pendants are immune to all magic. The trees themselves couldn't do this. I mean, how could they? It's not damaged. How could I have damaged it anyway? It was working normally last night. Huh... if any of this is normal...*I sighed and closed my eyes, feeling so sick from not having eaten or having anything to drink for nearly two days. *It's like it's just stopped. Kind of like when it led me to the shipwreck, and to the road that led to Travarna. It just went dark like this once it got me to where I had chosen to go.* I frowned, my eyes remaining closed. *But how does that make any sense? There's nothing here, just a clearing. We're not out of the forest, we're not safe. I don't understand...*

Then Amethyst growled a low, warning sound that made me open my eyes and look up at her.

She was standing with her four legs evenly spaced and her claws planted firmly to the ground. Her head was raised and her back high with her neck, her wings pulled up as she showed her true towering stature. The damage to her left wing was more obvious with this stance, curled tighter than her right wing and with definite rips showing through the soft magenta folds.

"Amethyst? What is it?" I asked anxiously, dropping my hands to the ground beside me.

At first she didn't answer me, her orange eyes locked hard on something in the mists behind where I sat. Her jaw set, tightening her muscles visibly beneath her purple scales, her jaw-webbing stretching wider like how a creature might stretch its limbs to appear bigger to scare off predators.

"Amethyst?" I got to my feet and touched my hand to her large, scale-plated shoulder worriedly.

She growled lowly in response.

"Where?" I asked uneasily, darting my eyes towards where she was looking.

Her head lowered and her eyes narrowed, a threatening snarl pulling from her lips and sounding from her throat. If she had been able to breathe fire, I knew without doubt that she would have burned the trees to cinders along with whatever was out there.

"It's all right," I tried to ease her, rubbing her neck and shoulder gently. "We'll hide and watch out. If we're threatened..."

She snapped her jaws savagely, adding her own part to what would happen.

"Right," I gulped at the thought of the Dragon snapping someone in half.

I moved quickly and braced my back against the tree I had sat by a few moments ago, dropping to one knee to make myself as small as possible. I watched Amethyst as she moved backwards slowly into the mists of the forest, never once taking her snarling eyes or her vicious grimace from where she watched.

The moments were slow and tense as I crouched behind the tree, listening to the silence of the forest for any sign of what she had warned me was coming. My breathing was a little too loud and it took me a few moments to ease the sound to a quieter tone. That's when I heard it, my mind freezing and no thoughts crossing me.

Footsteps crunched through the leaves and underbrush, twigs snapping lightly. The steps were heavy, those of a human man, just from what I had learned over the last few years. I could already tell he was bigger than me, which meant I would struggle fighting him off on my own.

Thankfully, I have a dragon.

Movement to my right made me push myself farther back into the tree's black bough, my eyes following the shape as it moved into view.

The man was tall, definitely taller and broader than me. He wore a dark brown cloak with his hood drawn, as expected, he had a bow and quiver filled with steel arrows across his back. Bracers covered his forearms and he had high topped boots laced up his shins, his body dressed in a grey shirt, leather jacket and dark trousers. There was a sword at his left hip and a number of daggers stowed on his belt. I caught sight of one behind his hip as he moved, his cloak swishing aside to his right just enough to let me see its sheathed blade.

The man moved cautiously, his back to me so that I couldn't see his face. He was studying the ground the way a hunter would, his movements slow and deliberate, like he was tracking something.

He could just be a hunter, but that doesn't mean he's a friend. He could still try to hurt me if he got the chance.

The stranger crouched low and ran his right hand along indents in the soft earth, tracing out the shape.

That's my footprint! Oh no! I stifled a gasp.

"Hm," he murmured to himself, studying my footprint. "She came this way."

His voice is very familiar... I ignored that thought more or less, another quickly entering my mind. *If I can just get that dagger...*

I kept my eyes locked on the dagger at his back, watching as he turned his attention along the ground farther from where I was.

"What's this?" he mumbled, his gaze now on another indent in the dirt.

I just have to be careful. I have to get it while his back is turned. I can do this.

As quietly as I could, I edged my way towards the man, closing faster than I had anticipated. He had looked so far away, and I realised that it was the apprehension within me that had made the distance seem greater.

"It can't be..." he was studying the other indents and I recognised them as Amethyst's prints.

I reached out, my fingers grazing the pommel of the dagger, nearly grasping its hilt...

The man spun around so fast I couldn't even remember the movement. He was suddenly glaring at me over his cloth mask, brown eyes locking onto my uneasy blue ones. His hand was closed around my wrist tightly, his other put to my mouth and dropping me back to lay on the ground.

I recovered from my shock and tried to struggle free, my fingers grabbing at his hand on my mouth, my screams of panic sounding muffled as they tried to slip free from behind his large, grimy fingers.

"Shh," he whispered to me. "I'm not going to hurt you, girl."

I stared wide eyed up at him, squirming beneath his body as he crouched on top of me, pinning my hips under his legs.

The masked man from Travarna and Blackwood! He followed me! How?! Why?!

He studied me for a few moments, looking into my eyes with a strangely gentle gaze. I couldn't figure it out, but he was so incredibly familiar to me, and by his stare, I was to him too. I struggled again and he pinned me harder to the ground, his hands rough and hot, their strength hurting me.

A bellowing roar ripped the air behind us, and the man barely had time to turn. He let go of me as Amethyst charged through the mists, her eyes blazing with fire in their depths. He was so distracted by the Dragon that he forgot about me and I took my chance.

I grabbed the dagger from his belt with a quick stab of my hand, yanking it free with a loud grind of steel. He turned to me as he felt the movement, but before he could react, I threw my left fist straight into his face.

"Argh!" he staggered off me in a crouch, hitting the ground in shock.

I got quickly to my feet, pointing the blade at him with my right hand as he recovered and turned towards me. He seemed to reach for his sword and Amethyst took it as an immediate threat. She roared and hit him hard with her right claw, throwing him to the ground a few feet away, his body tumbling with the loud breaking of underbrush.

The Dragon was after him in only a few moments and stood snarling down at him as he turned over to look up at her with wide, terrified eyes. I quickly joined her, holding the dagger hilt with both hands, keeping it level at his face.

"Wait, wait, wait!" he shouted in alarm, flicking his eyes from the Dragon to me.

"Who are you?!" I demanded, glaring at him. "Why have you been following me?!"

"I haven't..."

"I saw you in Travarna and then in Blackwood!" I cut him off quickly, my heart pounding in my chest as adrenaline sped through my body. "You were fighting the soldiers each time! Why?!"

"You needed help," he said, pulling back as I edged the blade closer towards him.

"And you just helped me out of the kindness of your heart?!" I shook my head at him. "Do you serve the Witches?! The Shadow Lord?!"

"No! No, neither!" he shook his head, his hands up in surrender as Amethyst snarled at him deeply.

"You tracked me through the forest," I frowned at him suspiciously, my voice lower and quieter now. "If you don't serve either of them, then why follow me?"

"To help you, Princess," he replied, jerking back as I jabbed the dagger at him harder.

"How do you know who I am?" I glared at him, gritting my teeth.

He slowly reached his hands to his head, withdrawing the hood and pulling his mask from his nose and mouth. Long reddish blonde hair fell free and the bearded face of a man in his thirtieth years I knew too well looked up at me.

I gasped, my muscles tensing hard at the sight of him.

"Because we know each other, lass," he said quietly.

"Tristan?!" I cried out in disbelief, anger filling my heart, my eyes going wide.

"Aye, girl," the Wanderer nodded morosely, shame in his eyes. "It's me."

More suddenly than before, Amethyst roared a viciously hysterical howling shout, her eyes burning with utter rage. She bared her teeth as she kept shouting at him, stomping and roaring after him.

Tristan scurried backwards frantically, his eyes wide with terror as he faced the enraged dragon. Somehow, he managed to scrape himself to his feet, though he didn't stand for long.

I watched on in stunned silence, not able to move quick enough to even react to my dragon's charge.

Tristan grunted loudly in pain as Amethyst slammed him hard against a large tree with one of her clawed hands, pinning him by his chest. He coughed and grabbed at her large hand helplessly, his feet dangling nearly a meter from the ground. The force was so much that the tree shook, and leaves rained down towards the forest floor.

"Gods, that's... uh... that's scary!" he choked out as he stared into the Dragon's flaming eyes.

Amethyst roared right in his face, the sound so loud and enraged that I was glad I wasn't the one it was focused at. He was shaking hard, his hair and clothes blown back with the power of her voice. Then she settled and just snarled at him, never taking her eyes from his face.

"Eh... Lass?" Tristan coughed and choked under her immense grasp as I moved to stand close beside her. "You... you think you can... argh... call off your... your dragon?"

"Why?" I demanded, tightening my grip on the dagger at my side, glaring at him with all the anger I had for him. "So you can betray me and sell me to the Shadow Lord again?"

"That... that was nothing... ugh... nothing personal," he struggled to reply, pushing his hands against the Dragon's fingers to attempt to relieve the crushing pain he must have been feeling.

"I spent two years in that tower," I told him, fighting the tears of rage that were trying to break past my eyes and strike down my cheeks. "*Two* years! *Alone!*"I shook my head in disbelief, twisting my jaw as it now ached with the stress that seeing him filled me with.

"I... I didn't..." he tried weakly.

"You didn't know what they were going to do to me?!" I nearly screamed at him, stomping closer quickly so that I was only a few feet from him. "You have no idea what they did to me! The Witches tortured me! They tortured me because it amused them! I watched them kill people! I was beaten, starved, humiliated, threatened and nearly raped! Because of you!"

"Now... that's... that's not fair..."

"FAIR!" I screamed, seeing red and feeling so sick with rage. "WHAT HAPPENED TO *ME* ISN'T FAIR! THEY TOOK *EVERYTHING* FROM ME! YOU SOLD ME OUT AND I SPENT TWO *HORRIBLE* YEARS SUFFERING! THEY TOOK MY DRAGON, MY PENDANT, MY FRIENDS! EVERYTHING!"

Amethyst responded to my hurt and anger, pressing her clawed hand harder against him and growling viciously while showing her teeth. Tristan cried out a groan of agony, his head lulling back.

I took a few breaths and closed my eyes, trying to calm myself down. I needed to find my composure, or I knew I would collapse, my hunger, thirst and exhaustion taking a heavy toll on me now that only worsened with my anger.

I opened my eyes, feeling tears slip free as I met his struggling gaze again, my voice softer now and wobbling: "They took *everything* from me, Tristan. And you let them. I trusted you as a friend... and you betrayed me. You gave me to *him* and he... violated me in worse ways than those concerning my intimacy..."

"I understand you hate me, girl," he said quietly, nodding as he stopped his struggles and just held onto Amethyst's claws. "You have every right to..."

I looked up at him angrily through my tears and put the blade to his throat, the tip touching his skin. He tilted his head back, keeping his eyes locked on mine as I gritted my teeth, twisted my lips and trembled with hurt.

"Why shouldn't I kill you right now?" I asked in a cold, shaking voice.

He smirked knowingly. "Come now, Princess. If you were capable of that kind of fun, you'd have done it back in Gorth'lak when you had the chance."

I blinked, staring at him, my resolve fading and my shoulder hurting from keeping it so tightly straight.

He's right... I... I can't. I can't kill him. I've never killed anyone, even at the Citadel. Not one of my arrows dealt a killing blow to any of those Scourge...

"You're not a killer, lass," he went on gently. "You're too good for that, too sweet and innocent. And you know what?"

I looked back up at him, frowning and fighting back tears.

He smiled softly, speaking in earnest: "That makes you so much stronger than a wretched bastard like me. It takes real strength and courage *not* to end someone's life. Anyone can kill. But not many can spare a life like you can."

I dropped my arm to my side, still staring at him, breathing hard as I backed away, clutching the dagger tight. He watched me uneasily as I came to stop a few feet away.

"Amethyst," I murmured, drawing her gaze. "Let him go."

She growled and snorted at me incredulously.

"Just let him go," I directed her softly and tiredly, all of my anger falling away. "He's not worth it."

There was a tense moment as the Dragon turned her glowing orange eyes back to the Wanderer, staring into his soul with a distrustful anger. For a few seconds I thought she might kill him out of spite, but she wasn't that vicious. She withdrew her claw quickly and stepped back, dropping him hard to the ground while keeping her eyes locked on him the whole time.

Tristan choked and coughed as he sat there on his hands and knees, spitting on the dirt as he tried to recover from nearly being crushed to death by an enraged dragon. He sputtered a bit more, then started to breathe a little easier, sitting back on his haunches with his eyes closed and his head back.

"If you're not hunting me for the Witches and the Shadow Lord," I started slowly and quietly, still glaring at him suspiciously, "then why are you following me?"

"To help you," he replied, opening his eyes and facing me. "Didn't I make that clear already?"

I half snorted incredulously at him: "What makes you think I would even *want* your help?"

"Listen, lass," he said, getting to his feet achingly, "you may not want my help..."

He moved slowly towards me, Amethyst's snarl and threatening posture making him pause a moment. I gestured with my right hand towards her, signalling her to wait.

Tristan continued slowly, standing tall and looking down at me. He seemed taller than I remembered, finding myself staring at the base of his throat and needing to tilt my head to meet his gaze. I felt intimidated, but I held my ground, determined not to give him the upper hand again. I became suddenly very aware of the dagger I still held in my right hand, coiling my fingers to get a firmer grip.

He nodded casually at me: "But you need it."

"I don't *need* your help either," I replied through my teeth, glaring at his face.

"Really?" he smiled sardonically. "Because in Travarna it looked like you weren't handling things very well, Leander."

"You don't get to call me that," I hissed quietly, shaking my head. "We're *not* friends, so don't use my name."

"Fine then," he glowered, "*Princess.* The fact remains that you *only* got away from Travarna and Blackwood because I helped you by distracting the soldiers."

"What do you want from me?" I demanded coldly and quietly.

"A thank you would be nice, for starters," he replied curtly and a little sarcastically. "Gratitude goes a long way, Princess. Or weren't manners apart of your rearing as a noble?"

I scowled at him and shook my head. "Thank you, then. Now, we'll be going."

"Going where?" he asked as I pushed past him.

"Away from you," I snapped without looking back at him.

I just had to get away from him, my every impulse telling me to keep moving and leave this wretched traitor behind me. My thoughts were chattering like demented songbirds all at once. I needed to find some kind of peace and silence that didn't involve him.

"You know, I could guide you through this forest," he called after me.

"For the last time," I threw a glare over my shoulder and through my long dark hair at him, "I don't *want* or *need* your help!"

"Fine then," he said as I kept going. "You go on. I don't care. Wander aimlessly through the forests until you starve, or something kills and devours you."

I slowed my pace, his words pulling at me.

No! I won't listen to him! He's trying to make me doubt myself! I got this far on my own and now Amethyst is with me! I don't need him!

"We'll be just fine," I replied, though I was sure it sounded weaker and less confident than it had meant to.

"How long do you suppose a young girl and a wounded dragon who can't fly will last out here?" he considered as if he were staging to an audience. "There are a lot of predators out here; dark spirits, draugar, trolls, dire wolves, groundmerks, just to name a few."

Ignore him! Just ignore him! I kept walking, blinding myself to everything but the ground and trees in front of me.

"Then there's the dangers of the forest itself," he stated darkly, chuckling a little and I imagined he was shaking his head. "Never minding the beasts and monsters that lurk amongst these haunted boughs, the forest itself is full of nasty little surprises for a girl out of her depth."

I realised I had stopped walking, standing with my hands at my side and my eyes staring at a spot on the ground in front of me relentlessly. I tried to make myself move, but my body refused to even flinch.

Could I survive out here? I don't have supplies; no water or food, no weapons, just my clothes that I'm wearing. How long would I last in the forest?

Tristan continued to speak: "This forest is full of bogs that will suck an unwary traveller down to be crushed and drowned in the mud. There are vines that will strangle and choke the life from you, and flesh-eating trees that shred your bones to their whitest in minutes. And there are even worse things out here. And what about food and water? I'm sure you haven't eaten since you fled Blackwood. Am I right?"

I didn't answer him, squeezing my hands into tight fists and pinning my lips into a grim line as I drew in slow, but shuddering breaths.

"Notice how there are no animals or birds," he stated obviously. "See how there are no plants with berries or streams of water beyond the stagnant little puddles and pools. Everything here is poison to a traveller with no survival wits. Heh, you'd probably eat something and die a slow death as it rots your insides."

I turned over my shoulder to look at him, feeling suddenly less confident than I had before.

Tristan was leaning against a tree with his arms crossed, one foot pressed back to the trunk, his attention on everything except me. He had a knowing expression and a lightly nonchalant gaze.

I noticed then that Amethyst still hadn't moved from where she had stood, her orange eyes watching me curiously. My gaze flicked back to Tristan as he shrugged heavily.

"Ah, but you don't want *my* help," he said offhandedly, turning away from me. "Why would you? You probably think I would lead you into a trap or something of that vile nature. That's fine. Well, you have a nice time traversing these treacherous woods on your own, little girl," he started walking back the way he had come, very casual in his movements, adjusting his clothes as he went.

No matter how much I hate him, he's right... Oh, to the Void with all this!

I swallowed my pride, knowing that there was no real choice. I closed my eyes and forced myself to turn to face him, building my voice within me to speak. It was so much harder to do than it should have been, all of this against my better judgement and taking all of my willpower.

"Wait," I choked out softly, opening my eyes.

He turned and faced me, crossing his arms and looking at me with a light gaze that I remembered as a mocking one my parents used to give me as a child when I had misbehaved. That only made things worse and I struggled harder still to push myself to do what I knew I had to.

"You're... you're right," I said in a small voice, meeting his gaze and shaking my head with a tiny shrug of one shoulder. "If I stay out here alone, I'll never find my way out of this forest, even with Amethyst at my side. Without someone to show me the way... I'm dead."

"Probably," he nodded then shrugged as he rethought that. "No, *definitely*."

I grimaced and took in a deep breath. "Will... will you... will you help us?"

Gods, why is that so hard to say? I mean, I know I hate and distrust this man, but it shouldn't be so hard to ask for help. I watched him uncertainly, not sure what would happen next.

Tristan slowly strode towards me, his walk more like a subtle swagger. He came to stand over me again, looking down at me with those dark brown eyes.

"That depends," he said lowly.

"On what?" I asked softly, looking up at him uncertainly.

"Whether an Aldegaadian girl like you can trust an Ivanstenian man like me," he responded evenly.

I shook my head faintly, never once taking my eyes from his: "That has nothing to do with this."

"Doesn't it?" he stood a little closer over me.

I shook my head more fully, feeling so small and weak next to him."No, this has *nothing* to do with our nationalities," I murmured.

"Then what is it about?" he raised an expectant eyebrow at me.

"How do I know you won't betray me again?" I kept my gaze firm with his, refusing to take it away and give him the chance to trick me.

He smirked and shrugged. "Well, I guess that's the problem then. Isn't it, little girl?"

"What's the solution?" I asked quietly, looking up at him distrustfully through my black eyelashes.

"Ask yourself this," he suggested, keeping his arms folded in front of his large chest, "what's more important right now: *trust* or *need*?"

I stared at him in disbelief, flexing my jaw with open lips as I tried to find the words.

"What good is need if I can't trust you?" I finally asked gently.

"How about if I give you my word?" he offered.

I shook my head. "Your word is worthless to me."

He shrugged. "Take my help or go on your own. Your choice."

I hesitated, flicking my eyes to the ground, then back to him repeatedly. *Damn it all! Why can't I just accept his help?! I am making this so much harder than it needs to be!*

"If you get us through this forest safely," I said slowly, meeting his gaze again, "then *maybe* I'll trust you. *Maybe*."

"And if I turn all evil and try to hand you to the Witches again?" he questioned me, though I was certain it was more out of jest than seriousness.

I shrugged lightly: "Then Amethyst gets to eat you."

Tristan's face suddenly drained of all colour and his eyes widened. He turned around and looked at Amethyst, made even more uneasy when she imitated licking her lips in anticipation. I would have cracked a smile if I wasn't feeling so sickeningly uneasy.

He cleared his throat as he faced me again: "All right. That's a good deal. I'll take that one."

"All right," I nodded, feeling slightly relieved.

"Give me that," he grabbed my wrist with one hand and forced the dagger from my fingers with the other.

He held it up in front of me, waggling the weapon as if he were talking to a little child. I felt insulted but stayed silent.

"Best let me hold onto this, lass," he said derisively. "You're more likely to lose a finger or an eye," he released my arm and pushed past me.

I breathed in a relieved sigh, closing my eyes for a moment before turning my gaze to follow him as he walked towards the trees. He was looking up at the sky, studying the deepening black of the clouds and the gentle droplets that were beginning to fall. They felt cold where they managed to hit my skin, making me shudder.

"We'd best get moving," he stated, turning over his shoulder to regard me. "There's only a few hours until dark and we need shelter."

I nodded and hitched my skirt hems into my hands as I made to follow him.

"Just do as I do and stay close to me," he instructed, starting to step through the boughs and underbrush, pushing vines and branches away with his large palms. "The forest has a tendency to sneak up on you. By your tracks, you've already encountered the flesh-eating trees."

"I got away from them," I pointed out, ducking under a low branch as I kept up behind him.

"Only because Shadow Knights and their Shadow-Steeds are a bigger threat than one unarmed girl," he responded with a shrug. "You got lucky, just as you did with the groundmerks."

I stared at him in shock. "How do you...?"

"Your tracks," he said, cutting me off. "I've wandered the wilds for decades. You think I've not learned some useful tricks in that time? Now, let's go or else the sun will fade on us."

As we walked, Amethyst came up beside me. I looked up at her, the Dragon growling and grunting softly to me.

I shrugged. "I don't know if we can trust him. But we have no choice. He's our best chance at finding our way out of this forest."

She questioned me with a growl.

"It isn't what I would have chosen," I confessed with a sigh, "but with so few options it's all we can do. We'll just watch him."

The Dragon grunted another serious statement, eyeing me sternly.

"I know you would never eat him," I said, meeting her eye. "I just said that to make him think twice about double crossing us."

She seemed content with that answer.

I turned my eyes to my pendant, holding it in one hand as my other kept my dress lifted from the ground: "I wonder if he's what the Pendant was leading us to when I asked it to find us a safe way out of here."

Amethyst grunted and shrugged.

"Yeah. Maybe..." I sighed as we continued to walk, following on behind the Wanderer, who either hadn't heard our exchange or simply chose not to acknowledge it.

In truth, I didn't believe for a moment that he could be trusted, but that didn't make his reasoning any less valid. I needed his help and whether he could be trusted or not didn't enter into it right at that moment.

I just hope he's true to his word, or else I'll end up regretting all of this... Just like before...

Chapter Thirteen
The Wandering of Hearts

For hours Tristan led the way through the very depths of the forest, his focus on nothing more than the objectives he had set his mind to. He moved with the ease of a man who knew these strange overgrown paths, his attentiveness to the forest seeming unlike any I had ever known before.

I followed on behind him quietly, careful to watch my step as I kept my dress hems gathered in each hand, staggering to keep up. Regardless of his intentions to help me, he still didn't seem too concerned about keeping me close to him. At least that meant that I had control over how much distance was between us.

Amethyst crunched through the underbrush evenly, staying close behind me and keeping me between her and the Wanderer. Though she trusted him as much as I did, the Dragon obviously saw the value in using him to protect me in such a way. She said as much when I questioned her about it, and so I chose not to argue, going along with her urgings.

I noticed that Tristan glanced over his shoulder at us whenever I conversed with my dragon. He seemed perplexed by the very nature of us speaking, though he kept this to himself in words while I saw it in his gaze.

Night was drawing near, and we were running out of time to find somewhere safe to rest.

Are there any safe places out here to find? I wondered as I staggered through the vines and dirt awkwardly, managing to stay on my feet. *I mean, this forest doesn't seem welcoming, especially after all that I've seen so far.* I sighed gravely. *I just have to trust that Tristan knows what he is doing and that he'll find us shelter very, very soon.*

It took another hour, but at last we came upon a quiet clearing under a rocky alcove and Tristan began setting up a very simple makeshift camp. Once again, he surprised me as he had at Ironbark Falls, withdrawing a bag of supplies he had stowed here. I didn't need to question him about it, deciding that it was better to keep the conversation between us as minimal as possible.

The camp was nothing fancy; a pair of bedrolls made of furs and linen, a campfire he prepared awkwardly in the dark, and an old canvas pulled up over the opening to the outcropping meant to shield us from the rains plunging from the night sky.

We sat in silence, Amethyst and I shielding ourselves in the shadows of the outcropping, watching Tristan as he tended the fire. Amethyst kept her right wing around me to gift me some of her infinite warmth, which I was grateful for as I huddled up against her. Since his arrival, she had seemed even more on edge and protective of me. I didn't blame her.

I lay there deep in thought as I watched the misty darkness of the forest outside our encampment, silently wondering what horrors yet lay within the swirling shadows. I had seen so many fearful things in my infinitely young life already, but those I had yet to encounter left me ill at ease for our inevitable meetings to come.

There was nothing to eat and Tristan merely tended the fire without speaking or even looking to us. I don't think he even knew what to do as we sat in the protection of the outcropping from the rainy shadows that night. I know I didn't.

My mind wandered back to Carden, and I imagined being with him in Eilath again, smiling as he turned to see me walk out onto the garden porch in the dusk lit air, just as he had that wonderful summer so long ago.

Why couldn't it have been Carden who found me instead of Tristan? This awkwardness would not exist, and I would feel so much more at ease. With Carden all the world seems right. With Tristan there is only doubt and suspicion. The Gods have a sense of humour, that's for certain, dark and twisted though it may be.

I sighed as I pulled the blanket of the bedroll further around me and snuggled into Amethyst's arm.

Still, it is much better not to be alone in this forest. Though I question whether I can trust him, at least I know Tristan is not lying when he says he can lead us through this place. All the same, I wish Carden was the man here with me...

I closed my eyes and - even with Tristan moving around, and my suspicion at his activities growing - I soon drifted off. Perhaps it was the knowledge that Amethyst was my sentry with her restless vision certain to watch for all threats to me, both without and within, that granted me the ability to sleep that night.

I dreamed of walking through a great marble and stone castle, one I had never seen before. Its grandeur was beyond all of my imagining and I found myself wandering with blissful awe.

Large tapestries of royal purple hung on the walls with the embroidery of a great dragon, its wings spread in gold while three crescent moons arched above its horned head in silver. I had only ever read of that standard once in my life during my tutoring when I was a child. It was the standard of a united High-Realm of the past, a High-Realm made by men and women with great honour for each other. Seeing it now only made me realise how such a thing seemed more and more impossible.

Following the white and gold halls brought me soon to a great balcony overlooking a valley of tremendous beauty beyond anything else. Sapphire waterfalls fell like gleaming crystals from the many cliffs to pool in the greatest lake that ever laid before my eyes. Trees so lush and green stood proud throughout the verdant lands of sprawling grass and flowers. The sky above shimmered with magic as its celestial lights flowed with greens and blues against night's wonder, three clear crescent moons illuminating everything below them.

And within this land there were Dragons. Hundreds upon hundreds of Dragons, all different and all beautifully majestic. They swept and dived through the crisp night air, mothers teaching the young broods of dragonlings to take wing while young dragons took to the fields and lake to wander and frolic. Their scales gleamed in the moonlight's gentle glow; their calls like a song all their own.

This is... incredible... I must be dreaming if I am seeing a place such as this.

I turned to a mirror within the room connected to the balcony, stunned to see myself. I wore a gown of royal purple with golden detailing, more like the dress of a queen than a princess. On my dark-haired head, I wore a crown of gold, delicate and yet regal, with sapphires and amethysts set into the metal.

I've never looked like that... What in the...?

I heard a sound from across the hall, looking up to the doors as a male figure passed through, shutting them behind him. It was Carden.

I took a breath and made my way across the hall, my slippers padding softly on the golden carpet. I gingerly pushed open one of the doors and stepped into a bedroom of golden splendour, the bed dressed in purples and gold with curtains of the same royal colours.

My eyes set on Carden instantly, ignoring all other feasts of sight. He stood with his back to me, looking out the windows that led to an identical balcony to the one I had just walked from, but the doors were closed. He wore black and dark red, his hands clasped at the small of his back, his body so perfectly still.

"Carden?" I called softly, gently making my way towards him. "Carden, it's been so long since we were last together."

"Not so long for immortals," he uttered quietly, not turning to me.

I raised an eyebrow at his remark, nearly right behind him now: "Even a day without you is a lifetime for me. Two years has been an eternity of agony without seeing your eyes, holding your hand, tasting your lips, or hearing your voice..."

"So it has been for me as well, my love," he said softly, still not turning.

"Why do you not turn to me?" I asked uncertainly, fidgeting my hands together. "I've dreamed so often of seeing your face again, and now that we are together, I don't want you to conceal yourself from me."

"Do you truly believe you are ready to behold me as I am?" he responded darkly, though calmly. "To face that which lurks beneath?"

I frowned uncertainly. "What do you mean?"

"Are you ready?" he repeated.

I nodded. "Yes. Of course, Carden. Anything for you, my love."

He turned to face me, and I gasped, staggering a little as his eyes locked with mine. That was all I could see, the rest of his face hidden from my gaze by my singular focus. The green of his eyes was gone, a deep unrelenting crimson replacing them. They shimmered with a power so inhuman that I had never seen anything like them before. They seemed to be able to stare right through my living skin into my eternal soul and reveal all that I truly am.

Before I could react further, he was suddenly right in front of me, his lips parting ever so slightly as his pale face came close to mine. With the darkened bruised skin around his eyes and the chill on his flesh, he seemed more like a being of death than the man I had known since our first meeting in Arvon.

He smiled darkly, his eyes glowing brightly as he held me so tight that I couldn't move.

"I love you, Leander," he whispered. "Always..."

The sound of movement woke me from my dream - or perhaps nightmare - bringing me back to the waking world. I opened my eyes to find that I still lay amidst Amethyst's wing and arm, the Dragon watching me with worried orange eyes.

She asked me what was wrong.

"I'm not sure," I replied, sitting up and letting the furs of the bedroll slide down my hips. "I dreamed of Carden, but he was... different... darker..."

She croaked out another question.

I shrugged. "I can't explain it yet."

She cocked her head and spoke gently, concern in her beautiful voice.

I shook my head, frowning as I thought about the dream. "No. I wasn't afraid... just... unsettled, I think."

Movement caught my attention and I turned to see Tristan rolling up his bedroll, the fire already out. He was moving quickly as he worked, his eyes on his task. He had also taken the canvas that had shielded us and was using it to bundle up our small number of supplies.

"So, you're awake, girl," he said with a nod, binding the bedroll to make it easier to carry. "Good."

"What are you doing?" I asked, turning more fully towards him.

"Breaking camp," he replied simply. "Best you get off that bedroll so I can bundle it up. We'll need these to make it through the forest and to safety."

I obeyed his suggestion, but only because I knew we needed to keep moving.

My stomach growled and I thought to ask about food, but I chose instead to keep my silence. I knew that if he'd had food to share, he would have already done so, just as he did when we first met. Still, he seemed to possess an ability to know my thoughts as he bundled the second bedroll up, something that never ceased to surprise me.

"We'll seek out food when we next make camp," he explained his planning without need of my prompting. "The way we take today will lead us to far safer grounds to scavenge what we need, and towards waters not so bitter to drink. And before you ask, lass, no, there is nothing in these areas that we stand in that is safe to ingest. We spend the day with a starving belly and heavy thirst, then feed ourselves with dusk's return."

I didn't speak, simply nodding and standing with Amethyst as she rose to her four legs. There was nothing to be said and I trusted that leaving Tristan to think he was acting his desired role would be better than questioning him further.

He knows these lands better than I do. It is much safer for me to follow and remain silent than to question his every comment and action. Unless it offers me threat as his deeds in Eilath inevitably did.

It was not yet daybreak when we set out from our resting place, Tristan insisting that an early start only aided us in making it through the forest in better time than if we waited for the sun's rays. The day came as it had every day prior in this dismal forest, the mists blocking all sight of the light beyond a miserable greyish hue. The trees lurked within the swirling clouds like black ghosts, every moving vine that reached for us hacked down by the small axe Tristan carried with him.

He is very well armed, I considered as I watched him. *A long sword, daggers, an axe, a bow, magic of his own... What does this man not carry with him?*

We stepped through the boughs and fallen logs slowly, very careful to watch our steps as we went. I knew if I fell that I would not get up again with ease, already tripping once and stinging my palms and knees with the impact. I studied the red grazing on my left hand, feeling the bite of the injuries to my knees continuously for a while. Still, I could always have suffered worse and was glad as the dismal grey day wore on that I didn't seem to.

Some hours after taking our leave from the outcropping, Tristan led us through the brush and to an open area where only a few trees without leaves stood.

"Ah... lovely," he muttered, nodding to himself.

I pushed up beside him and looked out at what lay before us.

Firstly, the smell was pungent and like stagnant water mixed with rotting flowers, among other things best not mentioned. I gagged a little, though only once. As for the sight, it is difficult to describe. The land was a festering marsh that led on for some way, the trees still thick around us, though not as thick throughout the expanse of the grassy swamps. Fat bulbous pods as large as my head sat atop the murky waters and thick mud with large dragonflies fluttering around as the only visible life in the area. The chirping of insects and the croaking of toads permeated the air, giving life back its sound after the forest's crippling silence so far, though it didn't seem a relief. Spiky reeds stood tall in shades of faded yellow as black weeds sprouted everywhere. It was like a once great lake had come to this place to die.

"There are marshes like this one all over this forest," Tristan explained, surveying the way ahead. "The ground is never certain, so stay close to me and do exactly as I do."

"Can't we go around?" I asked, touching his shoulder and drawing his gaze.

"Sure," he nodded, "if you don't mind going a hundred miles north or seventy miles south."

"Uh," I said simply, nodding. "I see your point."

"Best cut through," he patted me on the back and smiled lightly. "Don't worry, Princess. You've got me to show you the way."

"Be still my heart," I muttered sarcastically under my breath as he turned back to the swamps.

It seems his arrogance knows no bounds. Does this man never know failure or despair? Must he always see only his own success and self-assurance? Gods, I would truly love to bring him down a few notches and see him humbled for what he has put me through. I owe him that much.

The passage through the marshes was difficult and slow, slower even than those we had made through the wilds and boughs of the forest thus far. Our footing had to be sure and our path clear or else we would sink deep into the hungry mud that yearned to devour us. Even Amethyst seemed to worry that she would plummet to a suffocating end.

Tristan was very cautious as he worked his way along the only paths safe enough to cross, using a long stick he had snatched up to feel the way through. Though he knew the marshes well enough to judge the safest ways by sight, he still had a need to feel out the weaker ones in case of a collapse into the muck.

The water and mud were up to my ankles, making it difficult for me to move very quickly. I hitched my dress hems higher as I tried to stay close to him, though I knew it was a struggle in itself to do so. The sucking pressure surrounding me only made my progress that much harder and I began to silently worry that I would fall in at any moment.

I looked back to see Amethyst working her way behind me. Her greater size meant she had to be even more careful with each step she took, her movements making her look like she was trying to balance on a narrow beam with one foot in front of the other. The Dragon snorted and grumbled her annoyance, though I didn't say anything, determined instead to focus on not falling into the marsh.

We must have been at least halfway across by now, the way seeming only to increase in difficulty. With every step I took I felt my feet sink, the water trying to rise up my shins towards my knees.

I noted that Tristan was slowing now as well, sluggishly pulling his way through the murky swamp with the aid of the stick in his hands. His cloak was dragging in the water behind him and the portion that touched the surface was dirtying and becoming soaked. My own skirt hems were much the same, the blue of my dress and white of my slip tainted with a gentle staining, my teal velvet over dress catching dirt granules along its hem.

I turned my gaze to the way ahead, the trees looking much closer, though still so very far away. *How much farther do these marshes extend? It seems as if we won't reach the other side before the failing of the day.*

Suddenly, my foot sunk and I cried out, trying to keep myself from falling.

"Princess!" Tristan spun around and came trudging quickly towards me.

"I'm stuck!" I cried out, trying to tug my leg free.

"Hold on, I've got you!" he swung around behind me and grasped me in his arms.

He added his strength to mine as he squared his shoulders and set his legs apart, one arm curled tight around my waist. Together we fought and tugged at my leg, battling to pull me free. It felt like the mud had formed into a pair of arms that had secured my ankle between their grasping, crushing hands. Every movement I made only seemed to tighten its hold on me and I cried out in panic as I fought even harder to free myself.

"Stop panicking, lass," he warned me as he reached his free hand to my shin. "It pulls you in faster if you struggle."

I nodded and forced myself to be calm, ceasing all movements I had been making.

Tristan grasped my leg tight and - holding the fabric of my black leggings for support - began to slowly slip my foot back towards the surface. It took a few long moments, but my foot and boot came free and I was able to settle myself onto more solid ground, breathing out a heavy sigh of relief.

"There you are, lass," he smirked, turning my chin with his fingers to make me meet his gaze. "Still in one piece."

For a moment, I met his gaze and locked hard on his dark eyes. I could see that there truly was an affection there meant for me, though it wasn't something I desired from him. I drew in a sharp breath and yanked my arm out of his hold, stepping back and turning away from him to seek out the next way to go.

"Thank you," I grumbled back at him, reminding myself once again of his crimes against me.

"Gods, girl," Tristan quietly exclaimed, shaking his head as he walked up beside me. "Can you not show me even the smallest amount of courtesy?"

"I just did when I thanked you," I replied grimly, narrowing my eyes at him. "Now, can we *please* just get out of this swamp and back to dry land?"

He sighed and nodded. "Right."

For a few long, awkward moments we didn't speak, nor did we meet each other's gaze as we continued on our way through the marshes. I had no desire to enter into conversation with him, feeling that to do so would be disastrous.

What am I to even talk about? Anything I say to him will ultimately be cold and unkind. Not that he deserves my kindness anymore. Still, I'm better off not speaking since I have nothing nice to say.

After a few moments more, Tristan called back to me, digging his path forward with the stick he carried: "You have a mighty amount of trouble trusting others," he glanced over his shoulder and past his long golden red hair at me. "Is that not so, girl?"

"Trust is not given, it is earned," I met his gaze as I stepped heavily over a gap of deep water and onto more solid ground, feeling only contempt as I looked at him. "And what trust you earned from me in Aldegaad you cast away when you betrayed me in Eilath."

He rolled his eyes and growled under his breath before answering me: "Come on, lass. Do not judge me on that single moment between us..."

"I judge you on the deeds you sought to carry out," I told him sternly, continuing to move through the marsh with a little more ease now. "When first we met your deeds appeared honourable. Yet, that night in Eilath showed me the truest deceit within your heart and I can't simply forget that it ever happened."

"You could try," he reasoned.

"Your actions cost me two years of my life," I retorted strongly, but calmly. "Do not try to justify yourself to me after leaving me to the cruelty of those fiends..."

"It... was nothing personal," he murmured, wading onwards with his eyes towards the tree line.

"Of course not," I responded sardonically, rolling my eyes. "Clearly friendship and trust could never outweigh the worth of gold. What was it they promised you? How much gold did Keilantra line your pockets with for imprisoning me?"

"That is no concern of yours, girl," he growled quietly, standoffish as he continued to make his way through. "All you need know is now I seek only to offer you aid in escaping them."

"Why now?" I demanded, staggering a little, but catching myself. "Why help me now and not when they sought my capture two years ago? Why not warn me of their intentions in Eilath and spare me the tortures I have had to endure all this time?"

"Because now is when I could do something," he snapped, glaring up at me briefly before watching the way ahead.

"Altruism doesn't suit you," I said quietly, shaking my head and watching the ground as I placed my feet gingerly with each step. "Were the Shadow Lord to appear before us now and offer you a hundred sovereigns, I've no doubt that you would hand me over. Gods, you'd probably do it for a single sovereign, or even one silver piece."

"All right," he turned and stopped before me, meeting my gaze hard.

I pulled up and looked into his face, studying his expression. I didn't see anger, though I could tell his gaze certainly held some measure of it. If anything, there was hurt and regret, though the hurt wasn't caused by my words, but something deeper and far sharper cutting.

"Listen now, girl, for I am not the gold hungry monster you believe me to be," he pointed one finger at me, scowling, though his expression was soft and saddened. "Were that I'd had another choice I would have taken it..."

"Fawkner once said something much the same to me," I told him coldly, tightening my grip on my dress and refusing to unlock our gazes. "All that separates you from him is that he elected to cast aside gold for what was right when he saved me at Averet. *You* gave me to that monster for your reward."

"Death," he said sternly, "would have been a kinder reward for me than what I ultimately got for gifting you to them. There is no gold enough in this world to appease my afflicted spirit. And now seeing you before me, though I was granted my prize and permitted to depart from their dark company, I am reminded of my crimes."

He leaned over me and stared deep into my eyes, making me feel that if he came any closer, I could stumble and fall backwards into the mud.

"Watch your judgements," he warned me sternly, but with sad eyes, "for you know not what dire things may motivate those who cause you harm."

I just frowned back at him, breathing swiftly from his sudden closeness.

"Now, let's continue on ere the sun fades," he directed, turning and starting back on our original path. "We've still much ground to cover and few hours left to do it in. I'd prefer not to linger in the marshes when night comes."

I could only stand there watching him for a few moments as he started off again. So many thoughts swirled through my mind as I studied the Wanderer.

I am being very hard on him. I'm not sure if too hard, but then again, Fawkner had been much the same with me when we first met. Now I trust him more than most.

I started walking again, following Tristan's path through the swamps and back towards solid land. I kept looking from my feet and their gentle search for a sturdy foothold to his back, watching him with a new curiosity.

There was no doubt in my mind that he was repentant now that he was with me again, and perhaps he really did mean only to help me. It had seemed true enough when first we had met in Aneuran.

There's something in him that makes me think perhaps he wasn't meaning to be so cruel, despite his actions. Could it be that like Fawkner, Tristan is a victim of circumstance? If that's so, then whatever leverage the Shadow Lord held over him was enough to urge him to complete his part in that monster's plans...

* * * * *

We made the solid ground of the forest on the other side of the marshes an hour before dusk, our way slow, but speedier than it had been through the waters and mud. We remained silent as we moved, neither of us desiring to be the one to break the quiet. It seemed that being the one to do so would invite more criticism from the other and I didn't wish to add to that. Even Amethyst didn't speak as she stayed near my side, her eyes focused only on surveying our surroundings for any possible dangers.

At last, Tristan picked a spot beside a small stream for us to make camp. He secured the canvas between some trees to make a temporary shelter, then laid out the bedrolls as I crouched to drink from the stream. I hadn't realised how thirsty I was until the cool water touched my lips, guzzling down all that my cupped hands could hold.

I turned over my shoulder as Tristan took his bow and stalked out into the woods again, muttering something about hunting. I watched him leave, then looked to Amethyst. I truly felt like the worst person at that moment for being so hard on him.

As night was falling, Amethyst and I gathered wood for a fire, setting up a circle of rocks to contain it. I was setting the last pieces of kindling to the pile when Tristan returned with what I could only guess was venison he had carved from his kill.

"I'll get to that in a minute, lass," he said, moving to set his weapons down and prepare the food.

"It's all right," I replied as I knelt before the rocks and took my pendant from my neck. "I've got it."

I closed my eyes and held the Pendant close in my hands, speaking silently to it. *I need to light this campfire. Please, light it for me?*

The familiar heat rose in my hands and I opened my palms to once again see the purple flames and electricity dancing across the Pendant's heart-stone. Like I had before, I turned the stone towards the wood and the flames leaped out from it into the kindling, setting it ablaze before turning orange and gold as the Pendant's energy retreated once more.

Tristan was staring wide eyed at the fire, watching me as I refastened the necklace around my neck. I don't think I had ever seen the Wanderer so stunned by anything I had done before.

"How did you do that, lass?" he asked in a hushed voice.

I glanced up to him and gently held the Pendant between my thumb and forefinger.

"My pendant," I explained evenly. "It holds the heart-stone of an Amethian Dragon, one of Amethyst's forebears, in its centre. Since dragons breathe fire it seems the heart-stone can conjure it for my needs just by my thought and will."

"Then... it is no fantasy that what you carry around your neck *is* one of *the* Dragon Pendants," he looked awed as he studied it.

I nodded, staring at the stone. "My uncle and father told me it had magic meant to aid and protect its wearer. Since my escape from Castle Ortagaad it has been the only thing that has kept me from harm. It guided me like a compass across the frozen sea and through the Labyrinth of Dol Amor. It conjured fire to keep me warm amidst the cold winds. It cast those who would harm me to the ground to protect me. And it brought light to the darkness when I needed it."

"You say it acted like a compass?" he raised an eyebrow at me.

I nodded. "It's what led me to you. I asked it to show me the safest way to escape these forests, and where it led me was where we met."

"Truly? Then it seems your Pendant is more forgiving than you or your dragon are," he started tending to the meat as he set up a spit over the fire.

I looked down at my hands in my lap, feeling ashamed all of a sudden. While a part of me told me, I should still hold my anger against what he had done to me, there was this other part that urged me to find my compassion.

Slowly, I sat back and rested my shoulders into Amethyst's side where she lay behind me, hugging my arms around my flat stomach and drawing my knees up. I just watched the fire as Tristan worked to prepare our food, losing myself in the exquisite dancing of the flames.

"So," he spoke up after a few long moments that felt like minutes, "is that bauble what lets you understand her?"

"Huh?" I blinked out of the mesmerizing flow of the fire and looked to him.

He looked up at me as he sat down nearby and took his sword up to begin sharpening it.

"Your Dragon," he clarified. "You two seem to talk a lot, and you seem to understand her when I can't. Is it your necklace that lets you hear her in words you understand? Or do you speak Dragon-tongue like the scholars of old?"

I shrugged uncertainly. "I'm not sure. For as long as I've known Amethyst, I've been able to understand what she says to me, though no one else does. It's strange, because Fawkner and Carden could speak with Eamnonn, the Dragon in the Guardians' trials at Coastwatch Keep, but not her."

"Do you hear words when she speaks to you?" he frowned, working on his blade.

I shrugged again, deep in thought as I tried to comprehend my strange speech with Amethyst. "It's... difficult to explain. I know the words she speaks, yet I can't understand them in our human tongue. It isn't like knowing a foreign language and not being able to respond. It's more like... *sensing* what she means."

"Sensing?" he frowned.

I nodded, staring at the fire again. "Like I understand her without understanding. I don't know the language of the Dragons, yet I know what Amethyst says to me when she speaks it. Maybe it's because we're bound to each other through the Pendant."

He nodded, focusing his eyes on his work now exclusively. "A useful trick, if you ask me. And it is truly a gift to have such a loyal friend by your side, even if you understand her words only through sensing and not hearing."

I looked up at him, watching as he worked. His words betrayed the hurt in him once again, but this time it certainly was not because of anything I had said. There was a sense of loss in his voice, of lonely longing and of heartbreak.

He buried himself into the maintenance of his weapon to ensure that he needn't face Amethyst and I as we sat there in the cold darkness of the forest. Our friendship was a fire glowing bright, and I could feel that he was staring at it like a sailor trapped at sea, unable to reach the light on land signalling safety.

I took in a slow breath, looking to my knees and brushing my long dark hair from my eyes.

"I'm sorry, Tristan," I said softly and honestly, looking up to see him pause his work. "For before. I didn't mean to be so harsh. It's just that so many people I've trusted have hurt me now, including you, and... well," I sighed and shrugged, "I just don't know if I can let myself get hurt again."

"It's all right, girl," he turned his gaze towards me, his expression soft and sincere. "You have every right to hate me. By the Void, I hate myself for what I brought upon you for my own gains, and I've spent every day since last I saw you in that castle wishing I could undo my deeds."

He sighed and closed his eyes, setting his sword down and covering them with one hand.

"But I can't," he murmured remorsefully. "I let my own desires cloud my mind and I cost you so much to gain them. For that, all I can do is say how sorry I am, though I know it is barely a small comfort now after all you were made to endure, lass."

We fell silent for a few moments as I let his words of sincerity absorb into my heart and mind. I knew he was honest in his regret now, no longer doubting that he was a good man pushed to do terrible things. No evil man would speak such words of truth to their victim or feel such remorse for the wrongs he had inflicted upon her.

"What was it?" I asked softly, drawing his gaze. "The reward you sought to gain for me, what was it they gave you?"

"I'm not certain you could stomach such a story of that kind of ill," he replied, settling his elbows on his knees and staring into the fire. "Having endured it firsthand doesn't yet lend my mind to believe it."

"Please, Tristan," I urged him gently. "You can tell me."

He took in a shaking breath as he got back to sharpening his blade, seeming to need the task to relive his tale.

"I wasn't always a wanderer," he started, eyes on the blade as the occasional sparks fell from it with the grinding of the whetstone. "I had a wife and a child once, many years ago. She... Gods... she was the most beautiful woman I had ever known; fierce and strong, but then that is the way of your people."

"Your wife was of Aldegaad?" I was surprised by this.

He paused his work and nodded, smiling fondly. "That she was. Her hair was the same colour as yours, her skin like snow and her eyes blue as the sea," he looked to me then, studying my features. "You remind me so much of her."

I shifted uncomfortably where I sat, the comparison not helping me to feel at ease.

He sighed, thinking on the past: "She was young, and her family hated that she loved me, an Ivanstenian soldier, yet she cared not. Her heart was mine and it was with me that she longed to be. So, we left for Ivansten and along the way she grew heavy with child. Soon our little daughter was born, with her mother's auburn locks and my brown eyes. We settled in a small village where I worked as a woodcutter at the mill. Every day we would tend to our child and our family home, at night finding comfort in each other's embrace."

"It sounds like you had a happy life," I observed, already knowing in my heart that there was no happy ending.

He nodded, blinking back tears. "Aye... that we did."

"What happened?" I was hesitant to ask, hugging my knees tightly now and noting that Amethyst was listening intently at my side.

He drew in a shuddering breath, struggling to contain himself as he went on: "Fairy tales so rarely end with *"and they lived happily ever after"*, despite what people may think. My beloved wife was picking flowers one day with our daughter in her care," his expression paled."I heard her screams from the mill..."

I gasped, staring wide eyed at him, too afraid to ask what it was that had happened.

He closed his eyes, his face showing the pain that yet lingered within his chest as he ceased his work on his blade: "I... I ran... ran from the mill, weapon in hand. I thought of so many beasts or bandits harming her, of all the terrors that she might endure. But the truth... it was so much worse," tears slipped from his eyes and he dropped the sword to the ground with a clatter."She had been walking back to town and a merchant had been thrown from his carriage when the horse was spooked by a snake," his voice cracked as he spoke."It... ran her down... Her... and our child..."

Amethyst let out a mournful gasp, turning her eyes to me as my heart broke for the poor man.

"Oh, Gods," I covered my mouth, fighting back tears of sympathy. "Tristan... I'm so sorry..."

"I never even had a chance to say goodbye," he wept, covering his face with one hand.

I began to understand him better now, seeing the grief and the pain within him that he had surely shielded from me when we first met.

"What... uh... what did you do?" I asked softly, almost too afraid to speak at all.

"I had heard rumours," he replied, lifting his head and staring into the fire. "Though I had laid my wife and child to rest, I learned there might be a way to return them to me. At least for the chance to say goodbye. So, I journeyed into the Bargoth Mountains, north of where we now sit, to the town of Raven's Rest..."

"Where the Witches are from..." I realised with quiet terror.

He nodded. "I sought them out, the sisters who held the power to offer me the one chance I had left to see my beloved wife and child again, and to say goodbye. That was all I wanted. And Keilantra offered to free me from my grief..."

"What did she do?" I felt my tears for him and hate for the Witches growing slowly, my body shuddering from the cold that surrounded us.

He chuckled in his sobs: "She tried to bed me. When I denied her and demanded only what I wanted, offering her anything else she desired, she refused. I asked that she end my life and send me to my family, to do as she'd promised and free me from my grief."

"But she didn't," I guessed.

"No," he shook his head and met my gaze. "She cursed me instead for spurning her, condemning me to be hers in another, crueller way."

He paused for a moment, then opened his shirt. I gasped at the long, ugly scar that ran over the left side of his chest, the wound faded now, but the scar still strong in itself.

"Did you ever see their sanctum in Castle Ortagaad, girl?" he asked me.

I nodded, but couldn't speak, my eyes locked on his hideous scar. Though the thought to touch it occurred to me, I couldn't bring myself to do it, my stomach churning at the very sight of it.

"Then you saw her collection," he grimaced. "Each of those living hearts is that of a man who spurned Keilantra, while her sister, Manth, torments young girls because of their beauty, stealing it from them before ending their lives. My heart... was once among them..."

"She took your heart?!" I felt so sick as my voice gasped the words out.

"And yet, I lived," he confirmed what my terrified thoughts had already dreaded to know. "She said she would keep me alive to punish me for refusing her, to keep me from my beloved. She said I would never know death until I had fulfilled her use for me. And no matter how I tried to take my life, I could never succeed, her magic restoring me to what you see before you. That... was nearly seventy years past."

"You've been this young for seventy years?" I couldn't believe what he was telling me.

He nodded, closing his shirt again. "And I have suffered every moment of that time. For *seven* decades of this world I have yearned for death, prayed for Azmerath to take me into his kingdom, and begged Thringar to grant me his justice, yet neither came to me. So, I served the Witches as they desired, killing and stealing for them, unable to age... unable to die."

I just stared at him in bewilderment, trying to even comprehend what he had been through, but failing.

He sighed and met my gaze with regret. "My reward for bringing you to them was not gold or riches, but the return of my heart and with it my mortality. *That* was what I received for gifting you to them for their Master. Keilantra has allowed me to die."

He was right... His tale is one of such tragic ill. Gods... how could he have endured it? How could anyone?

"Then... why do you help me now?" I asked the only thing I knew to ask.

"To atone," he replied morosely, his eyes turning to the fire anew. "The Witch may have returned my heart and my mortal coil, yet, because of her I have lost my soul. Perhaps if I can make amends to you, girl, then I can find redemption, and at long last I can have peace in my wife's waiting embrace when I do pass from this world into that of the God King of Death."

I just nodded, knowing him better than ever I had before.

He was no monster, no traitor, only a desperate man looking for a way to end his decades of agony and sorrow. Regardless of what he had done to me, I couldn't hate him anymore. And it was now that I knew he spoke the truth, his words sounding so much sweeter than the lies he had told in the past.

"Forgive me," he cried into his hands, slouching where he sat. "Forgive me!"

I stood slowly and walked to where he sat sobbing. I knew only sympathy for him now and sat by his side, placing my hand to his shoulder.

"I forgive you, Tristan" I whispered gently, putting my arm around his back as he wept desperately.

There was nothing else left to say. His broken heart had spoken all that needed to be told. He didn't deserve what they had done to him anymore than I deserved what had been done to me. There was no hatred between us now, no resentment or mistrust. There was only the truth.

"I'll get you to safety, Princess," he looked up and met my gaze through his tears. "I'll get you to the High Elves in Silvervale. I swear to you, girl. I will. Oh Gods... I will..."

I just nodded and held him in my smaller embrace as he let out all the grief he must have held for so long. And we stayed like this for some time, my heart aching for him and his lost loves while fearing that my fate was turning to be the same.

I truly hope it doesn't. I could never survive such torments. I doubt I'm as strong as him...

Chapter Fourteen
A Clash of Scales and Stones

The rest of the night was spent in total silence after Tristan's confession. We simply ate the meal he cooked, took some water from the nearby stream and proceeded to settle in for our latest nocturnal rest. I didn't dare to continue my conversation with him, not wanting to add any further anguish to his already weeping heart.

There is no more I need to know of his past. To even try to make him speak of it would only be needlessly heartless. I wouldn't wish to delve into the tragedies of my past at someone else's insistence, so I won't do the same to him.

Rest wouldn't so easily be ensnared in the chilling darkness, the rustling and groaning of the trees surrounding us enough to keep anyone awake. I kept waiting for some unspeakable horror to emerge from the shadows of the forest to attack us, my heart racing without provocation.

I'm being paranoid. If anything came for us in these woods, we would be warned by both Amethyst's unflinching senses and my pendant's mystical alarm.

I lay down on the bedroll my once misguided companion had laid out for me, pulling the blanket around me and closing my eyes. I yearned for nothing but sleep at that moment, though I wasn't so certain I would achieve it with the deep dread permeating the air around us.

Surely, I am not the only one of the three of us to feel this. I can't be alone in my perceptions. Then again, it could simply be the fearful paranoia that this wicked place works in people.

I rested for a short while, not really certain how long my eyes lay shut in a dreamless sleep. Against all the unease in my heart and my body, I had come to rest in comfort on those furs, feeling the warmth of the fire fuelling me with its gentle embrace. This didn't last, however, a rough, callused hand gently shaking my shoulder to wake me from my sleep.

I blinked awake, my vision blurred, though the darkness didn't lend me much to allow my eyes to see.

He was crouched over me, his sword at the ready, his other hand perched on my arm as his eyes surveyed the forest around us. His gaze was alarmed, his jaw set severely, and I instantly felt that something was wrong.

"Tristan?" I moved to sit up.

"Shh..." he hushed me, looking out to the trees around us. "Be silent, girl. They're out there."

"What's out there?" I frowned, trying to follow his gaze.

"Shade Seekers," he whispered.

My heart was instantly filled with panic as I sat up from where I lay, forcing myself to remain silent. I could find no words, my throat tight with fear as I sought Amethyst's protection, the Dragon pulling me close to her with one large, clawed hand, her fire coloured gaze severe.

"They'll see this fire," Tristan uttered worriedly, then waved his hand, a blue flash casting from his left palm and snuffing out the flames. "We need to hide."

He stood quickly and took me by my arm, leading me swiftly into the cover of the unearthed roots of a large, gnarled tree. Amethyst disappeared as Tristan dropped me into the narrow dug out area, laying over me and watching carefully.

"Just stay quiet, girl," he warned me softly.

I let my eyes flick from him and out into the forest beyond this low shelter. The rain had given way to icy mists that fogged all sight of the world, the trees like black spectres amidst the ghostly murkiness. It seemed that the thick vapours were giving the impression of a bluish light over everything, yet I knew there was none.

I felt a warmth at my chest, gazing down to see the heart-stone in my pendant flashing rapidly. I swiftly closed my hands around it, hiding the purple light from sight.

They might see such a light...

I heard them then, the ghastly, wheezing death-rattle of the ethereal creatures filling the air. I just waited, holding my breath as they moved unseen around us, my blood running cold in my veins.

Slowly, like wraiths in the mists, their black robed shapes began to emerge from the murky air, tattered and floating. The glow of their eerie blue eyes shone dully from their skeletal eye sockets, their corpse-like fingers grasping at the air. First there came two of the hooded spectres, then another, and another, until at last there were seven of the floating black clad horrors drifting over the forest floor. They were searching with those glowing eye holes, their screaming jaws currently concealed behind their deathly wrappings, silent save for the wheezing gasps they were making.

They were getting close... too close for my liking.

"Come, quietly," Tristan took me by my arm and pulled me up, slipping out from under the tree and away from the monsters.

We crept from the tree as they began studying our campsite, their bony fingers grasping at things like curious beings that had never seen such objects. Their blue gazes were like searching lights, shining over everything they stared at, almost as if they could illuminate anything hidden to be revealed.

Tristan rushed me quietly beside him to the cover of another large tree as one of the creatures began surveying our previous hiding place. He turned me and pressed my back up against the trunk, holding me there by my shoulders.

"Right," he spoke in a hushed, urgent voice, keeping his eyes locked with mine, "here's what I need you to do. Do *not* move from this very spot, or else they shall see you."

"What are you going to do?" I questioned in a whispering, worried murmur, feeling so afraid that tears had begun swelling in my eyes.

"I have to get them away from here," he explained, peeking out of cover to check where they were, then turning back to me seriously. "Just do as I say and stay put right here. You understand, girl?"

I nodded swiftly with a few quietly rushing breaths, bracing my palms back against the tree firmly.

"Good girl," he smiled faintly, then moved out of my sight.

I stood there shaking, trying to control my shivering trembles as they broke through my limbs. All I could do was hold still and wait for him to return, my fear of the Shade Seekers too potent to allow me to move even an inch, though I actually wanted to run.

My breath caught in my chest, my body hurting with the tension pulling my limbs fearfully. I could hear them scraping around beyond where I stood, my eyes wide and my heart pounding so loudly I was frightened they would hear it. My senses were vibrant with awareness, painfully taking in the presence of the dire beings slouching through the mists surrounding me. I swallowed back hard, trying not to make a sound, though fearful whimpers slipped past my firmly pressed lips.

Suddenly, I could feel one of them near me. It was moving up beside the tree I hid behind, my senses screaming in panic at the coarse, grating, gasping breaths it was emitting. A deep chill filled me, making me shiver even harder than I already was with the frosty air.

I glanced up slowly, edging my face around to my shoulder and my eyes towards the edge of the tree. I saw the pale, white, bony fingers hook around the trunk, cracking some of the black bark under their points.

Oh no! Please, no! Don't... don't see me!

The hooded head of the creature slipped past me, looking away from me. I sunk lower down the tree, my heart in my throat and my breath caught in my chest. It needed only to turn to find me, my safety mere moments from being destroyed.

Suddenly, there was a loud sound and a flash, something drawing the Shade Seeker's attention. It turned around completely away from me, floating there for a few moments as it studied the world around us. Another bang and flash, and the creature's wrappings dropped, its elongated jaw ripping forth with that eerie glow and that ear splitting shriek. A chorus of shrieks tore the foggy air asunder as the other six joined their seventh in screaming, their attention towards the source of the noise and light.

The Shade Seeker swept away from my sights, vanishing as it chased after whatever it was that had made that sound. I just lay there, frozen on the ground where I had slipped unknowingly from my feet, my breaths now rushing out of panicky relief. I slowly pulled myself up and peered around the tree, catching a glimpse of the deathly black creatures spiriting away at an incredible pace.

"Lass," I nearly screamed as Tristan appeared behind me, startling me and making me skid in a jump.

"Gods! You scared me!" I exclaimed, feeling flustered from all the stress.

"Sorry," he said, sheathing his sword and placing his hands on my shoulders. "You all right? You hurt?"

"No," I shook my head. "It didn't see me."

"Good," he smiled softly, leading me back to the camp as Amethyst emerged from the thick brush behind me.

"What did you do?" I asked, frowning as I followed him back to our camp.

"A little spell I learned," he answered, moving to reignite the fire with a flint and striking stone. "Those blighted spectres will chase that illusion unto dawn's light and burn themselves to dust."

I crossed my arms as I stood over him, raising an incredulous eyebrow. "Why didn't you use a sun spell as Aldwyn did?"

"Since I am untrained and hardly the mage Aldwyn is, such spells are beyond me," he confessed, awkwardly relighting the kindling and setting more wood to the fledgling flames.

"I would think it to be a simple spell," I murmured, watching him through my dishevelled hair as he worked.

He glanced at me: "Are you a mage?"

I shook my head. "No..."

"Casting a little illusion such as what I did is small in comparison to harnessing and producing the power of the sun," he stated, leaning back on his bedroll with a sigh as the fire took to the kindling. "Best you do not assume knowledge of arts you are not practiced in, girl."

There was nothing to say to that, my mind blank as I settled back onto my bedroll and wrapped myself in the blanket. Even as Amethyst once again settled down beside me and shielded me with her warmth, I felt the cold of unease fill me.

After all this I'm not sure I can sleep easily...

* * * * *

The next morning, I awoke from an awkward, nightmare filled sleep to more dark storm clouds above the trees. I squinted up at the tarp above me, the dull light enough to sting my eyes.

We broke camp an hour later after refreshing ourselves with water from the stream, Tristan once more leading the way through the dull, murky mists of this dread forest. He kept his sword at the ready, cutting away vines and branches that got too close, clearing a path to allow me an easier trip through.

I was tired, the night before having left me with an unease that disturbed my rest. I carefully followed on behind Tristan, brushing aside twigs and vines with my palms as I walked. The forest felt as if it were drawing tighter around us, the air so close now. The immense age of the forest was without question, the size of the trees and the thick foliage surrounding us a true testament to such.

As we traversed the overgrown forest paths, I began to worry that there was no escaping its depths, but I tried not to think such things. *Stop thinking such foolish things! Tristan knows his way through this forest, he can lead us out safely. I'm just letting my fear take hold where I should be denying it.*

Suddenly, I felt something tighten around my wrist and I snapped out of my thoughts. A vine was coiling around my arm as if it were a snake, tightening its hold on me. I tried to slip free, then felt the grasping reach of more vines. They were a dark greenish grey with thorns, snatching at my clothes and enwrapping me at a moderate speed. I cried out in panic, struggling to get free of them, my eyes darting across each groping limb helplessly. I tried to slap them away, but they were reaching to pin my arms to my body, slithering over my skin and clothing with no sign of relenting. Another panicked cry slipped past my lips and I tried to thrash free, this only hastening their wrapping tangle around me.

A flash of steel gleamed and there was a squeaking hiss as a vine was cut away from me, the severed end oozing green sap to the ground. Tristan swung his sword, cleaving the vines with each strike as Amethyst clawed at the ones behind me. The man easily broke them apart, casting the hardening plant limbs to the dirt with deep focus. He grabbed my hand and pulled me free as Amethyst uprooted the two trees that had been the source of the reaching, strangling vines, crushing them to the ground as she passed them.

I breathed out a heavy sigh, staring wide eyed at the mess of destroyed branches and vines.

"Wow," Tristan remarked, shaking his head with a smile. "You really are easily found by trouble. Aren't you girl?"

"Too easily it seems," I agreed, following him with my gaze for a few moments before walking after him, Amethyst staying close at my back.

We continued on for a few metres, my attention on not falling to the ground or being snagged by another of the strangling vine trees.

"Can I ask you something?" my voice broke the silence that was otherwise given sound only by our crunching footfalls.

"If you'd like, lass," Tristan responded, cutting through some more branches and clearing the way further still.

"What do you know of Silvervale?" I studied him as he walked, squeezing my dress hems in my fingers firmly. "Have you ever been there?"

"A few times," he confessed with a nod. "The High Elves are very hospitable, perhaps more so than the Wood Elves. I've never known elven kind to be as gracious as they are in that silver city."

"How far is it from where we are?" I wondered, staggering a little as I navigated over a fallen log and under a thick low hanging branch.

"We're still some ways, unfortunately," he stated, turning his gaze to me momentarily before continuing forward. "Were that we'd taken the Elven Road we would be beyond the forest the day after tomorrow. Yet you were chased so far from it and so we must make our way there carefully, lest we fall to the hazards of this place."

"Then, Silvervale isn't far?" I felt hope spring up inside me.

He chuckled a little too darkly. "No, girl, only the edge of the forest would we reach the day after tomorrow on the road. It would be another two days hence to the Elven City."

I was a little afraid to ask. "So... how long until we reach it by *this* path we take?"

He shrugged. "A week."

"Really?" I gasped. "Is it truly so long?"

"Aye, that it is," he confirmed, hacking down a few more branches. "But don't worry your pretty little head. You may reach Silvervale later than you'd hoped, but you *will* reach it."

Amethyst growled behind me, drawing my gaze and lifting a gentle smile to my lips.

"You're right," I agreed with her. "It is better than staying lost out here."

She chuckled in her long throat and I shook my head at her. *Such a brazen dragon, you are. How funny.*

After some uncounted length of time, we stepped out of the thicker forest, casting our gaze across yet more trees. There was another deep stream and a downed tree which formed a natural bridge over it. I wasn't overly confident at crossing it, yet I knew that it was better than braving the swift stream.

Tristan moved up to the tree bridge, sheathing his sword and kicking it experimentally. He paused, studied it, kicked it a few more times then nodded with satisfaction.

"All right, it's sturdy enough to cross," he turned towards me then. "Are you all right to traverse this?"

I nodded, not so frightened and incapable as he seemed to assume. "I should be just fine. I used to balance on the walls of Castle Arvon's walkways. I think I can manage this."

Amethyst chirped something and I turned to her as she edged towards the shallow river.

"Are you sure?" I asked her.

The Dragon replied affirmatively and began crossing through the rushing waters. They only came to her ankles, hardly causing her any trouble.

I turned to see that Tristan had already climbed onto the tree bridge, carefully balancing himself despite its great width. He offered me his hand and pulled me up, my boots sliding on the mossy bark, causing me to wobble until I managed to gain my balance.

"It's a wee bit slippery," he warned me, turning slowly towards the other side of the bridge. "Just take your time, girl."

I simply nodded, choosing not to speak as I focused on my balance. The rushing of the water beneath me was disconcerting, yet I managed to keep my calm, my hands out to my sides as I traversed the uneven wooden surface. It felt like it took ages, but in truth it was not but a minute before I jumped both feet down into the dirt again. Tristan steadied me as I landed, smiling down at me.

"Nicely done, Princess," he praised.

"Thank you," I replied, the two of us starting towards the trees ahead of us as Amethyst re-joined us.

As we walked, Tristan suddenly spotted something, drawing his sword in response. He moved slowly towards a pile of white sticks sitting amidst the mud. My curiosity got the better of me and I followed him, gasping as he crouched before the sticks.

Not sticks! Bones! Human bones! Oh Gods! That's just... ugh!

"Whatever did this was big," he noted, studying the bones as he nudged them with the tip of his sword. "*Very* big."

"What could do something like this?" I asked uneasily, squeezing my arms around my queasy stomach.

"A few beasts," he answered, moving lowly as he studied tracks that lay there nearby. "Oh... no..."

"What?" I felt so alarmed, Amethyst now moving to stand right at my side.

"We need to move!" Tristan hurried to me, snatching my arm in his hand and quickly leading me away from the tracks.

The look in his eyes was one of terrible fear, his gaze darting like a frightened animal waiting to be hunted. His grip was tight and was hurting me, his steps too wide and quick for me not to fall. Somehow, I managed to avoid hitting the ground, though I staggered heavily.

"What is it?! What's got you so scared?!" I cried out, trying to ease his pace. "Would you please slow down?! I can't keep up!"

"We can't linger here!" he exclaimed swiftly, dragging me onwards without care of my struggles.

"Tristan, stop! You're hurting my arm!" I struggled, planting my feet and managing to slip free, drawing his gaze as I paused. "Tell me! What is it that you're so afraid of?!"

"Lass..."

"No, tell me! *What* kind of beast did this?!"

Suddenly, the ground shook beneath my feet and I heard the snapping of trees. I shivered as a low growl filled the air, instantly regretting asking that question.

I shouldn't have wanted to know.

I looked at Tristan, the fear in his eyes strong as his face paled, his gaze aiming up higher than I'd hoped. He held his sword ready, though it was shaking hard in his trembling hand.

Slowly, fearfully, I turned around, facing the great behemoth that had emerged from the trees behind us, Amethyst snarling at my side with her eyes ablaze and her teeth bared. I gulped hard, feeling my heart sink and my body shake in fear at the great monster now glaring down at me with dark, beady eyes.

The creature was huge, maybe twelve feet tall and shaped like a large, heavy set man. It was bald with gigantic hands, a heavy brow, flaring nostrils and sharp teeth behind thin lips. Its back looked scaly, its skin like tough rawhide and a deep grey colour. Its shoulders were hunched, and it leaned forward on its fists, knuckles to the ground. Mossy growths covered its back and it looked almost like it had a shell of stone, its tiny, angry eyes as black as onyx. It wore a ragged garment which was only enough to cover its modesty from the waist down, its hefty chest heaving over its large belly.

"That, little girl," Tristan coughed uneasily, grasping my shoulder tightly, "is a troll."

I had never seen a troll before, only ever having read stories about the creatures in my family's library at home. In all truth, seeing one face-to-face couldn't be compared to the horror described in the books, the words falling short of the real creature and its monstrous terror.

"What... what should we do?" I stammered, unable to take my eyes from the monster.

"Very, *very* slowly... back away," he urged me, pushing me behind him and trying to lead me away from the creature's sights.

I just nodded, staring wide eyed at the Troll as it sniffed the air, glaring at us with a fiery stare. Something didn't feel right about this, the beast seeming less animalistic than I had expected it to be. It was almost like it was... studying us.

As Tristan pushed me yet further behind him and farther back from the creature, its nostrils began to flare. The Troll growled more and started chomping its massive jaws agitatedly. With a terrible bellowing howl, it threw its head back, then charged, the ground shaking at its thunderous passage, the trees nearest it buckling and groaning with the heavy thudding.

"Nope, run!" Tristan shouted, spinning me around and throwing me forward.

I hitched up my dress hems in both hands, sprinting as fast as I could, panic thrilling my body with the Troll's racing strides. I cast my gaze over my shoulder through my swirling auburn hair, catching sight of it as it gained ground in mere seconds.

"Run, girl!" Tristan kept shouting, rushing to keep between me and the Troll, his sword ready to strike.

There came another roar and a flash of purple collided with the great grey monster. Amethyst clawed her front hands into the Troll's left shoulder, snapping at its face with her mighty teeth. The Troll howled and started trying to fight her off, swiping at her with its other hand as she attacked to protect me.

The Dragon and the Troll staggered and thrashed, fighting wildly with the crashing of stones and the shattering of branches. Amethyst's tail whipped up, striking it across the throat, the Troll roaring and snapping at her with its stone jaws.

"Look out!" Tristan screamed, grabbing me and pulling me away.

We hit the ground, just barely managing to avoid being crushed by the rolling bodies of the two enormous creatures. I covered my head as dirt, stones and dust rained down over me, a small cry of alarm escaping my lips as I closed my eyes.

The racket of the two creatures went on as they met in a clash of scales and stones, the sound moving from us swiftly. I propped myself up, glancing to my left to see that Tristan was already in a crouch. He was watching the battle with astonished eyes, his jaw dropping wide at the spectacle that was sure to have never before been seen by human eyes in this age, or perhaps any other.

The Troll swung its arms, swaying on its stump-like legs, roaring and grasping as Amethyst swept herself up onto its back. She held on with both claws, her tail wrapping around its waist to get a firmer grasp. She roared and snapped at the Troll's throat viciously, managing to coil her neck away each time its grasping hands snatched at her.

Tristan seized my wrist: "Come on, lass."

He dragged me to my feet and ran with me to where another tree had fallen, its roots up in the air and offering a perfect hiding place. He shoved me into this space, ushering me to get on the ground.

"You stay put, girl," he directed me. "I'm going to see if I can't help your dragon."

"You can't fight that thing!" I cried out, grabbing at his wrist in panic, fearing what such a large troll could do to someone. "It will kill you!"

"I think my chances are a whole lot better with a dragon as my fighting mate," he flashed me an unconvinced smile, then patted my shoulder. "Just stay here, girl."

"Tristan!" I grabbed at his hand as he pulled away, missing him.

Gods! He's going to get himself killed by that thing!

I turned and watched around the edge of the tree, grasping the bark with one hand, the other curling around the Pendant at my neck, seeking comfort.

Tristan rushed forward, reaching the fight just as the Troll managed to grasp hold of Amethyst's injured wing. I had never heard the Dragon scream so horrifically, releasing her grip on the Troll as she began worrying about her pain. The Troll hurled her to the ground and struck her across the face, dropping her to the earth in a tumbling roll. It then turned its attention towards Tristan as he let out a fierce yell, his left palm suddenly aglow with magic. He cast his hand forward, the icy white glow striking the Troll's face, causing the beast to howl as it staggered. It scratched at its pointed face wildly, the magic clearly hurting its eyes.

The Wanderer took his chance, leaping forward with his sword and swinging it with a bone splintering rush. The clang on stone and the cleaving of flesh echoed in the air, the Troll roaring in alarm, turning its enraged eyes down towards the man and trying to crush him.

Tristan managed to slip away, but just barely, three massive fingers and a huge thumb nearly grasping onto him. He swung around as he came out of his roll, his cloak swirling behind him as he slashed with his sword, tearing a gash across the Troll's wrist.

The Troll bellowed and struck out, hurling Tristan into the air to crash into the river with a heavy splash.

"TRISTAN!" I screamed in panic, fearing that the distance to the river and power of the blow had killed him.

The Troll jerked its head around and narrowed its eyes my way. It began stomping towards me, growling as drool slipped from its jowls.

I staggered backwards in panic, falling to the ground onto my back as I tripped on stones around where I hid by the downed tree. The Troll was nearly on me, snarling and gnashing its teeth. Panic filled my chest as I tried to scramble away, but there was no escape. The Troll reached down, and I was suddenly in the air. It had wrapped one enormous rocky hand around me and now held me tight.

I braced my hands against its rough, tough skin, staring up at it in fear and struggling to free myself from its powerful hold. I froze and stared up into its black eyes, my heart racing as short breaths wheezed from my chest. I faced the slobbering jaws, the stench of rotting meat hard on its breath.

Oh, Gods! I'm dead! It'll eat me!

A roar broke the air and Amethyst half flew with her wings spread to once again assault the Troll, desperate to free me. She drew the Troll's attention, clawing at its back and slashing at the forearm of the hand that held me. The Troll howled and swatted at her with its other hand, the Dragon burying her teeth into its neck and biting down hard, drawing a shriek of pain from the monster. I was afraid that the Troll would crush me in its hand or drop and fall on me, but I knew Amethyst would make sure that didn't happen. Almost as if she were trying to confirm this, her tail snapped up and lashed the Troll's face with its barbed tip in an attempt to pull the beast backwards.

The Troll roared in rage and suddenly managed to crush its free hand around the Dragon's long throat. She groaned out a cry of surprised anguish, releasing her hold on its skin as it tore her from its body. The Troll swung Amethyst through the air and let go, hurling her towards the river where Tristan was trying to recover. He gasped and fell backwards into the river as Amethyst crashed through the tree bridge, splintering and destroying it. Water and wood exploded around the Dragon as she landed on her back, her wings and tail flailing wildly in the chaos.

"AMETHYST!" I screamed in panic, then turned my gaze to the Troll.

The Troll snorted in a final sounding tone, then began lumbering away from the area, still clutching me in its hand. In no time it had carried me away from Tristan and Amethyst, separating me from them...

* * * * *

I struggled and squirmed as I had for what felt like hours since it had taken me. I was determined to get free, but my human hands and arms were no match against the strength of a troll's stone hard flesh. I looked up through wayward strands of my long dark auburn hair, huffing out breaths of exertion as I fought to slip loose.

All around us were the same twisted, dark trees that were all over the forest, their gnarled, pointed limbs snatching at us as we passed them by. Those hits were getting more frequent as the Troll climbed higher up the foothills, the number of trees thickening in their closeness. It was beginning to rain a little and the cold was only growing as the Troll shuffled through the underbrush, every step a thundering boom that shook the ground.

The Troll was grumbling in the way trolls do, drool slipping from its ugly lips and nearly hitting me.

"Ugh!" I shied away in disgust, bracing my hands against his flesh and closing my eyes to repel the sickening thought of the slobbering mess.

*I have to get free! This thing will probably try to eat me! I can't let it! But how?!*Then it hit me, and I righted myself so that my pendant was facing the creature directly. *Get this thing off me! Now!*

The purple energy shone from the heart-stone and a great force erupted up at the Troll. The Troll was staggered for a moment, but it didn't let me go, instead just dazed and confused. It looked around for what it was that had hit it, then continued on grimly. I willed the Pendant again, the shield lashing at the Troll hard, but still only momentarily slowing the beast. On the third blast of magic, the Troll got angry.

"Ugh! UGH! ARGH!" I cried out, arching my back and squirming as it squeezed me tight around my midriff and hips, pinning my thighs together painfully.

It jerked me right up to its face and roared at me, the strength of its stinking breath enough to throw my hair wildly behind my shoulders. As it stopped roaring and my hair settled down - though now messier - I breathed heavily, staring up at the Troll in terror. It squeezed me again, making me cringe and cry out another weak moaning gasp as I felt that my ribs and hips might break from the pressure.

"All right!" I cried out breathlessly, trying to look up at it. "I... unh... I won't try to fight! I'll... I'll... s-stop!"

The Troll nodded with a grumpy grunt, then continued on its way, still holding me firmly, but not crushing me.

Where is it taking me? What is it going to do to me? I have to find a way to escape it...

After some time, the Troll broke through the tree line with its free hand to the ground, the one holding me now up at its shoulder height to keep me in its sights. It brought me to the cliff face beneath a large craggy hill, overgrown with vines and guarded by the forest's black trees.

I looked around at where it had brought me, not really sure in which direction we had travelled. Then I noticed that there was a cave in the cliff, a strange wooden door set into a ragged looking frame and wall that sealed up the entrance.

Oh... this can't be a good place...

The Troll dumped me to the ground, the impact of the solid dirt meeting my torso stunning me. I coughed as I lay face down, my palms pressing to the ground, my hair fanning around my face and shoulders to hide me for a few moments. I heard shuffling footsteps, a chill slashing down my spine that I knew all too well yet couldn't place.

"Well done, my pet," a croaking, aging, female voice spoke as I saw fraying and old fabric moving before me, the pointed toes of boots peeking out from beneath it.

I looked up slowly to see a hunched, hooded figure standing over me. She was hiding her withered and aged face, barely any of it visible to me where I lay, her long white hair hanging from beneath the cowl across her cloak wrapped form. Long, gnarled fingers twitched at her sides from beneath the broad sleeves of her worn, tattered, brown robe, a shawl pulled tight across her shoulders and around the lower half of her face. Her eyes were green, fiery and fierce, staring out from beneath the shadows of her cowl and the wrinkled white skin of her face.

Oh Gods! A gasp of panic escaped my lips as I stared at the wilds woman, frozen in place where I lay.

The woman studied me with those piercing green eyes, twitching her head crookedly the way a raven would. She just seemed to exude magical power and I had no doubt that she was dangerous, especially given her communion with trolls.

"Yes, yes, well done indeed," she cooed at the Troll, studying me in her strange way as she did. "You found her. Just the girl I was looking for."

The Troll growled behind me and I glanced up at it as it showed her its wounds.

"You rest, my pet," she hissed softly in a raspy voice so much like Manth's. "Heal your wounds. I shall take care of the girl."

She lashed out one talon-like hand, snatching her coarse fingers around my right wrist firmly. I tried to resist, but she was stronger than I would have believed an old woman could be.

"Don't struggle, girl!" she snapped, hauling me to my feet and glaring sharply into my eyes. "I will not tolerate a child making such a fuss!"

She turned, dragging me along behind her, stretching our arms as I continued trying to resist, grasping my wrist with my other hand in an attempt to gain more strength against her. But my efforts were useless, and I knew it, my fear intensifying as she forced me towards the open door to her dark lair...

Chapter Fifteen
The Witch in the Wilds

We entered the cave, which wasn't as large as I might have first thought. It was the size of a cottage's living area, but certainly not as friendly. A cauldron bubbled away over a fire set into the far wall, a table positioned before it up against the naturally formed rock column. Racks hung above the table - which was littered with all kinds of unnerving ingredients and containers - various leaves, dead rabbits, pheasants and other things hanging there.

There were a few rooms off from this main space, curtained with old cloths to keep what looked like beds hidden away from sight. Candles glowed in various nooks and crannies in the walls, one whole wall taken over by shelves filled with dusty old books. Another was choked with items that looked to be of a magical nature and I silently worried even more in case this woman was of a dark alignment.

The woman closed the door and dragged me to where a small table large enough to accommodate six people was set in the centre of the space. A pile of candles flickered in the middle, wax covering its top as if she had no care to clean it.

"Sit," she ordered me, forcing me into the seat she'd indicated, which was facing the fire and the cauldron.

The woman turned from me and hunched her way over to the cauldron, cackling as she began stirring whatever it was that boiled within its heated iron belly.

I turned my eyes around the poorly lit space, feeling so uneasy as I grasped the seat of the chair with both hands. *This is so much like the fairytale about the witch that eats children! This is beyond frightening! What am I supposed to do?!*

She had taken the shawl from her face now, but the bad lighting still didn't lend me anymore than a few fleeting details of her aged face. She glanced over her haggard shoulder at me briefly, snatching something from the bench and casting it into the pot with a loud fizzling splash.

I swallowed hard, trembling in fear. *What is she going to do with me?*

She was scrambling through her kitchen like some kind of frantic creature, searching out her ingredients and casting them into the cauldron. She would study things, shake her head and throw them over her shoulder carelessly as she went on to the next thing, constantly searching for what she wanted.

"I knew you would come here," she muttered as she fussed in her dark kitchen, "knew which paths you would take. So *very* lucky... Yes... yes..."

"You... you were expecting me?" I murmured, trying to hide the fear in my voice.

She turned to me, nodding her hooded head: "Watched you enter the forest through ravens' eyes. The birds see all and so do I. I saw them chase you, saw the draugar knights pursue you where the fearful men dared not."

I just frowned at her, not really sure what to make of the old woman and her strange ways.

She went on as she scoured through more items messily: "You ran from my sisters, their eyes set on you even now. Yes, I saw Manth at the forest's edge. Hm, you are so important to her Master, I see..."

"Wait. Your sisters?" I stared at her in utter horror. "Manth and Keilantra are your...?"

She interrupted me as she confirmed: "Yes... The Sisters of Raven's Rest. Mother was so kind to us. How vile that my sisters turned out to be so wicked!"

A terrible, fearful sickness plunged through me as I stared at the old woman in horror. *Manth and Keilantra are her sisters... Then she truly is a witch! Oh, Gods, how much worse off could I possibly be?!*

The Witch shuffled towards me now, her approach making me cringe back in the seat. My breath hitched as she stood over me, her weathered lips twisting as she studied me again. A swiftly shaking breath heaved my chest as she cupped my chin, my eyes falling shut for a moment at her unnaturally strong touch. I forced myself to look back at her as she turned my head to get a better look at me, my hands clenching around the seat harder and my muscles tightening to the point of hurting.

"Such a pretty girl," the Witch said thoughtfully, releasing my face and hovering her claw-like hand before me. "So very pretty and innocent, yet I see the tortured hurt within you, too. Death, pain, humiliation... love..." she suddenly snatched a hair from my head with a painful tug.

"Ow!" I put my hand to where she had pulled the hair from my scalp, turning my gaze to her with annoyance.

The Witch leaned over the table, stretching the single long auburn strand out above the light of the many candles stacked there.

"You are of strong blood, girl," she mused as she seemed to read my hair. "Royal blood. The blood of two worlds... Ah... your legacy is powerful... You are a princess."

"And you're a witch," I replied nervously, grasping the chair firmly again.

She smiled beneath her hood. "Such a perceptive little girl. Intuitive and observant, quite smart too. How lovely to find a noble to be intelligent and innocent for a change."

"What do you want from me?" I asked softly, watching her as she studied my hair again in the candlelight.

"To set you on your way," she answered evenly, still eyeing off the single auburn strand. "To show you what lingers in that which has not yet come to be."

"You're... you're not going to... to hurt me?" I felt a splintering shudder slither through me as I stared worriedly at her.

The Witch turned her gaze back to me sternly, her jaw setting. "You will come to no harm here, girl."

"But... that troll..."

"My familiar," she explained simply. "Did he hurt you, child?"

I shrugged lightly. "A little. He hurt my companions, though..."

She shook her head in disappointment as she turned back towards the kitchen: "I instructed him not to cause you any harm, nor to harm any with you."

She paused then and turned back to me, reaching one gnarled hand to my chest. I braced myself back into the chair, watching her touch my pendant, but she didn't take it from me.

"You carry a dragon's heart around your neck," she murmured, then nodded. "So, you are *she* who I have seen in my foresights..."

The Witch turned away and slithered into her kitchen again, going through yet more items and even a few books as she searched for something.

"What do you mean you saw me in your foresights?" I asked, feeling slightly braver.

"I saw you in my mind's swirling mists," she explained as she continued her search, "the girl with the dragon's heart and a royal's blood. I knew I had only to wait for you to find me, and so you have."

"What for?" I frowned at her.

"For my aid," she said simply with no further explanation.

"You want to help me?" I was surprised by this.

She flicked her gaze to me sharply, flashing me her teeth. "I am *not* like my sisters. I am neither good nor evil. My allegiance is my own."

"How can you be their sister?" I wondered, studying her visage. "You're so much older than either of them..."

She paused and studied herself, then cackled lightly. "I let your young eyes see the truth of us and not the illusion my sisters prefer. Strange how such things slip one's mind with solitude such as mine."

The Witch raised her hand and there came the shimmer of magenta coloured magic glowing across her fingers. She coiled it around herself and I stared in complete awe as she seemed to change before my eyes. In moments, the haggard, hunched shape was gone, replaced by one that stood much straighter and moved with greater ease.

"There," the Witch spoke with a younger voice which was stronger and without a rasping husk. "That's much better, is it not?"

She slid back her hood and cast aside the heavy brown over-robe, stepping into the light to reveal herself. The woman before me was beautiful and tall with long dark hair that hung past her shoulders; pulled back neatly with strands weaved into intricate braids that crowned her head. Her skin was no longer pale, but now a warm creamy white a little darker than mine, her eyes sharp and filled with a living energy as her full lips pressed together into a stern expression.

She wore black leggings with brown high-topped boots, straps holding them firmly shut. Close fitting black sleeves clung to her wrists and seemed to glimmer with shimmering dust, a black corset pulled on tight around her midriff. She wore a dress of dark crimson that was almost brown, her shoulders left bare as the fabric sat lightly at her neck in a high collar. The dress hung to her shins with a tattered cut that leaned more towards her left knee, a deep purplish-grey fabric filling in the gap on the right side. Lastly, she wore a light cloak of black across her back, seeming attached into her dress with a hood hanging freely from her neck.

How did she do that? I wondered in awe.

The Witch moved to stand before me, her green eyes alight with her powerful aura."Perhaps now you will feel less frightened of me, girl?" she raised a sharp eyebrow at me, a smile tugging at the corner of her mouth. "And perhaps now we may be civil to one another?"

I just nodded, blinking away my stunned silence and swallowing back my apprehension.

"Allow me to introduce myself," the Witch said with a calm sternness, her hands on her hips. "I am Danika, youngest of the Witches of Raven's Rest, sister of Manth and Keilantra. And I intend to help you."

I stared up at her in bewilderment, in no way having been prepared for any of this. The very thought of this witch and her intentions for me far surpassed any expectations that I'd had. Still, I didn't fully trust her, and my heart ached with the fear of what she might yet do to me.

I shouldn't be rude. If I can keep myself from harm through pleasantries, then that is a better choice compared to the alternative.

"I'm..." I went to introduce myself but didn't get to finish.

"I already know who you are, girl," Danika cut me off sternly and almost rudely. "While your intention to offer me such civil niceties is certainly appreciated, it is unnecessary."

"Oh," I nodded, biting my bottom lip and twisting my hands together in my lap.

She studied me with narrowed eyes as she slowly stalked around the table, moving to my left side. Though she spoke of benevolent intentions towards me, she still carried that same frightening air as the other witches I had so far met.

"Yours is a curious tale," she said, considering me as if she knew me long before we had ever met. "Descendant of the Great Heroine of High-Realm, daughter of Arvon's ruling prince, and niece of Aldegaad's good king. Destined, it seems, to take the throne upon your uncle's passing, yet such is *not* the case. Is it, child?"

I flicked my eyes to my hands where they rested in my lap, subconsciously thumbing the velvet and silk edge of my dress.

That she knows such things about me is hardly a surprise. I doubt that there are those in High-Realm who don't know these details about my life. Such is the legacy of my family...

"Hm..." she murmured, seeming to use her powers to almost take what she needed from my mind itself, as if my thoughts were her silent informants."So much darkness haunts you," she perceived, not moving from me. "The blood of your line has been spilled in a great torrent that has wiped Arvon from the face of the world, and left Aneuran under the rule of a cruel tyrant who undeservingly bears *your* crown."

She drew in a sharp breath, the sound shaking behind me as I stared at the wood grains in the table, my eyes weakening in the candlelight.

"You have been made to flee for your own life's sake," she said slowly, "to seek refuge beyond the borders of your homeland, guarded by the only ones capable of defending you..."

"This is all... *very* interesting," I let out a shaking breath, edging my gaze up through my auburn locks to glimpse her dark visage. "Yet it's common knowledge and I am hardly surprised that you have come to know it. Even here, in these dark, forebodingly evil forests far from civilisation..."

"Civilisation is an illusion, girl," the Witch responded with her offhanded casualness, moving around to stand over my right side. "Such things only mask the truth of the world..."

"Which is?" I gave her a questioning gaze and a raised eyebrow.

A small smile pulled at her lips: "That we are *all* merely wild things. That *all* is chaos and that mortal beings seek to bring order to such things where it can never be. All things are yet fluid, the future not truly assured and the past capable of being rewritten. Yet, there are *some* things that *must* be."

"Like what?" I felt my chest moving quickly, though I tried to remain calm.

She paced a few feet towards the other end of the table, then turned to face me through her raven-coloured locks."You," she said softly, almost as if it were some great secret she was trying to whisper without others overhearing.

"Me?" I frowned hard, vividly feeling my chest and shoulders moving with my heightened breaths, quiet though they were.

"And all that you have done, and all that you are yet to do," she answered, lifting a crystal ball up in her hand from the table and studying it with her dark sage eyes. "You have a destiny you *must* come to face, yet many have sought to blind you to your path."

I shuddered a little and leaned myself back in the seat, pushing my shoulder blades hard against the uneven wood of the chair. My hand instinctively reached for my pendant again.

"It has come to you," the Witch seemed distant as she stared into the smoky, murky white orb which shimmered with some greyish light in her claw-like hand, "the Heart of a Dragon, now bound to your own. For too long it has waited in silence, yearning for its new Holder to be revealed. You were born to such..."She snapped her gaze to me, a deep knowing burning in her expression as her eyes widened with life: "And the Dragon... she calls to you as you do to her..."

"I... I don't know what you mean," I tried to lie, not really sure I could conceal much from her strange knowing.

The Witch nodded softly, studying my eyes and keeping my gaze locked with hers in such a seemingly easy way: "Please, do not assume to take me for a fool, girl. I *know* you and your dragon share a bond between you; one that allows her to seek you out at your silent urging. The powers of the Dragon Pendants are very well known to me, much as they are to my sisters. This, I am certain you already know after your less than welcoming *stay* in Castle Ortagaad."

"How... how do you know about that?" I was shocked, fearful as the thrill of panic filled my heart once again, trying to choke me.

"I am a Seer of many things," she answered softly and slowly, every word deliberate. "I see things that *are*, things that *were*, things that *may yet be*, and, of course, those things that are *destined* to be."

"You... you must have... j-just heard of me from others these past weeks..." I tried, not convinced myself that this made any real sense.

"Come, girl. You do not *truly* believe such self-wrought lies, do you?" she frowned at me curiously. "Your woman's mind - young though it is - knows what I say is true."

"H-how... how much do you know?" I stammered, my fear at her incredible power refusing to leave me.

She straightened up; her eyes cold with the knowledge, she then began to speak: "I know of *all* the pain you have suffered since reaching the eighteenth year of your birth. I know of the tortures inflicted upon you for two years, of the loneliness and cold that bound you in that tower. Of the betrayals and how one of your last remaining blood sought to control you through carnal torment and forced nuptials. Of the lies of one you called a friend; the man who cost you your mortality to regain his own..."

I sighed and nodded, feeling a tear trickle down my cheek. The horrid memories of the Shadow Lord's dark ritual returned to my mind and my heart immediately wept as the pain assaulted me anew.

"I know of the fantasies that once gave you such hope for your days to come, yet now fill your young heart with eternal grief," she went on gently, almost sympathetically. "And of the man your heart yet calls to..."

"Carden..." I gasped his name through my tears, meeting her gaze.

Danika nodded gently. "You long for your reunion, for him to embrace you once more and offer you his tender, loving touch. You fear you shall never see him again... That he shall spurn you for what was done to you... Do you not, girl?"

I nodded with teary eyes at her, whispering: "Yes."

She smiled softly and stroked my cheek. "Do not fear, child. I shall offer you the hope you need. But after."

"After what?" I frowned.

The door banged open and I spun in my seat as Danika watched with a hard gaze. Tristan stood in the doorway with his sword drawn, Amethyst peeking her head through behind him. I felt overjoyed to see my dragon and a little gladdened to see the Wanderer.

"After this most rude interruption," Danika growled disapprovingly, folding her arms in front of her chest with an icy glare of green.

"Princess, are you all right?" Tristan demanded of me, aiming his sword's point at the Witch fiercely. "Did this Void harlot hurt you?"

"Oh yes! The Fool rushes into *my* Sanctum offering only threat and insult!" Danika exclaimed angrily, glaring at him.

"Be quiet you!" he ordered her, edging closer with a fiery gaze and a hardened jaw. "We will not be bewitched by a she-devil who cavorts with trolls!"

"How brave you must think you are!" she responded sarcastically, rolling her eyes at him. "You think by rushing in here to snatch the girl from my *wicked* claws to redeem your past betrayals and thus gain her favour! Yet, all you will find is disappointment and the knowledge that you are nothing more than a prudent fool of the highest form!"

"How about I take you outside and set a fire in your flesh?!" Tristan threatened, brandishing his sword further towards her. "Hm?! See if witches truly are made of wood?!"

"ENOUGH!" I shouted, standing up and flashing my hard gaze between both of them before finally turning to Tristan. "She hasn't hurt me, all right? She's offered her help..."

"Help?" he scoffed, looking at the woman as if she were filth. "This... this... *hag* would offer us help?"

"I would offer *the girl* help," Danika clarified harshly. "Should you benefit as a result of my efforts is merely coincidence."

"Truly? You would deny me, yet aid her?" he raised an eyebrow, smirking incredulously.

"I do not aid betrayers, liars and fools," she stated, then smirked. "Sadly, you happen to be *all* three."

Tristan chuckled and shook his head, turning towards me. "Whatever you say, woman."

"You should be more courteous to those who hold greater command of this place than you do, Tristan of Ivansten," she said, drawing his stunned gaze. "Without my knowledge and aid, you would fail in your promise to the girl."

"How do you know who I am?" he looked so pale and frightened.

I grabbed his arm and looked up into his haunted gaze before she could reveal any more secrets to him, knowing it would only hurt him: "She has some kind of magical seeing power. I'm not sure how, but she knows things..."

"I have the gift of foresight," Danika explained evenly, no pride, only her same almost sarcastically bored tone in her voice. "I also see things that were."

"So, then the legends are true," Tristan nodded, sheathing his sword. "You are the one they call the Witch in the Wilds."

"Yes, that is what the peoples of Gorvenna and Dorvana have come to call me," she nodded thoughtfully. "Many also assume that I am allied to the Revenant of Arnath since both of us occupy the same forest. Such foolishness."

"So, you're not evil?" he seemed doubtful.

She threw him a hard stare. "My allegiance is to neither the good or the evil, only to myself. I only aid those in deserving need."

"Then why help us?" he asked.

"As I have *already* stated, I am helping *the girl*," she responded warily, bored with this.

"What help would you offer, Danika?" I asked with genuine interest before Tristan could speak again.

"That needed to set you on your path," she said with a shrug and gestured to the chairs. "Sit and I shall reveal to you all that you need to know."

Tristan snorted and laughed, shaking his head. "Oh, wonderful! A fortune teller!"

"You believe my power to be the falsehood of a trickster? You would think magic nothing more than a cheap hoax to dazzle the weak minded?" she almost seethed.

"Magic, I believe to be real," he clarified. "I've seen its power firsthand, but do not hold stock in fortune telling. Our fates are our own to be made."

"That is most certainly true," the Witch agreed with a nod as she sat at the head of the table, her back to the fire. "Yet there are those moments in our lives that must come to be, and those are what I foresee."

"Right, come on, lass," Tristan gestured to me, nudging my shoulder and jabbing his thumb towards the door. "We'd best leave before she asks for our gold... Well, *my* gold since I'm sure you have none."

I threw him a disapproving glare for that, folding my arms firmly. *Just because I am without any gold of my own, he would think to tease me like this? I should say "well, I didn't have a chance to ask anyone to spare me a few coins while I was running for my life!" Bastard!*

"You would do better to stay here until the storm passes," Danika said mistily, studying her crystal ball.

"What storm?" Tristan sniped at her with a glare.

Suddenly, there was the banging roar of thunder and we both turned to the door where Amethyst groaned, covering her head with one wing. Rain was pouring down so heavily that the instant we set foot outside we would be drenched.

Danika smiled victoriously at us. "*That* storm."

Tristan looked at me and shrugged. "Well... uh... I... suppose staying within shelter would be wiser than attempting to traverse the forest in this. Any camp we make would be drowned within minutes."

I just nodded at him, silently thinking on how foolish his attitude had been.

Danika set about getting us settled in for our stay with her, offering us blankets, as her cave wasn't exactly that warm, even with the hearth and the candles. She then completed her cooking in the cauldron, revealing that what I had first thought to be a witch's potion was in fact dinner. When I asked about the amount she smiled and said that she knew she would need enough for the three of us.

We ate together, Danika offering homemade bread and fresh water from her well, which both Tristan and I were grateful to have. Once we were done eating, she had me move to sit in a cushiony chair, wrapping a blanket around me to guard against the cold. She lit a small brazier that sat in the wall beside this strange sitting area, spreading heat through the space within moments.

"Will Amethyst be all right outside?" I worried, looking to the closed door and the little hole in the wall that served as a window, the light now gone outside.

"Your dragon will be quite fine," the Witch responded as she moved to sit in the chair opposite me, drawing her old woman's shawl across her shoulders. "Like my troll, she will have found shelter befitting her needs, yet she will remain close enough to keep a watchful eye on you."

I just nodded, satisfied by that answer. *I suppose dragons are such large creatures that they must be used to sleeping in the elements, much like trolls must be.*

"Now then," Danika rested her elbows on her knees, leaning towards me across the small gap left between us. "Shall we begin?"

"Begin what?" I frowned, flicking my gaze to where Tristan huddled in his seat and blanket by the brazier.

"I said I would guide you to find your true path; that which has been shielded from you by the designs of others," she answered softly.

I shrugged one shoulder and leaned forward as she beckoned for my hands. She took them in hers and turned them so that my palms were facing up towards the ceiling. She closed her eyes and started to concentrate, her grasp firm, but not painful. I glanced to Tristan worriedly, not really sure what to expect from this, then turned my eyes to the Witch again.

"Your path is filled with great turmoil," she uttered gently, but clearly, her eyes remaining closed, flickering beneath her thick black eyelashes. "I sense such terrible fear still plaguing your adolescent heart. The Great Heroine..."

"What about my ancestor?" I asked with a gentle frown and a curious tilt of my head as I studied her face.

"She offers her mantle to you from the Beyond," she said as if she were seeing such images with her darkened eyes. "Her foe has become yours and so too her responsibilities..."

I shook my head, my heart heaving in my chest and my breath catching. "No... No way..."

"I see you clad in armour with a glowing sword held aloft," she described distantly. "The Guardians themselves look to stand behind your standard, as do many others; the orders of old returning to once more face the evil which now threatens the world with *you* as their champion..."

"No!" I cried in fearful disbelief. "I don't want that! I *never* wanted to be like my ancestor!"

"The cloak of destiny enwraps you, girl," she went on, ignoring me. "You stand as the only one who can unite what is fractured, who can defeat what would destroy this world."

"There must be others," I said, determined to avoid this. "I'm no hero..."

"You would seek to avoid this destiny, yet it is only what *may* be," she expressed deeply, opening her eyes and looking at me.

"Then what *will* be?" I asked, hopeful that she would see something come that could bring light back to my darkened world. "What is my *true* fate?"

She let her eyes drift shut again and she began to seek through her powers, looking into the future.

"Close your eyes and I shall show you," she told me gently.

I let my eyes drift closed, trying to clear my mind until I could only sense the warmth of the nearby fire, the comfort of the chair and blanket, the scent of the herbs and the incense that drowned out the cave's stenches. A new warmth filled me, and light drenched my vision as I came to see a truly beautiful place.

It was that same intricately picturesque white palace high in the cliffs overlooking a great valley below. Dragons swooped and soared across the verdant green cliffs and splashed through the sapphire waterfalls as the sunlight played across their great scales. Snow capped the highest points of the cliffs and the peaks that surrounded the valley, a magic here unlike anything I had ever come to know in the world.

I was dressed in a flowing white gown, my arms left bare, the fabric of soft silk and sheer cloth. I felt my pendant around my neck, my exposed neckline, face and arms cooled by the sweet breeze of this wonderful place.

"Leander," I turned around, my long auburn hair catching around my shoulders as I faced the voice's owner, smiling as my heart warmed.

"Carden," I was so happy to see him.

He was dressed in dark clothes, almost entirely in black, his shirt left unbuttoned at the collar. His eyes were dazzling, taking on a golden hue through their green sheen, his skin so much fairer now.

He pulled me into his arms and gently kissed me. My arms hooked around his neck as his large hands pressed to hold my hips firmly, this vision more real than any other I had seen so far.

He let go of my lips and smiled as he gazed into my steel blue eyes, still holding me so close.

"Always, my love," he murmured earnestly, his smile so warm and true.

"Always," I agreed, and we kissed yet again.

I would easily have lived in that feeling, have stayed there until my last moment, but it was not to be. The image of that happiness and wonderfully warm future abruptly went dark and I saw only cold shadows that swirled around me. Blue flames suddenly erupted from the blackness and I felt such terrible fear flowing through me.

A great beast towered above me, its eyes glowing with evil blue fire, the same flames lapping up around its shadow and smoke wrapped body. Two enormous wings bigger than anything I had ever seen struck out above it and the beast roared, opening a great maw at me, its throat white and blue with fire. I turned away from it and saw the green eyes beneath the black cowl I feared more than any others. The Shadow Lord moved towards me, smirking as he reached for me, a strangled scream escaping my lips as I felt his hand close around my throat.

Behind the Shadow Lord, I saw Carden laying on the ground, face down, sprawled there with his sword at his right hand. He looked up at me with frightened eyes, reaching out helplessly. In the shadows behind him there stood a hooded figure with the black wings of an angel, a staff of gold in his skeletal hand topped with an Ankh. His blue eyes glowed out from the blackness of his hood, his left hand beckoning to me, calling me toward him...

The vision exploded around me and I felt a terrible pain, snapping back to the waking world and Danika's sanctuary.

"Lass! Lass!" Tristan had me by my shoulders, shaking me out of the trance, worry in his eyes. "Snap out of it girl! Princess! Come on!"

I fell back in the seat as I slipped from Danika's grasp, hitting the cushions hard. I couldn't breathe, tears burning my eyes as my chest heaved so swiftly, I feared I would choke.

"Are you all right?" the man worried, looking into my eyes. "Lass? Are you all right? Leander?"

My name broke the terrifying spell and I blinked as I met his eyes. I turned my gaze to Danika, her expression full of deep thought and a cold knowing as she held her palms together, fingertips to her lips.

"What... what was that?" I choked out fearfully.

"You asked that I should show you your fated future, the one that *will* come to be," she replied softly, almost sadly.

"I don't understand," I tried to make myself calm down, holding onto Tristan's arms for support. "*What* was all of that?"

"True love, happiness," she said, then met my gaze direfully, "and death."

"Death?!" I stared wide eyed at her. "No! No, not him! Please, don't let him..."

"The death is not that of your true love," she told me solemnly, almost hesitantly. "It is yours."

I couldn't speak, my throat tight and my voice missing as I felt my eyes lose focus. My tears slid free and chilled my cheeks, blinding me as sobs of panic began to break my chest. I tightened my hands on Tristan's arms, crushing the fabric of his shirt with my fingers.

It... it can't be real! Please... tell me it's not! I... I don't want to die! Please... no... I screamed mentally.

"I am truly sorry, girl," Danika sighed, standing and moving into the shadows of the column by her curtained sleeping area. "*This is* your assured fate. Love, happiness and death. It cannot be changed."

She disappeared behind the curtain as I started to cry, allowing Tristan to hug me tight in his large arms. I closed my eyes and nearly screamed my agonising sobs out with my aching heart, burying my face into his shirt's sleeve.

"Shh," he whispered, "it's all right, girl. It's not true. It's not true..."

I wanted to believe him, but couldn't, left now with only one thought: *I don't want to die...*

* * * * *

The storm raged outside for three long, silent days, its thunder tearing the sky and its rains flooding the grounds and swelling the rivers. I felt as if the sky knew what terrible fear now burned inside me and was expressing its own sadness.

I didn't speak on Danika's foresights with either her or Tristan again after that first night, choosing to find solitude in the small sleeping space behind the other curtain the Witch had graciously offered me. Tristan had been allowed to sleep in the living space on his bedroll, at his own insistence to grant me some measure of privacy.

Danika remained the gracious and courteous host, ensuring we were well fed before we would have to depart again. She was so much kinder than she let on, and so very unlike her wicked sisters.

The visions continued to plague me, and I suffered horrible nightmares, the old terrors of the Shadow Lord murdering me returning. I hoped so desperately that he truly didn't succeed in killing me as he'd promised, wishing that all that was true of the vision was mine and Carden's love.

At last, the storm passed and while the sun didn't shine as brightly as it could, the day dawned without the rains' wet touch.

Danika provided Tristan with the supplies we would need, then offered to lead us to where we could safely travel without fear of the forest's dangers. She drew her hood over her head and walked with her bone and feather topped staff in hand, a dark green gem its crowning glory. Her troll followed on beside her, lumbering through the forest without fear and pushing aside every obstacle that might hinder us.

I walked beside Amethyst, wrapped now in a grey hooded coat Danika had given me to keep me warm. Winter was beginning to creep in and there was frost on the ground, though only very little.

After some hours, we came to an overlook that allowed us to behold all that yet lay before us. I stared across it all in astonishment, the grey skies and far off coldness of the Bargoth Mountains doing little to diminish the majesty of our view.

The Forest of Arnath stretched on for so much farther than I would have believed, covering everything that lay between the much closer Nartarn'lath Mountains on our left and the far distant Bargoth Mountains to our right. Directly before us stood the greatest mountain I had ever seen; the Firehorn, the highest in all of High-Realm. Beyond it were more woodlands and rolling fields that were yellowing with winter's coming. In the far distance to my right, I saw a silvery glimmer and I guessed it could only be the City of Silvervale - or perhaps I hoped it was.

"Here we come to the border of Dorvana," Danika declared as she came to a stop at the great overlook's edge, leaning on her staff, "domain of the Rangers. Before you lies the Firehorn, High-Realm's grandest of mountains. Keep your path towards it and you shall find your way to the Elven Road," she turned to me and gave me a tiny smile, "and hence the safety you seek, girl."

"I...I," Tristan sighed awkwardly, then met the Witch's gaze, "was wrong about you. I had thought all witches to be wicked, yet you are kinder than any I have ever known."

She raised an eyebrow at him, surprised by his words. "Then your mistrust of me was not born of foolishness, but of the pains inflicted by experience."

"You have my thanks," he pressed a hand to his breast and bowed his head gently to her, "for all you have done."

Danika flashed him a tiny smile, then turned to face me, her gaze much kinder and gentler.

"I don't know how to ever thank you," I said softly, twisting my hands together in front of me beneath the coat's heavy sleeves.

"Your thanks is not necessary, girl," she replied, kinder than any other moment I had spent in her company for the past four days.

"Still, I wish I could repay you," I sighed.

"You are most welcome. Now, I must take my leave," she looked out to the way before us and nodded to it. "Follow the river trails. They are the safest and will lead you to your desired path."

"Thank you so much, Danika," I hugged her, surprising her with my embrace.

Danika hesitantly and uncertainly wrapped her arms around me, tightening her hold on me for a few moments. We separated and she looked into my eyes with a gentle smile.

"Know that not all is tragedy," she told me softly, brushing a few strands of hair from my eyes with her finger. "I have set you upon your destined path, and while there is still much to beware, there is also hope."

"There is?" I asked quietly.

She nodded softly and smiled brighter. "Trust that all shall come to be right, even with what horrors you have yet seen. You *will* be reunited with him. Sooner than you think."

"And what of my... my..." I couldn't finish, the fear too great.

"I shall simply say this," she responded gently, "*Love* conquers all, Princess Leander. Farewell."

She turned and strode away, beckoning to the Troll. He looked to us with a gentle growl, almost saying goodbye, then lumbered after the Witch, the two of them leaving us standing there on the rocky overlook.

"Well then, lass," Tristan drew my gaze, shifting his pack further onto his back as he smiled faintly down at me, "shall we get going?"

I nodded. "Yes. We should. Lead on."

"So, you trust me then?" he asked curiously.

I flashed him a small smile. "More than I once did."

We started down the sloping path from the overlook, making in the direction of the Firehorn as Danika had directed us. By nightfall we were below the trees once again where we made camp under the tarp Tristan carried.

I was content then to lay there by my dragon, wrapped in the furs and blankets of my bedroll. Tristan had cooked some of the food the Witch had gifted us, and we had eaten, but my need for food was less than it should have been.

My mind was wandering, and I found myself laying on my back, holding the Pendant in my hand. I turned it in my fingers, studying its shimmering purple heart-stone, the firelight dancing through its many facets as if the stone's own life-force were drawing it in.

Can you protect me from that frightening future, my silent guardian? With you, the Shadow Lord can't even see me, let alone come to bring me harm. Just tell me that you can keep me from meeting his promised end.

I let the Pendant fall to my chest, and I rested back into the furs of the bedroll, staring at the campfire and allowing it to hypnotise me into a drowsiness that would carry me to my rest. I dreamed that Carden lay with me, his large arms wrapped around me, his gentle kiss to my neck comforting me.

I know we will be together again, Carden. We can't be apart forever. True love can never be kept apart. I love you, my Carden...

Chapter Sixteen
Tribal Etiquette

T he next few days were long and silent, there was little for Tristan and I to discuss. He attempted to broach the subject of the Witch's foresights, but I truly had no desire to relive the terrible vision which yet haunted my waking and dreaming minds alike.

My nights were restless, spent squirming beneath the furs of my bedroll under Amethyst's concerned molten gaze. Dreams of horror would fill my sleeping eyes and *He* would come for me anew with my slipping into rest. I couldn't escape him, no matter how I ran or tried, every effort I made ending with the same nightmarish image. Screams would rip from my throat and lips as I was hurled back to the waking world, crying inconsolably where I lay. Each time, Tristan would be at my side, holding me close and crooning soft words meant to ease my fear-burned soul.

It was maybe the sixth day since leaving the Witch's company that we were once again trekking on towards the Firehorn, its great summit towering before us above the trees' thick canopies. I was sullen and silent; my thoughts numb now as a desperate means to prevent myself from thinking on the terrible visions haunting me like relentless ghosts. My only focus was on ensuring I kept my footing amongst the foliage and the ruins of the ancient forests.

It was after midday when we came upon a glittering waterfall rushing into a large pool that flowed into a gentle stream. The sound reached us along with the fresh scent before we saw the small sanctuary, inviting us in to find the respite we were desperately needing.

Tristan agreed it was a good spot to take some rest, setting down his heavy pack and stripping out of his long coat.

I sat on a rock with my hands clasped together in front of me, leaning on my knees as I let my eyes study the shimmers dancing through the calm water's surface. Amethyst grunted something about hunting, then lumbered off into the surrounding trees.

I glanced over my shoulder at her tail slithering into the underbrush as she left. *Just be safe, Amethyst. I don't want anything to happen to you.*

I felt her assurance that she would be fine without her needing to even call to me, a ghostly smile tugging at my lips as I returned my tired eyes to the pristine waters only inches from my feet.

Tristan looked to me as he rolled up his shirt sleeves, crouching on one knee by the water's edge.

"Where's your dragon?" he asked, preparing to dip his hands into the pool.

"Hunting," I replied simply.

"Hunting?" he queried.

I turned my eyes to him as he was washing his face and neck, shrugging in response: "Her hunger is far greater than ours, and much more than what little we carry in your pack can satisfy."

"Aye," he replied, wiping water from his eyes so he could open them again, shaking droplets from his large, coarse hands. "A beast as large as she must desire something my size to feel even a little relief from her hunger."

I smiled grimly and nodded.

As my eyes returned to studying the ripples in the natural pool, I could feel him watching me. I knew he was worried about me, his kindness all too clear in so many ways. I dreaded that he might once again try to coax me into talking about things I would rather leave unspoken, yet I felt the need to confess my fears all the same.

"Are you okay?" he asked.

Without facing him, I nodded. "Fine."

"But you're not, though," he stated, his observations of me over the past ten days never having been hidden from me. "I can tell."

I glanced at him as he stood up, his hands dripping at his sides, water staining his now yellowed shirt around the neck and edges of his sternum. His brown eyes were gentle as he studied me through his dampened reddish-blonde hair, his beard beaded with water after his attempt at something like a clothed bath.

"You cry out in the night, screaming whilst you sleep," he said, his voice soft, though still a little rough as he confronted me about my nocturnal frights, "and by day you are sullen like the deepest of storm clouds in Winter's bitterest of frosts. Though you have not deemed to speak on this cold vex, I know what it is..."

"Please... just don't," I whispered, closing my eyes and letting my head sink.

"Will you continue to burden yourself with this latest chain after all those you have previously cast off?"he was standing over me now, his shadow blocking the warming midday light from my closed sights. "Must you truly carry this burden alone, letting it devour your soul and the bright, beautiful girl you really are? That, to me, is a greater tragedy than any the Shadow Lord could ever inflict."

Slowly, I opened my eyes and met his gaze as he crouched down beside me. I felt tears starting to well up again, but I managed to keep them from flowing for the moment. I had grown so tired of crying.

"I know the Witch's vision frightened you," Tristan said gently, reaching forward and holding my clasped hands between his. "It would frighten any man or woman with a mind of sanity and a heart of good. Death... is not a thing faced easily, especially for one so young as you, girl. Especially your own."

I grimaced and cringed as he said that, wishing I could un-see all that Danika had shown me. But that isn't the way of visions.

"I can't get the images out of my head," I confessed, feeling a tear slip free. "They are so strong that I now see them with my waking eyes."

I closed my eyes against the urge to sob, drawing in a hard, sharp breath in an attempt to compose myself.

"As I have since first this began that day back at Averet, I find myself wishing for things to be as they were," I said, my voice wobbling sadly. "All that was good has been taken from me, and now the creature who hunts me means to take my life as well. And where I had hope and was determined to fight against him to save my life, I now find that this path is set, and that the fate which I struggle against is almost assured."

The pain in my heart grew as I said those words, a knot tying in my midriff and making me feel sick. All I could do was close my eyes for a few moments before I opened them again to meet his brandy-coloured gaze with grief-filled fear.

"How?" I asked in a soft, frightened voice. "How can I ever hope to battle Fate itself, Tristan?"

"I don't know, lass," he said gently, "but there must be a way."

I thought about it, staring at his coarse, sun tanned hands enwrapping my smaller, softer, fair skinned ones.

"Danika said that Love conquers all," I recalled softly. "If that is so, then it is Carden I need. Our shared love might be all that can spare me such a fate."

"Carden," he looked so solemn as he repeated my love's name, sitting back from me a little. "It is Carden you need..."

I frowned curiously at him, the way he spoke seeming... odd.

"Yes... Since first we laid eyes on one another, we have been in love, though we didn't confess such feelings until we were in Eilath," I said quietly.

"Then it is he who governs your heart?" Tristan's expression confused me, his stare like that of a man who had been struck with a sudden realisation of something unforeseen.

I nodded slowly, staring at him curiously. "Yes. I love him with all my heart. I only wish I could be with him now... I miss him so much."

Tristan blinked and smiled weakly at me. "Then I am happy for you, lass. Truly I am. You are such a girl who deserves only the truest of loves, and I hope that you once again find yourself in his embrace before much more time passes."

He stood then, and started back to where his pack lay, unrolling his sleeves and gathering up his other garments to don once again.

"I doubt we'll find any place as fine as this before dusk falls anew," he said, pulling on his jacket, then buckling his sword to his hip again. "We'll take the afternoon and rest here this night, then make for Silvervale again with the breaking dawn."

"Tristan, where are you going?" I asked softly, tightening my hands' grip on each other.

"Hunting, much like your dragon," he responded, taking up his bow and quiver. "The Witch's supplies have lasted us well this past week but will barely hold out on their own before we reach Silvervale. And I am in the mood for elk."

"Be careful," I urged him.

"Don't worry, Princess," he flashed me a toothy grin as he slung his quiver over his shoulder, "you shan't find yourself without your loyal guide. Stay by this pool and I shall return ere you begin to miss my company."

With that, the Wanderer vanished into the forests much as my dragon had, leaving me alone with only the trickling of the waters to keep me company.

As I turned my wandering gaze back to the shimmering surface of the pool, I found myself contemplating the conversation we had just had. Tristan's expression at the mention of my love for Carden was puzzling. Had I not known different, I would think that he had some secret yearning in his heart he hadn't yet confessed to me but longed to.

Think of what he has told you, I reminded myself, losing my vision to the waters. *His wife passed from this world and he has spent decades upon decades alone, cursed by that vile witch, Keilantra. He doesn't seek anything from me. He longs to have that which was taken from him. The mention of my love for Carden has reminded him of that which he shared with her.* I sighed as these thoughts made their case to me. *He must be so sad without her. I can only imagine the pain crushing his heart. Truly, I hope I don't find myself experiencing the same agonies as him. I hope I am able to be reunited with Carden again soon.*

Another slow breath slipped from my chest and passed my lips. I needed relief from the discomfort I felt. I considered the pool, stooping to my knees and sitting on my haunches then.

Slipping out of the grey coat, I cupped my hands and took water from the pool to satisfy my thirst before anything else. It was so soothing and tasted better than all other pools and streams the forest had so far offered us. I breathed in a comforted breath, letting my eyes drift shut as I felt the sunlight warm my soft skin.

Perhaps he had a good idea with his need to cleanse himself. A proper bath would be better, but for now I think I'll take what relief I can from this discomfort. And it has been so long since I've washed.

I loosened the cord of my bodice and slipped the shoulders of my dress down so that they nearly sat around my elbows, reaching into the pool and soaking my hands. If the sun hadn't been out, I would have felt a deep chill washing like this, but its light only helped to keep me warmed.

With each handful of water lapping over my skin, I felt more and more at ease, dampening my hair in an attempt to cleanse some of the grime from my dark auburn locks. Letting the water trickle over my soft flesh soothed so many more aches than I knew I had, and I started yearning to fully submerge myself.

A twig snapped, a gasp ripping from my lips. My eyes widened as I sought out the source of the sound, my chest heaving a little too quickly.

Calm down. It's probably nothing. Just Tristan hunting nearby.

"Tristan?" I called out, watching the forest for some sign of the Wanderer. "Tristan, is that you?"

Forcing myself to relax when there came no answer, I returned to bathing what skin I could, attempting to loosen my dress enough that I could wash more of my chest and midriff.

Another, louder snap and the definite stomp of footsteps startled me. I quickly pulled my clothing back together and tightened the lacing to shield my modesty, getting to my feet.

"Tristan?!" I shouted, panic rising in my chest.

Out of the underbrush came a burly green skinned man with tusks jutting from his bottom jaw. His heavy brow creased, and his black eyes narrowed at the sight of me. He had long black hair pulled back from his face, his immensely muscular torso exposed. Only a skirt of fur and hide around his hips, skin boots on his feet and hide bracers on his massive wrists served as his clothing. In his right hand he clutched a sword that reminded me of an oversized butcher's cleaver, human skulls worn as trophies on a strip of leather crossing from his shoulder to his hip.

I trembled at the sight of the mighty Orc, staggering backwards and bracing my hand against the rock I had been sitting on as I crouched awkwardly. All I could do was stare up at him, a few strands of my hair flicking in front of my eyes with my frightened breaths.

My thoughts were numb, my voice stolen away and my body rigid with fear as I waited to see what he would do.

The Orc twisted his jaw at me, glowering as he took in the sight of my frightened form before him.

"Hu-mon gul..." he growled in a low, snarling voice, then demanded: "Wop ca chu morvi na tetch sacra placae?"

I couldn't answer him, partly out of not understanding Orcish, partly out of unbridled terror of the burly, angry creature staring down at me.

He snarled at my silence, bared his teeth, then bellowed out a booming roar of rage.

I slipped and hit the ground as he rushed towards me, bringing his sword up ready to kill me. I tried to scramble backwards, crying out in panic as the threat of this creature drew rapidly nearer. That familiar heat warmed my chest as the Orc reached me, then suddenly a purple flash of light hurled him into the air. The

Pendant cast him away from me, his body landing with a thundering force into the water.

As I got to my feet, eyes locked on the creature now stunned and treading slowly in the pool, I thought *I am not so defenceless anymore. Not with the Pendant...*

"Hu-mon!" another bellow came from my left and I screamed as I narrowly jumped out of the chop of another Orc's war axe.

He turned his black eyes towards me, a groundmerk skull on his shoulder, hides wrapped around him and furs stuffed into iron bracers on his thick forearms.

"Kul hu-mon..." he snarled, showing his teeth as he wrenched his axe from the stone he had cleaved in half.

He swung at me and once again the Pendant shot its glowing strike from its heart. In only a moment, the Orc was slammed backwards into a tree, breaking it in half and dropping to the ground amidst the leaves and branches. He stirred, bewildered and dizzied by the sudden impact he had endured.

I have to get out of here!

I backed away, but before I could turn, a large green hand clamped around my mouth and jaw, pinning my lips shut as a startled scream was muffled behind my teeth. My fingers clawed at the creature's enormous knuckles, desperation and panic flooding all of my senses. His flesh smelled of dirt and many hours in the wilderness, a musk of his kind tainting my nostrils and making me gag.

I squirmed and struggled, feeling my pendant trying to strike out as I glimpsed its flashing, snapping and now wild energy illuminating beyond his fingers. Like me, it was lashing out in an attempt to free me from this third Orc who had ambushed me from behind.

No! I can't get free! Let me go! Let go!

The Pendant flashed more fiercely with my thoughts and I tried to protest as his other hand snatched at it. I felt the chain unclasp to spare itself from tearing, and the light of the purple heart-stone died in his fist.

My struggles increased and I sought to land a kick to whatever vulnerable parts of him I could blindly reach. He didn't seem disturbed even a little by me thrashing my heels into his shins and striking at his body with my arms. Then, his forearm crushed around my chest and I gasped as the air was choked from my lungs.

"Nonk strak anornk, gul," he hissed into my ear, his hot breath stinking of rotting meat. "Morg shil harkar chu ikk chu nonk reshek."

Fear overwhelmed me, increased by my inability to understand his demand of me. I fought and squirmed, tears slipping down my cheeks with each terrified groan and agonised breath.

He jerked me back hard and roared at me: "Reshek, gul! Or Morg kul chu!"

Stop struggling! He'll kill me if I keep struggling!

Still breathing hard, I let my squirming limbs fall limp and I held as still as I could manage as the Orc kept my head angled back against his bare chest. I glanced up at him out of the corner of my eye through tears, grasping his steel plated forearm with both hands helplessly.

The brutish man smirked down at me. He was scarred and had long black hair framing his lantern-jawed face.

"Gorr gul," he cooed in a way that was less than comforting, "gorr. Nar Morg shil nor kul chu."

I didn't know what else to do except nod to show my willingness to do as he said.

I have no idea what I'm nodding about. Gods, he might have asked me to do something I really won't want to. I wish I could understand these creatures.

The Orc started laughing loudly and I turned my eyes to the other two, who were now finding their way to join us. The one who had hit the tree retrieved his axe, glaring at me as the one who had landed in the pool was shaking himself free of as much water as he could.

"Amorka! Var amorka!" the Orc holding me chortled at them. "Chu markie braw-wers bekked ba e min hu-mon gul!"

"Shaltak, Morg!" the one with the axe snapped at him. "Gul ha mana!"

"Her mana ke dokk!" the wet Orc beat his chest with one hand, and I could only guess he spoke of strength... or possibly anger. "Yek, shi min! Lork rek her na cal!"

The Orc's gesture was violent as he imitated breaking something in half with his huge hands. I cringed back into the Orc holding me, terrified of what painfully horrid things his kinsman was saying.

"Lork shil nor rek gul!" the one holding me snapped like a dog guarding his food. "Lork shil lek-kaka Morg! Gul vitas! Wek chek her tor oog Gar-Chak!"

I squirmed as he brought his face close to mine, forcing me to look into his eyes. I held my breath, trembling as I stared wide eyed at his large, green face and sharp tusk-like teeth.

"Wek chek her tor Wokk-Jul," he stated, smirking at me.

I didn't know what any of that meant, but I could only guess they intended to do something terrible to me.

He turned his gaze to the one with the axe and seemed to order: "Borjik, tir her wrus an bar her ip. Wek chek her."

The axe wielding Orc nodded his head once, stomped his axe into the earth so that it would stay standing, then strode towards me. As he did, he took out a cloth from his belt and the one I could only guess was his leader released his hold on my face.

The Orc reached the cloth towards me and I begged: "Please... No! Don't... Mmmm!"

The cloth was wedged into my mouth and tied at the nape of my neck. Then he took a rope that hung on his belt and I was turned to face the lead Orc, his hands pinning my shoulders firmly. My arms were pulled roughly behind my back and my wrists were lashed together before a second rope was bound around my midriff, pinning my arms to my sides. With a third coiled around my thighs, securing my dress to my legs, I was left completely helpless.

I turned my eyes up to the lead Orc as he looked down at me, his gaze almost as if he were appreciating some work of art. I cringed at the gleam of cold cruelty in his eyes, watching as he tucked my pendant into a pouch on his belt.

"Borjik," he said, gesturing to me as he looked to the Orc who had bound me, "car-car jek gul."

The Orc nodded: "Borjik lek-kaka Morg."

The Orc secured his axe across his back, then bent down and scooped me up, hanging me over his shoulder. I cried out in panic as I thought for a moment that I was going to drop face first into the ground, but he held me tightly across my hips with his left arm, his large hand clutching at my backside. I tried to squirm against his touch but bound as tightly as I was there was little I could manage. Even screaming for someone to help me was useless.

The lead Orc was in front of the one who carried me, far out of my sights now, the other Orc picking up the pack Tristan had left behind with our supplies.

He turned to the leader and asked: "Wek chek?"

"Wek chek," the leader replied, then directed them: "Cor-kaat."

The three Orcs began trudging away from the pool, carrying me with them. They walked for what seemed like hours, the time feeling longer for me as I was hefted along on the brute's tough shoulder, which was digging into my midriff and hurting my ribs. I tried several times to slip my wrists free of the ropes, but it was useless and only rewarded me with what I guessed was a scolding from the one carrying me.

They took me up an incline through the forest, crunching their way to higher ground and soon breaching the tree line enough to bring us to a clearer space. Here was where we came to what I thought looked like a permanent encampment with sharpened logs forming stockade walls.

Orc guards stood on either side of large gates before my eyes as I was carried through them, the feeling of going backwards dizzying and disorientating me as much as the constant thumping into my stomach made me feel sick. By my guess of what I saw, there was a tribe of maybe thirty Orcs living in the encampment, their shelters one room huts made of bark and logs with animal skins serving as doors.

I was brought to a central area and in moments a rope was bound around my ankles after the Orc carrying me had hurled me to the ground without much care. There were grunts and I was dizzy as the ground was suddenly half of my height above my head.

They left me hanging upside down by my ankles, moving off and allowing me to take in a full view of their camp. A large fire burned in the middle of the central space, a pair of Orcs tending to it as they snapped large branches in their hands as if they were little more than twigs. There was a spit set over the fire, some unrecognisable slab of meat skewered there to be roasted. I cringed at the sight of it, fearing its human body sizing might be more than just appearance.

Across the way I could see a large Orc with steel shoulder plates strapped around his otherwise bare torso. He was surrounded by gnarled, twisted, rusty looking weapons - mostly jagged swords and razor pointed axes - all hung up under the open hut he sat in. As he sharpened one vicious looking axe he growled and sneered at the sparks shredding against the grindstone and blade.

Vicious barking snapped my gaze back towards the gate into the wood encircled encampment where two large, feral looking hounds were fighting over the remains of what looked like human bones. As they shattered what could have been a thigh bone, I closed my eyes and tried not to scream, biting the cloth gagging me in an attempt to fight back frightened tears.

Please tell me they're not going to eat me! Oh, please, tell me they won't!

I turned my eyes towards my right, seeing that there was a sort of makeshift dais set there on the natural rocks that faced out towards the entrance of the encampment. There was a large wooden throne with jagged spikes set around its back, many different skulls mounted on the spikes. It was cushioned in furs to serve as a more comfortable seat for its user, a large iron shield set into its back with the skull of a troll hung above it, clearly a trophy.

The three Orcs who had brought me there stood before this throne, their feet on the earth just in front of the first stone step. Their attention was on the figure lounging back there, watching them with a severe gaze.

"Wokk-Jul," the one who had led the other two spoke, thumping his fist to his chest and swiftly bowing his head before meeting the man's gaze. "Wek filn tetch hu-mon gul ba jek sacra puul. Shi ha dokk mana. Wek broog her tor Gar-Chek, Wokk-Jul."

The Orc on the throne simply eyed him down with his only good eye, the other closed with fierce, angry looking scars that scratched over his cheek and forehead. He twisted his jaw beneath his heavily greying beard as he rested his right elbow on the throne's arm, his closed fist at the edge of his green lips.

He wore a crude circlet with animal horns, the two largest at the sides of his head, a ragged half cloak draped over his left shoulder held in place with a spiked steel shoulder guard. Across his broad, bare chest he wore a leather cross belt; skulls hanging around his waist with his fur skirt, his forearms and shins guarded with iron armour plates. In his left hand he carried a great war axe decorated with another skull, this one an Orc's.

He had several female Orcs sitting at his sides on furs laid on the ground, two flanking him where they stood by his throne, all as vicious and armed as the men. There were even a few children sitting there, and I remembered my history lessons that only the Orc Chieftain in tribes like these was permitted to take wives.

"Jek hu-mon gul ha dokk mana," the Chieftain said slowly, turning his gaze towards me.

"Ya, Wokk-Jul," the hunter nodded.

"Wop mana, Morg?" the elder snarled, baring his sharp teeth and tusks fiercely.

I watched as the Orc fumbled around in the pouch on his belt with one hand and produced my pendant, holding it by the chain. It dangled as he held it out to the Chieftain, the glow of the fire bouncing off its silver form gently, the purple stone shimmering with its own inner light.

The Chieftain reached out and snatched it from the other Orc with his right hand, growling so that he backed away. He held it in his palm and began studying it, turning his single yellow eye towards me and glaring me down.

I cringed, instantly worrying what this greatly ferocious man-beast was thinking of doing. I immediately began trying to free my wrists from the coarse ropes holding them, but they seemed to only tighten and make me feel even more helpless.

With a low growl and a flex of his jaw, the Chieftain got to his feet, my pendant in one hand, his vicious war axe in the other. He stomped towards me from his throne, his movements purposeful, his shoulders hunched, and his brow creased into an angry curve. The clink of his armour was relentless and loud, his focus as threatening as the rest of him.

I struggled harder, trying to find a way to free myself, whimpering as he neared me. In a few moments, my body froze, and I was staring up into the Orc's single remaining eye.

A low gurgling growl issued from his throat, a little drool gleaming as it slipped over his bottom lip and past his pointed tusk-like teeth to touch his beard. He launched his right hand forward and yanked the cloth from my mouth, freeing my voice again.

I gasped a cooling breath into my heated and dry throat, staring fearfully at him all the while.

"Hu-mon gul," the Chieftain said lowly, studying my features before locking onto my blue eyes, "markie an dokk, yek min an weech. Gul tretchar na Ork larr. Orks sharv kul gul."

I was shaking hard, feeling the wetness of tears in my eyes as I recoiled at his foul, hot breath and threatening tones.

"Please don't hurt me," I pleaded desperately. "Please... Please..."

"Whey gul tretchar na Ork larr?! Torq! Torq, gul, or wek kul chu!" he demanded loudly. "Gul torq nar! Nar!"

"Please! I don't understand what you're saying!" I cried out, panic filling me at the sight of his enraged glare. "I don't know what you want from me! Please!"

The Chieftain snarled loudly, almost roaring as he pressed his axe to my throat.

"NO!" I closed my eyes hard and tried to pull away, trembling at the chill of his axe's blade.

"Gul torq nar," he said threateningly.

"Please... please don't kill me!" I whimpered, fighting the tears that were now wetting my face in the wrong direction.

I opened my eyes as the blade moved away a little, but still stayed close enough for me to feel it against my soft skin. I looked up at the Orc leader, shaking so hard as he glared at me. The Orc who had led the ones that attacked me stood at his back, watching on with a horrid gleam in his eyes.

"Gul ha mana," the Chieftain stated evenly. "Dokk mana."

"I... I don't understand," I replied so meekly, afraid that my ignorance would anger him anew.

"Gul mek mana porr Wokk-Jul," he said severely. "Mek mana nar."

"I don't know what you're asking me," I pleaded, my heart frantically racing and my mind running with the terror of meeting a gruesome fate because of his rage.

"Gul mek mana nar!" he roared, holding out the Pendant at me. "Mek nar! NAR!"

"You... you want to know h-how the Pendant works?" I guessed by him holding it before me.

He seemed to understand, straightening his back and smirking a little. "Mek mana, gul."

"I don't know what you're saying," I murmured up at him, feeling so lightheaded, "but if you want to know how that works," I shrugged, "I really don't know. It just does."

He was narrowing his eye at me, listening carefully to the words I had cautiously selected to answer him. Again, his axe came towards me and my eyes darted to it, my body tensing up as the blade neared my throat.

"N-no... Don't..." I whimpered and tried to pull away uselessly.

He snarled and growled, staring into my frightened, tear choked eyes viciously, almost as if he were watching to see if I would break further than I had.

"Wokk-Jul!" a voice shouted from behind the large, grey haired Orc, drawing his gaze away from me.

Two more Orcs dragged a beaten figure between them from the encampment gates. They brought him forward and threw him to the ground before us, my heart sinking and my horror increasing.

"Wek filn tetch hu-mon mear jek Gar-Chak," one of the new arrivals explained to the Chieftain. "Har tri tor mek braw witt oos."

The Chieftain snarled down at the figure on the ground lowly, glaring as he tightened his grip on his staff-like war axe.

"Oh, Gods," I gasped as I finally saw the man's bruised face. "Tristan..."

The Chieftain snapped around and threw his gaze at me again, my body stiffening as I stared at him fearfully. He then turned back to Tristan and pointed at him as he tied my pendant to his belt.

"Paa hem witt jek gul," he ordered them, then turned and walked back to his throne.

The Orcs tied Tristan up the same way as me, then hung him by his ankles beside me to my right. They turned away and went off to tend to their camp.

I turned my head to Tristan, worriedly studying his face. He had several bruises and a cut over his eyebrow that still oozed a little blood. He was moving though, his gentle groans enough to reassure me that he lived.

"Tristan?" I whispered, trying to bring him back to the waking world. "Tristan, can you hear me?"

He groaned again and his eyes fluttered but didn't open.

"Tristan, please," I tried more urgently. "Please, wake up. Please."

His eyes fluttered again, and this time opened, their brown pools a little glassy at first. He blinked and groaned as he shifted against the ropes binding him.

"Ah... I feel like I spent the night in a tavern with too much ale," he commented, then turned his gaze to me and frowned. "Lass? What's..."

He took in our surroundings and groaned.

"Okay, that's *really* not good," he said, then faced me again. "Are you all right, girl? Have they hurt you?"

"No, to both questions," I replied honestly, feeling ever more nauseous as I hung there. "But you..."

"I came back to where I left you," he explained, "but you weren't there. I found Orc tracks and saw the signs of a struggle, so I followed. Then I got ambushed by two of these green bastards."

"Why are they doing this?" I wondered, my voice trembling as much as my body, the air now getting chilled with the falling of night.

"Orcs are territorial," he replied, surveying the encampment. "My guess is that pool is part of their territory and they see us as trespassing."

"But we didn't know!" I exclaimed in desperate panic.

"Orcs don't give a damn," Tristan responded, trying to test his restraints now. "They're... eh... easily slighted creatures... ehem... with no sense of... ugh... civil niceties. Their land is theirs... ugh... eh... and anyone who passes on it... ehem... is a trespasser..."

"What are they going to do to us?" I mumbled, looking to him through the new edges of fresh tears.

"Looking at that fire, I don't like our chances," he swallowed back hard as he focused ahead of us.

I followed his line of sight towards the fire and the spit turning with the unknown meat cooking there. The Orc who had been sharpening blades was now standing with another by the fire, inspecting the weapons.

"They're... they're not..." I couldn't finish.

"Orcs will eat anything and... ehem... anyone who crosses their path," Tristan said grimly. "That includes wayward humans... like us."

"They're going to eat us?!" I cried out a little too loudly, the Chieftain and the Orcs surrounding him all flashing me their hard stares before returning to their conversations.

"I think now would be a great time to call your dragon, Princess," the Wanderer suggested with more worry than he could manage to hide from me.

I shook my head, still fighting the ropes on my wrists, the pain of the tight coils crushing my skin becoming unbearable. "I can't. They took my pendant from me. Without it... ugh... I... ugh... I can't call to her."

"But surely she can..."

"No, Tristan," I eased my struggles to soften the pain pressing through my limbs. "Without me touching the Pendant, she can't sense my need. Don't ask me how that is because I truly don't know, it just is."

"I'm certain she'll seek us out on her own," he tried to sound hopeful. "Though, by the time she does we'll likely be in several Orc bellies."

"Oh, well, that's really very comforting!" I snapped, trying to free myself desperately again.

"I think our hope just drew its last breath, Princess," Tristan murmured, his eyes set forward.

I turned my gaze to see the two Orcs who had been preparing the fire moving towards us. The one who had been sharpening the weapons carried a huge cleaver in his hand, his eyes set on us as he licked his coarse, green lips.

"Oh, no!" I gasped in terror. "Tristan?!"

"I'm thinking, lass, I'm thinking," he tried to reassure me, but to no avail.

The large brute came up to us, holding the cleaver ready and close to our faces. He sniffed us and stared each of us down, trying to decide who he would choose.

"Gul," he pointed the blade at me, drawing my frightened stare, then moved it to Tristan's face, "or marn?"

I didn't need someone to translate that for me, the sounds of the words so similar to "girl" and "man" that to think they were anything else was foolish.

"Marn borkek tourk an chargy," the other Orc commented, grabbing Tristan's shoulder and shaking him to sway on his ropes.

"Hey! Back off you savage bastards!" Tristan shouted, struggling to get free of the Orc.

"Ya, nor marn," the Orc with the cleaver turned to stare hungrily at me. "Gul ke soo an mels gorr. Et gul."

"Ya! Et gul!" the second agreed.

"No! You leave her alone, you swines!" Tristan yelled at them, trying to fight to free himself, but the second Orc backhanded him hard in the face.

The first grabbed me by my hair, making me scream as tears flowed from my eyes once again.

"Gul mek gorr merrl," the Orc smirked viciously down at me with hunger in his eyes.

"No! No, please, no!" I sobbed, struggling and thrashing my shoulders, trying to break free of his hold. "Please! Please, don't! Don't!"

The Orc brought the cleaver to my throat, resting it just beneath my jaw, the sharp edge pressing softly to my skin. I froze as I feared that the slightest movement would tear my flesh and spill my blood, but then that was probably why they had us hanging upside down the way a butcher hangs a pig for slaughter.

"Please, spare the girl!" Tristan pleaded desperately. "Spare her! Please! Kill me instead, just spare her!"

"Quittoo marn!" the second Orc backhanded him once again, drawing a yelp of pain from his lips and dazing him.

I closed my eyes and thought of Carden one last time. I imagined his smile, the gleam of love in his green eyes, and every other handsome detail about him that made me love him all the more. My heart ached and I felt myself start to cry even harder knowing that I would never see him again.

Please, don't let this happen! Please, please, oh, please!

I felt the Orc press the blade into my throat, whimpering through my sobs and tightening my already closed eyes even more. All I could do was brace for the agony that would surely come from my throat being sliced, then the torture that would follow from drowning in my own blood.

Please... don't let this happen...

"Stoog!" a voice shouted loudly, speaking Orcish, but soft and feminine. "Stoog nar!"

I opened my eyes slowly as I felt the pressure of the Orc's hand - which had moved to squeeze the back of my neck - ease off, the blade still at my throat, but now hovering above my skin instead of pressing into it. I looked up at him to see that his attentions were now over his shoulder, his gaze set upon several figures standing silhouetted by the fire.

The figures were nowhere near the size or burliness of the Orcs surrounding us, all of them more completely dressed as well. They wore green cloaks, the hoods drawn to shield their faces, their clothing consisting of leather wilds armour over simple tunics and hosen with high topped boots. They each carried a bow and quiver with either a sword or twin daggers, the unmistakable sheen of golden hair shimmering from beneath their cowls in the firelight.

The female figure standing nearest us turned towards a male with her and spoke quickly to him. He nodded and turned to the Orc Chieftain, who was now moving swiftly from his throne with a terrible scowl twisting his scarred face.

"Wokk-Jul," the human man addressed the Chieftain in Orcish, "reshey tetch gul nar!"

"Tays hu-mons tretchar na Ork larr!" the Chieftain roared in response, beating his chest hard and stamping the base of his war axe into the ground heavily. "Wek rek an et tays hu-mons! Jek gul ke oog tor et! Wek et gul nar!"

"No!" the female snapped, stepping up and glaring from beneath her hood at him. "Chu shil nor rek an et jek gul! Chu shil reshey jek gul nar!"

"Chu dormaan Wokk-Jul?!" the Chieftain bellowed with rage in his eye. "No Raanger dormaan Ork Wokk-Jul! Etsark e gul Raanger!"

The woman snatched the Pendant from the Orc's belt, making him hiss and bare his teeth as she held it up fervently at him.

"Tetch ke hers!" she exclaimed at him, showing a strange dominance I had never imagined any human could show to an Orc. "Tetch ik knoo! Shi ke e fridek an un ik projek! Reshey her nar!"

"Dou ar shi seys," said the male in the hood. "Wek broog maank tor trede witt Orks. Maank gorr tor trede, Wokk-Jul."

The Chieftain considered what they were saying, then nodded and gestured to the Orc standing in front of me. "Reshey gul! Nar!" he commanded.

"Wokk-Jul?" the Orc frowned incredulously at his leader.

"Nar! Reshey her nar!" the Chieftain roared at him.

Begrudgingly, the Orc with the cleaver turned around and cut the ropes binding my ankles, dropping me to the ground hard. He stood over me as my head swam with the dizziness that hanging upside down for so long had brought on. He cut my thighs free, pulled me up to kneel, then began cutting the rest of the ropes as I patiently and nervously held still.

I don't understand. What's happening? Who are these people? Why are the Orcs untying me? As the ropes around my arms and midriff were cut away, a terrible thought entered my mind. *Are... are they giving me to these people? Why? What could they want with me?*

The Orc freed me and stepped away as the man and woman approached. I rubbed my wrists as I looked up at them uncertainly, my eyes darting for a moment to the Pendant in the woman's hand, silently wondering if I could make an attempt to snatch it back.

"Are you hurt, your Highness?" the man asked in common.

"I... uh... Who... who are you?" I stammered, still unsteady and dizzy.

"Forgive me," he said, pushing back his hood to reveal a handsome face near thirty-five winters, with long blonde hair and hazel eyes. "I am Ranulf Landrace, a Dorvan Ranger. You have nothing to fear, Princess."

I frowned at him. "Landrace?"

He smiled and nodded. "Yes. Know that you truly are among friends."

As he said this, the woman at his side withdrew her hood, letting her long blonde hair fall free. The strands were now longer than when I had last seen her.

"It is so good to see you again, Princess Leander," she smiled.

"Oh, my gods!" I got to my feet and threw my arms around her in a tight hug. "Tallinn! I can't believe you're here!"

"Nor I you, Leander," Tallinn replied, hugging me tightly, then pushing away, keeping her hands on mine as we met each other's gaze. "However did you manage to escape Castle Ortagaad?"

"It wasn't easy," I confessed, "and to hear it told it isn't readily believed either."

"It is just so good to see you, my friend," she smiled at me.

"Ehem, excuse me," we both turned to face Tristan where he was still hanging. "While I hate to interrupt you ladies enjoying your reunion, do you think perhaps I can be let down? It is rather dizzying being like this."

Tallinn scowled and snapped her sword from her belt, jabbing it at him angrily. "Why?! So that you might betray the Princess to her enemies once again?! Becoming an Orc's next meal is too good for *filth* like *you*, Tristan!"

"Tallinn, wait!" I stepped in front of her, drawing her attention. "Set him free."

She stared at me incredulously. "This *man* is the reason you were imprisoned, the reason we all were! He betrayed you!"

"If it weren't for him," I confessed, knowing in my heart that I was doing the right thing, "I would never have made it this far through the Forests of Arnath, or managed to evade the Witches' soldiers."

Tallinn flashed a vicious glare at Tristan, so desiring to stab him with her blade.

"Please, Tallinn," I urged her gently, drawing her hazel eyed gaze once again. "He is trying to make amends. Please."

She sighed and nodded. "Very well. But if he should show the *slightest* sign of betraying us again... I *will* kill him."

She nodded to Ranulf, who spoke with the Orcs, the Chieftain snarling, rolling his eye and gesturing towards Tristan. As the Orcs moved to do as instructed, Tallinn sheathed her sword and smiled at me, handing me the Pendant.

"You truly have a way about you, Leander," she said as I took the necklace back. "I do not know whether it is innocence, foolishness, or wisdom beyond your years, but you have a way."

"Thank you," I replied, looking at my pendant in my hand gratefully, then glancing at the Orcs. "How have you come to be here? And why do the Orcs not try to kill you as they did us?"

"Tribal etiquette," she answered, folding her arms. "The Orcs see us Rangers as valuable trading partners. We travel and hunt, then, when we come across one of their enclaves, we offer to trade our bounty with them, and so we are welcomed."

"I am so glad you came along when you did," I said with obvious relief.

"As am I, Leander," she smiled.

There was a yelp and a bang, and Tristan muttered: "I'm all right..."

I tried not to laugh at his hard landing, turning back to my friend.

"Come, let us rest," she suggested. "And perhaps we can talk on all that has happened since last we met."

"I'll just call Amethyst to join us," I said. "Perhaps you should warn the Orcs so they don't think she means them harm."

She nodded and did so as we moved to the fire. I fastened my pendant around my neck again, raising my hand to summon my dragon. Soon enough, her familiar call echoed in the air as her silhouette appeared at the gate, bringing me greater comfort...

Chapter Seventeen
Where the Dead Walk

It was strange going from being the intended dinner of an Orc Tribe to being their welcomed guests all in one evening. After Tallinn and Ranulf had explained to the Chieftain who I was, the Orcs were more than accommodating to us.

We were seated in a circle surrounding the fire, Tristan staying nearer me, though Tallinn and Ranulf decided very clearly to place themselves between us due to their lack of trust for him. I couldn't blame Tallinn for feeling such towards him, yet I did silently wish that she would not make her distrust so well known.

I sat with my back against Amethyst's shoulder, my dragon lying with her head resting at my side so that I could easily stroke her cranial scales with my palm. She was so easily soothed by this touch from me, much like a very large, very scaly puppy seeking its person's affections.

I was watching as Morg - the Orc who had led the ones who brought me here - was sitting beside Tristan, offering him a goat's horn filled with some strange liquid.

"Corgg," Morg urged him, holding the drinking horn towards the sceptical Wanderer. "Corgg tetch, briikek jidot marn."

"What does he want?" Tristan frowned, looking to the two Landrace siblings.

"He says drink this," Ranulf was smiling as he was cutting some venison to eat. "Is that not true, sister?"

"It is," Tallinn smiled, then winked at me.

"It seems like he said more than that," Tristan noted, studying their faces.

"Just drink it, Tristan," Ranulf urged him. "You wouldn't want to insult him."

"Corgg. Corgg," Morg offered Tristan the horn again, eagerly watching him.

Tristan threw me an uneasy glance then shrugged. "Well, I wouldn't want to offend the nice cannibals. Now would I?"

"Orcs aren't cannibals," Tallinn chuckled a little at him. "They only eat other races, not their own kind."

"There's a difference?" he gave her an incredulous look.

Morg tapped his shoulder with the back of his hand and urged again: "Corgg."

"All right," Tristan nodded and took the horn.

He hesitantly sniffed it, then drank deep. Suddenly, he choked and shouted, spitting out some of the liquid with a yelp, his eyes watering as he coughed violently. The Orcs and Rangers began to laugh raucously. I laughed too, though softer and less rowdily than those around me, feeling a little sympathy for the Wanderer.

Morg beat Tristan on the back as he chortled: "Briikek jidot marn corgg libb habb hii mels!"

"Yeah... ehem... that stuff's smooth," Tristan coughed and looked to the Orc. "What's in it?"

"Arckar witt hoowl urilnar," Morg answered, smirking. "Chu corgg hoowl urilnar roo darn!"

Tristan spat and squinted. "Well, whatever it was, it tasted like ale mixed with piss."

"Because it was," Ranulf started to laugh, though he tried not to. "From a wolf, to be exact. So Morg here says."

"Ya, ya!" the Orc nodded vigorously. "Hoowl urilnar! Ya!"

"Ugh! Bastards!" Tristan started spitting and snatched up a cup of water sitting by his feet. "You green skinned, pointy eared... ugh!" he drank and spat on the ground, then drank again.

"It means they like you," Ranulf chuckled, patting Tristan's back. "He's just amazed you drank it all right down."

"Var amorka! Var, var amorka!" Morg laughed loudly and hit Tristan hard on the back again.

"Never accept a drink from an Orc," Tristan grumbled with watering eyes as he wiped his face on his shirt. "Treacherous bloody bastards."

"Ke jek briikek jidot marn angorvva witt oos?" Morg asked Tallinn.

Tallinn shook her head. "Jek briikek jidot marn ha no lorfftu na hii sool. Har ke e markie braw-wa, yek, har ke e var dokk jidot!"

Morg laughed loudly and nodded. "Ya! Ya! E var dokk jidot! Var amorka jidot!"

"And what's he say now?" Tristan asked.

Tallinn smiled and shook her head. "He says you're an idiot, but a very amusing one."

"Ya, var amorka jidot!" Morg agreed ardently, smiling and striking Tristan's shoulder strongly again.

"Well... how nice," Tristan grimaced and looked to the large Orc. "Right back at you."

The Orc leaned forward, smirking and very awkwardly tried to repeat his words: "R...rye beck et... *you!*" he burst out laughing with the other Orcs.

"Great," Tristan forced a grimacing smile, then raised his cup vaguely at the laughing Orc.

I smiled and shook my head, folding my arms around me. I looked back to Tallinn as she turned towards me, seeming so different and older to my eternally young eyes than she once did. Though she was only two years more senior to when last I had seen her, she seemed more aged.

I knew this sense that I could now see the aging in others where it no longer dwelt within me had to be from my unwanted immortality. I could only guess that such is the way of immortals, a truly terrible thought in itself. My heart felt that familiar hardness again as my mind drifted to recall the distant hurts of knowing that I would never grow beyond my teenage years. Once more, I silently and tearlessly grieved for my lost humanity.

The woman smiled at me, completely unknowing of my hidden truths, so very different here with her own people compared to with the Guardians. She seemed much more content with this life than that of a travelling protector. And she smiled more.

"It is good to laugh like this together once more, Leander," she said to me with such deep honesty and more feeling than I had ever seen in her.

"It is good to laugh again at all," I confessed with a small sigh. "I haven't had reason to smile in more than two years, my every waking moment spent in fear of what torture the Witches planned to inflict on me next."

"Clearly you were not fed well," she observed gravely. "Your frame is so much slighter, and your bodice tied tighter than when last I was in your presence."

"The starving stomach was a lesser torture than the others employed in Keilantra's attempts to take control of my pendant, and of Amethyst," I felt a deep, sickening dread as I spoke those words, Amethyst growling softly and pressing her cheek closer into my hip to comfort me.

"Those Witches are foul, wicked, demonic creatures," Tallinn remarked coldly, an anger behind her eyes. "I cannot imagine what horrors you've suffered at their hands. Especially after all that their dread Master already inflicted upon you in Gorth'lak."

"You are very fortunate to have escaped as you did, Princess," Ranulf joined our conversation with sincerity. "Though your tale of how is... incredible."

I half laughed and nodded as I thought back to all I had experienced since fleeing from Ortagaad's West Tower:"I can scarce believe it was real myself. It truly sounds like a story of fantasy to my own mind, let alone what I think it must seem to others. I must sound mad..."

"I would never think you mad, Leander," Tallinn assured me, drawing my distant gaze from the fire again to her blonde framed face. "In all the time I have known you since first arriving in Arvon three years ago, I have seen some truly bewildering and incredible things. I have also grown up in these forests and know the dark magicks that plague them. So, don't fear that I think you mad, because I don't."

"Though, that part of falling from the castle battlements, swimming from Culler Sharks and walking across the ice-covered sea is certainly one of the most fantastical parts of your story," Ranulf smiled and nodded at me. "It is also my favourite."

I offered him a small smile in response, the thought of it all feeling as tiring to recall as it had been to endure.

"So, it was because of your pendant that you made it across the ice?" Tallinn asked curiously, studying my necklace.

I nodded, instantly running my fingers over the Pendant and gently thumbing its purple stone.

"It seems to respond to my thoughts as if it can read them," I explained distantly as I thought on all of the magic I had seen it use. "In all honesty, when my uncle and father gave it to me, I was sure it was just a pretty thing with a wonderful story attached to it, but now it has shown itself to be so much more. When I am lost it shows me the way, when I am in need it brings me to what I require, and when I am in danger it protects me just as Amethyst does."

"Then, Ser Mithras was right about it," Tallinn thought aloud, her forearms resting on her knees. "The Dragon Pendant is as a living being and is loyal to its wearer. Loyal to you, Leander."

"I guess so," I sighed, my heart aching at the thought of Mithras.

I wish he were still alive. He would know what to do and he would never have allowed me to be taken as I was. How I miss him.

"Enough about me," I decided and forced a weak smile as I looked to her. "What of you, Tallinn? The last time I saw you the Revenant was taking both you and Carden to Arnath."

There were suddenly hisses and growls from the Orcs that startled me, all of them showing their teeth and looking more vicious.

"Ar-Nak!" the Chieftain hissed and spat at the word. "Taatch placae ke horfar!"

"The Chieftain is right," Ranulf agreed gravely. "Arnath is a foul, vile place."

"It is, brother," Tallinn turned to me grimly, fear and hurt in her hazel eyes. "And it is one that I am so grateful to have escaped."

"What happened?" I asked, a little fearful now that I had seen the very vocal and physical reaction the mere mention of the dreaded place had caused.

Tallinn swallowed back and turned her eyes to the ground as she thought on the words she would use. She looked haunted, damaged, as if what time she had spent with her captors had nearly destroyed her. How easily I could relate.

"We were taken from Castle Ortagaad and back across the sea to Travarna," she recounted slowly, almost perilously, as if she expected her words to manifest and attack us. "Carden and I were bound and led on foot with other prisoners who had been offered up to the Revenant. They marched us for days, killing any who fell from hunger, thirst or exhaustion. To sleep was to invite a torturous death."

I shuddered hard as I imagined what she was explaining, my stomach churning and my heart aching.

She shook her head, her eyes so dark: "We came within sight of the Labyrinthine Fortress of Arnath, the dead themselves our escorts from the border of Gorvenna, Gathlorks joining them to keep us in line. Gods... seeing that place so close... it... it was like the Void itself was reaching out to devour us."

She closed her eyes as a tear managed to break past her eyelashes and strike down her cheek.

"Carden had managed to free us in the night and we sought the opportunity to flee," she went on coldly, opening her eyes again. "We began to fight, trying to free the other prisoners, leading an uprising against the Scourge and the shambling dead. And... that is when... *He* appeared..."

"W-who?" I was actually afraid, feeling as if I could see all that she described like I was viewing the past.

"The Revenant," her voice was low and frightened as she shook at the very thought of him. "He appeared as if out of the darkness that choked the world around us. Every person he touched he drained to a withered husk and resurrected to swell his ranks," she closed her eyes, crying without sobs, guilt now taking hold of her. "Carden... he told me to run... He... I did... I ran as fast as I could..."

I felt sick. So many terrible things were burning my mind and I feared what might have happened to my love.

She tried to regain her composure, watching the flames for strength: "I must have walked for days before collapsing. That is when Ranulf and his hunting party found me. And I have travelled with them ever since."

"What... what happened to Carden?" I asked, feeling as if the answer could destroy me and bring forth all the tears I had in me.

"He lives," she nodded, relief flooding my heart instantly, but her gaze also offered more dread. "As far as we know, he did not escape the Labyrinthine Fortress. He yet remains as the Revenant's prisoner."

I stared blankly at the ground beside the campfire, numbness flooding through me and silence filling me whilst my heart screamed in agony and terror. While I knew that he lived and was relieved, I was also terrified to hear this horrible truth.

Tallinn, seeing my expression, immediately added: "I wrote to Aldwyn in Eilath and informed him of everything that had befallen the three of us. He and Fawkner were devising a plan to rescue you, yet I insisted that I must stay and find a way to help Carden. I could never forgive myself if he met the same fate that our elder brother and father met at the hands of the Revenant."

"And so, we have sought to help him all this time," Ranulf said earnestly, his long, blonde locks falling messily to his jaw, his hazel eyes looking so dark in the firelight. "No one should have to endure the horrors of Arnath's Labyrinthine, or the Revenant's whims."

"Is that why you're out here?" Tristan asked solemnly.

Ranulf nodded to him. "Yes. We regularly make recognisance trips around the edge of the fortress to view the situation and find a way in. Thus far, we've had little success."

"We have to get him out," I murmured shakily.

"No," Tallinn shook her head at me. "No, Princess, *you* need to make for Silvervale as you and Tristan have planned...

"I won't leave him, Tallinn," I said, my mind made up, my eyes locking with hers. "I can't. You know what he means to me."

She sighed and nodded. "I do, just as I know there is no talking you out of your decision. But it won't be easy."

"Whatever it takes," I replied softly with a small nod.

"Hu-mon gul," the Chieftain drew our attention, gesturing to me with a gentle wave of his hand, the other holding his staff axe. "Chu yould journek na tor Ar-Nak, tere jek horfar angorvva kelnik logrund dwill undet tass sistenarvark mortril's pooshnar?"

"What did he say?" I asked.

Ranulf translated: "He said: Human girl. You would journey into Arnath, where the foul angered walking dead dwell under their sinister master's power?"

The Chieftain hissed and shook his head. "Sek e tranok ke forgaast!"

"Such a task is foolish," Ranulf repeated to us in common.

The Orc looked at me, shaking his head questioningly: "Whey yould chu cashissk chor lastkarvi rashold vor carvishka?"

"Why would you cast your living-form aside so carelessly?" Ranulf looked between me and him.

The Orc nodded, his single eye so concerned and gentle for such a hardened creature.

"Tallinn," I looked to my friend for help. "Please, explain to him why I must go there."

"All right," she nodded and faced the Orc to speak in his own language. "Shi yould yol tor Ar-Nak beekchak her martil ke ishkvarnishk wostish taatch darshka placae ar shi shaas unastarr. Taass horshts daasbard taatch bir renostey. Ba chor horkvar ar e braw-wa, Wokk-Jul, hishk oos reshey hem."

I held my breath as I waited for the Chieftain's answer, my heart thundering inside me with the fear that he would refuse.

"Wek Orks shil hishk chu Raangers an jek gul reshey chor fridek," he said with a bow of his head, all of his tribe bowing in time with him.

Tallinn nodded, looking relieved as she smiled at me: "He said they will help us free Carden, Princess."

All I could do was nod and breathe a sigh of relief. It was impossible at that moment to describe how grateful I truly was.

*****

The journey to the Labyrinthine Fortress of Arnath would take a day and a half from where the Orc Tribe's Enclave rested in those hills. We spent two days preparing, the Chieftain sending three of his best warriors with us, the same three who had brought me to him in the first place: Morg, Borjik and Lork.

The three Orcs heavily armed themselves, Borjik and Lork eyeing me down with a serious disdain. They still dreaded the magic of my pendant after it had defended me against them, which I now understood was the cause of the Chieftain's questioning me when first I arrived at the enclave.

Ranulf and Tallinn led us with their six accompanying Rangers, Amethyst remaining by my side as the skilled Dorvans flanked us protectively, their hoods drawn to shield their faces. The three Orcs walked ahead, their weapons of choice always unsheathed and ready for use as they guided us. It seemed to be the way of their culture.

I looked to Tristan as we walked, my body buried in the coat he had recovered for me. He was watching the way with his bow at the ready, his right hand twitching as if he were waiting to snatch an arrow from his quiver and shoot. I couldn't help but feel uneasy, focusing instead on holding tight to the hems of my skirts and not tripping on the uneven ground we traversed.

We broke to make camp just before sunset, the Rangers sheltering us under hide tents, some of them taking watch with the Orcs while we tried to rest. But in truth, there was no rest to be had so close to such a terrible place of power.

I suffered horrific nightmares, crying out in my sleep as I saw ghoulish visions, fearing even more for Carden's safety. When I woke from the terrors of my sleep, Ranulf explained that this close to the fortress the power of the undead necromancer held such sway as could disturb our very subconscious and turn our dreams into enemies. Holding the Pendant in my hand, I tried to sleep again, and this time rested with some peace at least, the Pendant's magic reaching out and enwrapping me in its protection from the Revenant's influence.

Sometime after late noon, we arrived at the edge of the Labyrinthine Fortress' perimeter, cautiously making our way along the high cliffs that surrounded the great valley beneath. The black steel and stone structure was unlike any terrible nightmare I had seen, a monstrous tower set at the heart of its spider webbing shapes. It looked more like the ruins of an ancient stone fortress than a functioning one, its battlements scarred from combat as many of the structures seemed damaged or incomplete from attempts to rebuild it.

The Orcs said something I didn't understand, Ranulf and two Rangers going with Morg and Lork as the rest of us took refuge in the cliffs overlooking the fortress. I knelt down here, hidden amongst the rocks and sparse shrub coverage that we had, holding onto a boulder as I took in the terrifying structures and causeways before me.

The only way in obvious to me was the large causeway that linked the Labyrinthine Fortress with the cliffs below. The valley beneath it was dark and filled with jagged rocks, all else nothing more than a barren waste caked in mud. But the worst part about being so close to the Revenant's stronghold was how silent it was, only the wind offering any sound at all.

I couldn't see anyone moving along the walls; no guards visible, no shouts or screams from the prisoners certain to be held within. The whole place might as well have been abandoned, already seeming as if it had been taken by nature with the dead vines that claimed the stone walls.

Gods, Carden, where are you? I shuddered in fear as I thought of him languishing in there under the gaze of some terrible monster.

"This place seems empty," Tristan noted, speaking aloud what I already thought as he and Tallinn knelt behind the boulder with me. "How is this supposed to be an inescapable prison with no guards?"

"Oh, there *are* guards," Tallinn answered with unease in her voice and fear in her eyes. "The shambling dead prowl the labyrinth-like halls of this stronghold under the guidance of Shadow Knights. We have even seen a breeding ground for the Scourge housed in a cavern we found beneath."

"I saw the same thing in Castle Ortagaad," I recalled, turning my gaze to her worriedly, feeling as though I needed to whisper so as not to be heard. "Manth showed me before I escaped. She said it is all a part of the Shadow Lord's plan."

"It is?" she frowned at me worriedly.

I nodded. "He plans to launch an attack against High-Realm using these new Scourge forces being bred in different parts of the lands. He's building an army, and the Witches and Revenant are helping him."

"Then truly we need to reach Silvervale," she stated darkly, turning her gaze back to the fortress. "We must inform the High Elves and the Wizards, then send word to the other Guardian strongholds."

"The Kingdoms must be warned," I murmured.

"No easy task," Tristan observed with a sour breath and a shake of his head. "Many of the Kingdoms are at each other's throats and will hardly consider stories of a Scourge Army being bred for war against them all."

"We'll warn the High Elves and the Wizards," Tallinn reiterated sternly, her long golden locks catching in the breeze. "At least they can decide on a course of action to confront this threat."

I turned and looked back to the fortress, sucking in a shaking breath: "I can't believe Carden is in there."

"If we can enter, then we'll free him, Leander," Tallinn said earnestly. "I promise you that we will."

"Largy Raanger," Borjik called to us, drawing our gaze to where he leaned his back against the cliffs with his arms crossed.

Tallinn got to her feet as Ranulf, Morg, Lork and the two other Rangers returned, Tristan helping me up as she moved to join them.

"Ranulf?" she looked to her brother curiously and with a soft air of urgency. "What word do you bring, brother?"

"The fortress is quieted, my sister," Ranulf explained, one hand on the pommel of his sword, his hazel eyes flicking to me, then back to her behind wayward strands of his otherwise tied back blonde hair. "It seems that the guard presence is greatly diminished."

"Why? What possible reason would there be for that to happen?" Tallinn frowned, crossing her arms in front of her chest.

"The Revenant has departed," Ranulf replied uneasily. "As we have seen during past investigations of the fortress, he seems to have left to confer with his dark ally in Gorth'lak."

"Then, we can just walk right in?" I asked with a foolish hopefulness.

He shook his head. "No. The main ways in are still well guarded by warding magic as well as the shambling dead he has armed for the task. As for the Shadow Knights, we think there only to be a handful left to garrison the stronghold."

Tallinn nodded thoughtfully as she turned to gaze at the fortress again.

"If we are to do this, then it is with stealth," Ranulf added seriously. "Even with this lessened force, we will still face a dire battle if we move against the stronghold directly."

"Is there another way in?" she turned back to her brother, her hand to her chin, her other arm held around her middle to brace her elbow.

"Wek knoo un," Morg stated with a nod, clicking his large jaws. "Teess ke e wak ba jek clookas wek kaar yaas."

"Morg says there is a way by the cliffs we can use," Ranulf translated, the Orc nodding his approval.

"Te laskkas tor e karvarnaak witt e wak na tor jek horfar morgarthakish's Gar-Chek," the Orc explained.

"He says it leads to a cavern with a way into the 'Raiser of the Dead's' enclave," Ranulf relayed.

"Very well," Tallinn nodded. "Then we'll take that path." As Ranulf gestured for the Orcs and the Rangers to follow him, Tallinn turned to me:"Stay close to me, Princess. We have no idea of the dangers that lurk within those dire walls."

"Don't worry about me," I assured her, my hand to my pendant. "I'll be fine."

She nodded and began towards the cliffs.

I turned to Amethyst where she watched on, knowing the Dragon was too large to join us this time.

"Stay here until I call you, Amethyst," I directed her gently.

She didn't argue, merely nodding and grunting her agreement to do as I'd asked.

With Tallinn before me and Tristan following, we traversed the difficult, narrow ledges of the cliffs towards Arnath's dark walls. We were so high up that to slip would mean a certain death on the sharp rocks in the barren valley below.

Don't look down... Don't... look down...

I turned my eyes to the way ahead, carefully negotiating my footsteps into the crags and crevices of the rock face, staying close to my two companions. I remembered how I had climbed along the ledges of Castle Ortagaad's keep, trying to keep my focus as I had then.

If I could do this with soldiers shooting arrows at me, I can certainly do this now.

We soon found our way to the opening into the caverns as Morg had told us, carefully climbing down into the short depths. In only a couple of minutes, we were entering the darkened, dusty, decrepit hallways of the fortress.

Stepping through the gaping chasm in the wall, I found myself staring at a ruined corridor of dark stone, very little light filtering through the gaps in the walls to show the dust thickened air before us. The air tasted stale and old, a stench of ancient death permeating the atmosphere of this sinister place.

Ranulf and Tallinn took the lead, he with his sword drawn, she with an arrow laced to her bowstring. I heard the familiar grind of steel at my side, glancing to my right as Tristan drew his own sword in his right hand, snatching a dagger from his belt with his left in a dual wield. All around us, the other six Rangers had their bows at the ready, the three Orcs brandishing their weapons in anticipation.

"We must go carefully, yet we must also be swift," Ranulf said, watching the way ahead. "Though the Revenant himself does not linger here at this moment, his minions still do and will descend upon us should they discover our intrusion."

"You four go back outside," Tallinn directed the four Rangers she selected. "Be prepared with the Dragon to secure us an escape route should things turn badly."

The four nodded in response, turning past us and heading back through the gap we had entered by.

"Stay near me, lass," Tristan urged me, trying to give me a gentle smile, but producing more of a grimace.

I nodded, grasping the hems of my dress and following close by his shoulder.

It seemed that we spent hours wandering the long stone corridors, the light of day starting to dull as we found our way further into the fortress' twisted depths, the occasional torch all we had to illuminate our path. Seemingly in minutes, what outside light we saw was darkening as the sun was setting, a terrible dread filling my chest as we traversed a narrow stairway with a great drop into darkness below it.

Being inside the Revenant's fortress at night doesn't feel safe. What terrors could lurk in the darkness of this evil place? What could begin stirring in these dire halls now that night has fallen? My heart ached and I resisted my eyes' desire to free tears once more. *Carden... where are you?*

After what felt like a small eternity wandering the twisting, curving passages, we stepped out into a hall... and I felt a scream tearing up through my chest. A hand slapped over my mouth to muffle my cry, the warmth of the palm almost a comfort as I turned my eyes over my shoulder and through my long dark hair to see Tristan's worried stare.

The Wanderer shook his head to me: "Shh... Don't scream, lass. Don't make a sound louder than a whisper, or else they'll turn on us."

I just nodded fearfully at him, holding my breath as he carefully took his hand from my mouth. My eyes fell back on the way ahead past Ranulf and Tallinn, both Rangers looking ill at ease. Ranulf was silent as Tallinn cringed back with her lips pinned tightly shut to prevent her own cries.

The corridor before us was the same as all the others we had previously past through; the torches lit with a dull flame producing a bluish hue, lighting the space with an eerie air. There were ruined sections of ground and walls, debris everywhere like in every other part of the fortress we'd seen, but there was one difference. Terrifying figures lurched and shambled along the length of the hall, their arms limp at their sides, their heads hanging forward or back. They wore the clothing of men and women, of nobles, knights, commoners, merchants and rangers, all tattered and dirtied from their time here. But what was most terrifying was that these creatures were not people anymore.

Their faces were sunken and sallow, their eyes well back into their skulls and white as pearls, their mouths hanging open to emit the most awful moaning I could imagine. Their skin had become leathery and stretched across their bones, their bodies emaciated beyond the ability to live, yet here they were, shuffling through these corridors like the maddened patients of an asylum.

I cringed, knowing I would have nightmares of these distorted, twisted beings for months to come.

"What... what are they?" I voiced my thoughts as softly as I could manage.

"Lost Souls," Tallinn responded quietly, keeping her bow ready, but her voice was shaking. "Those poor innocents the Revenant has taken and condemned with his dire powers."

"Like our father and brother," Ranulf said sadly, gaining Tallinn's own grief filled gaze and nod.

"How can these poor people be alive?" I asked uneasily, trying not to look at their twisted, gawking faces.

"They aren't," Tallinn replied gravely. "These are the resurrected husks of all those that were brought here. The Revenant and this place have drained their souls and their life force from them, leaving only these walking draugar."

"Do they... do they know... what's happened to them?" my voice shook, and I wasn't sure I truly wanted to know.

Tallinn shook her head. "N-no... All that they were has been taken with their life force. These wretched creatures before us are purely instinctual, acting out only when they hear movement or sense something they might try to devour."

"Which includes us if we're not careful," Tristan remarked darkly and I shivered in gruesome fear.

"As long as we're cautious and slow," Ranulf explained, edging his way forward, "and as long as we do not make any loud, sudden moves or sounds, they will simply let us pass by unnoticed."

"Stay close to me, lass," Tristan said, putting his arm around my shoulders after stowing his dagger.

I just nodded, my breathing already swift, my heart racing as we began our slow movements forward into the shambling gathering.

The Rangers led our small group cautiously, every step taken slow and deliberate. Tallinn paused in front of Tristan and I as I held my breath at the draugar that shambled slowly in front of us, blocking us from Ranulf for a moment. Once it had passed enough, she directed us with her hand, leading us forward again.

This passage amongst the dead was awkward and terrifying, every obstacle that surrounded us moving slowly at a lumbering pace, each one capable of alerting the others to our presence. I silently feared that we would collide with one and cause the monsters to howl out and attack us, images of being torn apart by their grasping, skeletal hands haunting my thoughts.

Another set of twisting halls led us forward, the dead still surrounding us as they lingered in their open prison. Now I understood why there didn't seem to be many guards. Then, suddenly, there came heavy, armoured footfalls echoing from ahead.

"Hide!" Ranulf warned at us and we all took cover in the dark alcoves that flanked the corridor.

I pushed back into Tristan and covered my mouth to silence my rapid breathing, the man holding me tight to his chest to keep us both hidden. We watched then as two large Shadow Knights stomped past us, their black cloaks swirling behind them, their pointed ebony armour gleaming coldly in the eerie light. Their glowing eyes surveyed the corridors from behind their terrifying black helms, scouring the shadows for any sign of anything out of the ordinary... well, at least what was ordinary for a place like this.

They shoved aside some of the shambling dead, dropping them to the hard stone floor with soft thuds and languishing moans, not caring for them at all. The draugar didn't seem even disturbed by this, simply pulling themselves back to their feet and continuing their lumbering in the Shadow Knights' wakes.

These monsters truly know no bounds when it comes to their cruelty. How can there be beings as evil as this in the world? Of course, some humans can be worse...

The Shadow Knights vanished around the corner we had just come by; the sound of their stomping passage soon falling into silence, leaving us only with the draugar's moans and whines.

"Nasty bastards," Tristan growled as he stepped back into the corridor, bringing me close behind him.

Tallinn, Ranulf and the others re-joined us, all of them - even the Orcs - on edge from the near encounter with the terrible supernatural knights.

"It seems with the draugar's inability to perceive beyond instinct, that only a few Shadow Knights are truly required to guard this place," Ranulf surmised uneasily. "Had we known sooner..."

"We might have attempted to free Carden before now," Tallinn agreed a little too harshly, her desire to leave this fortress and her guilt over being the one who was free all too clear. "Come, let us hurry and find him."

"I can find him quicker," I said without thinking, drawing all eyes to me.

"How, Princess?" the woman turned to me curiously.

"My pendant can lead me to him," I reminded her of what I had told her at the Orc Enclave. "That's how I found my way across the Ortagaad Sea and through Dol Amor."

She nodded. "All right then. Do what you must."

I nodded and stepped in front of the group, both Tallinn and Tristan remaining close at my sides. I held the Pendant in my palm, studying its stone for a moment as I thought on what I needed to do.

"Help me find Carden in this place," I whispered to it, the stone immediately beginning to do its hot and cold flashes as it had before. I studied its flickering as I searched the ways, finding the strongest indication and turning to the others: "This way."

We carefully made our way forward, passing out of sight of the draugar and into another long, dark corridor. The Pendant kept directing us with a strong, clear pulse, telling me which way to go. My heart started racing at the prospect of finding Carden.

We'll find him soon. I know we will. Then I can go with him and leave this all behind.

Suddenly, there came a grinding of stone and I let out a startled yelp, falling forward as the wall slammed towards me from my right. I hit the ground as I heard the screams of the others, seeing their recoiling forms just moments before the walls closed, leaving only dust falling then before me.

For a moment, I was stunned into staying still, staring wide eyed at the wall that had just sealed in front of me. Then, panic set in and I jumped to my feet.

"Tallinn! Tristan!" I banged on the wall with my palm desperately.

"Leander!" I heard Tallinn's voice call from the other side. "Leander, are you all right?!"

"What happened, Tallinn?!" I asked frantically.

"The fortress is known to change its layout at a whim!" she responded through the wall. "That's why they call it the Labyrinthine Fortress of Arnath! It's a labyrinth that moves its passages!"

"What do I do?!" I worried. "I... I can't get back through!"

"We'll find our way to you!" she assured me. "There's sure to be an open place near the centre we can meet! Head there!"

"All right. I'll try to find Carden, then meet you there!" I replied.

"Be careful, Princess!" Tallinn warned and I heard the scraping of boots as they started moving quickly.

I turned from the wall slowly, my eyes searching out the way ahead. The passage lay dark before me, the way seeming so much more frightening now that I was alone. The only light I had to see by was the purple glow coming from my pendant's heart-stone.

I'm on my own again... Okay... This isn't frightening at all...

I swallowed back against my fear, stepping forward and slowly continuing my way along the dark corridors. I kept flicking my eyes to the Pendant's flashing light, always seeking out the faster blinks that indicated I was going the right way.

I found no resistance to my passing through the myriad of darkened, crumbling stone passages, no guards crossing my path. My progress had to be slow to avoid moving down the wrong turn or passing by the wrong corridor, my eyes constantly seeking my pendant's glowing guidance.

I turned down a corridor and stifled a scream, slamming one palm over my mouth, my fingers curling tightly to my cheek. Yet more draugar shambled before me, desiccated and looking as if they could fall apart with the slightest gust of wind. As before, they didn't acknowledge my presence, but the way ahead looked so daunting with so many shuffling through the long space.

I drew in a shaking breath, trying to compose myself, then looked at the Pendant as I let my free hand drop from my mouth to my side. The Pendant's glow was now strong and steady. This was the way to find my beloved Guardian.

I can do this. I just need to take it slow...

I edged my foot forward, trying to be so very careful not to draw the attention of the shuffling dead. The stench was revolting, and I drew in shallow breaths past my lips, trying not to breath in the moving rot of the dire corpses I now found myself surrounded by.

The way was slower than before, my awareness heightened as I navigated my way amongst the moving obstacles. One stared in my direction and howled, reaching with grasping hands. I dropped against the wall, stunned as it swept past me and knocked over another draugar, the two monsters fighting. It was in no way interested in me, thankfully.

I reached the end of the passage in what felt like countless ages, pausing there to decide my next direction with the Pendant's guidance. It pointed me to my left and I entered a chamber full of darkened cells, a single torch glowing on a pillar in the centre of the space. The cells were left open, which seemed odd for a prison, more draugar lurching and lingering within.

The Pendant glowed brighter as I faced the single cell with a closed door, a lone figure sitting hunched on the floor. I strained through the darkness and past the bars of the cells to get a good look. The figure was broad shouldered with long black hair, dressed in a sleeveless leather jacket trimmed in silver, a forest green shirt pulled on beneath it.

My heart skipped joyfully inside my breast and I felt a smile form on my lips: "Carden," I breathed his name softly.

I tried the lock, but it didn't budge. Instinctively, I aimed the heart-stone of the Pendant towards the lock and thought of it being burned open. A jet of purple flame lanced forth from the stone's smooth surface and broke the lock, leaving a melted husk of metal where it had been.

Letting the Pendant fall to my chest, I pulled open the door with a squeak of aging metal, setting foot into the dully lit cell.

"Carden," I said softly, so happy to see him. "Carden, it's me, Leander."

He didn't move, simply huddling there on the floor, my heart aching and my worry for him growing.

The Revenant must have done terrible things to make him behave like this. Oh, my poor beloved Guardian.

"Carden?" I frowned worriedly, edging towards him, his soft groans so strange. "Are you all right?"

I reached out my hand slowly, my fear growing as my heart felt a strange ache. A tingle warmed my chest, and I felt those warning vibrations begin to course through me from the Pendant's silvery coils. Something was truly very wrong.

"Carden?" I touched his shoulder. "Can you hear me? Carden?"

His hand slammed around my wrist and panic filled me as I saw how gnarled and aged his skin was. I started trying to pull free, gasping and crying out in panic as he turned towards me. My eyes widened and my heart shattered as tears flooded my vision instantly at the sight staring up from beneath that black hair at me.

His eyes were white without pupil or colour, his face pointed and skull-like, his teeth gnashing at the sight of me. He smelled of rotting flesh and ancient dust, his movements slow and jerking.

"No! No, Carden, no!" I cried, tears slipping down my face as the draugar that had replaced him slowly stood, still grasping my wrist. "No, please, no! Not him! No!"

The Carden-Draugar opened his mouth and let out a husking breath, reaching and grasping at me desperately, my struggles barely enough to keep him from biting me.

As the ghoulish face snapped at me, there came that familiar warmth and the sheen of bright purple light. The Pendant flashed and he was hurled away from me, slamming into the far wall as I landed hard on the floor on my back.

Slowly, I propped myself up and watched as he clambered to his feet. He let out a terrible, shrieking howl, then charged at me. Another flash of the Pendant and he was thrown so hard against the wall that he exploded into a cloud of corpse dust and bones.

Silence followed and I closed my eyes, sobbing at the pain that filled my chest as tears ravaged my eyes. *He's dead... Oh Gods! Carden's dead! No...*

There suddenly came howls and shrieks from all around me. I didn't have the time to sit and grieve now, the Pendant flashing wildly against my chest at the danger that was erupting all around me. I pulled myself to my feet, gathering my skirt hems in my hands and rushing from the cell, tears flooding my cheeks as I left the dusty remains of my beloved behind...

Chapter Eighteen
From Darkness into Light

E ven with the screams of the wretched undead filling the way behind me, I couldn't help crying as I fled, the image of my beloved's corrupted and cursed form so fresh in my mind. I thought of what horrors he must have faced to have come to such a terrible fate, my heart now nothing but shattered, the broken shards stabbing me from within with a razor-sharp pain.

I can't think of this now! I have to get out of here or I'll be joining him in that dread fate! But, oh, Carden... Why?!

I brushed my tears away with my sleeve to clear my vision, watching the Pendant as it was now trying to show me the way to safety.

"Help me find my allies and escape this place!" I urged it desperately, looking over my shoulder as I ran, the shadows of the draugar charging after me.

The Pendant started flashing as it did when searching, pointing me to my right. I followed, running and screaming as a grasping group of hands snatched at me. They seized my arms, scratching at my skin as they pulled me back against the bars from behind which they reached. I fought and struggled, feeling their hot, foul smelling breath savaging my skin, their claw-like hands tugging on my hair painfully. My legs thrashed and planted my heels to the stone floor as I battled to free myself, but the draugar were far too strong for me.

My eyes locked on the five shuffling, hunched figures that now lurked towards me out of the shadows, their dead white eyes staring through me with a hunger so terrifying that to describe it would cause nightmares.

"No... no... please..." I closed my eyes, so terrified of the pain they would be wrought upon my soft flesh.

I felt one coarse, leathery hand close around my throat as the hissing breath issued from the draugar's sunken lips, its teeth close to my face.

Please... someone, help me! That was the last thing I thought, then waited for the biting to begin.

Suddenly, a golden flash drew me to open my eyes and I watched as a glowing sword carved up through the air, dispatching the draugar that held my throat. The undead thing crumpled to the floor, a golden knight in a black hood standing before me, his shield slamming into a second draugar that threw itself towards him.

Behind him stood four more golden armoured knights, all with their hoods drawn to hide their faces. They were now fighting the onslaught of draugar as the first knight freed me, the cracking of undead limbs with the sweeping of steel sounding around me.

The Knight pulled me from the draugar behind the bars and turned his hooded face to me. I couldn't make out his features beneath the hood, glimpsing only two familiar eyes that I couldn't place having seen.

"Go, child," the Knight urged me in a rough voice, gesturing with his sword to a doorway. "We shall dispatch these foul creations of evil."

"Wait!" I was so stunned, staring up at him as he tried to push me towards the doorway. "Who are you?! Why are you helping me?!"

"There is no time for questions, girl!" he stated, swinging his shield and knocking back another draugar. "Go! Find your friends! Flee this wicked place!"

"But I..." he shoved me further towards the door and looked down at me severely, cutting me off.

"Run, Leander!" he ordered me sternly. "Now!"

"Thank you," I said, then turned and ran through the doorway, catching a glimpse of him as he began swinging his sword into the fray.

*Dragon Knights! They were Dragon Knights! But why would Dragon Knights have come to the Revenant's fortress?! And how does that one know my name?! I can't have met him before... Could I?!*I shook my head, snapping out of my astonishment. *Don't worry about that now! Run, like he said! I **have** to get out of this place!*

I ran as fast as I could, the sounds of the screaming draugar still tearing up behind me. I knew the knights who had suddenly appeared - as coincidental and fortuitous as that was - could only hold back so many of the undead fiends, my single hope now to keep moving as quickly as I could.

The Pendant kept showing the way, its purple light my only salvation in this dire place, my legs carrying me as quickly as they could to its promise of safety. I was getting breathless, ducking and weaving through the many passages of the labyrinth fortress, my heart now so stressed that pain shot up my arm, through my chest and into my neck.

A howl drew my gaze and I instantly regretted turning to look as the floor vanished beneath me. Air rushed around me, a hard thud went through me and a sickening snap brought pain to my leg. I screamed; my left ankle filled with a splintering agony whilst my head throbbed with the impact of the fall.

Awkwardly, I pulled myself to sit up, turning my gaze to the way above me. I had fallen from a destroyed ledge that I'd not seen, the sky above me clear now that there was no ceiling. I turned my gaze about me, seeing that I lay there on the floor of a rounded courtyard built up beneath the great domed tower that presided over the dreaded fortress.

Haunting statues stood there, ruined with fractures in their stone skins, their lifeless eyes staring through me as they clutched at their swords. Broken stone littered the ground, creeping vines climbing every wall with their brown coils and sharp thorns.

I cast my attention to my ankle, sitting up properly and reaching my hands tenderly along the length of my leg. Pain shredded through my nerves with the gingery touch of my fingers, my ankle surely broken as I seethed at the pain.

How am I going to get out of here with a broken ankle? I need help...

"TALLINN!" I shouted into the wind. "TRISTAN! HELP!"

I listened, only the wind replying with its gentle whispers, the crescent moons casting an eerie pale light down through the night's clouds.

"SOMEONE! PLEASE, HELP!" I shouted again, desperate for them to reach me, but still there was no sign of my companions.

What do I do? What can I do? I can't walk on a broken ankle...

"*Princess...*" a voice hissed, deep and metallic from the darkness that surrounded me.

I looked up from my hands, still clutching my ankle, my fingers curling around the straps of my boot at the sudden hiss. My eyes started searching the shadowy arches and passages that led into the courtyard, my heart racing with fear as I felt a familiar nausea that made me feel like I would pass out.

Oh, no... Please, no...

"You are a foolish girl," the voice mewed in its harshly terrifying way, "coming here when you had the chance to be free of us. How very foolish, Princess..."

I know that voice...

I began trembling, my eyes flicking to every walkway frantically in search of the dreaded owner of those frightening words.

"Your little escapade has angered my Master greatly, child," the voice went on, filling me with a cold, icy terror. "Escaping Castle Ortagaad... Fleeing across the ice sheets of the sea... Your little scene in Travarna... The efforts wasted pursuing you to these forests... How very incredible you have revealed yourself to be for a mere girl."

"What do you want from me?" I asked in a shaking, terrified voice.

"Your life," the monster responded, and he appeared.

I drew back in terror as the Revenant emerged from the shadows of the tower, his wine-coloured robes and cloak swirling around his black armoured form, his white eyes staring at me from behind his hideous skull-like helm. He looked like some terrible obsidian king wreathed in robes of blood, his undead gaze locked squarely on me.

"You have no hope of escape now, Princess," the Revenant said, stepping slowly down the steps towards me. "Fleeing is impossible."

I dragged myself backwards painfully, turning my eyes to the arches surrounding me. Terrified gasps and whimpers escaped my lips at the black figures that stepped from the shadows, their swords drawn, their eyes set on me. I was suddenly surrounded, ten Shadow Knights closing every possible exit I could have taken if I could have walked, trapping me before the Revenant.

I braced my back against the central statue in the courtyard, a single image of the Revenant himself, my palms pressing to the ground, my good knee bent while my broken ankle lay out before me. I didn't know what to do, not even sure that my pendant could protect me from so many powerful enemies all alone. And my nausea was worsening with his presence, like every other time we had met.

"You have no weapons, no friends to help you, no power you can use to save yourself," the Revenant hissed through his mask down at me. "Even with your pendant you cannot last long, girl. You are *alone*..."

Suddenly, there came a loud boom and a bright flash of green light that exploded from behind me. The Revenant recoiled, shielding his face with his gauntleted wrist as the Shadow Knights hid behind their shields. The light dimmed but did not go out and I turned over my shoulder as a voice spoke.

"She is *not* alone, Revenant," that very familiar wise voice from the tower in Ortagaad spoke, filling me with cautious relief.

I looked up as the Green Wizard stepped up to my right, his gnarled staff in his hand, its stone glowing bright with green light. He peered out from under the wide brim of his pointed hat at the monster before me, his hazel eyes stern and strong with conviction.

"You continue to interfere in my Master's affairs, Wizard!" the Revenant growled viciously, red energy crackling across his gauntleted fingers.

"Neither you nor your Master shall touch this girl again!" the Wizard declared.

"You can do nothing to stop us!" the Revenant bellowed.

The Shadow Knights all stomped forward at once, but before they could reach us the Wizard stamped his staff against the floor, a green wave of energy rippling out all around us from its strike. The ten Shadow Knights were destroyed, shrieking as they evaporated like black steam in the power of the Wizard's magical light.

The Revenant snarled behind his mask, stomping forward, his gauntlets cracking and his right hand snatching his sinister black sword from his hip. The Wizard drew a silvery sword of his own, the two lashing out and battling in the middle of the courtyard with the clashing of thunder from their strikes.

The Wizard swept through his strikes like a green wind, hitting back against the Revenant's assaults with both his glowing staff and his silvery singing sword. The Revenant looked almost clumsy next to the old man's astonishing grace in battle. I had never seen anything like it.

As the Wizard shouted and grunted, and the Revenant shrieked and howled, I heard footsteps, turning my gaze up to see Tallinn, Tristan, the Orcs and Rangers.

"Leander!" Tallinn called, running to my side.

"Tallinn! Oh, I am so happy to see you!" I felt as if I could cry as she and Tristan dropped down beside me.

"Are you all right, lass?" Tristan asked.

I shook my head. "My ankle... It's broken."

"It's all right, Leander," Tallinn tried to reassure me as she assessed the damage with a cursory inspection.

"Tallinn," I couldn't help my tears as I looked up at her. "Carden... he's... he's dead..."

"Oh, Gods..." she gasped with grief in her eyes. "Leander, no, I'm... Gods..."

"I'm sorry," Tristan said softly, looking from me, then to Tallinn. "Truly I am."

Tallinn sucked in a wavering breath, recovering her composure. "We'll have time enough to grieve him later. For now, let us get you out of here. Tristan..."

"Aye, I've got her," Tristan scooped me up, supporting me around the waist and helping me to stand on my uninjured leg.

Wiping my eyes, I turned my gaze to the battle still going on, watching with my friends in awe. The Wizard slashed and dodged another of the Revenant's attacks, a green shield of light enveloping him now as the monster turned his dark red power onto him. The Wizard responded with his own staff's magic, the green and crimson colliding in a storm of energy between them.

"You cannot hope to destroy me, old man!" the Revenant snarled, pushing the magic stemming like a powerful river of red lightning from both hands at the Wizard. "You haven't power enough to accomplish such a task!"

"I needn't destroy you, Revenant," the Wizard retorted sternly, pushing his staff further towards the Revenant, the green energy pulsing and growing brighter. "I need only keep you from the girl."

"The girl belongs to my Master!" the Revenant roared, pushing harder, but struggling now against the power building between them.

"I'm afraid that you will be leaving your Master very disappointed," the Wizard remarked and struck with a powerful beam of magical light that seemed to illuminate the whole courtyard.

The night glowed bright with green power, the Revenant staggering and straining as his hold against the Wizard's magical might was breaking.

I clung to Tristan with my left arm, shielding my face with my right and trying to see through the emerald glare.

The Revenant staggered backwards, desperately trying to hold on, his red power now only around him as the Wizard's green light overwhelmed his position. He screeched and yowled like some terrible thing, unable to hold for much longer as the Wizard stepped closer and closer, his staff powering even greater against the Necromancer's own magic.

"This girl is protected!" the Wizard declared in such a loud, booming voice that it echoed around us as if he were a chorus instead of one man. "Return to your Master and reveal to him his folly in pursuing her!"

"NO!" the creature shrieked.

"BE GONE!" the Wizard bellowed and gave one final, powerful shove with his staff.

The green energy exploded forward, and we watched on in awe as the Revenant shrieked, then was launched from his feet. The terrible armoured necromancer flew high into the air, red lightning crackling wildly as he flailed amongst the green light, then disappeared far beyond the tower of his fortress.

The light died away and the Wizard turned towards us, seeming more like a wise old man now that his power had receded.

"Come," he said gently. "We best not linger here, ere the remaining denizens of this place converge upon us with their blight."

"But we know not the way out," Ranulf said, coming to stand at his sister's side.

"Follow me and I shall lead you safely from this labyrinth back to the free world," the Wizard said, then sheathed his sword, lifted his staff and strode forward towards an archway in a swirl of green and brown robes.

We made our way swiftly through the labyrinth, the Orcs eagerly following the Wizard. It was almost as if they knew him very well. All I could do was hobble along, holding onto Tristan as we moved, our focus on keeping up.

I feel so useless like this! Why did I have to break my ankle?! Oh, Gods, it hurts so much!

The Wizard led us quickly, stomping his staff's base to the floor each time the draugar closed in on us, the power of his green magic seeming to ward them off. The glowing green light kept us safe as we made our way towards the entrance to the fortress. The courtyard before the bridge across the vale was filled with undead archers and Shadow Knights, blocking our way.

The Wizard shot them down and cleared our path with ease, the Rangers dispatching as many enemies as they could with their bows while the Orcs knocked back all enemies that got too close. The whole event was a blur to me as I desperately hoped we could escape across the bridge and make our way to freedom.

"Call on your Dragon, Princess!" the Wizard commanded as he threw down a pair of Shadow Knights. "Her aid would be greatly appreciated!"

"She can't breathe flames and she's too hurt to fly!" I replied, shying away as an undead attacked us, Tallinn slashing it down with her sword mere feet from me.

"She need not be able to for the task I have for her," the Wizard responded.

I nodded and squeezed my pendant tight: "Amethyst! We need you!"

In response, there came her familiar roar from the forests, and I saw my beautiful purple and silver scaled dragon appear, charging down the hill towards the bridge.

"Over the bridge! Swiftly!" the Wizard directed, Tristan helping me as Tallinn and Ranulf ran with us.

I focused only on Amethyst where she stood, the other four Rangers still with her, their arrows flying past us to find their marks. I dared not look back for fear of what I might see, knowing that many draugar pursued us under the whip of their Shadow Knight commanders.

We reached the other side of the bridge, the Wizard and the Orcs the last to cross.

It was then that the Wizard turned to Amethyst and said quickly to her: "Tear this bridge asunder, dear Dragon! Protect the girl you are bonded with from the dire evil crossing it!"

"Do as he says, Amethyst," I permitted when she gave me a questioning look.

Amethyst nodded, turned her back and attacked the bridge with a sweeping strike of her barbed tail. She turned and stomped with her front claws on the stones, the bridge rippling as if it were water, then shattering and falling. The shrieks of the wretched draugar and the dreaded Shadow Knights echoed as they plummeted with the ruins of the bridge, their forms vanishing into the darkness below.

The Wizard pointed his staff towards the portcullis gates of the fortress and struck with a ball of green fire, the stonework and steel exploding with the strike. The courtyard collapsed and we stood there staring at the devastated fortress, which was crippled now and unable to spew forth any more dire soldiers to pursue us.

"Very handy to have in a fight, this fellow," Tristan remarked, impressed by the Wizard's skills.

"Indeed," Ranulf agreed, glancing to his sister, but Tallinn looked as dark as I felt.

"Come, we must move on," the Wizard said, turning and striding up the hillside. "It will not be long before the Shadow Lord learns of what has transpired here."

"Where do you suggest we go?" Tristan asked, drawing the old man's gaze, bracing me closer to him as I continued to hop at his side.

"The City of Silvervale," the Wizard responded, "fortified province of the High Elves, and the very place you had intended to lead your young charge since you began this trek."

* * * * *

Our group travelled for some hours before reaching a place we could be safe from the terrors of all that yet lurked in the forests surrounding us. The Rangers set up our camp while Tallinn sat on a fallen log, staring into the fire from beneath her hood. Her grief was silent, but no less potent than mine as Tristan helped me to sit on the furs that had been laid out for me.

"Let's take a look at that ankle, lass," he said, un-strapping my left boot and carefully freeing my foot from it.

I cringed at the pain the movement caused me, watching with my hands braced to the ground behind me. I felt Amethyst laying against my back, glad for her to be so close to me at that moment. My foot came free, the Wanderer rolling back the cuff of my dark leggings to reveal the horrible purple bruising that had swollen up through my skin.

Tristan seethed at the wound, shaking his head. "That's really bad, lass. How does it feel?"

"It really hurts," I murmured, cringing back against the pain that now felt worsened with it being free of the boot. "I've never broken a limb before."

"It's never fun," he sighed, studying it. "I'll fashion a splint and find some herbs to take the pain away. It's the best I can do for now."

"The pain of this is nothing compared to the other scarring my heart," I sighed, feeling as if I could cry.

Tristan looked into my eyes sympathetically: "I'm... uh... I'm sorry about Carden, lass. Truly, I am. I know you cared for him."

I just nodded, trying to hold back my tears.

"How is the Princess faring?" the Wizard asked, drawing our attention as he stood there before us.

"She has a broken ankle," Tristan replied, looking over his shoulder at him. "I have not the skills needed to heal such an injury here, yet I can at least aid her enough until we reach the Elves. Perhaps their magicks can help."

"Go attend to the meal, Tristan," the Wizard instructed him. "I shall take care of the girl."

"You're going to use your magicks then?" the reddish-blonde haired man questioned curiously.

"I know of something that will help her," the Wizard replied cryptically, then gestured for him to go.

Tristan nodded and stood, throwing me one final gaze before turning to join the others by the fire.

I watched as the Wizard took off his hat, revealing his kindly, wise old face and hazel eyes as he took a seat on a rock beside me. He set his staff and hat down, studying my foot for a moment with great thought behind his calm eyes.

"How will you heal me?" I asked softly, wishing for the pain to go away and hoping he could do it quickly.

"With the magic you yourself hold," he replied.

"I have no magic," I said despondently, staring at my broken ankle. "There isn't a magical bone in my body."

"Ah, but you are wrong, child," he said knowingly, drawing my gaze, "for you carry the greatest magicks ever known, both in your heart and in the Pendant around your neck."

I looked up at him, feeling the tears that yearned to flow from my eyes and the tiredness that accompanied my grief. "I don't understand."

"The Dragon Pendant possesses many powerful abilities. This - I am sure - you are now aware of," he explained evenly. "Your pendant has demonstrated its powers many times now. It has shielded you from harm, guided you when you have been lost, been the light you needed in the darkness, given you warmth to sleep by in the nights, and even gifted you the friend you have found in your dragon. Yet, this is not *all* that it can do."

"What do you mean?" I frowned, feeling lightheaded from the pain coursing through my injured limb.

"Not only can the Pendants do all these things you have thus far seen, they can also aid you in many more ways," he told me with a sense of reverent awe and knowledge. "Whilst you wear this pendant you will not die from harsh elemental conditions, accounting for your survival on the frozen seas, just as it makes you immune to the pain and destruction of which Dragon Fire is capable."

"Really? You're... you're saying even a dragon's flames can't hurt me?" I was stunned and curious all at once.

He nodded. "Yes. The wards within your pendant shield you so strongly against all such powers. Only those of physical origins may cause you harm, yet with time and practice, you might even cast the very arrows shot at you from the air and cleave a man's blade into melted steel. Such are the powers held by the Dragon Pendants and those they choose to wield them."

I met his gaze sternly, the pain feeling as if it were worsening yet again: "And... ugh... and what can it do to help me now?"

He smiled softly at my question, clearly noting my growing impatience and discomfort: "Not all of the Dragon Pendants' powers are defensive or used in battle. Some, many that you have seen, are for other more varied uses."

He reached out and gestured to my ankle. I just frowned at him, my eyes flicking to the injury, then back to his face uncertainly.

"Place your right hand upon your injured ankle," he instructed me gently, taking my hand in his and setting my palm against my skin, causing me to seethe in pain. "I know it is painful, my dear girl. Next, hold your pendant with your left hand."

I nodded and did as he instructed, grasping my slender fingers around the silver coiling designs and the smooth purple stone. I felt my thumb begin to caress the stone gently, finding a small comfort in this simple action.

"Good, very good," the Wizard nodded. "Now, close your eyes and think of the brilliant light the Pendant issues from its stone. As you do this, silently ask the Pendant to send its energy through you to your hand and allow it to repair the damage done to your bones. Imagine that the pain and the injury will fade with the casting of its power."

"Okay," I whispered, letting my eyes fall shut.

In my mind I thought of the light that shone from the Pendant's heart-stone whenever I had need of its help, feeling that familiar warmth beginning to spread through me. I visualised it flowing through my body, reaching along my right arm and slithering out of my fingertips to cascade into my skin and fill my broken ankle bones.

Let me heal this wound. Let all the pain it brings leave me. Restore my body to the way it should be before this hurt came to be upon me. My strange thoughts of invocation surprised me, and I half wondered if they were my thoughts at all.

I began to feel clicking and grinding in my ankle, groaning and seething as I did, tears watering behind my eyes with their wet heat.

"Do not lose your focus," the Wizard urged me gently. "The pain is natural in this, just as it is in normal healing, but more rapid than usual. It *will* pass."

I nodded, pushing aside all thoughts other than my invocation to heal. From beneath my eyelids, I caught the shimmer of that purple light, resisting the urge to open my eyes and look. The pain soon faded, and I felt the Pendant's heat recede, opening my eyes to see its glow fading from me. I turned my gaze past the Wizard to see the others all staring at me in astonishment.

What did I just do?

With the purple light once again returned to the Pendant's heart, I turned my gaze to my ankle. There was no mark, no bruising, all the swelling gone as well as the pain. I twisted it to see if it hurt, but there was nothing, only the normal feeling I was used to.

"It's... the pain's... gone..." I was beside myself with amazement.

The Wizard nodded. "Indeed, it is."

"How?" I asked, looking to him curiously.

"The Pendants hold many gifts," he replied, leaning his elbows on his knees as he met my gaze. "The power to heal oneself and any others you would choose to is but one, and certainly a great one."

"It's incredible. It's as if I never broke it," I ran my fingers along my ankle once again, feeling that everything was as it should be.

"You have much to learn of your gifts, my dear girl," he said kindly, smiling as I looked back towards him. "Yet, it is evident that you learn quickly."

I brushed a hand through my hair, clearing my eyes as I studied him for a moment.

"How is it that you know so much of the Pendant and the gifts it has given me?" I asked curiously.

"Because my dear," he said, reaching into his collar and producing a chain, "you're not the only one with these gifts."

I stared at what he held before me; a silver necklace hanging from his neck, the chain pinched between his thumb and finger. From its loop hung a simple oval shaped pendant with an emerald stone at its core, many etched designs arcing around it to create beautifully carved shapes within its silver skin.

"You... you have a Dragon Pendant too?" I was stunned as I glanced from the silvery necklace and its emerald heart-stone to the Wizard's face. "Who are you?"

"A friend come to help you in your time of need, Leander," he responded gently. "One who intends to aid you where I can and, for the moment, help you to ease the pains that plague you."

My heart panged at his words, grateful though I was for his intentions to assist and protect me. There was a yet deeper pain that ran in me than that of the now healed broken bones and torn sinews of my ankle.

"I fear that not all my hurts can be healed as easily as my bones," I confessed, feeling my tears slip free down my cheeks. "The pain now known to my heart can't be taken away by any kind of magic I could ever hope to wield."

I closed my eyes, seeking to see Carden as he was, but only seeing the monster that had been made of him. All that my love had been was gone, destroyed and corrupted by the Revenant, then shattered into dust by the Pendant in its efforts to defend me.

I felt two coarse, warm fingers touch my chin, opening my tear-filled eyes as the Wizard lifted my face to meet his gentle, comforting gaze.

"Not all things are what they seem, Princess," he told me softly, his words so sincere. "Especially not those things shown to you by our enemy. Do not lose hope or faith in the love your heart possesses."

I nodded softly, no words coming to my mind to answer his gentle counsel.

"Take what rest you need, my dear girl," he urged me as he got to his feet and took up his staff and hat once more. "Your strength will be much needed on this last leg of the journey to reach our safe haven."

* * * * *

The journey to Silvervale was no more than three days from where we made camp that night after fleeing Arnath. Three miserable, rainy, wet days filled with bitting cold and harsh winds across a difficult forest path. Huddled under my hood, I cursed the deluge that fell upon us, wishing for the rain to cease, even if the sun didn't shine.

I pulled the grey coat further around me, my hair slicked by the rain as I tried to stay shielded by my hood. It felt as pointless and futile fighting the rains as much as it did fighting the everlasting grief that choked my heart.

Amethyst knew of my hurt, never leaving my side, a constant purple presence out of the corner of my eye. She had become the closest thing I now had left to a family, and I wouldn't allow myself to lose her after all that I already had. My heart couldn't bear the pain.

We made camp that night, my exhaustion leading me to sleep without my evening meal. My dreams were plagued by the nightmarish images of what I had experienced in Arnath, tearing at my heart with bladed claws like some rabid beast bent on causing me greater harm. I woke in tears, looking up from beneath the furs of my bedroll to see those comforting molten orange eyes gazing down at me. Amethyst nuzzled her nose's horned tip into my shoulder, urging me back to sleep. While this didn't prevent the terrible dreams, it did offer me some comfort.

The last morning of our journey I woke to a curious sight. The Wizard, Tallinn and Ranulf were quietly talking to the three Orcs at the edge of the camp while Tristan and another Ranger tended to our meagre breakfast. The Orcs bowed their heads and beat one fist to their chests before turning and trudging off into the woods.

I sat up as the Landrace Siblings and the Wizard turned to re-join us.

"Where are the Orcs going?" I asked curiously, watching their bulky green shapes disappear into the forest depths.

"Back to their enclave," Tallinn answered me, her hood pushed back, and her blonde locks tied into a neat braid.

"They're leaving us?" I wasn't sure how I felt about that.

"The Orcs will not enter into Elven territory," she explained evenly, almost too coldly for her, but that had to be because of her own grief. "They do not venture near to Silvervale out of respect for the treaty they share with the High Elves, just as they will not travel the Elven Road through the forest."

"Which is our decided path today," the Wizard stated as he leaned both hands on his staff. "We shall eat, then set out upon that road for Silvervale. We should find ourselves at their gates before dusk."

An hour later, we were soon making our way through the woods again, the Wizard guiding us to the Elven Road. It was paved of warm coloured stones and had a more inviting air to it than the rest of the forest did. Even all that surrounded us seemed more vibrant and alive as we began following its gently winding trail.

The forest began to thin as hills surrounded us, the road sloping down at about four hours after midday. We were soon walking through the gentle faces of cliffs and great pines, birds singing brightly above us. I hadn't realised until that moment how much I had come to miss the sound of birds singing.

We walked through the curving corners of the canyon, soon stepping onto an overhang that looked out over a wide expanse of vast green country. Beautiful forests and wilds stretched all the way to the Nartarn'lath Mountains to our left, which we were now closest to, and north to the edge of the familiar blue of the Ortagaad Sea. Far off in the distance I could see Ivansten, a place I had never sought to go, hidden behind rolling hills and gentle miniature mountains. Yet, this was hardly the single most impressive sight of all that I saw.

So very near to us on the edge of a great lake and beneath the shadow of a verdant mountain capped with snow stood a glimmering city fortress. It was silver in the late afternoon light with golden domed roofs glinting brilliantly as many spires reached up to the sky.

"Here lies the City of Silvervale, home of the High Elves," the Wizard declared proudly. "And there, on the mountain's feet, the Broken Towers: sanctuary of the Elemental Brotherhood, my brothers in magic."

I followed his description to see that there were five black towers that stood on the mountain cliffs above the fortress city, all of them seeming broken.

I never thought I would ever make it here. It's so beautiful.

"Hey, we did it, lass," Tristan nudged my shoulder, gaining my gaze as he smiled at me. "We made it."

"We did," I returned a weak, saddened smile, turning my eyes back to the city.

I just wish Carden could have been with us.

We made our way down the hillsides, setting foot on the grounds below the cliffs we had emerged from. These vast fields under the shadows of the mountains were more alive than any I had come to know in so very long that I had forgotten any such beauty could exist.

The sun was falling slowly towards the horizon when we at last came to the doors of the city, passing over an intricate and elegantly carved bridge high above the river that fed the lake. We crossed, Amethyst ducking her head so as not to collide her horns with the woodwork, entering the enormous silver and white gates set into the white stone walls that surrounded the city.

Upon entering the gates, I looked to my left to see a drop barred by a carved wooden barrier that looked down on great gardens and waters pooling there. The lake had been allowed to enter under the castle walls of the city to form a second, smaller lake that fed the flourishing gardens.

My eyes drifted to a guard post by the gates where there stood three silver armoured and masked Elves in flowing charcoal-coloured cloaks. They each carried a bow and a curved long sword, the plates of their armour set over a fine chainmail unlike any I had ever seen in human armouries.

The Wizard led us forward easily, his welcome here assured. The stares of the silver, white, mauve and pale blue robed elven citizenry did nothing to discourage him, though their attention was on us. Like the Wood Elves I had met in Galvenin, these Elves were beautiful, though less like hunters and woodsmen than their Galvenin cousins and with skin tinted a golden-cream. They looked more like nobles, many of the women wearing delicate silver circlets with emerald leaves, the men just as fair faced and beautiful.

We walked the roads along the cliff, turning slowly to the largest house that stood tallest of all. As we reached the stairs, I caught the beating of great wings, turning as a shadow fell over us. I stared in shocked wonder as a great green dragon landed on a large rocky platform above the gardens. The Dragon considered me with his orange eyes and bowed his head, his wings held up above him, all of his four feet set to the stone beneath him.

I know that Dragon...

Amethyst bowed her head to him, the other dragon watching her softly as we came to a stop.

"Princess," the Wizard drew my gaze from the Dragons back to the stairs, "may I present to you Lord Selwyn of Silvervale, leader of the High Elves of High-Realm."

The Elf that stood before us had long dark hair and a young, but wise face. He smiled and bowed his head in welcome to me, dressed in fine cobalt robes over silver, a gold circlet of Elven design around his head.

"Ish irr manarhia," the Elf smiled warmly. "You are welcome, Princess Leander."

"Thank you, my Lord," I responded, feeling so tired from the journey to get there. "May I ask, how do you know who I am?"

"You have been long known to us, your Highness," Lord Selwyn said evenly, speaking with such age and wisdom beyond the perceived years his face showed. "We have sought your arrival here for quite some time. Ever since the others you know came in search of our aid."

"The others?" Tallinn frowned, staying close by my side. "What others?"

"The others of your order, Guardian Tallinn," Lord Selwyn responded evenly, his hands clasped together before his stomach.

"You did not think us to abandon you so readily, did you, my friends?" a female voice asked.

I turned and smiled as familiar red hair and turquoise elven eyes appeared before me. Ellora stood there dressed in her huntress' leather armour, her weapons not with her, but her appearance impressive all the same. She hardly looked any different and to see her again was beyond words.

"Ellora!" I exclaimed, hugging her tightly.

"It is so very good to see you, Princess," she beamed as she hugged me, then stepped back to take in my features. "We had feared that we might never see you again."

"As I feared the same of you," I told her.

"It is good to see you too, Tallinn," Ellora stepped past me and hugged Tallinn, who merely smiled softly in their embrace before parting again.

"Bless my eyes!" I turned to see Dolin striding towards me, his black beard neat and his blue tunic perfect over his armour as he approached. "Lassie, is it really you?!"

"It is," I confirmed with a smile and a nod. "It's wonderful to see you again, Dolin."

"We feared you lost forever to those foul folks that night," the Dwarf confessed gravely, then smiled as his ever-dishevelled twin came up beside him. "But to see you with my own eyes... Oh! What glad tidings!"

"We gave them our best, girlie," Holger assured me with a gruff nod, his arms crossed firmly as he tried to be stern and hard. "Truly we did."

"I know, Holger. And I am so glad to see you too," I leaned down and kissed his cheek, then did the same with his brother.

The Dwarf blushed and chuckled lightly. "Oh... uh... yes, well..."

I turned my gaze to the three remaining figures that stood with them now.

Aldwyn looked as wise as ever, his staff in hand and his black and silver Guardian robes flowing with the wind, his gently greying dark hair catching in the breeze with them. Fawkner smiled softly at me, his scar over his left eye suddenly remembered after all the time I had spent trying to imagine his light brown haired and bearded face. He was dressed in a black and silver Guardian jacket over a greyish blue shirt, his sword at his hip. And, of course, Joran had never seemed bigger to me as I saw him again, imposing and powerful, his arms at his sides. Dressed in brown leather armour over a grey cotton tunic and dark trousers, he still looked intimidating, the golden markings burned into his mauve skin on his face seeming so vibrant now.

"Joran," I hugged him instantly, feeling so like a child in his mammoth embrace.

"I am gladdened to see you again, Sarissi," the Storvari stated factually as he always did. "Too many days have passed since you were under my care."

"No more will, Joran," I said hopefully, looking up at him. "Never allow me to be without your protection again. Please."

He nodded solemnly. "By the honour of the Carethanes, it will be done, Sarissi."

"It truly is wonderful to see you safe, Princess," Aldwyn said, stepping away from hugging Tallinn.

"What brought you here to Silvervale, Aldwyn?" I asked of the Mage, releasing myself from Joran's embrace.

"An urgent missive sent some months after your abduction," Aldwyn explained evenly as horns echoed in the distance. "For near a year we had no means to seek you out until word reached us in Eilath."

"So, we came here to Silvervale as requested," Fawkner added, smiling warmly at me. "Ever since, we have been making plans and searching for the means to free you from Castle Ortagaad."

"A task apparently accomplished without our aid," Aldwyn said as another horn blew. "One moment, Princess," he stepped past me as horses and riders came through the gates into the city.

I twisted my hands together, watching my fingers grimly as I thought on this reunion. I felt truly safe and lucky with such friends, both old and new, yet there was an empty place in my heart.

As always, Fawkner seemed to know the state of my emotions, stepping forward and gently tilting my chin up from my distraction.

"What troubles you, Leander?" he asked softly.

Looking at him I instantly started to cry, his very presence the comfort I needed to openly release all the hurt that lingered inside me. He pulled me into his arms and held me tight, so like a father.

"Why do you cry, girl? What has hurt you so?" he sounded so concerned.

"Carden," I sobbed, burying my face into his shoulder to hide my tears. "He's... he's dead, Fawkner..."

"Oh, Leander," he cooed, lifting my chin and looking into my eyes with sympathy and a small smile as he shook his head. "What cruel visions have plagued you?"

I frowned, sniffing back my sobs as I met his gentle, pale eyed gaze.

"What word do you bring?" I heard Aldwyn ask from behind me, drawing my gaze before Fawkner could speak any further.

"The Witches keep the way through Gorvenna guarded, Travarna far more fortified than even the capital," a voice explained, a deep tenor that started my heart racing as I turned.

I gasped as I saw him perched in the saddle of his black stallion, the reigns gripped in his hands, Elven riders on white steeds all around him with their hoods drawn. He threw back his own darker hood, his black hair shorter than I remembered, now cut neat, but still caressing his forehead and neck lightly. His green eyes were hard, but so full of a desperation and fear that he tried so ardently to hide. He looked so different dressed in Guardian armour, his sword at his hip and gloves on his large hands.

Carden shook his head glumly at Aldwyn, sighing grimly: "I fear that we will never find a way to reach her with the Enemy so well guarded."

"Carden, it's all right," Aldwyn tried to assure him as Tallinn came up beside him.

"It's good to see you, Tallinn," he nodded to her.

"And you," she responded, "but listen to Aldwyn. It *is* all right."

"How I wish that were so," Carden responded, shaking his head gravely. "I mean to return to Gorvenna once I've rested to continue searching for a way to free her from those vile women. I will *not* abandon her..."

"Carden," Aldwyn interrupted him, gaining his frowning gaze. "Someone would like to see you."

The Mage gestured towards me as I pulled from Fawkner's arms, Carden following the movement with his gaze. His eyes widened and his jaw dropped, his face paling at the sight of me. He looked bewildered, frozen in place for a moment as he looked upon me with his jade stare.

"Leander?" his voice was small, his movements swift as he took from his mount to the ground, casting off his gloves and handing them to Aldwyn.

"Carden?" I murmured, walking towards him as if living in a dream. I couldn't be sure this was real.

We faced each other, then he rushed towards me in a few long strides, pulling me into his arms and kissing me deeply. My arms slid up around his shoulders tightly, my body pulling into his so eagerly as I cried with joy.

He broke his lips' embrace, allowing me to breathe as he looked into my eyes with wonder.

"I thought I would never look upon your beautiful eyes or taste your sweet lips again, Leander," he confessed. "Gods... I am so happy to have you back in my arms."

"I've dreamed of this moment for so long," I told him, not releasing my arms from around his shoulders, tears and sobs slipping free of my eyes and lips. "I thought I'd lost you in Arnath. I thought the Revenant had..."

"I am here, my love," he said softly, leaning his forehead against mine. "I'm here with you and I will *never* let you go again."

I looked up into his eyes and nodded, trying to smile, but still so shocked just to be with him again. I was afraid this was all a dream, and I would wake up at any moment to once again face a harsher reality in which he was dead.

"Come, let us get the Princess some much-needed food and rest," Aldwyn suggested. "I am sure after which she will be all too happy to tell you about everything that she has experienced until returning to us."

"Yes, of course," Carden nodded and smiled softly at me. "Come, my love."

I just nodded, letting him lead me with an arm around my shoulders up the stairs, the others following us close behind. I couldn't even begin to think of how happy I was in that moment, just glad to be with the man I love and all of my friends once again after spending so long alone without them. Finally, I had been freed from darkness and into the light again.

Chapter Nineteen
The Silver City

The hospitality of the High Elves was truly something to experience, Lord Selwyn having not only welcomed us into his beautiful city, but also into his home; and his generosity didn't stop there. I was shown to a beautiful room with white silk drapes and golden wood floors, the view from the balcony spectacular as it looked out over all the city and its constructed valley. The High Elf Lord showed me to the room himself after convincing Carden to take what time he needed from his travels to rest and get cleaned up.

"These rooms shall be yours, Princess," he said as he opened the silvery double doors into the beautiful room. "I perceive that you shall be staying with us a goodly length of time."

"Thank you, Lord Selwyn," I offered him a tired smile, turning from the room over my shoulder to meet his gaze. "It's so very kind of you to offer me so much."

"You are most welcome, your Highness," he bowed his head lightly, his hands clasped at the small of his back. "I have taken the liberty of arranging clothing to be brought to you. I trust they will meet your needs."

"I'm sure they will. My thanks."

"Take what time you require, your Highness," he bid me gently, watching me as I studied the intricate details of the room. "I am certain you would be in need of a proper bath and bed. When you have done all you desire, your attendant shall lead you to the dining hall. I hope you will join us for evening meal."

"Of course," then I frowned. "My attendant?"

I looked past the Elvish Lord and nodded as I saw Joran standing by the door. In truth, I had come to miss seeing the Storvari always standing by my door to guard me from harm.

"Right. Thank you," I said to Lord Selwyn.

"I shall leave you to your rest, your Highness," Lord Selwyn bowed his head, then turned and swept gracefully from the room with his silvery and blue robes trailing behind him.

Joran reached into the room, bowed his head to me, then closed the door to grant me some much-needed privacy. I turned to take in the late afternoon view of Silvervale's crystal city and waterfall abundant vale with a breath of ease.

We made it. At last, I'm safe from the Shadow Lord and his allies. Gods, I've forgotten what it feels like to be safe with people I care about.

I slipped out of the grey coat Danika had given me, then proceeded to undress as I went into the bathroom. I ran myself a bath then relaxed as I gratefully washed away all the grime and aches the journey here had left me with. The warm water was so nice on my skin, soothing the chilled pains that had plagued me since Castle Ortagaad.

Once I was clean, I got out of the deep square bath set into the marble floors, dried myself, donned a long flowing silver bathrobe, then took to the bedroom again. I brushed my hair, the silky strands feeling so much better now that they were cleaned and without knots, then I sought out something to wear. Only my dirtied dress remained to me and I chewed on my bottom lip as I thought on what to do. That was when there was a knock at the door, and I permitted two beautiful Elven women dressed in silver to enter. They brought with them clothes that had been tailored from Elven fabrics of silk, linen and velvet.

One of the women assured me that they would see to replacing my own dress with one very like it that the Lord's tailor would begin working on immediately. In the meantime, I was offered the most beautiful Elven dresses I had ever seen.

I selected a soft mauve silk dress which left my arms and shoulders bare, only gentle loops of its glittering silver fabric left to hold it around my upper arms. Over this I put on a teal velvet over-dress, the bodice similar to what I was used to, but with flowing sleeves that hung around my arms, still leaving my shoulders exposed but for the strap that held each sleeve in place. I laced up the silver cord in the front and put on the soft white slippers I had been offered before meeting my reflection in the mirror.

The two Elves fussed with my hair and set a silver circlet with the Elvish arrow and coil designs running over it onto my head.

For so long I've looked like a broken girl who has lived in a cave. Now I look like a princess once more. I'll never be so cold towards my birthright again. I will embrace who I am and be the Princess I should be.

Joran soon led me from the room, actually commenting on my appearance: "You look most beautiful, Sarissi."

"Thank you, Joran," I smiled softly up at him.

The Storvari led me down the long stairs inside the lordly house's main hall, then took me to the right, past the doors we had entered from the city. We passed by many silvery crystal rooms and white wooden arches before coming to a low set of wide steps that ran the length of the wall behind four large archways.

Before us was a balcony dining room with wide eaves that reached over to keep the rain from falling on those who dined there. A long silver and gold table was centred in the space with many chairs of intricate Elven carving set all around it. There was an Elven Woman in white and pale mauve stringing a harp softly, an Elven Man dressed in similar colours playing a pan flute gently in time with her, their music hauntingly beautiful. The remaining Elves in the room were either serving the table or were the silver armoured guards that stood at the arches onto the balcony; their faces covered by their helms with only their chins and lips visible, the high crests of their helms gleaming in the late sunlight.

As I entered the balcony, I heard all the chairs move, my friends were gathered there and dressed so neatly. Lord Selwyn stood at the head of the table, now wearing a golden robe over his silver one and a welcoming expression on his beautiful, yet masculine face.

I was surprised to see Ellora wearing a gold and green flowing robe with a circlet of her own, never having imagined the Huntress in anything other than her armour. She sat to the left of Lord Selwyn; a seat left empty by his right for me. Carden had the seat beside it with Tallinn at his right next to her brother. Aldwyn and Fawkner were seated opposite them with Ellora and Tristan. The two Dwarves had the seats beside Ranulf, the remaining seats taken by Elves of noble standing.

"Your Highness," Lord Selwyn greeted me and offered me the seat at his side. "Please, be seated."

I nodded and made my way slowly across the space to the seat he had offered me. As I walked, I took in the view of everyone there, all the Elves wearing mostly silvers or whites while many of my companions dressed as they normally did, but more formal.

I was glad to see that Tallinn had exchanged the furs and leathers for her own Guardian garb once again. She wore a black corset over a dark silvery tunic, the corset trimmed in silver with cords of the same colour, black and silver fabric hanging from its waistline down to her knees. She had her blonde hair pulled back neatly; the majority of the strands cast to hang over her left shoulder.

I smiled as I looked at Carden, gaining his smile in return. He was dressed in a long silver quilted tunic, a black shirt pulled on underneath it. Though he wore a brown belt at his waist, he didn't carry a sword or any of his throwing daggers. I had to admit that I really did like his new shorter hair style, his face looking so much clearer and more handsome than I remembered and his eyes more emerald now than jade.

He pulled out the chair for me and I took my seat, the rest of those gathered there doing the same once I had done so. Two years imprisoned in a tower had taught me to appreciate the respect I had always been offered with my royal upbringing, and I no longer cringed at the thought of it. It was better to accept that respect than to be abused with cruelty in its place.

"I trust that your room and the clothes we've offered you are to your liking, your Highness," Lord Selwyn smiled at me.

"Yes, thank you very much," I said honestly, feeling so well at ease with my hands folded in my lap. "I can't tell you how much I appreciate your hospitality, my Lord."

"It is very much the way of my people, Princess," Lord Selwyn stated, taking up a crystal goblet as a server filled it with clear water. "We High Elves have always offered our hospitality to those who truly need it, just as we have always defended the realms from the forces of the Shadow."

I cringed a little at his mention of our enemy. I would so gladly never think of those I'd had the misfortune of spending such a long, dark and painful time in the company of ever again. Yet, I knew that this wasn't over. The Shadow Lord was still looking for me after all.

"Am... am I safe here?" I asked uneasily. "From the Shadow Lord, I mean?"

"My Lady, you have nothing to concern yourself with," Lord Selwyn assured me after taking a mouthful of his drink and setting it down, the servers bringing us our meals.

"Forgive me, your Lordship, but I have been made these promises before," I said softly and unconvinced.

"Your path here to our city has been arduous and not without peril," the Elf Lord nodded softly, clasping his hands together in a steeple before him on the table as he studied me with his turquoise eyes. "However, I can assure you that you will find no threat here. Never have the forces of the Shadow ever set foot within High Elven borders, and never shall they. The enchantments of my people, as well as those of the Wizards who reside within the Broken Towers, keep *all* evil at bay where the Forests of Arnath come to their end. I doubt that there is any safer haven for you in all of High-Realm, your Highness."

"Even I have to admit the power of these pointy-ears," Holger surprised me, still not standing on ceremony as he ate his meal. "Not once since arriving in this city have we ever seen even the smallest hint of evil rearing its ugly head."

"No, indeed not," Dolin agreed, setting his drink down and gently picking at his food. "And it is no easy thing for a Dwarf to admit such of Elves."

"Then, we are honoured by your words, Masters Dolin and Holger," Lord Selwyn said appreciatively.

"May I ask," I looked to Ellora and Lord Selwyn, "did my ancestor ever visit this house?"

"No, your Highness, she did not," Ellora replied in earnest. "In truth, I believe you are the first Aldrich to set foot within the grand walls of Silvervale proper."

"Although, Leander the First did indeed visit the Broken Towers," Lord Selwyn confessed as he began eating, "though not for very long. Her business was with the Wizards, not with my people."

"Speaking of the Wizards, where did the Green Wizard go?" I wondered, noting that he wasn't at the table. "Will he not be joining us?"

"My old friend decided that it was best he confer with his fellow wizards, though I am very certain that you shall get your chance to meet with him again," Lord Selwyn replied evenly. "I would not be surprised if they would ask for an audience with you, Princess."

"Why would they want to speak with me?" I wondered, picking at my meal, very grateful for the fresh salad for a change.

"You were inside the walls of Castle Ortagaad," Aldwyn stated, drawing my gaze to his face, his aging surprising me. "You are also the only prisoner to have escaped from its cursed walls..."

"I wasn't the only one," I confessed with a shrug of my bare shoulders. "The Green Wizard was there as well. I don't know how he managed it, but he escaped too."

"Why was he imprisoned?" Tallinn asked curiously.

I chewed and swallowed my food before answering her with a vague shake of my head: "I'm not entirely sure. He said he was captured trying to help free King Thoralf's mind from the Witches' spells."

I noticed Fawkner's smile of amusement and the glimmer in Aldwyn's eyes, frowning as I looked to Lord Selwyn.

"Whilst this was indeed one of his intended tasks within the castle's dark halls," the Elf Lord confirmed with a nod, meeting my gaze, "he was also to determine your location and discover a means to rescue you. A task, it seems, *you* were more capable of accomplishing than us."

I was stunned and at the same time validated hearing such words. I'd had the feeling that they were trying to help me, that the Wizard had been there not only by chance of aiding the Gorvennan King.

Of course it makes sense. Anders said that he had a friend who had been attempting to free me. The Wizard makes the most sense.

"Nevertheless," Aldwyn went on, returning us to his first point, "you have seen so very much within that castle of what Manth and Keilantra intend, and have even been the single prisoner they have attended to the most. That gives you valuable insight the Wizards will seek to know, Princess."

I nodded as I thought about what he was saying, knowing he was right and remembering all that the Witches had shown me in their Sanctum.

"Will I have to go alone?" I asked a little nervously.

"Hardly," Aldwyn shook his head, eating his meal.

Carden touched my arm and drew my gaze to him, his eyes instantly filling me with a warming comfort and calm."We'll be with you. That is, all of us who are Guardians will be," he explained gently, his hand reaching up and his thumb caressing my chin. "I'll never let you endure such questioning alone."

I smiled softly at him and nodded.

"You are, of course, among friends once more," Fawkner added evenly, swallowing down some food with a sip from his goblet.

"And I could not be happier to be so," I said in earnest, receiving his gentle smile and nod, then looking to Carden. "I have missed you all."

Carden's smile and the hand that cupped mine on the table said infinitely more than his words ever could. I simply lost myself in his matured emerald gaze, swimming there in the comfort of his presence. Had I a choice, I would have remained there for the rest of my now incalculable life, but that thought alone was enough to pierce my heart with ice at the knowledge of all that I had lost.

"The question must now be asked," Tallinn's voice broke me from my loving stare and my haunted thoughts back to the dinner table, "what are we to do next? What course shall be taken?"

"For now," Aldwyn said, setting his goblet on the table after downing a large mouthful, "nothing."

"You would do nothing?" Tristan demanded gently, eyeing him dubiously. "The girl is yet still hunted by the Witches and their vile Master. I don't think it a good idea to sit on our laurels in this beauteous place with such evil at her heels..."

"No one asked your opinion, *Wanderer*," Carden hissed venom at the man, his eyes more a poison green than their normal hue as he gritted his teeth at him.

Tristan turned to him with a soured expression, almost hurt, though I could hardly believe for a single moment that he could have expected a warm welcome from my friends and protectors.

"Aye," Dolin agreed with Carden, pointing one accusing finger at Tristan. "Given your past allegiances, we can scarcely consider counting on your aid to protect the Princess from harm."

"I am the only reason she yet lives to stand in these halls," Tristan argued as calmly as he could manage. "Were it not for me, she'd have died weeks past in the forests, regardless of how far she had come on her own..."

"Were it not for you, she would never have found herself the prisoner of those foul witches and their wretched master," Tallinn scowled at him. "Nor would Carden and I have endured both the peril of facing the Revenant, or the fear for the Princess as she was taken from us."

"Had I a choice back then beyond that which I had been given, I'd have gladly taken it," Tristan sighed gravely, looking so tired. "Even taking my own life would have been preferable..."

"Not only to you, whelp," snapped Holger.

"There is little to be gained from this bickering," Aldwyn declared sternly, gazing around the table at us. "The past is the past and may not be changed. All we might focus our efforts on is the here and now, which I suggest we do."

I sat there feeling so tense from all the animosity that lingered around that table. To look at Carden and Tristan staring each other down was to look into the very eyes of hatred and jealousy, though the second emotion I couldn't understand.

"Master Aldwyn is correct," Lord Selwyn stated, seeming able to spread a calm unlike any other in the room. "Our priority at this moment is to maintain the safety of the Princess within this city, and so it shall be done. All petty squabbles will be left unattended until such a time as she is no longer under threat. As for what course to be taken next, I would suggest that we await the words of the

Wizards, as it is they who understand such things. Would you not agree, your Highness?"

I merely nodded, no longer interested in being a part of this conversation.

"Come," Ellora spoke warmly, "let us think on happier things. We are, after all, reunited once more, and I for one would celebrate and cherish such a wondrous event."

"You're right, Ellora," I smiled at her, blinking out of the daze the argument between the men had left me in. "I couldn't be happier to be with all of you, my friends, no... my family, once again."

The Elf nodded with her warm smile as she held up her glass in toast to our shared feelings.

"To family," Fawkner added, offering his goblet to the air in kind.

"To family," the others chimed in, all lifting their glasses in toast.

* * * * *

With dinner concluded several hours ago and our joyful reunions coming to a restful end, I bid my host goodnight, then made my way to the rooms he had provided for me. Joran stayed at the door, to my great ease, and I closed myself away, lighting the lamps and candles before seeking a means to relax my tremulous thoughts and heart.

Though I was safe in this Elven Kingdom and reunited with my friends, I could scarcely bring myself to rest at ease. That relentless shadow lingered on the edge of my thoughts, refusing to depart from my waking mind even with all the distractions I could manage to find. I couldn't even confess my fears to my own self as my thoughts inevitably turned to the visions the Witch had shown me.

Something caught my attention in the candlelight, and I turned to the bed to see a book wrapped in a hard leather cover sitting there. I sat down beside it and, with one hand, delicately turned it so that I could read the title: *Tales of Dragons*.

My favourite book... A smile tugged at my lips and I took up the folded parchment that had been left atop the cover. Unfolding it I beheld a gently scrawled handwriting I had never seen before, yet strangely found to be very familiar.

My dear Princess Leander,

I thought an old comfort might be welcome. Perhaps reading the words upon the pages of this book will ease the burden within your young heart for a time. If you should seek your beloved friend, you need only go to the gardens. Amethyst awaits you there.

We shall speak soon, my dear girl. But for the moment take what rest you need and embrace in the Love you have long dreamed of sharing once more with your Beloved young Guardian.

Yours,

That single initial "R" left me curious. At first glance I had thought the note to have been from Carden or Fawkner as both men knew of my love for literature and especially this book in particular. Yet, the language and the handwriting alone were so clearly not of their hands or tongues, and I doubted that Lord Selwyn would have written to me in anything other than Elvish, though I didn't read a word of it.

Who could have written this note and given me this book? No one I'm familiar with has the initial "R" except Tallinn's brother, but it couldn't be him. He hardly knows me...

As I sat puzzling over who the mysterious author of the note might be, there came a gentle, yet strong knock at the door.

"Come in," I called and looked up over my shoulder and instantly smiled as he entered. "Carden."

He stepped in gingerly, nodding thankfully to Joran for allowing him entrance to the room. As the Storvari gently closed the door, Carden turned to me. He still wore the knee length silver quilted doublet over his dark pants, his black shirt unbuttoned around the collar to show his strong neckline and throat.

"Am I intruding?" he asked softly.

"Not at all," I shook my head, setting the note back on the book and turning where I sat to face him. "I'd hoped to see you, actually."

He flashed me a small smile as he casually strode into the room, surveying all the silvery and gold trappings the Elves had dressed it in. To behold him lit with the warm glow of the candles made him all the more real, every dream and fantasy I had conjured over the past two years seeming cold in comparison to the truth.

"I... need to apologise to you," he said softly, pushing his right hand into his left awkwardly as he came to stand some feet from where I sat.

I frowned. "Apologise?"

"For my behaviour at dinner," he clarified. "Seeing Tristan has... There are too many hurt feelings left, I think. Among many of us."

I nodded. "I understand that. Even I have to confess my misgivings of him... but I truly think he means to only help now."

He frowned deeply and dubiously at me. "How can you say such a thing, Leander? He betrayed us. He betrayed *you*," it was as if the fact that Tristan had hurt me was the worst point in Carden's mind, greater even than his betrayal of Tallinn and himself.

"He did," I nodded with a sigh. "Since meeting him in the Forests of Arnath, he has explained his reasons to me..."

"What possible reason could he have had?" he almost demanded with a snort, his green eyes flaring with a strain of red that I could only guess was the firelight. "Was it gold? Hand an innocent girl to a monster for some measly sum of sovereigns?"

"The reward was his mortality," I confessed, meeting Carden's hard gaze. "The Witches took from him the ability to pass from this world and join his wife in the Beyond. For gifting me to Morod, he was freed from their curse, nothing more."

He seemed shocked: "A curse?"

I nodded. "From what I saw in their sanctum in the castle, it was a truly wicked and agonising one the sisters have placed on many men. The one, I now realise," the thought made my heart ache as I looked into his green eyes, "that Keilantra had intended to force on you when we were first brought to her..."

The fact that his left hand clutched at his chest told me that he had come to understand what curse I spoke of - a twinge of pain on his handsome face.

"That... that day," he murmured with distant eyes to the past, "as she clutched at my chest with those claw-like fingers, I felt as if... as if my heart were being pulled from my chest... Is that what she..."

"Yes," I sighed, trying not to call up tears. "*That* is the curse Keilantra inflicts on men; one you were spared only by the Shadow Lord's promise to me. Imagine it: a life unending, your heart taken, yet still beating; no aging, no death...no escape..."

As I said those last words, I felt my own heart ache in a different way, remembering what the Shadow Lord had done to me. *My curse is different. There is no curing me of the Shadow Lord's influence, no recovering my mortality or my changing. I... I can't tell him... I can't...*

Carden nodded thoughtfully, moving to take a seat on the bed beside me.

"If that is the curse the Witch inflicts," he said softly, watching me as I stared at my hands in my lap, "then I am so thankful not to have suffered Tristan's fate. This doesn't absolve him of his past transgressions, but perhaps redemption is in his future."

"Maybe," I murmured.

After a few silent moments, he lifted my chin with his forefinger, making me meet his softened gaze.

"Why are you so sad, my beloved girl?" he asked me with all the earnest truth in him.

I can't tell him! I can't! He must never know that I am changed! He mustn't!

"I... I've spent so long wishing you were with me," I decided to say instead, "that to finally have you here, *really* here, touching me... I can hardly believe this isn't a dream..."

He reached out with his other hand, caressing my shoulder gently as he hushed me lovingly.

"I'm real, Leander," he assured me. "I'm really here with you. Can't you feel my skin against yours? Can't you see me with your own eyes?"

I shuddered at the feeling of his touch, my eyes drifting shut for a few moments as my breath laboured from my lungs. It had been so long in dreaming that I had felt such a sensation, that to experience it in reality once more drove my body beyond all sense, every small touch aching in me and driving a painful pleasure I'd never known into the depths of me.

I opened my eyes and looked up at him longingly as he leaned his face so close to mine that all he needed to do was inch a little farther and we'd embrace. My breath caught, my heart raced, my lungs ached, and my blood boiled with such a powerful yearning beyond all else that I had ever known.

"Gods, Leander," he breathed in my very scent, his eyes drifting for a moment before locking with mine once again as he caressed my cheek and throat. "I can't express the desires I've had since we were parted more than two years ago. Every night that I lay in that Labyrinthine hell amongst those shambling corpses, I felt my humanity waning, saved *only* by my loving thoughts of you."

I nearly sobbed at the mention of that wicked place: "How... how did you ever escape? I saw one of those undead things wearing your clothes and my heart broke thinking it was you..."

He smirked a little. "Escaping Arnath was no difficult feat for me. I simply exchanged my clothes with one of the dissolute creatures newly abandoned in those dark cells by that dread necromancer. The fortress is hardly well guarded against escape, and after some effort exploring in silence through the throng of undead, I found a gap in the walls that led to a cave."

I nodded, listening intently as he weaved his simply stated story, running one hand through my long dark hair to cast it from my face.

He looked thoughtful. "Funny how even the Shadow Knights seemed disinterested in my passage through the fortress. Although that might be because..."

His sudden pause and glance of concern to me made me frown.

"Because of what?" I asked curiously.

"It... isn't important," he deflected and continued on. "Once I'd navigated my way to the cliffs beyond the fortress' walls, I wandered for some time, my thoughts of you all that urged me on. I kept thinking that I would see your beautiful eyes and your bright smile again, even if only for a moment. I would have been content to see you one last time as my body grew weaker."

I blushed a little.

"I was discovered by chance on the edge of the Elven Road," he told me. "Lord Selwyn himself passed by with his hunting party when they discovered me. I was barely conscious from thirst, hunger and exhaustion. When I awoke, I was here, Aldwyn at my side. His Lordship had sent word to him after the Green Wizard had told him who I was."

"And you've been here ever since?"

He nodded, cupping one of my hands in his larger one, the other to my face and neck: "Once I was healed enough, I insisted upon seeking my way back into Castle Ortagaad. I had intended to rescue you from whatever dread fate was being inflicted upon you in that cold place by those wretched creatures masquerading as women..."

"But I escaped first," I sighed with a small shrug of one bare shoulder.

He shook his head, astonished. "To hear your telling at dinner of all you have endured... Gods, I am beyond astonished with you. Never have I heard of even a single Guardian of the greatest renown ever achieving so immense a challenge."

He brushed a wayward strand of my hair from my eyes and gazed deeply into them, studying every facet of my face as if he desired to memorise me should we be separated again.

"Truly, you are the most remarkable woman I have ever met in all my life," he said with an air of admiration. "How did you ever survive so much?"

"You," was all I said.

"Me?" his thick, sharp eyebrow raised curiously.

I nodded, my breath shuddering at his continued touch as my palm cupped over his hand, holding it to my neck.

"Every moment I spent suffering in that castle," I confessed softly, my voice barely more than a murmur, even to myself, "and every second spent running for my life, I thought of you. I imagined that you ran with me, hand-in-hand, that you urged me on against all the pain, all the tiredness, all the fear to save myself. Carden..."

I knelt on the bed then, placing my hands to either side of his face and drawing myself up to sit in line with his eyes. Instinctively, he coiled his arms around me, placing his large, broad, long fingered hands on my hips, his breath now as shaky as mine with our touch.

"...every moment," I went on with the strongest yearnings of love and lust that I had ever felt, "was spent pleading with the world to let me be with you again. I... I can't imagine my life without you, and to live for so long with that horror has only made me want you all the more."

He was speechless as I straddled his lap, my arms now coiling around his shoulders, my small heaving breasts pressing against his chest. The very depths of me were aching for him and all I wanted was to be with him, and to be his forevermore. Suddenly, all my cares and fears of the limitations of our standings were gone, all the thoughts of the nobility of my people condemning our union nothing more than foolish worries left behind in the snows of Ortagaad.

"Gods... I love you *so* much, Carden," I whispered, the feelings inside my heart and my body nearly agonising as a new kind of tears began threatening my eyes. "I've missed you terribly..."

"Oh, Leander..." he gasped softly, his face so close that I could almost taste his lips. "My Leander..."

Everything happened all at once then, my rational mind leaving me and my perceptions feeling separated from my body's workings. Our lips crushed in embrace, this kiss more passionate and truer than any I had ever experienced with him. His hands tightened their grasp on my slender, but tall frame, his arms so large that I felt dwarfed being amidst them.

I gasped in a breath as he continued his furious kissing, my lips barely parting enough to draw in air before crushing to his once more. My fingers curled into his dark off-black hair, the strands' new shortness a surprise at first, but easily adapted to. My arms tightened their hold, and I felt a swell growing deep within me at his closeness.

His desire for me was as strong as mine was for him, the feeling of his firmness only increasing against me as I pulled myself further into his lap. A quake of powerful loving need rocked through me and I gasped a moan of want against his kiss, my fingers now searching madly for purchase.

There was a snapping sound, and I felt the bare skin of his chest on my palms, so firm, yet soft and strangely cool to the touch. Another tearing echoed, this time from the straps of my dress as his lips departed mine and began furiously caressing my jaw and neck.

My palms ran across his muscular shape, sliding back to his shoulders beneath the fabric of his shirt, my gasping moan surprising me. His lips were now in the crook of my neck, his lust for me mounting so much that even our clothes could scarcely shield it from my nerves.

He continued his furious embrace, a soft cry escaping my lips as I felt his teeth catch my warm flesh. His hands strengthened their hold and his pressure on my neck and shoulder increased almost to hurting. But I couldn't ever have asked him to stop, every sensation - even those that I had been told were inappropriate before marriage- like a tidal wave of exciting pleasure and experience I never wanted to give up.

"No!" he suddenly snarled.

His hold on me released and he shoved me from his embrace, dropping me backwards to the bed with a soft, easy landing.

I lay there bewildered, breathing quickly as I looked up at him, his shirt and doublet open to reveal his chest down nearly to his naval, the lines of his finely carved muscles driving even more lust into my slickening core. But I could see the anger in his expression as he closed his eyes, turning them from me so I didn't see. Before he did, I glimpsed the red of the fire within them once more, concern now rising to consume my desires.

"Carden?" I tried to ease my quickened breaths as I leaned my elbows behind me. "What's wrong, my love?"

"I... that was foolish of me," he said softly, keeping his face turned from me as much as he shielded his lower half with his arm to hide his other reaction. "I should never have..."

My heart sank and rejection filled me."Do... do you not... want me?" the words sounded so stupid to my ears, so insecure.

He turned back to me, his green eyes now wide with worry and his face twisted with a pain I couldn't describe.

"Oh, love, yes! Yes, I want you!" he exclaimed as if rushing to make things right. "I... I just can't stand hurting you..."

"But, you didn't..."

"I drew blood..."

A thrill of fear coursed through me at those three words, my right hand reaching delicately to my left shoulder and my fingers gingerly dabbing into the crook of my neck. I felt something warm against my fingertips, studying them then. The small amount of crimson that was sparsely spread over my fingertips looked almost black in the candlelight, the smell of salt and copper drawing a light-headedness to me, but only mildly.

My heart skipped a little at the sight of my blood, my blue steel eyes darting to Carden's expression of tortured anguish.

"I am so sorry," he murmured, looking on the verge of crying. "I never should have given in to my lust for you..."

"Carden," I sat up and reached my other hand to him, caressing his cheek gently. "It's all right. It's just come from a moment of passion, not malcontent..."

"You don't understand," he hissed, pulling away from me. "I love you, Leander. I should be better than this..."

"It's all right..."

"No. It isn't," he sighed with a darkened expression. "Aldwyn was right to be concerned..."

"Carden..."

He turned from me and headed for the door.

"Carden, wait!" I cried out, kneeling on the bed once again. "Please!"

He paused with his hand to the door handle, turning over his shoulder to look at me.

"Stay with me," I pleaded in a whisper. "Just... just lay here with me. We don't have to do anything more than be together."

I could see the conflict within him, his eyes turning towards the door again, his hand tight on the handle. If he were to leave at that moment it would tear me apart and I couldn't bear seeing him in such anguish over something so small as an overzealous love bite.

"Please, Carden," I begged quietly, feeling I could sob at any moment. "Please..."

His expression softened and his large hand fell away from the door.

"All right," was all he said.

Slowly, he crossed the room and returned to the bed, gently seating himself down on the side and leaning his torso over me. He brought his face close to mine again, my eyes falling shut a little, but just enough to allow me to still see him.

"I'm so sorry, Leander," he whispered again, touching his hand to my cheek once more.

"I'm sorry, too," I murmured, feeling suddenly that I should take some responsibility. After all, I had been the one to start all of this.

He kissed me again, this time more softly and romantically, my own lips responding in kind to his embrace. Though this kiss lasted only a few moments before we parted to meet each other's gaze, it was well worth it.

He lay back amongst the palatial silver and gold pillows, drawing me with him to lie my head against his chest, my left hand resting on his sternum. His arm wrapped around my shoulders, holding me close to his body, and this is where we stayed.

Does it matter that we just lie here in each other's embrace instead of doing what our bodies yearned? Why should it? Maybe... it just wasn't the right moment for that yet. And truthfully, I'm not so sure that I'm ready for that sort of complete intimacy...

I looked up at him as he stroked my hair, his gaze loving and soft. I drew his smile with my own, then lay back to rest there in his arms.

As long as I'm with him, nothing else matters. Carden is my soul mate and I am so happy to be his in return. That's enough for me.

My body eased and I felt sleep starting to come on slowly. This was the first night in more than two years that I had actually felt truly able to rest without worry. In moments, I was drifting away, my body relaxing to the sounds of our breaths; mine soft and a little quicker, his deeper and slower.

That was the moment where I once again heard and felt our heart beats. At first, they beat individually, his once again a deeper beat than my lighter ones, but within moments they slowed and shifted until we shared our rhythm. Two hearts in love always seem to beat as one.

Finally at ease after all this time, I let myself relax and curled my knees closer to my body. I felt his lips gently peck my forehead and his hand draw a blanket around my legs and hips to keep me warm.

"I love you, Leander," he whispered gently and lovingly to me, still stroking my hair and the skin of my shoulder.

I think I replied in kind to him, though I can't remember clearly, for sleep's haze had come over me. All I know as I drifted off into my rest was that I was safely with my true love once again, and everything felt right...

Chapter Twenty
The Elements Gather

The morning sunlight woke me with a gentle nudge, its glow warm, but lessened with the soft clouds that promised a downpour still to come. My eyes opened experimentally to test the light's strength, squinting a little at first for no more than a few moments before easily taking in all that surrounded me.

A soft, soothing breeze fluttered through the windows and open doors of the balcony, casting the sheer white curtains loftily into the air. It was beginning to smell of a fresh spring day, though given the green of this beautiful place I could scarcely imagine it being cold and dreary.

I shifted a little where I lay, wrapped in a white sheet beneath a quilted blanket of gold, still resting where I had laid my head the night before. Now I could see the damage my dress had taken with our abruptly halted passions; both straps on the shoulders torn, the bodice barely managing to keep my chest concealed.

A soft breath and grunt drew my gaze to the man lying beside me, a smile spreading over my lips to see him there. He'd slipped from his tunic and his shirt overnight, his chest completely bared now and so well defined compared to how I had remembered him. He seemed to have grown into his masculinity, his muscles nicely carved into his cooled olive-white flesh, his shoulders seeming bigger yet again.

A swell filled me, and my very depths shuddered at the sight of this being that I considered closest to perfect. I had never felt such yearnings stir in me before last night and I could only guess that my time imprisoned had done this to me, along with my unbridled longing for him.

Gods, why do I feel this way?! It's madness!

Trying not to wake him, I slid up to sit, but such a task was futile. He stirred and his handsome emerald eyes opened to gaze up at me.

"Leander?" he asked gently.

"Um... good morning," I said, brushing my hair from my face with the fingertips of one hand.

"Morning," he squinted against the sun, propping himself up in the bed. "I think this is the first that I've awakened after you, my love."

"As far as I remember, it is," I confirmed.

"What is it?" he asked, pulling his arms around me, the skin of his chest pressing into my back with a cool warmth that made me shiver in delight.

"I... I feel strange," I confessed, shrugging lightly in his hold, my hands delicately grasping his strong forearms. "I'm filled with so many sensations my body has never yet known and desires I can hardly understand."

"I think I know," he kissed my shoulder, his lips so soft on my smooth skin.

"How could you know what things stir in me when I can't even comprehend them myself?" I glanced back at him, just seeing his face out of the corner of my eyes.

"Love," he whispered into my skin, still kissing me. "Lust. A desire for knowledge of each other intimately..."

I let my eyes fall shut, surrendering to his breath and kisses that caressed my heated flesh, my body responding with all the shivering, throbbing, quaking yearning it could. His hands crept to my bodice, finding the cord and unlacing it slowly, my heart racing excitedly.

"Carden... stop..." I whispered breathily.

"What's wrong?" he asked softly, still holding me close, his hands pausing their task.

"This was why you became so angry last night," I reminded him.

"Yes... I... I lost control of my be- myself," he said with guilt in his voice. "Can you ever forgive me, my love?"

"I already did," I unhooked his hands and looked to him. "But it is my own feelings that concern me. I've never felt such things before and I'm... ashamed."

"Ashamed?" he frowned at me, his black hair flicking over his forehead with the morning breeze.

I blushed, looking at my knees from his chest, trying to quash these intense physical feelings that stemmed from my core.

"Leander, you need not be ashamed for what your body desires any more than for the wishes of your heart," he tilted my chin and made me meet his gaze. "You're a woman and I am a man, and such sensations are natural."

"Have you ever had such feelings before?" I asked of him as if I were a small child afraid of the answers I would be told.

"I have," he confessed with a nod. "Yet, my first experience of such things was not made from love, but lust alone. Have you..."

"No. Never," I replied a little too quickly. "I'm... I'm a virgin."

He smiled and nodded, stroking my face and lifting my chin to once more gain my soft eyed gaze.

"But of course you are, for how else would you - a girl so virtuous, beautiful and true - be?" he seemed so genuinely pleased by that single truth of myself. "Oh, how I wish I could share in such virtues myself, yet such a state is long lost to me."

"When?" I asked almost suspiciously.

He lay back amongst the pillows, pulling me with him and pinning his right arm behind his head as his left cradled my waist to his side.

"Younger than you were when first we met," he said thoughtfully. "I was not but freshly fifteen winters, and I would sooner not think on that past."

"Was it so bad?" I asked curiously, hugging into him and enjoying the gentle caress of his fingers.

He sighed awkwardly. "The experience taught me that I ought have waited for the single one who would treasure my heart, not merely seek my virtue in lust," he looked down into my eyes with a deep regret. "Had I known that but a few years hence from that moment I would find you, I would happily have waited."

"I was just a child then, on the elderly edge of my eleventh year," I thought aloud, having calculated my age at that time. "I hardly came close to resembling a woman as my sister did."

"Yet a woman you now are," he said, looking into my face with such powerful love, "your twenty-first year reached whilst far from my sight. Strange, though I know your years have advanced, you look no older than when first I laid eyes upon you, my dearest love."

A shiver of fear flooded my aching heart. He could see that which I so desperately tried to hide; the curse of the Shadow Lord's will, painted into my very skin and imbedded into my bones and marrow with no way of being extracted. I stared into his love filled eyes, knowing that his honour prevented him from forcing me into any action that was not of my own desire, but also knowing that his heart yearned for what mine did too.

How? How can I tell him that the woman he thinks me to be is nothing more than a fantasy because I am unable to ever be a woman, but only a girl? By so many standards, to be seventeen winters is physically enough to be called mature, but my people's laws deny me such, casting my adulthood to this, my twenty-first year. Yet, I am hardly the form of a twenty-one winters passed woman.

I sighed deeply, sitting up and feeling him do the same to meet my hesitant gaze. I could see that he knew I was vexed, though by what I wasn't sure if he could tell.

I must tell him. I have to. Isnari, please, I pray he still accepts my love...

"There's... there's something I have to tell you," I started slowly, holding back my fear as fiercely as I might manage, yet to him I'm certain I appeared meek.

"What is it?" he frowned.

"When... when we were prisoners of the Shadow Lord...no... of Morod," I forced myself to say the monster's name, to reclaim some strength stolen by my fear of him, "I was made to be a part of his dark ritual. Remember?"

He scowled. "I could hardly forget. Watching you scream as that hag cut you and drew forth your blood into that vile cup. As they forced you to consume that wretched concoction against your will. As he..." he looked so angry, fighting back tears of rage, "as he... *dared* to lay his monstrous lips upon you... Had I my hands freed at that moment I'd have carved up *every one* of them for defiling you... I'd have slain *every last* lying, miserable creature in that hellish temple of death to spare you whatever horrors I could..."

"That's... that's sweet of you to say so, Carden," I smiled sadly at him, my hands in my lap as I knelt before him in the ruined folds of my dress. "But... had you been free or not, I doubt you could have spared me his curse..."

"Curse?" he looked haunted, as if he had thought me mostly unscathed but for the mental scratches left by that dark event. "You've been cursed?"

I nodded, trying to swallow back the hard lump lingering in my throat. "When I awoke, I was with him, with Morod..."

Those words alone were enough to draw a murderous rage from my beloved Guardian, though he somehow kept his control.

I continued hesitantly, choosing not to recall the Shadow Lord's lustful advances towards me: "He... told me that the ritual had gifted him physical form and all the power he once had in my ancestor's time... but at a cost..."

"What was the cost?" he frowned, trying to read my eyes as he leaned nearer to me.

I felt as if I could cry, seeing him before me only making this worse:"He took-"

The door to the room opened before I could finish, Ellora walking in dressed in her standard huntress garb. She took one look at us and our dishevelled appearances, then quickly turned her gaze away with a blush to her elfin cheeks.

"My apologies, your Highness, Carden. I should have knocked," she regretted, embarrassed as I held my ruined dress to my chest.

As terrible as it is, I was actually glad she had interrupted this awful moment of confession. Carden, red in his masculine cheeks, was up and recovering his shirt, quickly pulling it over his chiselled torso to regain the modesty he seemed to no longer have the need to shield in front of me. I confess, I wish he hadn't hidden himself.

"Yes," I nodded, quickly retaining the attitude of a royal, though only lightly. "You should have, but it's all right. What do you need?"

"We have been summoned, Princess," she responded evenly, turning her turquoise eyes to meet my blue ones. "The Wizards have called for us and we are to attend the Broken Towers. As soon as you are fit to do so, your Highness."

I recognised the crack to be about my clothing and the state of both Carden and I together with skin exposed and garments askew amidst the sheets of the bed.

"Nothing... nothing happened, Ellora," I stated quickly, embarrassed and blushing.

"Clearly not," she seemed more confident, meeting Carden's gaze as he fastened the front of his shirt. "If something had happened, he would not be wearing pants."

Carden gave the Elf a smirking scowl, the woman merely returning his smirk in kind, the nature of gentle joking clear between them.

She turned and nodded to me. "I shall wait with Joran to escort you, Princess," and she left the room.

"Ah," Carden nodded with a smirk, "the gentle ribbing of a wood elf. Don't worry, she's not going to go spreading it around like the Dwarves would."

"I don't care if people know we spent the night together," I said in all honesty, shrugging my naked shoulders as I clutched my bodice tightly. "I intend to spend every night of my life from now on in your embrace."

He moved back to the bed, fastening the last button of his shirt and taking his godly physique from my sight. He leaned one knee on the mattress and came to hover his face close to mine.

"And I intend to keep you in my embrace every night from now on, Leander," he kissed me gently on the lips, the moment agonisingly passionate in its briefness. "You should dress..."

He stood, swiping his ruined tunic from the floor and making his way to the door. He paused only to smile at me one last time, then vanished from my presence.

I slumped back into the bed, playing with the Pendant around my neck absentmindedly. *I came so close to telling him. His passion for defending me makes it seem as if he will just care for me no matter my tainted form. Maybe the curse will mean nothing to him...*I sighed and ran my hand over my head, knowing I didn't have time to lie there musing on the ways of my beloved's mind. The Wizards were expecting me, and I didn't dare to be late.

* * * * *

With my body washed and wearing a replica of the dress Carden and I had destroyed, but coloured of blue and pearlescent white, I walked to the door, once again donning the circlet of silver the Elves had fashioned for me. I was so glad to see Carden, Ellora and Joran awaiting me in the hallway, Fawkner joining them, clad in his Guardian garb as Carden now also was.

Ellora led us from Lord Selwyn's house out into the white and silver streets of Silvervale, passing amidst the great gardens and cascading waterfalls that swept through the city. Four silver armoured Elven guards joined us, less approachable in their heavy masked helms than the Galvenin Elves had been, but still kind.

We crossed an older bridge, this one of ancient stone with a blackish hue more like ebony than the grey stones of the rest of the city. This took us to the great stone steps that carried us up the long slope of the minor mountain the city was built upon the feet of. Here the Broken Towers stood, their tops looking as if they had been shattered by a god's wrath, their black stone walls as ancient as the bridge.

Once again, there were Elven Guards at the great archway atop these stairs, standing with elegant halberds and shields of graceful design, their charcoal cloaks swaying with the breeze. But as we came to the entrance, I gasped at the sight of black cloaked, golden armoured Dragon Knights in attendance as well.

"Dragon Knights?" Fawkner frowned as we reached the sanctuary's gigantic porch of black stone. "Why are they here?"

"The Dragon Knights hold an enclave within the southern tower," Ellora explained with the knowledge of one who had been here before. "The Wizards retain the central, eastern and western towers, whilst the Guardians have a base within the northern tower."

"There are Guardians here as well?" I asked as I clutched my skirt hem with one hand, Carden taking my other gently to help me over the last step.

"Here is where the Guardian Stronghold of Dorvana has long dwelt," she replied, her red locks blowing across her armoured shoulders, "though there are only a few Guardians in residence here. The Broken Towers and Silvervale have long hosted the powers of good and justice in High-Realm since before the times of the Shadow Lords began."

We walked past the numerous guards, only then noticing four Guardians in their black and silver armour standing as sentries with the High Elves and Dragon Knights. To see these three orders standing as one gave me a stronger sense of safety than I had ever known since all this began three years ago.

I felt a gaze upon me, turning to look towards the rocks and cliffs that overhung the great porch. There stood the majestic green dragon, his molten fire eyes proud as he watched me; a protector I'd not yet come to know. Amethyst came up from behind him, her mauve scales glinting in the sunlight, her darker ones seeming opalescent. She gently nodded her twin horned head, that one small gesture a great comfort.

I smiled to my dragon, then continued with my friends into the tower's great black stone halls.

The halls of the Broken Towers were unlike any place I had been before, more guarded than even my home of Castle Arvon or our capital's palace. Upon every wall there was a banner of pale ice blue trimmed in black, the symbol etched into its fabric that of five misshapen diamonds, the longest of all the points directed inwards. At the top of the group was a pearl white diamond, the others going from it clockwise being red, blue, green and finally gold.

I had seen this before, the symbol of the goddess Maveria, incarnation of the five elements of spirit, fire, water, earth and air in union. As I thought of it, this symbol made sense to be here.

They are the Brotherhood of the Elements after all and Maveria is the Elemental Goddess. Of course they would share her symbol, though I don't see any form of her likeness here.

We passed through the eastern tower at first, this the one that held the entry arch into the sanctuary stronghold. We climbed the winding stairs up until we reached a long, covered bridge that led us into the central spire. Another flight of stairs brought us into the very top level near the tower's seemingly shattered peak.

From what I could tell, the architects who had worked to repair the tower - if it had ever been damaged - had done their very best to make do with what structure lingered. This floor had one curving section thickened for the stairways, the rest open to the air with support columns of ebony stone spaced between arches to keep the frame of the ceiling above us. A second wall of columns and arches created two rooms: the first an outer ring with benches and meagre furnishings along with the Elemental banners. The second was a wider, perfectly circle space, the main floor of the tower's point.

In this central space were set black steel braziers positioned before each column, their gentle flames' glow illuminating the room. I gazed up at the wondrous domed stain glass ceiling, silently wondering how that had been done so perfectly. It boasted the four colours of red, blue, green and gold, but was clear and frosted where white was missing.

The only furniture in the room was a set of curving tables that were organised into a circle with a large brazier in the middle, much like the one I had seen in the Dragon Knights' fortress of Mountain Falls. A chair was seated at each place, perhaps twenty in total, but the five that faced the stairway had colours. The centremost chair had a white carving and cushioning laid into its dark wood, the two to its right red and gold, and the two to its left blue and green, all the same design.

In each of these five seats there sat a wizard, each one dressed in robes of the corresponding colour. I recognised the gentle eyes of the Green Wizard immediately, feeling so much more at ease seeing him. To his right was a wizard in blue, his robes like the ocean with designs of gentle gold and deeper blues waving through the fabric, his hair and beard an almost bluish grey.

The Golden Wizard was not of High-Realm's people, but a Harredi with black hair and a twisted, knotted beard, his eyes a caramel colour. He had the darker complexion and fuller lips of his people, tints of grey touching his hairline, and a hood cast back across his shoulders with an indigo lining. To his left was the Crimson Wizard, for his robes were like blood with the orange of flames sewn in; his long flowing hair free down to his hips and shimmering a silvery ash grey. His beard was short and neat, his eyes as black as coals, and he had the gaze of a man who could incinerate someone with one glance.

The final Wizard wore robes of purest white and silver, a little gold trimming some parts. His skin was as pale as the snows, his long white hair and beard completely free of any other colours. Around his neck he wore a talisman that bore the emblem of the Elemental Goddess, his face severe, yet calm and wise.

All of the Wizards had a hat which rested before them on the table, wide brimmed and pointed. Each carried a staff: The Green's like a gnarled branch with an emerald stone, the Red's like hard charcoal steel with a claw grasping a blood red gem. The Golden's staff was like flowing silver wood coiling around a topaz stone at its peak, while the Blue's was a gentle green, smooth and like the seaweed of the ocean with a sapphire stone in the parting of the leaves. Finally, the White's was a coiling of silver and gold with cobalt at its centre, forming three fingers that held a smooth, perfect pearl-like gem at its top.

As I passed the archway into the chamber, I came to see Aldwyn standing there waiting, his own blue topped staff in hand, the rest of my companions with him. He bowed his head in greeting to me as my eyes took in the last of the faces gathered there.

Lord Selwyn stood next to the Green Wizard, dressed in silvery blue robes with a kingly Elven circlet upon his head. Beside him stood a blonde-haired woman in the armour and cloak of a Guardian Warden, her face beautiful, yet harsh from the many years she had taken to gain her role.

Across from them I glimpsed Ser Callenhad of the Dragon Knights. I was suddenly so gladdened to see him, the injuries he'd taken whilst fighting the Revenant long healed. At his side stood another Dragon Knight, just as the Guardian woman had a blonde Guardian man with her. I could only guess that these were their seconds, the ones who aided them in their duties as leaders. With Lord Selwyn was also a young male elf with long dark hair and dressed in flowing robes as well as an elf with long blonde hair dressed in guardsmen armour.

"Your Highness," Aldwyn drew my gaze, gesturing me to a chair directly in front of the White Wizard. "If you would."

I nodded softly, pausing as Carden drew out my seat, then sat, allowing him to push it in. He took the seat to my right, Fawkner joining him, while Aldwyn and Tallinn sat to my left; Ellora, Dolin and Holger taking the last seats beside her as Tristan and Ranulf were left watching from behind Aldwyn. Joran remained at my back, always guarding me and a constant protective comfort.

"Princess Leander," the White Wizard spoke in a deep booming voice despite his fair, yet aged appearance, instantly making me cringe a little, "I bid you and your companions welcome to the Broken Towers and our meeting chamber. I am certain that you are apprehensive before so many you do not know, therefore, allow me to make the much-needed introductions," he gestured with one long finger to his right: "To my right are the Dragon Knight representatives, Ser Callenhad and Ser Sigmund," then he gestured to his left. "To my left are Lord Selwyn, General Gailan of the High Elven Guard, History Keeper Tenzin, and the Guardian representatives of the Broken Towers: Guardian Warden Alessa and her second, Master Guardian Aswin."

I looked to each of them in turn as he introduced them, then followed his attention back to the Wizards.

"Then, I would introduce myself and my brother wizards," he stated evenly, again gesturing right, then left. "Brother Samhir, the Golden Wizard of Air, Brother Lucilius, the Red Wizard of Fire, Brother Ragdobar, the Blue Wizard of Water and Brother Ranzel, the Green Wizard of Earth."

My eyes fell to the Green Wizard as the book and the note left in my room suddenly made perfect sense. "R" stood for Ranzel.

"I," the White Wizard concluded, drawing my gaze to him again, "am Brother Xzharn, the White Wizard of Spirit. We are very pleased to meet you, my young Lady of Aldegaad."

I was too uneasy to speak yet, but as always, I was glad to have Aldwyn willing to speak for me until I was.

"And her Highness is pleased to be here and to be able to meet with all of you in the safety of this great city, and this ancient renowned sanctum," he stated in his usual calm, diplomatic tone.

"I'm sure she is," Ranzel offered me a warm, comforting smile and a gentle wink of reassurance.

"As you know, we have been in deep discussions since your arrival here within the safe boundaries of Silvervale's borders, Princess," Xzharn stated, leading this conference of orders. "Dark events have transpired in the past few years that cannot be ignored. Especially given what Brother Ranzel has perceived during his incarceration within the walls of Castle Ortagaad."

"The rise of this Shadow Lord," Lucilius spoke direfully, his charcoal eyes like burning black embers staring out from his ashen face, "is a dread development. Far too many portents of doom are yet laid before us as we behold the darkness once again flowing from the Maw of Gorth'lak's foul black lands and grey ashen wastes."

"Such activity has not been seen from the dark lands in more than a millennia," Samhir spoke in his dark voice with his thick Harredi accent, his caramel eyes surveying all of us present with great worry and severity. "The return of the Scourge and of the dreaded Shadow Knights is a blighted sign that war may once more be upon High-Realm, if not all of Therras."

"I'm afraid that war may be unavoidable," Ranzel spoke with deep concern, clasping his hands together on the table before him. "As you all know, both the Princess and I were imprisoned in Castle Ortagaad under the wretched custodianship of the Sisters of Raven's Rest. We were shown many terrible secrets within that castle, including the breeding grounds of a Scourge army lingering beneath the skin of that frozen sea locked atoll."

"Truly?" Lord Selwyn frowned deeply, concern in his turquoise eyes.

"Yes," the Wizard nodded grimly. "And these are not the first such breeding grounds I have encountered throughout High-Realm over the past two years. What resurgence of the beasts that have been seen in the Dwarven Tunnels over the past twenty-one years has been but a portent of the calamity yet to come. Given that the Darkest Shadow's most powerful and destructive general has returned from the Netherworlds, we can only assume the worst."

"Is it indeed Lord Morod who haunts us once more, my friend?" Xzharn asked gravely.

Ranzel nodded again and sighed. "Though I've not encountered him myself, I do believe it is he. No other Shadow Lord in all the history of this world - beyond Gorth Lavelle - has ever managed to amass such a force, nor has ever made as powerful an alliance with dark warriors and casters such as the Sister Witches and the Revenant of Arnath."

"If it is indeed he we face," Ragdobar spoke in a voice so full of age it made him seem frail as he sat there shrouded in his blue robes, "then High-Realm could be about to face the greatest calamity of our time. It could reignite the spark of the War of the Shadow."

"Do we know what it is Lord Morod seeks most?" Samhir asked thickly, stroking his knotted black beard, his golden robes seeming to shimmer with the light.

"What all of his kind seek, brother," Lucilius growled with fire in his eyes and sulphur on his tongue, "the destruction and domination of all the world that lives beneath the skies."

"If this Shadow Lord is the dreaded Lord Morod of legend," Warden Alessa spoke slowly, her harsh, but beautiful features remaining strong despite the edge of fear that must surely have tainted her, "and he is breeding an army of foul creatures to come forth, then the Guardians *must* and *will* unite to stand against him and this rebirth of the Shadow Dominion. Whatever the cost."

"As will the Dragon Knights," declared Ser Callenhad firmly, his white hair looking so less grey as he had aged. "However, our first priority at this very moment must be seeking out all holders of the Dragon Pendants and placing them under our protection, so that we might stand a chance against this threat."

"The Dragon Pendants are lost to the pages of history," Lord Selwyn stated grimly, his hands folded on the table before him, "save for the two which happen to sit here in this room in the possession of Brother Ranzel and Princess Leander, as evidenced by their dragon protectors."

My hand instinctively slipped up over my chest to caress the smooth, cooled skin of my neck and collarbones where the Pendant hung by its delicate silver chain.

"Then, given that we know she has been imprisoned by the Shadow Lord's disciples," Warden Alessa spoke with a coldness that I didn't like, "and without any other possible motives or designs for what it is he yet plans, the girl is our only avenue to deny him the victory he must surely be seeking."

"She is not merely some objective!" Carden snapped, slapping his hands against the table and glaring with passionate anger at the woman. "Can you not see that she is a girl in need of more than simply being safeguarded as a means to deny our enemy his victory?! Is she nothing more to you than a mission, Warden?!"

"Watch your tongue, boy," Warden Alessa slowly hissed at him. "You accuse me of caring not for her safety when that is not the case..."

"You do not see a girl in need, a human being who has had to face great trials simply to survive many tragedies and a greater threat," he seethed with quiet rage, baring his teeth as he spoke. "All you see is a tactical method to keep Lord Morod at bay. You would use her to draw him out, to force him into conflict! That is *not* the way of the Guardians!"

"Carden, sit down!" Aldwyn snapped at the younger Guardian, his dark brown eyes hard and severe.

Carden jerked his gaze swiftly towards the Mage, seeing the seriousness there before slowly retaking his seat by my side. He looked to me with a pained expression, yearning to reach for me as I did for him. But both of us knew that to do so at that moment wouldn't be a good idea.

"Your suggestions that Warden Alessa does not have the Princess' best interests in mind are unfounded," Aldwyn told Carden firmly, meeting the woman's gaze. "Like us, she is a Guardian and is sworn to protect those in need. However, it is important to note that the Princess is indeed the only objective we know of to be within Lord Morod's views of interest."

"Then, her protection is all the more important," Ser Callenhad decided, turning then to look to me. "When first you came to us in Mountain Falls, your Highness, you departed our guardianship in order to warn your uncle, King Aric, of the traitors near to him."

The mention of my one good uncle left a reminding pang in my heart as I felt his death in my mind anew.

"Now, however, there can be no more allowances for you to leave our safe keeping," he went on, urging me to listen. "You are the last holder of a Dragon Pendant born of a champion's bloodline, and the single-minded focus of the very enemy we face. You *must* remain in our protection."

I just sighed and nodded. What was there for me to say when all those around me had already decided what needed to be done, and when I had nothing to return to beyond those fortress walls? To argue the contrary would only make things worse.

"If only we could determine the designs of this Shadow Lord, we might stand a chance to create a defence," Xzharn considered, interlacing his fingers and resting his hands upon the smooth dark wood tabletop. "Princess Leander, you were the prisoner of him for some time. You must have some understanding of what he intended for you."

I shook my head, chewing my lip uncertainly as I thought of all that I could.

"Carden and I were taken with her when we were betrayed in Eilath," Tallinn spoke, drawing my gaze to see her hazel eyes. "Though I can't say what further designs he had intended for the Princess, we *did* witness some dark events during our captivity."

"What did you see, my dear girl?" Ragdobar asked in his elderly, soft toned voice.

I knew what she would say, and I would have screamed for her to keep it from them for the mere shame of what I had been forced to endure. But I could only look at my hands in my lap and try to stem the tide of tears that were once more threatening to cascade down my cheeks.

"The Shadow Lord's allies took us to his seat of power," she described with a cold fear and a dark hatred too harsh for such a kind person. "We were brought to the fortress of Grishk'kinnar, the Black Doorway of Gorth'lak, and here he detailed a ritual..."

"A ritual?" Samhir frowned, still stroking his beard in thought.

Tallinn nodded gravely. "It was designed to restore a Shadow Lord in spectral form to the physical planes of this world, and gift him all his mightiest powers anew."

Carden was trembling beside me, his rage at the memory of that night as potent as my guilt and shame. Fawkner kept a steady hand upon him, trying to ease him where he could.

Tallinn went on: "We were taken as a means to ensure that the Princess obeyed all instructions commanded of her by the Shadow Lord. We learned that... that the attacks against the Custodians of the Past was the combined efforts of both him and the Revenant of Arnath, all set towards preparing for this ritual."

"The theft of the Nempanarth from Eilath, the desecration of Leander the First's tomb, the attacks on Coastwatch Keep and the Citadel of Dartaren," Ellora looked horrified as she realised the truth, "this was their plan? This ritual?"

"Yes," Tallinn sighed, keeping her eyes to the Wizards: "They forced her to participate in the ritual, to give her consent under duress for some guarantee of success; a perversion of theirs meant to hurt her. It was here that we watched as the Darkest Shadow consumed the lives of eight innocents as an offering in order to gain its favour..."

"The Demon itself was there?" Lucilius almost erupted at the very mention of the beast we had faced. "It has taken a new interest in the world?"

"Taken a new interest," Ranzel mused dourly, "or continued to show such over all of this time?"

"Go on, Guardian," Xzharn urged Tallinn.

"I would not think to cause the Princess any further distress by recounting the rest of the perversions in detail," she said to my great relief. "Once the ritual was completed, Carden and I were taken to cells to await transport to Travarna, then Castle Ortagaad. All I know for certain is that the ritual succeeded. Lord Morod has regained the power and physical form he desired."

"This is most distressing news," Ragdobar spoke with a gentle worry, looking to Xzharn.

"Indeed," Xzharn agreed with a dark thoughtfulness. "Yet we can be certain that this ritual was not the full extent of his interests if he kept the girl hostage for so long."

"Why?" Lord Selwyn asked thoughtfully, looking to me as he spoke. "Why keep her alive if she had already served her purpose for him?"

"Because he is a befouled, perverted creature!" Holger declared with a harsh snap of his fist to the table. "A beast with no decency or sense of sympathy! We'd do well to cut his head clear from his shoulders for what he did to the lassie!"

"Be calm, brother," Dolin urged him gently, patting his arm.

"I would hear from the Princess," Xzharn decided, to my dismay, turning his nearly black eyes to look at me. "You have survived much for a girl of so few winters, your Highness. That you escaped the confines of Castle Ortagaad when no others have before you is monumental in itself. However, to have made it here to this city and sanctuary with so little defence and aid is no less than a miracle."

"That it is," Samhir agreed as Ragdobar nodded behind his square framed eyeglasses.

"Tell us, girl," Xzharn leaned back in his seat, his right hand curling like a claw around his gold, silver and cobalt staff, "how did you survive? Regale us of your venture from the impregnable Castle Ortagaad."

I took a deep breath, feeling so much more at ease for having Carden at my side. I wanted to reach over yet again and take his hand in mine for comfort, but I didn't, once more reminding myself of where I was.

I was selective in what details I confessed, choosing to keep Ulric's depravity towards me to myself. Even thinking of what he'd intended to make me do made me cringe and gag with disgust. So, once more I told the story of how I had fled Castle Ortagaad, of the strangeness of surviving not only the fall from the castle walls, but also the freezing waters below it, then everything else that had followed. When I had completed my telling, I simply sat there with my hands in my lap, looking around at the faces studying me.

"Remarkable," General Gailan mused, his silvery armour and stern expression seeming mismatched with his gentle elven voice. "Simply remarkable."

"It seems that you have overcome many challenges that a man twice your size and age could not," Ragdobar said thoughtfully. "Simply astonishing."

"Tell me, Princess," Xzharn drew my gaze with his deep voice, his eyes peering fiercely from beneath his perfectly white flowing hair, "however did you survive the trials you faced?"

"My pendant," I replied simply, touching my fingers once more to the silver coiling designs surrounding the purple stone. "It's the only reason I survived any of it."

"Before this escape," he chose his words carefully as he spoke, "did you possess the knowledge of your pendant's abilities?"

I shook my head. "No. No, I had only seen my pendant protect me with an energy shield on two occasions. I had never experienced any of its other abilities until these past few months."

"Intriguing," Ser Callenhad spoke up, having listened to my tale with all ears. "Never in the histories of our order has a Dragon Pendant Holder ever used a pendant's abilities so completely through instinct alone."

"She is certainly a unique Holder," Ser Sigmund commented, studying me thoroughly from where he sat.

"I honestly have no idea how I even came to do this," I confessed with a shrug of my shoulders and a shake of my head. "It just... happened..."

"And when you were in Castle Ortagaad," Lucilius took his time, each word deliberate as his scorching gaze lay on me, "why did you not use these powers to escape your captors? Surely such powers could have freed you much sooner."

I cringed at his snideness, choosing to answer as honestly and calmly as I could: "My pendant was taken from me by my captors. They seemed to know a great deal about the workings of the magicks it possesses and took it so that I couldn't defend myself."

"How would the Witches have known about the powers of the Pendants?" Samhir questioned, almost rhetorically, yet expecting an answer.

"Keilantra, the one sister who has claimed the title of Gorvenna's Queen, has a Dragon Pendant of her own," I explained with a tremble of fear spiking down my spine and neck.

"How?" Ragdobar looked horrified. "How can a Pendant have fallen to one with such a black heart?"

"It is impossible for those of cruel wills to wield a Dragon Pendant," Lucilius growled at me as if I were simply a foolish child who didn't know what I was talking about.

"I... I don't think she or sister started with darkness in their hearts," I said, thinking of what little I had been told during my time there. "I think they were pure once, then corrupted by evil."

"And how did this witch come to possess a Dragon Pendant?" Lucilius demanded grumpily, waving his hand dismissively.

"It was given to her by her grandmother," I recalled the Witch's story. "From what little I know; the Dragon Pendants can only pass to the descendent of a Holder. Isn't that right?"

"It is, your Highness," Ser Callenhad confirmed with a gentle nod, the flames of the braziers reflected in his golden armour.

"Was a dragon present?" asked Ser Sigmund with a cold curiosity.

I nodded. "Yes. The Witch has a golden dragon named Kuldar who serves her, and the Shadow Lord a black dragon named Cathal. I had the displeasure of a... a pretty long conversation with them when I tried to flee the Shadow Lord's fortress at first."

The stunned expressions and gentle, yet panicked murmurings of the room only served to heighten my own fears.

"Then there are two Pendants arrayed against us?" Ser Sigmund looked very worried.

"It is common knowledge that Lord Morod has long possessed not only the Obsidian Pendant, but also the ability to summon a dragon to it," Ranzel stated in such a factual tone.

"But if the legends of Lord Morod possessing the power of a dragon are true," Warden Alessa shook her head grimly, "then battling him may be impossible."

"No," Ellora shook her head sternly. "No. During the War of the Shadow I stood with the Great Heroine herself and faced this very same Shadow Lord we now find ourselves contending with. We tasted victory then, so I assure you it can be done again."

"If only we could secure more Dragon Pendants and the Holders to wield them," Ser Callenhad stated, "then we could certainly defeat him..."

"Keilantra has other Pendants," I murmured, suddenly realising I had spoken when they all stopped their grumblings to look at me.

"How many?" Ser Callenhad frowned.

I shrugged lightly and shook my head. "Um... including hers, she has five."

"Five?" Ser Callenhad was startled.

"Had we but known that five of the thirteen pendants were located in her keeping we might have acted sooner!" Ser Sigmund exclaimed, banging his fist hard on the table. "It is the sacred duty of the Dragon Knights to secure *all* Dragon Pendants that are not held by a Holder! We *must* act!"

"You cannot!" Ranzel snapped, drawing all eyes to him. "Though four inert pendants are gathered together in a single place, we cannot simply hope to retrieve them. That I escaped Castle Ortagaad is a monumental task in itself, that the Princess did so beyond fathomable. But to assault that fortress is impossible."

"We should know," Fawkner commented sourly, then looked to me. "We tried."

My heart leaped in my chest. The knowledge that my friends had at least planned an attempt to free me was beyond all the hoping I had possessed while trapped in that castle. Now I realised that while I had felt alone there I really wasn't.

"And we have more dire concerns at the present," Xzharn declared, turning his black eyes to the two Dragon Knights. "Though I recognise your sacred duty to the Dragon Pendants, at this time it is more important that you attend to your other duties to defend this single Holder as we ascertain the Shadow Lord's intentions."

"Of course, Grand Wizard," Ser Callenhad conceded, placing a hand on his second's arm to ease him back into his seat. "The Witch cannot wield the powers or dragons associated with the others she has taken, limiting her to the use of her own single pendant."

"Child," Samhir drew my gaze to his caramel stare, leaning his folded arms on the table, "how did you come to discover this secret of the Witch?"

"I was taken to the Witches' Sanctum," I explained slowly, still feeling a thrill of fear as I thought of that dire room and its hellish contents. "Keilantra intentionally showed me the Pendants she had collected herself."

"Why?" the dark-skinned wizard asked.

I shook my head, hesitating. "They... they told me... what the Shadow Lord intends to do with me..."

"Why have you not said so before in this convening?" Warden Alessa demanded harshly. "We have sat here questioning his very intent and here you, a mere girl, hold the key to..."

"I don't know what he intends," I cut her off, quickly clarifying my meaning. "I know what he intends to do with *me*."

"What is that?" Lucilius asked quietly.

I felt my body shaking, tears burning the edges of my eyes without falling, my lips trembling as I held them in a thin, grim line.

"He... he's planning to kill me," I said, my body shuddering and my tears slipping free. "That was why I was taken to the sanctum. Keilantra and Manth told me that I was to die in a ritual, though they wouldn't tell me more than that."

"What ritual, child?" Xzharn asked with the most severity he had yet wielded, gripping his staff tighter as the other wizards all now held their own defensively, almost as if fearing my words could conjure our foe.

"I... I don't know..." I confessed.

"Think, my dear girl," Ranzel urged me gently. "Think back to what you saw, to what you heard."

I thought carefully of the time I had spent there, more time than I cared to count left alone. I remembered the shelves, the horrible jars, the black mirror, the tall windows, the cauldron, the display case, the books strewn across the desk amidst the rune covered scrolls... *The books! Why didn't I remember?!*

"There were books," I translated my thoughts to the conference of warriors and wizards, slowly picking at what I could remember. "The Witches intended me to see them, telling me it was how I would die."

"What did you see, child?" Ragdobar queried, peering over his eyeglasses at me.

"Passages of ancient texts, drawings, etchings... runes... strange markings," I recalled with effort, shaking my head as if to rattle the memories loose. "There was a single passage I read, though I can't remember it."

"What do you remember, Princess?" Samhir urged me on.

"Only a few words," I confessed, really concentrating. "Lunar Joining... Seals of... of Ankorect, I think... World Ender..."

"The Beasts of Ragnarok?" Ranzel frowned at me with deep dread in his eyes.

I took in a shaking breath as I nodded.

"Are you certain, girl?" Xzharn questioned with a dire expression, his grip on his staff tightening even more.

I nodded. "Ragnarok... I remember that word, though I have no idea what it means."

"It is an ancient word," Ranzel explained dreadfully, "meaning The End of All Things."

"Morod wants to end the world?" I couldn't believe it, my own words of realisation sounding horrible and foreign to my ears.

The hush and unease that fell upon the room was beyond deafening. The tension was so thick that there couldn't have been a knife or even a great sword capable of cutting it. I looked to my friends, the fear in their eyes so alien, so haunting. Never before had I seen such terror in the faces of these people I had trusted for so long now. For once I could see the dread in Joran's expression, the end of the world a prospect that must have shaken the Storvari's iron strong resolve where nothing else would.

"You have been most helpful, Princess Leander," Xzharn stated slowly and carefully, trying to shield his own unease. "We must consult upon this information you have provided us. Please, if you and your companions would take your leave."

I was numb, standing only when Carden leaned over me and offered me his hand. He took me around my shoulders, his hand against my back as we made for the doorway beyond the arches to the stairs with Fawkner and Joran close behind me.

"Master Aldwyn, Huntress Ellora," Xzharn called to our two elder companions as I looked over my shoulder to his voice. "I would ask that you both remain."

"Aldwyn?" I looked to him worriedly.

"It is all right, your Highness," he turned to Fawkner. "Keep an eye on her."

"Of course," Fawkner nodded, placing his hand to my shoulder in addition to Carden's.

Tallinn, Dolin, Holger, Ranulf and Tristan reached the stairs as we turned and followed, Joran remaining at my back.

"It's going to be okay," Carden tried to reassure me, but there was no comfort I could find now that I knew the Shadow Lord's plans for me... and for the rest of the world...

Chapter Twenty-One
Soul Kindred

Days had passed without any sign of either Aldwyn or Ellora, though I am certain they must have returned to the house to rest and eat. My nights were restless, though not as much as they had been before coming to the Silver City. Sleeping in Carden's unflinching embrace only comforted me, and while I didn't tell him what it was that I dreamed of, he woke when I cried out in fear and calmed me back to my rest. Still, the nightmares came, hard and strong with each eve that fell.

I saw *Him* standing above me with that sinister dagger aloft in his clenched fists, the blade gleaming as it thirsted for my blood. Carden's cries of panic rang in the dark place as the Shadow Lord stood ready, the strange hooded, angelic figure watching on as he ever did, his staff of gold in hand and his eyes glowing blue.

Then, above the Shadow Lord I saw the shimmering of haunting eyes glowing with an evil blue flame so unholy that all things withered and died before it. I heard the Beast snarl, saw the flames behind his teeth as he scowled at me, impressive in his monumental wickedness.

"Kill her," a terrible, snarling, deep voice spoke from the shadows that surrounded me. "Kill her that I might devour all... Kill her and I shall serve you, Master of Shadows..."

The Shadow Lord looked down at me, taking in a lingering breath. "Goodbye, Princess..."

The knife came down hard, pain tearing my chest and blood erupting through my vision as the terrible shadow in the flames roared maliciously...

I woke up with a terrified start once again, this time the dream was worse than it had ever been.

"Leander?" Carden sat up beside me, his shirtless chest silhouetted in the darkness of the room, his green eyes scanning my scant nightgown clad form.

I trembled, feeling the straps fall from my shoulders as sweat beaded my skin, sticking the light fabric to my body. Tears choked my eyes as my breathing laboured hard in my heaving chest and fear cracked through my heart.

"Leander," his touch startled me, making me jump where I sat. "It's all right. It's just me. You're safe."

I blinked back my fearful tears, my sight clearing to show me the Elven bedroom we lay in, the cool breeze flickering the sheer white curtains that framed the open terrace doors. I looked to my handsome Guardian, stunned to see him so scantily dressed and frowning sleep from his eyes.

"Carden...?" I gasped hoarsely.

"You've had nightmares almost every night since your arrival here," he said softly, concern in his gentle emerald gaze. "Will you please tell me what it is that frightens you so much, my beautiful girl?"

I took a shaking breath as I looked at him. "A dream... a dream I've had since meeting that strange woman in the wilds..."

"The Witch? This... Danika you spoke of?" he recalled with distaste in his mouth and snapping from his tongue, but he didn't say anything coarse.

I nodded slowly, trying to ease my frantic breathing and my panicking heartbeat. "She showed me my future..."

He frowned darkly. He never did trust such things. That is, except when it came from me. For some reason, he trusted my premonitions more than any other's.

I went on: "She showed me that you and I would be together again. That we would know happiness and love in a kingdom where dragons roam free, and all is prosperous. But then the vision turned dark, and I saw the Shadow Lord standing before me as you screamed in terror. And as you watched on... I... I beheld Azmerath himself..."

"The God-King of Death?" his frown deepened, and his jaw set firmer.

I nodded as tears fell from my eyes and my voice was broken by sobbing breaths. "He... he stands there, watching as... as you plead... as you scream to save me from the Shadow Lord. But you can't... He... he slays me... with a cold dagger while a terrible beast watches on, urging him to end my life..."I looked up at him, filled with sorrow and fear."He kills me... in front of you and you can't stop him, though you try. I'm... I'm afraid I'm going to die, Carden..."

"No," he shook his head, pulling me into his large, muscular arms and holding me to his exposed, firm chest, his right hand to my hair as he tilted my head to rest on his shoulder. "No, you won't. It was nothing more than a bad dream conjured by a witch..."

"She showed me a vision..." I whispered.

"No," he shook his head as I looked up into his eyes. "If she is the sister of those vile women who imprisoned you as you claim, then all she showed you was an illusion. It was a deception to make you weak and allow them an easier chance to reach you. Nothing more."

"Carden," I sniffed, looking down at his chest, "part of it is already true. We *are* together in a kingdom of prosperity where dragons roam freely. I have never been as happy as I now am here with you..." I was hesitant to add the rest. "And... I've had these dreams of my death long before I ever met Danika..."

He grabbed my chin and made me meet his gaze again, our faces only inches apart, his height overwhelming mine despite sitting on a bed together. He shook his head, his fear of losing me so clear in his eyes.

"It *won't* happen," he said so certainly. "Leander, I will *never* let it happen, nor will any of our friends or all those here that now protect you. You *are* safe, my love. Nothing can hurt you here."

I just nodded as he cradled me, resting my head to his bare chest again. I wanted to believe him, to trust that what Danika had shown me was nothing more than a vile fantasy. But I couldn't. In my heart of hearts, I knew that what I had seen was not authored as fiction, but was Fate showing itself to me. Yet, with Carden, I couldn't help but feel an unbreakable sense of safety.

"*You* make me feel so safe," I confided in him, allowing him to lay back with me, snuggling into his side. "No one makes me feel like this but you."

He stroked my bare shoulder with his large, warm, coarse fingers, making the caress seem like silk.

"I *will* protect you, Leander," he pledged, looking down at me against his torso. "Always and forever, my darling girl. And I will *always* love you, no matter what comes."

He kissed my forehead as I closed my eyes, his gentle touch soothing me back to sleep. I didn't dream of that wicked scene again, instead resting comfortably with him now through the rest of the night...

* * * * *

We woke to knocking at the door, Carden slipping from the bed and donning his dark teal shirt as he crossed the room. He permitted two Elven women to enter, carrying clothing, which they told me was courtesy of his Lordship.

I stood and looked at the garments, each one a replica of my own dress. I thanked the women and asked that they pass on my compliments to their Lord and the tailor. They left with a bow of their heads and I chose one of the blue, teal and mauve gowns, deciding on a colour change for now.

Carden and I took breakfast out on the terrace overlooking the gardens, enjoying our time alone. We had decided to spend some time together today without the company of the others until after midday, just to grant us a little reprieve from all the waiting we had done so far.

After midday meal, which we shared with the others, we took to the dining room balcony. Tallinn was speaking with Ranulf just beyond the doors of the dining room, the Rangers who had accompanied us now with them. Fawkner and Dolin sat together by the barrier of the balcony playing a heated game of chess, the man and the dwarf daring each other to make their next moves. They both looked oddly calm, Fawkner turning only to feed strips of meat to Farsight, the falcon perched on a branch set in a stand beside his chair.

Tristan leaned his elbows on the barrier as he watched the gardens, a pipe to his lips, blue smoke puffing from its end. He looked to be deep in contemplation as he studied the gardens and the waterfalls beyond, his reddish-blonde hair tied back in a neat ponytail, his clothes less dishevelled now.

Joran remained near the archway onto the balcony with his arms crossed and his eyes roving the room. Unlike the others, he never set down his twin scimitar-like swords, keeping them sheathed at his back at all times. He was the picture of the Storvari ideal of readiness. And Holger was pacing erratically, his pipe held in one hand to his lips as he muttered to himself. He stroked his knotted black beard feverishly, his dark brown eyes gazing upon the white marble floor.

I sat back on a long love seat with Carden, my shoulders resting against his chest, my hair left untied to hang across my shoulders and the blue velvet of my dress. I had my knees up with the book the Green Wizard had left for me perched upon them, my eyes taking in every word on the pages as I read.

Carden sat with his jacket off, one arm around my waist, watching me read as his other hand gently rubbed my shoulder, soothing my tension. It felt so good to be so free with him, to just sit so peacefully together like this.

"Blast it all!" Holger grumped, drawing my gaze from my book. "It has been days! Nearly twelve by my count since we have heard anything from the towers!"

"Patience is a virtue, my brother," Dolin advised him, making his next chess move and leaving Fawkner frowning at it in thought as the dwarf puffed his own pipe.

"Even in all the days we have lingered in this city, ere the lassie's return to us, never have we been so idle!" Holger grouched, turning his eyes to his twin brother.

"Would you truly wish danger to befall us?" Dolin questioned his logic with a raised bushy eyebrow. "Would you want foul beasts to attack when at last we have a safe haven for the wee lass?"

"I would not waste my prowess and worth sitting on my hands, Dolin," Holger responded gruffly, ceasing his movements. "I would revel in an opportunity to be of use now and find myself bringing the fight to our enemy rather than sitting stagnant as a pool with no flow."

"Do not look so eagerly for a battle when one is not necessary, Master Dwarf," Fawkner played his move, then turned his grey eyes to the angry dwarf. "We need not seek out danger when it so readily seeks us."

"We are at no risk of it finding us, Lord Caradoc!" Holger retorted roughly, stopping his movements once more. "Whilst we remain in the realm of these high blood pointy ears, we stay feeble and useless!"

"We seek the knowledge of what course to take next, Holger," Fawkner reminded him, studying Dolin's next move thoughtfully.

"Aye," Dolin agreed as he sat back in his seat to allow the man his move. "That is the reason why Master Aldwyn and Lady Ellora have yet to return from their discussions with the Wizards."

"And how many days must pass, and nights must wane before their return, brother?" Holger demanded grumpily. "How long does it take to confer on such knowledge as that as the lassie has gifted them? Hm?"

"They will come to their decision when they come to it," Fawkner expressed wisely, making his next move on the chessboard, then glancing at the dwarf and feeding his falcon another strip. "The Wizards have their methods and more wisdom and experience than all of us combined. If the Shadow Lord's designs are such as these that threaten Leander now, as well as all of High-Realm, then we must be prepared..."

"Prepared?!" Holger snorted gruffly. "I say we take the fight to the bastard ourselves! Slay the Shadow Lord ere he can enact his evil desires and awaken the timorous beasties of Ragnarok!"

"I doubt such creatures as these that they spoke of are as nervous as you might think, Holger," Tristan remarked, turning over his shoulder from his view to look at him. "By all accounts, the Beasts of Ragnarok are nigh impossible to defeat in combat, save through magicks of ancient design."

"That's coward's talk," Holger snorted and returned to his pacing.

Tallinn joined us, her eyes harsh as they fell on the dwarf: "If I were you, Holger, I would hold my tongue in present company, ere you drive those around you to depart from your presence."

"Is everything all right, Tallinn?" Carden asked her as I looked up at her from my book.

She nodded, sitting down nearest us and crossing one leg over the other, her hands folded on her knee. "I was farewelling my brother and the others."

"They aren't staying?" I frowned.

She shook her head. "No. Ranulf and the others have much to do, their place is with our clan."

"Should you not be with them?" Tristan asked.

She threw him a death glare but looked to Carden and I before sighing: "My place is here, my duty as a Guardian foremost to all others. Leander's protection is my focus and remaining here in Silvervale makes such a task all the easier."

"I couldn't agree more," Fawkner nodded and smiled at Dolin. "Check mate, my friend."

The dwarf studied the board then laughed brashly. "Aye, that it is. Another game?"

"Another it is," Fawkner nodded with a smile, the two men resetting the board.

Tallinn turned her gaze to Carden and I, smiling a little. "I see you both have decided away with secrecy, instead embracing publicly."

I looked up, startled by her words, but Carden was the calmer as he spoke: "Is there any reason we should not be gladdened by our relationship?"

"No," she shook her head. "I am honestly so happy and relieved to see you so blissfully embracing."

"Indeed," Fawkner looked to us from feeding the bird another strip of meat. "It is good that you are together once more. Your love should be celebrated."

"Aye," Dolin nodded, focused on setting their heavy pieces to the board, "that it should."

I smiled and looked up at Carden, gaining his own warm grin back. He kissed my forehead and I set my book down, resting my head into his chest, his arms slithering around my midriff to hold me close. He made me feel so very safe and secure.

"As well as the lad and lass having embraced what is in their hearts is," Holger growled, looking to the others, "there is still the matter of the Shadow Lord to attend to."

I groaned and rested my head back against my lover's chest. *Can he not stop for just **one** moment?!*

"Do you ever stop with this subject?" Carden scowled at him. "Yes, we have waited near a fortnight for some word from the Broken Towers as to what is to be done about Morod's plans. And all that time we have implored you to be patient."

"Patience is no dwarven virtue, young Guardian," Holger responded coldly. "It is humans who place value on such, yet your kind struggles to embody it."

"As I am certain it has been said dozens upon dozens of times," Tallinn rolled her eyes at him, "but Aldwyn and Ellora will return when a decision has been reached. Griping about having to wait here in this comfortable house with all the leisure we could desire seems a poor way to spend your time."

"And is Lord Morod spending his time in leisure, Lady Guardian?" Holger asked harshly, folding his arms and giving her a hard stare. "No, he will be conjuring some new means to capture the Princess and achieve his aims whilst we sit here drinking tea and playing chess! While she reads stories of fiction in her lover's arms, her enemy rallies against her! This inaction will be our downfall, mark my words!"

"Enough!" Tallinn snapped at him. "Keep your vile thoughts within your perverted mind and your barbed tongue behind your ale pickled lips!"

"You would challenge me?!" he demanded as she jolted from her seat to glare down at him. "You?! A woman!"

She snorted incredulously at him. "Yes! *I*, a *woman*, would *dare* to challenge *you*, Holger!"

"ENOUGH!" Fawkner shouted, drawing both of them to turn to him. "Once again this bickering is tiresome and serves only to disturb those of us present! Keep your words to yourselves and your petty opinions sheathed as well as your weapons! Aldwyn and Ellora will return with a plan of action once the deliberation with the Wizards is complete! And *that* is the *last* time we shall have this discussion! Do I make myself clear?!"

Tallinn and Holger both fell silent, glaring at each other, then turning back to Fawkner. They both nodded gruffly.

"Good," he turned back to the chessboard. "That is quite enough of this subject for today."

Their bickering had worked into me, despite his rapid intervention. I couldn't help fearing what the Shadow Lord was doing right at that moment, imagining him preparing some terrible force to seek me out.

I need Amethyst. I need to see her.

I pushed myself to my feet, slipping free of Carden's embrace and gaining a frown from him.

"Are you all right, Leander?" he asked in his perfect, handsome voice.

I looked to him and nodded as the other's turned their gazes to me. "I just... I need some time to myself. I want to go and see Amethyst."

He nodded. "All right. Joran, go with her."

"I shall guard the Sarissi, Master Carden," Joran nodded and bowed his head.

"I'll see you at evening meal," I said as he stood.

"All right. Be safe," he kissed me softly and briefly, letting me go.

I smiled at him, then turned and left the balcony, crossing through the dining room to the main hall with my Storvari bodyguard following closely. I loved that despite the fact I was only going to the gardens that Carden still felt the need to tell me to stay safe. It was endearing and oh so sweet. How it made me love him more.

All the bickering had stirred up my insides, a sick nausea filling me with anxiety. I could thank Holger and his fear mongering for that. Perhaps it would have been better if he had taken to his flask and not his opinions, though his breath did have the odour of ale upon it.

I walked to the gardens, making my way down the steps behind the Lord's House into the vast, verdant sanctuary blooming brightly around me. I had come to know a gentle peace here, safe amongst the Elven grown beauty of Silvervale, and taking every opportunity I could to bask in the quiet serenity of this place.

As I walked amidst the flowers and trees, I came to feel as if Spring had arrived, though the chill in the air suggested we were still in beginning of Winter's grasp. A smile came to my lips as beautiful butterflies of every vibrant colour fluttered about, an orange and gold monarch landing on my shoulder. I took it gently on my left hand and carefully set it to a rose bush, smiling at its soft fluttering.

If I am to stay anywhere for my own protection, I couldn't ask for a more beautiful sanctuary than this.

The butterflies suddenly burst into a cloud of colour, flying up from their perches amidst the flowers and flowing into the air. Such beauty had been denied me for so long that seeing it here gave me a new appreciation for all that had once been so commonplace for me.

I came at last to the great pools that gathered at the foot of the city and its grand, towering silver walls, this grove another place I so longed to go when I had a need for oneness. Again, I smiled as I reached the water's edge to see Amethyst basking in the pure crystal lakes.

The Dragon was stretching her wings as she devoured fish that swam below the water's scintillating surface, their magenta skin finally looking all but completely healed with only a few scars remaining on her left wing. I was so happy to see that she was doing better, that injury having worried me so terribly ever since finding her all those weeks ago.

"Amethyst," I smiled as I called to her, brushing a few strands of my long dark hair from my eyes as the wind gust at my clothing.

She looked up from her fishing with water dripping like clear diamonds from her long scaly snout, her orange eyes instantly finding me. She let out a joyous, but reserved sound and trudged majestically through the waters on all fours, her long tail slithering through the lake's surface glittering with the droplets on its scales.

I slowly walked backwards, holding my dress hems so I didn't trip and keeping my eyes on her as she approached me. Then, once on land, she shook herself almost like a dog would, water spraying everywhere as my arms came up to shield me from it with a laugh.

She looked at me, now slightly damp, her expression one I would call a little bashful for spraying me, but I didn't mind.

"Are you feeling better, Amethyst?" I asked, looking up at her, my hands dropping to my sides.

She cooed a deep sound that I knew in my heart meant yes. She looked bigger than I remembered, but she was still only young and growing.

I reached up my hands as she brought her large face down to meet me, her head almost the entire length of my body. I ran my palms across the smooth, damp and cool, yet gently warm scales of her snout, rubbing her rough but silky skin softly. She continued to coo, looking down at me with the love of a loyal companion, which I gave back to her in turn.

"Do you like it here?" I focused on her fiery coloured eyes.

She responded in her gentle way.

I smiled softly. "Me too. This is the safest I've felt anywhere since Eilath."

She spoke as she always did to me, my heart knowing her words where my ears couldn't understand her gentle voice.

I nodded. "Yes. Everything we've been through since Eilath... since Arvon has been..."

She found the word I sought, and I met her gaze.

"Hard, exactly," I agreed with a small sigh. "I wish I had known what they planned for you. I wouldn't have..."

She cut me off with a scowling sound, her eyes severe.

I sighed. "You're right. Dwelling on it helps no one."

She asked me a question and my heart sank.

"I... I haven't told him my fears," I confessed over Carden. "I've tried, but like when we meant to confess our love, I find myself being interrupted."

She snapped her jaws lightly.

"Don't be like that," I said, looking at her disapproving expression. "I *will* tell him about the curse. I just... I don't know how. And..." I sighed, "and I'm afraid."

She spoke, knowing my fears as she always did, her gentle dragon sounds so clear in their meaning to my heart while no one else understood her.

I nodded glumly. "The nightmares are getting worse, and I'm afraid that the Witch's vision is coming true."

I felt the strong sense of protectiveness as she growled lowly in her craw.

I smiled weakly at her. "I know you'll protect me, Amethyst. Carden said the same thing when I told him last night. He doesn't believe that what I was shown is fate, but illusion."

She spoke her great wisdom beyond her short years of life.

"Not all fate is set, really?" I frowned.

She nodded lightly, once again promising me her protection.

I chewed on my bottom lip and turned my gaze from my hands to look at her eyes as I continued to stroke her scales:"Are you able to fly yet?"

She gave her dragon smile and responded cheerily.

I half laughed. "Only short distances but getting better. That's good. I'm glad you've had time to heal here, Amethyst."

She spoke of the other.

I frowned. "The green dragon helps you?"

She responded softly, explaining.

"Yes, I know the Wizard carries a pendant like mine," I confirmed."Believe me, when I get a chance, I will talk with him about this."

Amethyst lifted her face from me and looked over my shoulder, making me frown deeper again at her.

"It would seem, my dear girl," a familiar voice spoke from behind me as the soft thud of dragon feet drew closer, "that you have at last found your chance."

I turned around, looking past Joran to see the Green Wizard striding towards me, his hat and cloak missing, though his staff was in hand, and his green and brown robes were flowing gracefully around him. The great green dragon followed at his back, twice Amethyst's size and magnificent in his splendour.

"I... I didn't think I would get a chance to speak with you until the discussion about the Shadow Lord was complete," I confessed as the two reached us.

The Wizard stopped, smiling down at me, a full head taller than my stature. "Even we wizards need a rest from time to time, my dear."

I looked up at his dragon, smiling. "Your dragon is an Emeralian? Right?"

"Why, yes," he smiled, looking up to his companion and waving his hand to shake it free of his wide flowing sleeve, then reaching out to pet the magnificent creature's horned nose. "This is Gaspeite, and he has been my companion for several lifetimes of the world."

I smiled, watching him with Gaspeite, the Dragon seeming so content with the Wizard's touch. It was clear to me that they shared the same companionship that I did with Amethyst.

"Wonderful creatures, dragons," he smiled thoughtfully as he continued to stroke Gaspeite's snout. "Fiercely loyal to their own kind, yet even more so, it seems, to their treasures."

"I never liked the fictional image of dragons hoarding gold," I said, folding my arms and holding my hands around my elbows as I shrugged lightly. "It always seems that humans would vilify them as terrible serpents taking all that they could."

"Such is the image created by dragon slayers," the Wizard agreed, turning over his shoulder and smiling at me. "But dragons are fiercely protective of what they treasure most, whether it is a hoard of gold, their hatchling brood, their harem, their single true mate, or, in our cases, the humans they befriend. You, dear girl, are Amethyst's greatest treasure and so she will risk you no harm, protecting you to the very last, for such is the way of dragons."

I really liked that view, feeling that it was more noble and befitting of the wonderful creatures.

The Wizard continued to pet Gaspeite's nose, the Dragon cooing gently as Amethyst did when I tended to do the same with her.

"Never in all my years," he said gently and warmly, "have I known the friendship of any other as I have that of Gaspeite. Truly, those of us who hold Pendants are blessed beyond all imagining. What fortune we have."

I smiled, clasping one hand over the other at my waist now, blinking against wayward strands of hair that found their way to my face with the breeze.

"Gaspeite, take the younger and continue teaching her whilst I do the same, my dearest friend," the Wizard instructed the Dragon.

Gaspeite responded with a loud roaring bellow of affirmation, then turned and grunted a series of sounds that Amethyst responded to. I understood her, but not him, having to guess from her replies that he was asking her to go with him. I watched then as the two dragons took to the air, Amethyst a little unsteady as her injured wing was still on the mend but managing. The two of them then landed on a high rock perch above us and began conversing in their way.

I frowned, looking to the Wizard as he began to move towards a stone bench in the garden: "That's strange. I understand Amethyst even though she doesn't use words, but I had no idea what Gaspeite said at all."

"Nor should you," he replied, taking his seat as I followed. "Dragons do not speak to all in their tongue. That you understand Amethyst is a testament to your bond, and it is not an understanding you may share with any other dragon."

"But... Eamnonn, the Dragon in the Guardians' Trials of Coastwatch Keep," I recalled, crossing my arms as I stared at the ground in thought, "he spoke with me. I understood him perfectly well."

"Eamnonn has been visited by quite a goodly number of mortals in all his centuries," the Wizard explained, knowing the great Aquari Dragon just from my mention of him as if they were friends. "As such, he has learned the tongues of those who walk the earth in order to speak without fear of reprisal. Many dragons learn such words to communicate."

"But Amethyst doesn't speak our tongue," I pointed out.

"She has no need of it," he responded evenly, smiling. "Like Gaspeite, Amethyst is a Pendant Dragon and so her speech is reserved *only* for her own kind... and for you, dear Princess."

"So... I can't understand Gaspeite because..."

"Because his words are for me alone to hear," he nodded gently.

"I have met four dragons of the Pendants now," I told him uncertainly, "and only Amethyst and Gaspeite don't speak our tongue. Cathal and Kuldar..."

"Cathal and Kuldar have chosen to speak mortal tongues in order to intimidate and terrify," he expressed with dark distaste. "They embody the terrible villainies of their vile and wretched masters, for they are not bonded to Morod and Keilantra as Gaspeite is to me and Amethyst is to you. They are wretched evils in their own rights and thus have forsaken the ways of the Elder Ones."

"How did such evil beings ever come to hold Pendants?" I wondered without truly seeking an answer. "I thought the Pendants were powers of good."

"Come, my dear, sit," the Wizard gestured, waiting for me to sit to his left before explaining. "The Pendants respond to the wills of their wearers, and as such take in all that their wearers are at heart. If you are of purest heart, then the Pendant you carry, and the Dragon bonded to it will know only purest of intention and love. If your heart is darkened with hatred and wickedness, then so too are the Pendant and the Dragon. They are such powerfully empathic things, capable of feeling what their human wearer feels. Such has always been the magicks of the Pendants and of the Dragons connected to them."

"So, my pendant is good because I am?" I asked hopefully, a little fearful of being told the contrary.

"You are the purest of hearts I have ever known, Leander," the Wizard smiled warmly at me. "And the Amethian Pendant knows your heart, for that is why after nearly thirteen centuries and twenty-three generations beyond your namesake it has chosen you. Your purity and your innocence is what it yearns and adores."

"Do all the Pendants yearn such things?" I wondered, studying his expression.

He looked down at his own emerald stoned pendant, gently touching his hand to it.

"No. Not all desire what yours does," he turned his hazel gaze back to me. "The Emeralian Pendant - my pendant - has long desired wisdom and the willingness to guide those in need, and so I was chosen as it passed from my great-grandfather to me when I was but a boy. You see, each Pendant has its own desires for a wearer and so waits until the right person comes to it."

"And what do Keilantra's and Morod's Pendants desire?" I frowned, knowing I wouldn't like the answer.

He sighed. "Unfortunately, like people, some desire power and control. The Obsidian Pendant has been one of the less noble since it was forged, and so easily sought out one who would fulfil its needs. Its need for power was met by many a warrior over the ages, but when it at last came to Lord Morod it found an insatiable hunger for the darker powers he offers, and so quickly fell to his will."

"Is... is that why he was able to take it?" I asked uneasily.

"Take it?" he frowned at me. "Is that what you were told?"

"The legends..." I started.

"The legends speak falsely," he interrupted me calmly. "Lord Morod did not take a Dragon Pendant by force, as so many believe. He inherited it, like every other wearer in the history of the world."

Hearing that chilled my heart and made me wonder: *Was he a normal human once? Was he a good person who came to have the Obsidian Pendant and was then corrupted, or was he always so terrible?*

The Wizard went on with a dire sigh: "Lord Morod was once a child, once a mortal and, I am certain, once possessed a heart of goodness, but he had a kernel of darkness seeded inside of it, and that darkness yearned greater power. Every Shadow Lord who has ever lived took to learning the magical and arcane arts only to be seduced by the darker powers so many magic wielders fear."

"Then, if he had his Pendant when he discovered these magicks..." I surmised thoughtfully.

"Yes, my dear," he nodded. "As the powerful teachings of Lord Gorth Lavelle have corrupted many a soul, when Lord Morod discovered them, both he and his pendant were filled with the Shadow Lords' evil, his dragon soon following. As for Keilantra, a good heart was broken when she was spurned by her lover and her pendant felt her pain, and so changed with her to become hateful, as did her dragon."

"No one has ever explained how the Pendants work to me before," I murmured, staring at my hands folded in my lap. "Mithras tried, but he wasn't..."

"He wasn't a wearer," the Wizard nodded, drawing my gaze as he offered a soft smile. "The Dragon Knights, though we are descended from their bloodlines, are not wearers of the Pendants, merely guardians of them. Even so, many of them here are astonished by the instinctual prowess you seem to have with your pendant. Truthfully, it is incredible that one so young could wield such magic and power so readily."

"I don't know how I do it," I confessed with a shrug, holding my upper arms and leaning my elbows on my knees, "and I don't always get it right. I just do it."

"And that is why you astonish so many," he smiled at me. "But then, I have long known the kind of girl you are, Leander. Which is why I made a point of securing your most favourite book for you."

"Which you authored," I smiled knowingly, looking to him. "As you say, *Tales of Dragons* is my favourite book and I've read it countless times... Ranzel."

He nodded with an even warmer smile. "You know me then."

"As if the White Wizard introducing you by name wasn't enough," I shrugged, "though, I suppose the name Ranzel could go to anyone, but a wizard with that name gifting me the book written by a wizard of that same name..."

"Ah, yes," he smiled, nodding. "It is rather obvious, is it not?"

"Then I'm right?" I questioned with a little excitement, though I managed to keep it hidden. "You're Ranzel of Arvon?"

"I am indeed," he nodded with a sad smile, my heart aching as I also felt the loss of our shared home once again. "Although, I have not lived in Arvon for many centuries."

"Not since you raised my ancestor from a baby?" I asked.

He nodded, smiling reminiscently. "Yes. Some of my fondest memories are of watching her grow from a small babe into a beautiful young woman," then he looked to me knowingly, "a joy I have gladly repeated, though at a distance, with you."

I frowned. "With me?"

"Surely, you know I have been there," he said, not asking, but assuming.

I shook my head. "I remember you were in my father's study the day Uncle Aric gave me my pendant..."

"I have been there since you were born, coming and going, checking on you to ensure your wellbeing," he said, smiling. "That day I was merely playing my part in your future with your father and uncle, agreeing that it was time to gift you the Amethian Pendant."

"Really?" I frowned. "Why?"

"King Aric had long considered giving it to you; the heirloom of your kingdom, the most valuable possession of Aldegaad's first Queen," he explained. "He asked for my counsel as a close friend of the Aldrich Family on what I thought of the subject, and I said that if he felt it should pass to you then that was what needed to be."

"That's... incredibly perceptive of you," I blinked away my astonishment. "How did you know that I was the right person to carry it?"

"Just as I knew you were the right person to carry the Dragon Stone that I gifted you at the Festival of Light," he replied, "which now seems to have granted you your greatest friend; a soul kindred when you needed one most."

"Yes, Amethyst really is my greatest friend," I agreed, looking to where the two dragons were conversing in their tongue.

"Yet, there are many types of soul kindred in the world," he said, drawing my gaze back to him, "and it is another of these that weighs upon your heart."

I frowned at him. "What are you talking about?"

"The young Guardian," he replied, my face instantly heating with a feverish blush that I tried to hide under my hair while attempting to ease my thundering heart. "He too is a soul kindred to you, my girl, though of the romantic bond."

"He's... he's the One," I confessed, sighing as I sat up straighter, looking at my hands in my lap once again. "I... I love him so much..."

"Yet, you fear he will turn from you," his words drew my swift and startled gaze. "That if he should discover the affliction you hide from the world that he will no longer love you."

I felt myself choking on sobs, fighting not to let them overtake me. Tears were trying to force their way past my eyes as I met Ranzel's gaze, so confused as to how he could know that hidden truth that I had told no one but Amethyst.

"You... you know..." I stammered uselessly.

"That Lord Morod has cursed you," he nodded softly, sadly. "Yes."

"H-how?" I murmured, bewildered.

"I am a Wizard of the Elements, dear girl," he smiled gently at me, taking a clean white handkerchief from his sleeve and offering it to me. "There are far too few things involving magicks that I cannot perceive after all my centuries walking this world."

I took the handkerchief, feeling my tears flow down my face on their own: "He... he used me. Violated me in a way I never knew I could be. He's taken... so... so much from me..."

I felt myself break down, my tears flowing as I clutched the handkerchief in my hands, my sobs quiet and small. I felt Ranzel's hand on my back, a gentle comfort on its own.

"You have lost so very much," he perceived with silent grief and sympathy.

"I... I would have spent my life with him," I grieved, staring at my knees through my tears, my hair shielding my face from sight. "I would have given him a family... lived happily as his wife... grown old with him. But now... the pledges he made me in the grove that day... the promises we each offered..." I shook my head, feeling defeated. "What good are they? Though I can keep mine and I would, he cannot. I will never grow old, never change, never bear him children. And as he will change and his hair will grey, what will he think looking at me, still a girl of eighteen winters? I didn't only lose my humanity that day... I lost Carden too..."

I let myself cry, hurting so deeply with my confession.

"And then what?" I asked through my cries and sobs of heartbreak. "Once he has passed from the world into Azmerath's realm, what becomes of me? None of my companions, my friends, can understand, for they grow old and change every day. Each of them is two years older than the day of that ritual, while I am not. Only Ellora as an elf is as I am, yet for her a life is still possible, love and family still to be given to her. But me..."

I drew in a shaky breath, hugging myself as if to hold my insides from tearing from my body and spilling across the garden floors.

I shook my head as my tears fell heavily and silently from my eyes: "Immortality and eternal life is a curse. So many would wish for this as if it is a gift, but it isn't. How can it be a gift when you're alone? How can you endure eternity by yourself when your loves and friends are all ash? Why would anyone wish for this?"

He stroked my back with such care, tilting my chin with his hand to make me meet his gentle gaze.

"Oh, my dear girl," he said softly, "such burdens you carry, far greater than those of she for whom you were named. But know that you are not alone..."

"Amethyst is a dragon," I said, meeting his eyes and just letting the tears go without sobs, resigning myself to my sad fate. "Though I love her, it isn't the same as being with someone of my kind."

"It is not Amethyst of whom I speak," he replied simply. "The man you love will not turn from you, Leander. He is burdened with his own curses and he will never give up on the love you share."

"But I'm different," I argued fearfully. "I am not the girl he fell in love with."

"Is it aging and change that defines who you are, or is it your heart, your thoughts and your love?" he asked, gently brushing my tears from my cheeks with his thumb. "No, girl, you are no different as a person, only as a living being. The girl Carden loves is still you, the heart he holds still yours," he shook his head knowingly. "You have nothing to fear from him, and though I do see that there are those who would decide to take that from you, he is not one of them."

"Then... he'll always love me?" I asked, hope starting to rekindle in my immortal heart.

He nodded. "Yes. You and Carden are soul kindred and meant to be. Never forget that child."

I nodded, calming my heart as I drew in a deep, relieving breath. "Thank you, Ranzel."

"You are very welcome, Leander," he stood and offered me his hand, helping me to my feet. "But now, we must attend the Broken Towers, for I hear my brothers' call."

I just nodded and ran a hand through my dark auburn locks, trying not to feel both the uneasiness of the mention of the Wizards' decisions and the fear that yet lingered in my heart over Carden. While one I would certainly attend to later, for now the other had to be my focus, and I willingly, though nervously, followed the Wizard back through the vast beauty of the gardens as my eyes flicked to the black peaks of the Broken Towers in the near distance...

Chapter Twenty-Two
Misconceived Truths

Ranzel led me from the gardens to the great porch of the Broken Towers, and once more to the round, black stone hall at the peak of the central spire. We stepped through the archways in the centre of the great domed space, walking towards the rounded table. Ranzel left my side to stand now with his four brother wizards, my nerves hurting with the unease I felt. Not one member of this conclave was left sitting, even the Dragon Knights, High Elves and Guardians were on their feet.

I stood there, looking gratefully to Aldwyn and Ellora as they came to stand on either side of me, almost as if to protect me. Aldwyn offered me a simple nod in greeting, while Ellora gave me a gentle smile, and a soft, but brief touch of her hand to my shoulder.

"Princess Leander," Xzharn spoke in his deep, dark voice, his eyes focused on me, "this conclave has given considerable thought to the information you have provided us. We now understand Lord Morod's purpose for you, and as such have devised a plan for your defence."

"I'm sorry," I spoke softly, nervous, though I hid it as I turned my blue gaze to him, "but I still don't understand what it is that he wants with me."

Xzharn nodded, explaining evenly: "The passages you read in the Witches' Sanctum refer to the prophecies regarding Ragnarok. Four millennia, ago your predecessor, the first Dragon Knight to wield your Amethian Pendant, gave her life to imprison the Beasts of Ragnarok. Her sacrifice ensured that the brother of the Goddess Dragon Ankorect could not destroy what his sister created."

I nodded, taking in all that he said uneasily, my heart growing more fearful as he spoke.

"The passages written on the subject are the last warning left to us by Alura Salu, the Silver Wizard and creator of the Dragon Pendants," Xzharn expressed, gripping his staff in his right hand. "It was Alura Salu who designed the Fallen Ones' prison as no weapon had yet been devised to destroy them, or Lord Gorth Lavelle, who had intended to aid them in ending the world."

"What does this have to do with me?" I wondered uneasily.

Lucilius spoke harshly, his red robed arms folded firmly, his staff held under his left: "The Shadow Lords knew as we do that what was done by the first Dragon Knights to entrap the terrors that plagued the world could be undone at the right moment."

"The Lunar Joining," Samhir spoke gently, his golden visage a contrast to the Red Wizard's, "refers to the alignment of the three moons set to occur in this year. It is a natural event that we see every forty-two years and is magically bonded with the prison of the Fallen Ones; the very event on which your ancestor gave her life and imprisoned them."

"As such," Ragdobar spoke in his soft, elderly voice, his pointed blue hat upon his white-haired head, "this ceremony may be performed in contrast to the original in order to reverse the affect."

"Meaning, they will release these monsters," Ellora said darkly, making me shudder at the very thought.

"Why does he need me?" I asked fearfully, looking to the five wizards.

"You are the doppelganger descendant of not only Leander the First, Heroine of High-Realm," Xzharn declared coldly, "but also that of the very Dragon Knight who imprisoned the Fallen Ones with her death. You are the same age as she was when she gave her life. Thus, the Lunar Joining in your twenty-first year is the reason you have been chosen by the Shadow Lord to die upon the altar that imprisoned the Fallen Ones in order to free them."

I was shaking, unable to control myself. Now I understood and it didn't make things any better for me.

"Fear not child," Ragdobar said softly, "we have come to our decision. You will remain here until the Lunar Joining of your twenty-first year is passed, making you useless to the Shadow Lord and defeating his plans to awaken Ragnarok upon the world."

"How... how long until the joining?" I needed to know, though I didn't want to.

Xzharn replied: "The Lunar Joining will commence six days hence from now. We need only deny you from Lord Morod another seven cycles of the sun to achieve victory and ensure your safety."

"A week?" I nodded, trying to ease my frantic breaths and heart. "Just another week and I'm safe?"

The White Wizard nodded. "Yes. After which we will begin the process of hunting down the Shadow Lord and defeating him whilst you remain here in the safety of Silvervale's borders."

"There can be no safer bastion for you now, Princess," Lord Selwyn agreed with a gentle nod. "With the forces of the Dragon Knights, the Guardians and the High Elves present, you have an army between you and Lord Morod. You *are* safe."

I just nodded, not feeling so confident. I didn't dare speak my fears, shaking as I was, but I worried that he would somehow find his way to me. He always seemed to.

"It is likely," Ser Callenhad voiced at least one of my thoughts, "that the Shadow Lord, so pressed for time as he now is, will make an attempt to abduct her."

"If he does," Warden Alessa stated firmly, "then he will be met with the full force of both of our orders and that of the High Elves. This girl is our priority as much as she is his, and we will not concede her to his possession."

"Indeed not," Aldwyn agreed, placing a hand on my shoulder. "Myself, both my juniors and Lord Caradoc stand ready to defend her, as we have already pledged."

"As will myself, her Storvari bodyguard and the rest of our companions," Ellora added with a gentle nod.

My awareness was suddenly so strongly focused on Joran's silent form close behind me that I wondered how I could have forgotten he was there.

"And I will offer my aid," Ranzel stated, nodding to me gently. "I will stand with the girl to protect and guide her."

"You have always found yourself involved in the affairs of this girl's family, Ranzel," Xzharn turned a hard gaze to the Green Wizard as he spoke. "It is curious why you would show such an interest."

"Nevertheless," Ranzel said, moving to stand with me, "I will aid in her protection all the same."

"Very well," Xzharn nodded. "This council is concluded."

With Xzharn's words, the remaining Wizards, the Guardians, the Dragon Knights and the High Elves all began to depart. I stood there, letting out a slow, anxious breath at the thought of all that had been said as I was left amidst those protecting me. I had no words, no thoughts left to me, just a nagging tingle in my chest that made me worry for my safety despite the promises of these figures of power.

* * * * *

We returned to Lord Selwyn's house in time enough for evening meal, his Lordship attending to us as he so often had. I just sat in silence beside Carden, feeling his analysing gaze, but waiting for a later opportunity to discuss it with him. However, that would have to wait.

Aldwyn called Fawkner, Carden and Tallinn to a meeting, the four of them going with Lord Selwyn and Ranzel to the library and sealing themselves inside. I was left alone to my own devices with so little to focus on aside from the painful thoughts lingering inside me.

With Joran remaining nearby, I took to the balcony to watch the sunset and the moons rise. The silence felt welcome, as did the peace of this beautiful place, yet I couldn't help the fear in my heart as I rested my arms on the railing and stared down at the vast gardens below.

One week. That's all. That doesn't seem like too long a time. Soon I'll be safe, unneeded by Morod, just able to be a normal girl again and not live in fear. Gods, that's wonderful.

My heart felt the dark worry tugging at it and I felt my expression drop as my eyes turned their gaze to the ground.

A lot can happen in one week. Too much.

I fidgeted my hands, curling my fingers and pressing my palms together uneasily.

It wouldn't take much. All that needs to happen is for the Shadow Lord's minions to just get one successful shot and then what?

My breath hitched inside my chest and I felt pressure in my eyes that told me that tears loomed close to pushing their way free.

He'll kill me. If they succeed in taking me, he'll kill me and end the world. I... I don't want that to happen. It can't...

"You all right, lass?" I flicked my head around over my shoulder, my hand tugging my long dark locks from my gaze as he spoke.

Tristan passed the archway, silhouetted by the lamp lights within the dining room. He had left his golden red hair untied, but despite his dishevelled appearance he was rather neat.

He glanced to his left up at Joran as he walked onto the balcony, the Storvari regarding him calmly before turning back to his sentry duty, arms crossed. The Ivanstenian Wanderer just nodded and moved to my side, a flask in his hand, drinking, though not addled.

"Tristan... I'm fine," I lied as he came to stand beside my right shoulder, looking back at the gardens before me.

"You don't seem fine," he observed, just another who demonstrated to me that I am a terrible liar. "I hate to see you so vexed, Princess. That you take to loneliness whilst the rest of us are joined in celebration is troubling."

"Celebration?" the word didn't sound right to me.

"Aye," he nodded, leaning his right elbow on the railing as he watched me. "Ellora has told us how we need only keep you safe a week longer and we have victory over those monsters that hunt you. Is that not cause to celebrate?"

I sighed. "I don't see how it could be."

"Why not?" he questioned, gripping his flask with both hands. "Never have I known a simpler way to claim victory in all my years, nor a greater justice upon the Witches and their vile Master. We need not even battle them, lass."

"We haven't beaten them yet," I pointed out quietly, glancing at him through my hair while feeling the gentle, cooling breeze on my skin. "Seven days, Tristan. That is how long I must be protected for."

"An easy task..."

"No," I shook my head at him. "It's never so simple with Lord Morod. He isn't going to just give me up..."

"Then we will fight him when he tries to take you," he seemed so certain of himself and how things would happen.

I met his gaze, studying him curiously and seriously. "Seven days is an eternity for something like this. While my heart is so joyous to know this ordeal is nearly at an end, my mind knows that this is the most dire and dangerous time we must face. I can't just let myself feel relaxed knowing that he is running out of time. He won't just give me up. He will become even more desperate now."

I turned back to the view as the world seemed to darken with the sun responding to Sungar's call to give Kelos the night. My heart seemed to follow the fading light and grow dimmer as night began to slowly take the sky.

"I'm... afraid," I confessed, pressing my hands together, fighting the feelings inside me. "I'm afraid that he will succeed, that they'll take me away from everyone I care about... That they'll... kill me."

"Hey, hey," he lifted my chin with his coarse, hot, dirt scented hand, bringing my gaze to his. "You are *not* going to die, Leander. Okay? None of us are going to let them get you."

"You're so certain?" I asked, trembling.

He nodded. "Aye. That I am."

I tried to smile, feeling a comfort in his words. It was just good to know that I had so many willing to stand with me, to make sure that Morod and his loyal followers didn't hurt me. I could only feel tired trying to contend with all of this now, but at least here I was free to give in to the feeling and find the rest I needed.

Tristan had a strangely soft smile on his lips, his dark eyes gazing into my blue ones with an intimacy that felt... inappropriate. Suddenly, I was uncomfortable as I saw his stare, frowning at him uncertainly.

"You are so beautiful, lass," he whispered as if to a lover.

My frown deepened and before I could speak, I found myself bewildered.

I didn't have time to think, the man pushing me against the pillar that held the eaves above us, my back pressing to its firm, smooth wooden surface in seconds. His hands pinned to my hips and, before a sound could slip free from my throat, his rough lips were on my softer ones.

I blinked in utter shock, feeling his furious embrace, his hand cupping my neck from behind to keep me steady, his breath hot on my lips. My entire body tensed, and I felt my heart start screaming and thrashing violently where my arms and legs were only petrified.

No! No, this isn't happening!

My mind went back to our time wandering the forests and of his tale of tragedy regarding his family. Anger filled me and I blinked back tears of rage, pressing my hands against his shoulders and trying to push him away, my strength miniscule next to his.

Stop it! Stop! Get off me! Get off!

It felt like an eternity of screaming in my head, but at last Tristan released his hold, leaving a bitter taste in my mouth and a fury I had never felt before in my chest. He smiled as he pulled back, but that was on his face for only a moment.

I swung my right arm and balled my fist, the cracking impact hurting my wrist and knuckles as it echoed through the balcony. I seethed, shaking my hand as he staggered back from me, his flask clattering to the floor and spilling its foul-smelling golden-brown liquid across the white marble.

"OW!" he cried out, clutching his face. "What the Void was that for?!"

"Don't you *ever* touch me like that again!" I shouted, shaking my aching hand as I glared fire at him.

"Come on, lass, we have something, you and I..." he moved towards me as if I was being foolish and he were offering forgiveness.

I backed away from him, glaring fiercely, my heart thundering with rage. "There is *nothing* between us, Tristan! *Nothing!*"

"Leander..."

"GET AWAY FROM ME!" I screamed, hitting the pillar with my back again as he stood over me. "DON'T TOUCH ME! DON'T!"

Before he could utter a sound, there was a deep roar, and he was suddenly off his feet. Joran had him by the throat, pinning him to the opposite pillar to the one I had backed into, his violet eyes blazing with rage plastered over his broad featured face. I had never seen the Storvari enraged before and it was a little frightening.

"You would *dare* to touch the Sarissi when she has already gifted her *Lomenvara* - her heart's promise of love eternal - to another!" the outraged Storvari demanded viciously. "You would dishonour her vows, her desires, her heart for your own lusts, little man thing?!"

"Let... let... ach... let go..." Tristan gasped, his feet dangling off the floor, his face turning purple and his eyes watering.

Joran roared a sound so inhuman it frightened me as he slammed him back harder again, making the vile letch gag and look dizzy.

"She is *not* your soovirinark!" the Storvari hissed with a violent stare that made me think he might rip Tristan's head off with his teeth. "You are not as you humans would call the mate of her soul! You are a wretched piggaranavaraka!"

"Please..." Tristan wheezed, looking as if he would pass out.

"Joran," I glared at the wretched man, touching my protector's shoulder.

I didn't need to say anything else, the Storvari hurling him halfway across the room in an instant. Tristan hit the floor and lay there, coughing violently and painfully as he clutched his throat.

I stood over him, glaring with hatred at his vileness: "I am *not* yours, Tristan. I am *not* in love with you, and I *never* will be."

He gasped for breath, looking up at me.

I shook my head at him. "I'm *not* your dead wife."

I turned and quickly walked away from him, managing not to flinch as I heard Joran's bellowing roar and the frantic scrapping of a body on the ground. I was a little satisfied to know that the Storvari's bellow had terrified the Wanderer, leaving him daunted by the two of us as we left his lecherous company.

He kissed me! I can't believe he would do that knowing that I'm in love with Carden! Wretched bastard! I... I need to see Carden... I need to tell him...

Joran and I reached my rooms in silence after checking at the library only to find that the Guardians' meeting had concluded. I was worried, a dark feeling completely new to me now in my heart. The Storvari waited by the door as I opened it and walked in, closing it behind me.

I was relieved as I saw Carden sitting there on the bed with his back to the door, his view towards the window.

"Carden," I said, but he didn't look up, a frown replacing my smile quickly. "Carden?"

I moved towards him, sitting down on the bed next to him. He had a dark frown and a violent expression in his eyes. Something terrible must have been said in that meeting.

"Carden," I spoke softly, touching my hand to his, "what's wrong?"

He pulled his hand from mine and stood, moving to the terrace doors. He turned his gaze to me and once again I thought I could see a red glare in them. I had never seen him looking so... hurt...

Oh, no! No! He... he didn't! He couldn't think...

"Carden..."

"I don't want your excuses," he hissed, turning and storming through the terrace doors.

"Carden! Wait!" I got to my feet and chased after him, having to snatch up my dress hems to keep from tripping.

He saw everything! Oh my gods! He saw the kiss! But he... Why is he mad at me?! Didn't he see me punch Tristan or Joran defend me?! Doesn't he know the truth?!

I had to run to catch up to him, his much longer legs carrying him farther much quicker than I could get. I silently cursed my long clothes, desperately chasing him into the gardens down by the lakes as the dying dusk light was spreading a fiery orange glow over everything and making the greens look like blues and greys.

"Carden! Stop!" I ran, my chest hurting and my breathing labouring as he stormed onwards. "Stop!"

He came to the lake's edge amidst the great oaks and pines of the garden, stopping only as I finally got in front of him.

"Will you please just talk to me?!" I pleaded, out of breath as I stood in his way.

He scowled. "What is there to talk about?"

"I know what you saw," I started, catching my breath and shaking my head at him, "and it's not..."

"Not what I think, right?!" he half shouted, glaring down at me. "I misunderstood what I saw, is that what you're saying, Leander?!"

"Yes," I nodded, my breathing slow and painful.

He rolled his eyes, turning from me to glare at the lake. Then, without warning, he spun around and shouted at me, his eyes picking up the red hue of the light on the water.

"I saw you with him!" he ranted in rage. "You were in his arms! Kissing him! Just like her! Just like the woman I first gave myself to!"

"Carden, no..." I started, but he didn't let me speak.

"You deny it?!" he virtually screamed, scaring me and making me back step a little. "Do you have no respect for me at all, Leander?! Can't you at least tell me the truth?!"

"I *do* respect you..." I tried.

"Do you?!" he reeled at me. "After all the love and kindness I have shown you, you would find love's embrace in another's arms?! In *his* arms?!"

I felt like I was going to cry, tears pushing at me, trying to break my barriers and flood my face. I was hurting at his words, at his doubt of me, the feeling cutting into my heart mercilessly.

"I didn't kiss him!" I defended.

"I saw you!" he seethed, glaring rage and brimstone down at me, his green gaze now heated and full of anger. "I *saw* you kissing him!"

"*HE* KISSED ME!" I screamed back at him. "I *DIDN'T* KISS HIM! I WOULD *NEVER*!"

"YOU DID!" he bellowed back at me.

"DO YOU EVEN CARE ABOUT ME?!" I screamed, feeling the tears coming hot to my cheeks and slipping from my jaw. "DO YOU?!"

He scowled. "WHAT KIND OF A STUPID QUESTION..."

I cut him off: "YOU ONLY SAW WHAT YOU CHOSE TO! YOU DIDN'T STAY! IF YOU HAD YOU WOULD HAVE SEEN ME HIT HIM! YOU WOULD HAVE SEEN JORAN THREATEN HIM!"

"I SAW..."

"NO! IF YOU SAW AND CARED YOU WOULD HAVE DONE *SOMETHING*!" I was shaking, my heart hurting, my eyes burning. "YOU DIDN'T! YOU DIDN'T HELP ME! YOU BROKE YOUR PROMISE TO ME!"

He looked suddenly horrified, his voice softening its volume. "What?"

"I was alone!" I sobbed, feeling as if I was being strangled by the pain in my chest. "I was scared! I wanted you to come for me, but you didn't! You didn't save me! You promised!"

He frowned.

I looked up at him. "Two years I waited for you... Two years I called your name and hoped you would come for me... But you never did..."

"The tower..." he realised what I hadn't even worked out yet.

"You didn't come for me," I dropped to my knees, my hands in my lap and my cheeks drenched in the salt of my grief. "You... you left me there alone and they hurt me so badly..."

"I spent all this time trying to find a way back to you, Leander," he spoke harshly, but softly.

I looked up at him. "What does that matter if you can't recognise when I am being forced by another man, Carden? If you saw what he did, why didn't you stop him? Why do you keep leaving me to fight on my own?"

"I... I..." he was lost for words.

I looked down at my hands again. "I have been faithful to you all this time... I am not like some unfeeling woman from your past... Tristan thinks that I am like his dead wife. He doesn't care for me, only covets me because I am yours. He is a lecherous nothing, a liar, a heartbreaker! My heart belongs to you only, but you can't even see that!"

He was silent, not moving, his eyes to his feet. I couldn't even look up at him, so hurt that he would think I could ever betray him like this.

"All this time since we were parted," I explained softly, fighting not to sob and battling to stay in control of my own shaking voice, "all I have thought of is you. When I escaped the Witches all I wanted was to find you. I went to the Revenant's fortress looking for you. When I thought you were dead, I didn't know what to do. I wanted to die, to give up if I could never be with you again..."

He sighed sadly. "Leander..."

I looked up at him. "I am sorry that he touched me, but I didn't choose that. I would never choose anyone but you, Carden. You're the only man I have ever loved. Please... Please, believe me... Please..."

He dropped to his knees in front of me and looked into my eyes. I felt my tears still flowing, his face blurred by them as they choked my eyes.

"I'm sorry!" he whispered, pulling me into his embrace. "Gods, Leander, I am so sorry! I'm a fool and let my past hurts confound me! You would never... You couldn't..."

"I wouldn't," I promised him, knowing it was the truth. "I love you and *only* you, Carden."

"I love you so much," he kissed me feverishly, holding me tight. "Please, forgive me for my blindness, for my misconception of what is true? Please?"

"Just... never let that happen again," I said, managing to ease my breathing and slow my sobs. "Never walk away like that again..."

"I... I have always been jealous when it comes to you," he confessed, meeting my gaze with his now softer one. "I didn't mean to hurt you with my blind ignorance to the truth. Tristan has always been a deceiver, and you foolishly believe that there is good in him..."

I shook my head. "I... I believe there is good in everyone and that people make mistakes, but I would *never* betray you with him. You're the One, Carden, no matter our pasts, our status, our upbringing or anything that afflicts us. You are my soul mate."

"And... and you're mine," he forced a weak smile, his eyes red with their longing to release tears. "I... I'm so sorry, Leander. I've been a jealous fool."

I managed a small smile of my own as I looked up at him, feeling his large finger and thumb hold my chin.

"You aren't mad at me?" I asked softly, meekly.

He shook his head. "Only at myself."

"I'm mad at myself too," I confessed. "I shouldn't have trusted him."

I gazed into his eyes, feeling as if this could have all been avoided, but just glad that it wasn't the end of us. I could never endure that.

He smiled, then his eyes drifted to my neck, where his smile became a frown. He leaped up, his sword sparking as it snapped from his hip with his rapid movement. I was terrified, staring up at him, too scared to think why he suddenly glared at me with such fierceness.

"Your pendant," he growled.

I looked down, horrified to see the Pendant's purple stone flickering warningly. Then I heard the footsteps and the crushing of grass and twigs, turning over my shoulder to see them approaching.

Hurgarks scuttled, Gathlorks and Orcs strode, Erks lumbered and Gymphs slithered, their weapons ready, their hisses, squeals and growls animalistic and evil. The beasts came from the waterways where the city's docks were, somehow having gotten past the High Elven defenders.

"Get behind me!" Carden ordered and I immediately got to my feet, rushing behind him and grasping his shoulder fearfully.

It was just the two of us against a full Scourge attack force with forty Hurgarks, six lumbering Erks, four viciously vile Gymphs, twenty-six Orc warriors with eight leading Orc lieutenants, and twenty powerful Gathlork soldiers under the command of four fierce and heavily armoured Gathlork Captains. Leading them was a single Gathlork Field Commander, his brutish, heavy armour smeared with white paint and elvish blood, his putrid yellow eyes snarling above his jagged teeth, his long black hair swaying as he stormed towards us. He carried a deadly looking great sword across his back made of black steel and dripping with blood.

I snatched up a two-foot branch from the ground, the only thing I had to use as a weapon.

"You need to run," Carden advised me as we backed away.

"No," I shook my head. "I am not leaving you to fight them on your own."

"Leander!"

"No!" I snapped, glaring at him. "We're in this together. Always."

He knew he wasn't going to persuade me, turning his gaze and his sword towards the incoming Scourge forces. He gritted his teeth, and as the first of the beasts came at us, he swung his blade, casting them down. He was moving with a vicious speed unlike anything I had seen him use before, impressive and terrifying.

Hurgarks ran at me, my branch smashing the four-foot beasts in the face and staggering them as I swung hard. They kept coming, a Gathlork rushing at me only to be slain by Carden's swift skills with his blade.

A great roar echoed through the air as the six Erks rushed towards us in their demented charge, suddenly shrieking as the beat of wings drew their attention to the sky. Purple scales gleamed in the dusk light, Amethyst landing and lashing out with her claws, her teeth and her barbed tail at the brutes. The Dragon was determined to keep us from falling, her roars driving fear into the foes that charged around us. Yet, even with my dragon's help, we were overwhelmed.

The whistle of arrows shot past my left ear and I pulled back as two Orcs were slain. Tallinn and Ellora appeared, slinging arrows from their bows expertly into the throng to defend us. A shout came from behind me, Joran charging into the fray with his twin blades slicing and carving the horde of Scourge.

"Get behind us, lassie!" Dolin ordered as he and Holger came to flank me, their war hammer and battle-axe at the ready, both dwarves armoured up to fight.

Fawkner swung his blade past me, taking down a Gymph that attempted to attack Carden, joining my lover in the battle to now stand back-to-back. More arrows passed me as High Elves sped into the fight, their silver armour gleaming in the light, their elegant blades unsheathing to meet the Scourge's crooked weapons.

Green and blue energy struck down more Gathlorks and Orcs as Ranzel and Aldwyn came with the Elves, the Wizard drawing his sword as Gaspeite swept from the sky to help Amethyst. The two dragons had turned their attention to a great troll in heavy armour that the Scourge had somehow tamed, clawing it and biting at its weak points. Gaspeite belched flames into its face as Amethyst strangled it with her tail.

"Holger! Dolin! Get the Princess out of here!" Aldwyn shouted at the Dwarves.

"Aldwyn, no..." I tried protesting as Tristan rushed past me with more Elves and several Dragon Knights.

"Do not argue, your Highness!" Aldwyn barked, smashing down a Hurgark with his staff and setting alight several more enemies with magic. "Go! Now!"

"Get moving, lassie!" Dolin shoved me back.

I screamed as a sword came at my face, my pendant flashing as the branch I had in my hand was cleaved by the Gathlork's strike. The creature howled as it was thrown backwards by the Pendant's magicks, hitting a tree with a shattering force.

"Come on, girlie!" Holger hollered, slicing his hammer through the air to crush a Hurgark down.

I grabbed the hems of my skirt and followed. Aldwyn covered us as we backed away, Gathlorks and Orcs pursuing us. We just ran, the Dwarves and the Mage protecting me, my heart fearful that I was being driven back from Carden.

Please, don't let him die! Please!

The beasts howling behind us kept me sprinting as fast as I could, my focus now on reaching the house.

Suddenly, our way was blocked, Gathlorks surrounding us as a Gymph leaped at me. Dolin swung his axe up, catching the creature's leather wrapped shape and casting it down as I dropped to one knee.

"Stay down, girl!" Aldwyn commanded, turning with his sword and staff to fight those that had followed us.

I could only watch on helplessly as the Dwarves kept me protected. It felt as if we were facing a full-on assault of Scourge that would never end.

Aldwyn swung and downed a Gathlork that reached for me, my scream of shock dropping me further back. Then, I heard a terrible sound like steel breaking bone and flesh.

My eyes widened as I saw Aldwyn's expression, his mouth turning upwards painfully and his eyes flickering. He looked down, a sinister black blade breaking through his chest, splintering his light armour and tearing his robes. As his blood spilled and stained the blade, he looked over his shoulder at the Gathlork Field Commander snarling behind him. The creature shoved his arms forward, the force causing Aldwyn great and terrible pain, drawing him to cry out in agony.

No! I shrieked inside my mind, feeling a terrible heat flash through my head and chest at the sight...

Chapter Twenty-Three
Hearts Asunder

The Gathlork withdrew his blade, dropping the Mage to the ground before stepping back, chomping his jaws eagerly as he did. I felt absolutely helpless as cries echoed around me, footsteps rushing through the grass loudly. Aldwyn fell forwards and I jumped up, running towards him without thinking. I reached him as he rolled onto his back, his breathing difficult and his hands shaking. I turned my eyes up to the Gathlork, watching him sneer down at me, feeling like a deer facing a hungry lion.

The world seemed to slow down, the beast roaring as Dolin and Holger rushed forward, attacking him with swift and heavy strikes from their weapons. I turned away from the battle and faced Aldwyn, seeing the gruesome wound that was draining his lifeblood from him.

"Prin... Princess," his voice shook so very much, blood wetting his lips.

"Aldwyn," I gasped, pressing my hand to his chest and grasping my pendant. "Heal him. Please... Please, heal him. Like you healed me. Please..."

I felt utterly helpless, watching on as Aldwyn's life drained away, his blood staining into the earth and grass. I kept trying to will the Pendant to save him, desperately pushing all that I had into it, pleading with it to save this great friend and protector of mine. But ultimately it was useless as the Pendant's light glowed, then flickered and died. I felt horrible pain in my chest as I realised the truth.

I can't save him...

"Princess..." he gasped, reaching up and holding my right hand as my left clutched the Pendant, drawing my gaze to his paling face. "I... am... sorry..."

"Aldwyn... no..." I shook my head, tears returning as I felt a terrible hurt inside me.

I heard footsteps, the rushing of the High Elven guards like silver streaks passing us by. I could hear the Dwarves taking down the Gathlork, but my focus was on Aldwyn only, not the violence around us. I felt my tears run down my face and my heart lurch at the sight of my Guardian friend dying before me.

There must be something! Please, anything!

Suddenly, I felt arms hooking around my shoulders and midriff, pulling me backwards. I screamed and thrashed against the one holding me, trying desperately to break free.

"Shh, Leander, it's all right," Fawkner spoke into my ear, holding me tight. "I've got you. Shh..."

I settled my struggles as he pulled me away, Tallinn and Carden rushing into my view and dropping down on their knees beside their mentor, their faces twisted in terrible anguish.

"Aldwyn, no!" Tallinn was on the verge of tears.

"Ah... Tallinn," he smiled weakly, grasping her hand, leaving his blood on her skin.

"Ranzel!" Carden looked up pleadingly as the Wizard approached, the rest of our companions and the two dragons joining us as the Elves finished the last of the Scourge. "Please! Do something!"

"I am sorry," Ranzel said with all the sincerest sympathy and sadness he had, leaning on his staff with both hands. "There is nothing that can be done. He is beyond even the healing powers of a Dragon Pendant."

I closed my eyes, both hands gripping Fawkner's wrist as I felt the pain that came at this news. But what was more agonising than losing Aldwyn was knowing that Carden and Tallinn suffered so greatly as their hearts were torn asunder.

I looked up as Aldwyn spoke gently: "It... it is all right, my charges... It is how... how it must be..."

"No, Aldwyn, please," Tallinn pleaded with him as if that would do any good.

"Please... there... there is much I would say," he beseeched them, struggling to draw breath. "Tallinn."

He drew her near to him and met her gaze. She looked so dishevelled from the fight, her hair having slipped free of its tie. She met his gaze as sternly as she could manage, but her grief was clear in her hazel eyes.

"You... you must lead the others now, Tallinn," he told her gently. "You must take charge... Must take my place..."

"Aldwyn, I can't..." she whispered sadly.

"Do not be afraid, Tallinn," he said weakly, smiling as she held his hand in both of hers. "You are... ready to be a master. You are ready to lead. Do not abandon the mission..."

"I won't," she promised, a tear gleaming as it slid down her warm cheek.

"Good," he smiled, then beckoned with his other hand. "Carden..."

"Yes, Aldwyn?" he moved forward on his knees to take the man's other hand in his, his green eyes dry, but red with sorrow.

"I... I was wrong, Carden," he confessed in a shaking voice. "You will never lose control or... or hurt her. Your love for her is too great..."

Carden sighed and looked down, his breath shaking and his shoulders trembling. He turned his now teary gaze back to his mentor sadly, but calmly.

Aldwyn met his gaze with all seriousness and urged him: "Never give up on her. Be who you... who you really are, Carden. Be not ashamed of your birthright, and love Leander as you desire. You are... meant... to be..."

"I will," was all Carden said, and maybe all he could say.

Aldwyn laid back and managed one last smile at the two of them: "It... has been... my... my honour... to be your m-mentor... You are the son and daughter... I never had. I am so... very... proud of... of you both..."

We watched then as his last breath slipped from his lips and his eyes blanked to stare at the sky above.

Tallinn began to cry outwardly as Ellora crouched to hug her, the Elf woman's expression sympathetic and grief filled. She cradled the sobbing woman in her arms and soothed her as much as she could.

The Dwarves bowed their heads in solemn respect as Tristan looked away from the scene. Fawkner held me firmly as I felt my own tears falling in silence, my eyes set on Carden as he very gently placed two fingers to Aldwyn's eyelids and closed them.

"Vashabaravan Karvarn, Aldwyn," Joran bowed his head in respect, his hands making fists and his forearms crossing together over his broad, massive chest.

As the Dragons bowed their long necks and closed their orange eyes, we all sat there with Aldwyn until his spirit was gone.

* * * * *

It took a full day to make the arrangements for Aldwyn's funeral. It was decided that we would set a pyre for him as we had for Mithras, this one upon the great porch of the Broken Towers.

Two mornings after the battle, the pyre was built by the Guardians of the enclave in Silvervale, Warden Alessa leading all those there. Carden, Tallinn and Fawkner dressed in their ceremonial armour with their black and silver cloaks furling in the morning winds. They had a few scrapes and bruises from the battle in the gardens on their skin, but otherwise they were unscathed.

I stood with Ranzel, Ellora, Joran and the Dwarves, Tristan decidedly far from my presence. I was all too glad to have him stay away from me after his unwanted advances, the purple bruise on his cheek a reminder never to touch me again.

I had dressed in the black gown that had been left for me, my hair neat, though catching its lengths in the wind, the silver circlet on my head all that kept it in place. I held my hands to my sternum, my black clothing fluttering around me in the breeze, my eyes upon Aldwyn as Lord Selwyn presided over the scene. Even the Wizards and Dragon Knights had gathered to offer their condolences and pay their respects.

We all watched on in grief as Warden Alessa set the torch to the pyre and the flames enwrapped Aldwyn's black clothed and armoured form where he lay.

Lord Selwyn held his hands together before him and spoke: "Co harnarey bellorn, daimar tis alargathar wey paic'ee ne t'i Tulir'rael, torasnor t'i ris formarnagarta."

Ellora whispered to me: "Go honoured warrior, depart this living world with peace into the Realm of Twilight, there to rest forevermore."

Lord Selwyn continued, holding his hands to the heavens: "Mai Gaya tul'lurilish ra swisilil brii ish fro Lii'lur thas ish mai naorbana vaierre agassana. Ris wath paic'ee, hirraley, formarnagarta. Ish shono'beyfar."

Ellora took in a breath and translated as she watched the pyre: "May Gaya watch over you and swiftly bring you from Life's Light that you may never know pain nor grief again. Rest with peace, honoured friend, forevermore. You shall not be forgotten."

I looked towards Carden and Tallinn, seeing the expressions of determination to stay strong hiding the grief that they shared over losing their beloved father figure. It was a grief I knew too well, and I yearned to be the one to help them, to be of comfort to them as they had been for me.

Carden glanced to meet my gaze, my heart both leaping at his sighting of me and aching at his loss. But his eyes didn't linger, his expression cold and without love.

I turned my eyes back to the pyre, remaining there with my companions until the flames turned cold, the remains became ashes and the last embers fell to the winds. Then all those gathered began to depart, the Guardians retreating into their enclave.

I made to reach Carden, but he, Tallinn and Fawkner swept away from me, vanishing into the black fortress of the Broken Towers with the others of their order. I stood there, my heart aching, my tears welling in my eyes.

I felt a gentle hand on my shoulder, looking up to see Ellora standing by my side. She knew what had happened, the only one I had confessed my soul to after Aldwyn's death, the only one other than Ranzel who would understand.

"Are you all right, Princess?" she asked of me.

I shrugged, watching Carden vanish. "Carden has been avoiding me, though, I'm not sure whether it is because of Aldwyn's passing or... or because of what I told you."

"You refer to the event with Tristan," she nodded. "No. Carden's heart is heavy with grief, Princess, not hurt of betrayal from you."

"I didn't betray him," I whispered, feeling my tears slipping free.

"No, and he knows that," she confirmed, turning my chin gently with her delicate hand to meet her turquoise eyes beneath her red wavy locks. "As all who face grief must, he turns now to the support of the family he knows, to the Guardians who share in his loss."

"I understand," I nodded and sighed.

"Do not fear," she smiled softly to me, "he will come to you when he needs you, for his love is stronger than any other loyalty he has. Allow him his time to grieve."

I sighed and nodded, then took one last look at the Broken Towers and at Aldwyn's pyre, silently wishing the Mage farewell.

* * * * *

I returned to my rooms, changing into my preferred royal blue, purple and lilac dress, then laying on the bed. With the circlet on the table and my hair brushed free of all knots, I just lay there, my hand to my lips, my other held up at shoulder level, its fingers absentmindedly playing with the fabric of my dress.

Time passed slowly, all reckoning of it slipping from my wakeful thoughts. It was only when a servant came to offer me a midday meal that I had any understanding of its passage. I shook my head, telling her that I wasn't hungry, my heart aching so much that my stomach churned relentlessly.

I replayed that terrible night over and over in my head, thinking that if I had managed to fight off Tristan that Carden and I wouldn't have fought. And if we hadn't fought, we would not have been in the gardens when the attack came, and Aldwyn would still be alive now.

I knew this was guilt talking, but I couldn't escape the nagging gnawing of it in my mind. In only an hour everything had changed so drastically, and despite our pledges of love and forgiveness, I suddenly wasn't sure that Carden was truly still in love with me, though I would always be in love with him.

I'm being foolish. He does still love me, he's just heartbroken. I know this. I've felt this. Gods, why do I have to have such insecurities in my heart? Why can my mind not simply accept what is and know that there is nothing wrong between us?

I sighed, watching the gentle snowflakes through the window. They had slowed their fall some time ago but were still wafting a little in the breeze. It had grown so cold now that winter had come to the land and I had closed the terrace doors just to keep the chill from biting my skin.

My right hand lifted from my lips and sprawled into the pillows, my skin soothing from the softness of the cool sheets and linen. I let my body decide what to experience then, the tactile feelings at this moment better than those of my mind and heart.

There was a tapping at the window, and I sat up to see him standing there, his cloak pulled around him in the white of the falling snow.

"Carden," I felt a soft smile form.

"Could you let me in?" he asked gently.

I slid from the bed and walked to the terrace doors, opening them and allowing him to enter.

"Are you insane? It's cold outside. Why didn't you just come through the hallway?" I asked, astounded by him.

"Coming this way was quicker," he said, looking down at me with a soft gaze. "I... I needed to walk through the gardens..."

"Are you okay?" I reached up, brushing snow from his shoulder.

He nodded gently. "Yes. I... I am aggrieved, of course, but I'm all right."

"I'm so sorry," I felt as if I could begin to cry. "If we hadn't had that fight, we wouldn't have..."

"Shh, do not think of it," he urged me, brushing my hair from my eyes gently. "I... I just wanted to see you."

"Really?" I looked up at him, feeling a warmth in my heart that was stronger than the chill outside.

He smiled very softly and nodded. "I need your company and your love. I need *you*, Leander."

"Of course," I nodded, trying to be comforting. "Anything you need."

"Come outside?" he pleaded softly; his eyes warm. "Please?"

I raised an eyebrow, glancing at the weather. "It's... it's snowing."

"I want to show you something," he said, grasping my hands in his, his fingers strangely cold.

I thought about it, trying to decide if it could wait, but it was Carden, and I couldn't deny him.

"All right. I'll just get my cloak," I said, turning to the wardrobe and bringing out the royal purple cloak embroidered in gold that hung there.

Pulling it on, I followed him to the doors, walking together then onto the terrace just as there came a knock to the bedroom door. I frowned and turned to go answer it, but he seized my upper arm gently.

"I'm sure whoever that is won't mind us coming back later," he said, looking down into my eyes.

I nodded. "All right. Lead the way."

We walked together into the gardens, but away from where Aldwyn had passed. We made for the orchards where beautiful golden fruits grew strong all year round, even in the bitterest of colds. The trees were evergreen and reached great canopies out and around themselves much like apple trees, silver bark covering their tall trunks.

"It's so quiet here," I observed, only the sounds of our boots crunching the snow to be heard. "It's as if everything here is right."

He watched me silently as I moved through the orchards, looking at the softly powdered grounds and the far-reaching trees with their golden fruits.

"This really is a beautiful place," I said, turning over my shoulder to look at him.

"Only half as beautiful as you, my girl," he smiled, moving to stand before me and stroking my cheek with the back of his hand.

I blushed, looking up at him. "Is this what you wanted to show me?"

He nodded vaguely. "In part."

I heard footsteps crunching behind me, frowning at him, then turning and instantly gasping at the two women who stood before. I felt tears of joy trying to take my sight as the ones of grief and fear had so many times before.

"Aislinn!" I smiled at seeing my sister, then turned to the older woman who looked like her. "Mother!"

Aislinn looked so beautiful, dressed in a gown of purest sapphire blue with a silvery under dress, a circlet of gold upon her dark brown hair. She smiled at me; her cobalt blue cloak pulled close around her shoulders. She hadn't changed.

My mother smiled brightly as she saw me, her grey eyes twinkling. She wore a gown of deepest cobalt with a golden under dress, her hair pulled back and tied into itself to leave her neck free. She wore a golden circlet of her own, her cloak hanging wide as she opened her arms to me invitingly.

"Oh, Leander, my youngest," she smiled, looking as if she could cry. "It has been so long since I have seen you."

I looked to Carden with a smile, then ran into my mother's arms, hugging her tight.

"Mother, I have missed you so much!" I felt tears slip free. "They... they told me you were dead in Castle Arvon."

"No, my darling, no," she replied, shaking her head and smiling as she looked into my eyes. "I fled with the help of several guards. I wanted to come back for you, my daughter, but they would not allow me."

"They brought her to me," Aislinn said, drawing my gaze and hugging me briefly before continuing. "It was some time after the fall of Arvon that Mother's party arrived in Daamenhall. Sten and I have taken care of her since."

"How did you find me?" I asked. "Aislinn, the last time I wrote to you was two years ago..."

Aislinn explained: "The Guardians informed us of what had happened. Lord Caradoc I believe was the one who wrote to me. It was he who sent word only a week past to tell me that you were here, safe with the High Elves."

"The Gods be praised," Mother smiled, brushing my dark auburn hair from my eyes, "my little girl is safe and once more in my arms. I may have lost my husband, but I have regained both of my children."

"They arrived this morning," Carden stated, drawing my gaze to him where he stood with his hands behind his back. "I met them on my way back from the Broken Towers and we decided to surprise you."

"I am surprised, believe me," I smiled at him, moving forward and hugging him. "Thank you so much, Carden."

I kissed him passionately, feeling his gentle caresses and his firm hands touch my hips. Then I felt strange, a weird tingling on my lips. I pulled back, frowning as I touched my fingertips to my lips, feeling some unusual dizziness start to take me.

"W-what...?" I tried to speak, but my words vanished, and I felt panic as I fell to the ground, my legs suddenly numb.

I lay there on my stomach, looking up at Carden in deep panic, wanting to scream out, but suddenly unable to. My arms were getting heavy, and I felt so exhausted, every part of me beginning to tingle as my lips had. The only sounds I could make were desperate breaths and soft groaning moans.

What's happening?! My legs! My voice! My entire body is going numb! What's happening to me?!

"Poor child," Carden spoke so harshly, his eyes cold as I desperately clawed with my fingers to crawl away. "You have been confounded by love, blinded to our little trick."

"Yes," my mother spoke, moving to stand beside me and drawing my shaking gaze. "Foolish girl. I knew your lover, your sister and your dead mother would be the perfect disguises for us to reach you."

No... Who are you?! Why are you doing this to me?! What have you done?!

She kicked me with her foot, rolling me onto my back and effectively ending my desperate struggles. I lay there in the snow, my hands at my sides, my chest heaving as I lost all feeling in my arms now, completely paralysed.

Carden's features began to change and shift, smoothing out to become something else, something... foul and evil. His skin turned snow white, his eyes black and without whites, his nose becoming two slits in a flat face. His clothes changed and he became that gruesome bald-headed disciple that had been there during the Shadow Lord's restoration two years ago. A lizard-like tongue flicked its forked length out of its lipless mouth, then back in, making me feel sick that I had kissed that thing.

"The Lost has a wonderful ability to take on any form it desires; male, female, human, elf, dwarf, anything," my mother said, smiling coldly at me, then gestured to herself and Aislinn. "We, however, need to use illusion magic to change our appearances, but it is merely a glamour that the initiated of the magic world can see right through. How fortunate that you are no mage, Princess."

Both my mother and sister waved a hand in front of their faces, their visages vanishing in wobbling waves like a mirage. I stared in horror as their clothing became black dresses with dark cloaks, as their hair turned the colour of raven feathers and their faces were replaced by evil. Aislinn's eyes turned black while Mother's turned green, a golden pendant appearing around her neck.

My panic worsened as I saw the two Witches, trying desperately to make my body work, struggling to get more than a shuddering of movement from my shoulders.

"Having trouble moving, Princess?" Keilantra asked mockingly. "Oh, I am hardly surprised."

"It is a little balm for the lips I have concocted," Manth explained in her hissing, whispery voice as she strode towards me. "Derived from stone root extract and night bloom flowers. But a little upon the lips will do no harm if applied to a skin-changer like the Lost, yet, for a human like you to taste it, the formula paralyses the body. Fortunately for you, girl, the effects are temporary."

I groaned and whimpered, fighting to get my body to work, struggling to move and escape.

"That little attack that claimed the old Guardian into the Beyond was simply a ruse," Keilantra told me, snatching my pendant from my neck as it began to glow with my desire for help. "While the Scourge attacked, we slipped in and have lain in wait for you to be alone. How fortunate we saw that little row you had with your lover."

I felt tears slide from my eyes and into my hairline beside my ears as she said that. I hated to know that they had been watching us.

"Do you see now, girl, how men can betray you?" she asked with a victorious gleam in her eyes and a cruel sneer upon her lips. "Do you now understand how they might destroy you?"

Stop it! Please, stop! Just let me go!

"We have taunted her long enough, sister," Manth stated coldly, moving to glare down at me. "The Lunar Joining is but five days away and the Master grows impatient."

"Ah, yes, so true," Keilantra smiled down at me, holding my pendant in her hand. "Time *is* of the essence and we have a ship to catch. Lost, pick her up."

I turned my eyes fearfully to watch the tall, bald, white creature move towards me, its grasping hands grabbing me under my shoulders. It lifted me, holding me with one arm around my midriff, the other hand closed around my throat. Its chest pressed into my back as it turned me to face the two Witches.

I heard hurried footsteps and the crunching of snow, turning my gaze to my left where I could see easiest. Carden, Fawkner, Tallinn, Joran and Ellora came into view, stepping around the trees, Carden's face filling with terror the instant he laid eyes on the scene.

"Leander!" he shouted. "No!"

"Let her go, foul devils!" Fawkner drew his sword as Joran growled threateningly and the two archers turned their bows towards us.

"We've no time for this," Manth hissed, extending one claw-like hand towards my friends.

Magenta lightning lanced from her fingertips, nearly striking them all as it blocked their path and staggered them where they stood. Ellora's arrow slipped and managed to snag my pendant from Keilantra's grasp, the Witch scowling and casting my friends to the ground with an unseen force from a wave of her slender hand.

Dolin, Holger and Tristan joined them with their weapons ready as Amethyst charged through the trees from behind us. Keilantra threw the three men down in a pile with the rest of my friends and protectors as Manth turned her dark lightning on Amethyst, driving her to crash into a tree. All I could do was watch on in fearful helplessness.

"Keilantra! Manth!" I looked up from my Dragon to see Ranzel striding towards us, his staff's crystal glowing green and Gaspeite spreading his wings viciously behind him.

Manth turned to the Wizard and smirked a cold, vindictive grin. "You're too late, Ranzel. We're winning."

The black robed woman raised her arms and focused her powers, the snows beginning to spin as a black vortex surrounded me and my three abductors, magenta energy flaring and sparking through the clouds of the terrible magic tornado.

I could see my friends recovering, all of them shielding their faces as the great vortex gust around us and nearly blinded them with debris. Carden's eyes were wide, his hand reaching for me, the only one of all of them to fight to get nearer.

"Leander!" he cried out in desperate terror.

Carden! I screamed in panic in my mind as everything went dark...

Chapter Twenty-Four
Ragnarok's Redoubt

My eyes weakly fluttered and opened, my sight vague at first beyond my dark eyelashes. I felt like I was being rocked gently as if in a baby's crib, the scent of saltwater filling my nostrils. I frowned at the wooden room filled with crates and barrels, sunlight shining in streams through gaps between the planks in the ceiling. But this wasn't the hardest of sights before me. There were bars all around me, crossbars holding them together. The cage in which I sat was tall enough to stand up in, yet I couldn't.

I tried to move, my body chained to the back of the cage, ropes binding my wrists behind me. Panic began to rise in me as I felt a cloth wedged tight between my teeth, silencing me from screaming or pleading. I squirmed against the restraints, desperate and frightened, trying to slip free, but it was no use. The bindings on my wrists were too tight, the chain around my waist keeping me pinned to the back of the cage.

The urge to cry grew and I had to fight so hard not to give in, not to let the tears flow. Through my frantic, gagged breaths, I could hear the groaning of the ship around me, knowing that there was no escaping even if I weren't tied up and in a cage.

The door above the stairs opened heavily, light shining down into the hold where I sat, my struggles ceasing instantly. I pressed my back against the bars fearfully, anxiously watching as an armoured figure in a black and gold cloak stomped down the stairs. Ulric turned his gaze to me, smirking as he strode towards the cage, keys in his right hand.

"Well, well, well," he boasted, opening the cage with a click of a key. "Back with us at last, Princess. You know, you've been asleep for nearly two whole days."

I shuddered as he crouched before me, turning my face from him and feeling my eyes flicker against my tears. His hand touched my cheek and throat lightly, drawing a hard tremble of disgust from me.

"That was very naughty running away like that, girl," he whispered mockingly, grabbing my face in one hand and making me look up at him. "You gave me these," he indicated the four scarred up scratch marks that I had clawed into his face. "Didn't you? Hm?"

I whimpered through the cloth, looking up at the cage just above his head. *Please don't! Don't hurt me! Please! Oh, please, please!*

He slapped me lightly, drawing my eyes to him and a tiny sob from my throat: "Look at me, girl. Because of you, I was punished by the Master and the Mistresses. If I had my way, I would make you beg and scream as I forced the most intimate pains on your virginal little body."

I cringed and shook fearfully, yelping and closing my eyes as he slammed his hand against the bars by my head. I couldn't help the tears that slipped free now, knowing that it excited this monster.

"However," he said, drawing his hand back and unchaining my waist as I opened my eyes, "the Master has need of you as you are, so you're lucky not to gain my punishments," he leaned his face close to mine and smirked, breathing in my scent as he caressed my cheek with one rough finger. "At least I'll get to watch you die, girl. That will be most amusing."

He abruptly seized my left upper arm and dragged me onto my feet, forcing me from the cage. I struggled, but he backhanded me, nearly dropping me to the floor as I cried in pain.

The cruel man forced me up the stairs and through the hold door, then along a corridor full of Gorven soldiers until we came to more stairs. We passed up and out of a door onto the deck of a large galleon, the sails white and bearing the crest of Gorvenna as the black with gold flags flew in the breeze.

He brought me up to the command deck, forcing me to stand there at his side as the chilled sea air whipped at my hair and clothes, throwing the dark strands into my face. I held still, seeing the Witches standing there as the crew worked the ship forward.

"Ah, Princess," Keilantra smiled, turning towards me. "Awake at last. Such timing. I am certain you are wondering where we are going."

I watched her as she led us to the port side, gesturing out towards the way ahead. Struggling a little against my restraints and the man holding me, I turned my gaze where she directed me, seeing an island coming close into view with a towering mountain at its heart and a great plume of black smoke rising on the shores to my left.

"The Isle of Safferan," she said, turning to look at me as I stared in shock, "until recent days, home to the College of Mages. That black plume there is all that remains after Lord Morod arrived here."

Morod destroyed the Mages?! Oh my gods! There's no stopping him!

She took my chin in her hand and turned my face to her gaze. "You will be meeting him again soon, girl. When we reach Ragnarok's Redoubt."

I could only look at her with a fearful gaze, knowing what those words could mean.

She turned to her crew: "Make ready the boats. We go ashore to meet his Lordship with his prize."

The ship weighed anchor off the coast of the island in a matter of minutes, seven boats launching with a formidable force of Keilantra's personal soldiers, their armour a darker version of that worn by the Gorvennan Knights. I was set with the two sisters, the Lost and Ulric, the boat being guided to make landfall in a cove on the northern side of the island.

For what felt like hours without stopping, the group marched onwards, the Witches leading the way as the Lost hid its face beneath a black cowl of its own. The clanking of armour and stomping of boots was almost deafening as we trudged through the craggy rocks and sparse foliage of the island, the forests far from us on the northern side of the Safferan Mountain.

We climbed the foothills from the shores, the ground uneven as we made for the mountain, the way all too clear for my captors. All I could do was try not to fall, hoping against all hope that my friends could find a way to reach me.

As the afternoon waned and the sun was sinking behind the mountain, we came at last to a deep canyon that ran towards its base. Here the Scourge were in force, raggedy barricades and hastily built watchtowers set all around the canyon. The camps of the Scourge and Keilantra's forces were situated all through the ground between the cliffs, a path left open to the end of the deep ravine.

I stared up in wonder and terror at the redoubt that stood before me, its walls made of black stone segments with statues of fierce dragon heads adorning the parapets as if to ward off any who would dare approach. The terrible fortress was built into the face of the mountain itself, shrubbery dotting its feet as its immense shapes rose up from under the skin of the cliffs themselves. At its very heart was a mammoth dome with sinister looking pillars curving around its edges.

The Witches led the way as Ulric forced me up the vast and tall stairs at the front of the redoubt, the man taking me by my arm now. I was exhausted when we reached the top, passing through the great archway that was large enough for a huge dragon to cross under. Somehow, I doubted that design was by accident.

Within the redoubt, there was some dark and terrible door of strange design, rounded like the ones in the Guardians' Gauntlet of Coastwatch Keep. Shadow Knights stood guard as a group of ten mages - men and women, young and old - stood there in chains. They were trying to open the door, casting spells and reading from large books, fearful of the Shadow Knights that stood over them.

Ulric dragged me away and took me into a small room off to the side, a pair of Shadow Knights following us. He threw me down on the stone floor so hard that I cried out in pain, my shoulder and hip hurting from the impact. Then, he grabbed me by my neck and forced me halfway across the room to where a black stone pillar rose opposite the door.

My back was pressed against it, my arms forced painfully between it and my body, a length of rope now added to my wrists and being bound firmly to a chain loop bolted into the stone. He then bound another length of rope around my throat to lock me to the pillar and smirked before he left me with the two frightening Shadow Knights.

I was alone then for some time, struggling to get free, my arms and back hurting from the unnatural position. I tried to scream, but the gag kept my mouth restricted, stopping me from making a sound beyond a desperate murmuring cry.

Help me! Someone, please! Help me! I don't want to die! Please, don't let them kill me! Please! Please! Oh Gods, please! Carden! CARDEN! AMETHYST! HELP ME! HELP ME, PLEASE, HELP ME! HELP!

At last, I couldn't even mentally scream anymore, looking down at my knees beneath my long dress and staring at the black fabric of my leggings and the leather of my brown boots before me. I just started to cry, no longer trying to be brave, no longer determined to be strong.

It doesn't matter if I cry or not. They're going to kill me anyway... Oh, Carden. I'm so sorry. I'm so sorry that I let them take me from you again. Gods, how I would give anything just to see you again. Just for one last kiss. I love you so much...

I heard footsteps, looking up through my tears, my body trembling, my breathing quickening and my chest heaving beneath my laced up blue bodice. Movement from the doorway drew my gaze and I saw that most terrible sweeping black hooded form that I had suffered nightmares about for the past two years.

Lord Morod entered the room, his green eyes locking onto me from under his black cowl, his slender, bony, grey, long-fingered hands gently held together against his chest. His Obsidian Pendant gleamed with an evil hunger around his neck, yearning for my death as much as its Master did.

I tried to squirm away as he moved gracefully and terribly into the room, drawing my knees closer to my chest. I would give anything to escape this monster and his plans for me at that moment, my heart straining under the weight of my terror.

"Princess," Morod said softly, his smile so cold, so cruel, so mocking.

He crouched in front of me, reaching those cold, long, grey hands towards me, meaning to touch me. I cried out, thrashing against my restraints frantically, tears pouring down my face as I nearly choked myself on the rope binding my neck. I tried to pull away, but I couldn't, his icy touch soon on my flesh, his palms closing on my cheeks.

"Calm yourself, girl," he urged me gently. "You will do yourself an injury, and we cannot have that."

I stopped fighting, my muscles tensed almost to petrifying, a hard sob shaking through my torso. I had never been more afraid of this monster than I was in that moment. Every second I spent with him felt like an eternity, his presence a constant reminder of what he wanted with me. It took me a few moments and all of my focus, but I managed to calm down, slowing my breathing to a level where my chest didn't hurt when I took in air.

Morod smiled, the sunken grey skull that was his face seeming to not fit the expression.

"There now," he said, softly pleased, "that's a good girl."

I allowed myself a slow, deep breath, my shoulders heaving with my chest as I lay my head back against the wall. There really was nothing I could do. I was completely at his mercy. Again.

"Now then," he met my gaze, still managing to stand over me while crouching, "why don't we take this cloth out of your mouth so you and I can have a little chat?"

Slowly, fearfully, I nodded, letting out the tiniest whimper of an "uh-huh".

"Good girl," he prided, reaching those long, bony, grey fingers around my head.

I tried not to look him in the eyes as he meticulously loosened the cloth's knots, not wanting to see the cruelty or the pleasure that lingered in them. I felt his long talon-like nails scratch my neck, flinching instinctively, but not hard enough to gain his anger.

The gag was finally slipped free of my mouth and down around my neck, leaving me able to exercise my jaw and lips again. I stretched out my aching facial muscles with closed eyes, then turned my gaze slowly to him.

"Please," I begged instinctively, unable to control my desperation to survive. "Don't kill me... Please don't kill me..."

Morod frowned - at least, I think he did - his eyes studying me with their eerie green glowing irises.

"A death is required for what I intend here, child," he said evenly, watching me without flinching.

"But why does it have to be me?" I asked, sobbing helplessly.

"Would you ask another to take your place?" he questioned, raising the ridge on his face that would have been his eyebrow if he were still human. "Would you choose to kill another in your place so that you might live?"

I shook my head, feeling numb. "N...no... I...I couldn't do that... I could never..."

"Yet you wish that it is not you who meets this fate," he observed. "That your life would be spared such an ending."

"Y-yes," I nodded, silencing my sobs and feeling a painful guilt that wasn't meant to be there.

"You wish for your freedom... For your safety..."

"Yes..."

"Poor girl," he cupped my chin in his hand and made me face him again. "Do you not realise the gift that I am offering you?"

"Gift?" I stared at him incredulously. "This isn't a gift."

He stood suddenly, turning quickly as frustration filled his eyes. I don't know why he wanted me to accept this fate he had concocted for me, but I could see that my defiance - as usual - was upsetting him.

"You do not grasp the concept of what I am doing here, girl," he stated, turning back to me after a few moments. "I am offering you something remarkable."

"You're offering me death!" I retorted in fear and anger. "You mean to murder me and end the world! That's not remarkable! It's evil!"

"I offer you transcendence," he said as if this was supposed to be some higher calling for me. "You will give this world a new form, a new life... a new god."

I blinked back tears, shaking. "You're going to kill me and destroy the world all so that you can become a god?"

He straightened up, slowly showing me an expression of convicted reverence as he lowered his hands to his sides: "Yes. I am."

I fell silent, staring up at him as he began his even, purposeful movements back towards me.

"I will stand as creator of all life," he said, sounding like a devout madman. "Through me, this world will be reshaped and granted a new life, a new form to live in. It will be a paradise far surpassing any that has come before, or any that shall come after. With Ragnarok and the Fallen Ones, I shall burn the weakness and the imperfections from the world, allowing it to be reborn under my careful cultivation. A new world, perfect, flawless, beyond imagining. And I will rule as the God-King who destroyed all others so that even the Daemons themselves cannot rise against my might or that of the Darkest Shadow."

I stared at him in utter horror. He was fanatical, I realised, something much worse than just evil. He really believed in his cause, which made him even more dangerous than I ever imagined he was.

His eyes darkened along with his expression and he held out his right hand, bringing green flames magically to his palm. He stared into them, his eyes glowing with the same hue, his jaw set hard.

"At last, I shall fulfil the desires of all my forebears; of Lord Heskath, Lord Everild, Lord Gorth Lavelle and every other Shadow Lord before me. I shall succeed where all others have failed," he was talking more to himself now than to me. "And the dwarf-kin, elven kind, humanity and all others will bow on hand and knee before me and beg for my benevolence; that I may show them kindness in *my* new world, that I may be merciful to them as I rule over all creation, a god, everlasting."

I shook my head, terrified: "You're insane!"

He turned to me, closing his hand and snuffing out the mystical flame he held instantly. "And you, my dear, sweet, innocent, Princess Leander, will be granted the privilege of gifting me with this power. With your heart's blood, you and I will change the world. Is that not glorious, child?"

I felt my lips trembling as my heart lurched in my chest. The tears came stronger now, short, sharp breaths standing as my only sobs.

"I-I don't want to die," I whispered sadly. "P-please. Don't do this to me. Please."

With the mockery of sympathy, Morod crouched down before me again, meeting my tear-filled gaze.

"Do not grieve, girl," he said. "You have been chosen to give your life for the greater good. It is a wonderful thing."

"I don't want to give up my life!" I protested, breathing heavily. "I don't want to die!"

"Shh," he hushed me, stroking a finger across my cheek and making me shudder. "I offer you a great consolation, Leander: your life for the world's. I have taken your dull human existence and turned it into a grand purpose."

"Please," I begged softly, blinded by my tears. "Don't do this. Please. Just... just let me go. Please, let me go, please."

"I cannot do that," he replied softly, evenly. "I need you and you alone as the descendant of the one who imprisoned them, or it will not succeed."

I sobbed, shaking my head as I looked up at him. "How can you do this to me? It's cruel."

"You have no choice," he told me. "This destiny was put in place for you eons ago. Your death and my godhood are preordained. You will die, the world will end, and I will build it anew as its Creator."

"Please," I whispered. "I'll do anything you ask. I mean it. I'll do *anything*," I started sobbing harder, breaking down now. "Just don't kill me. Please. Please, don't kill me."

He smiled, shook his head and said: "Oh, Leander. How innocent and naive you are. There is no contesting Fate and Prophecy. Your death cannot be prevented. This *is* your destiny, girl."

"But... but I haven't even lived," I tried, desperately hoping to appeal to whatever humanity remained in him. "I... I'm in love. You know this. And you won't even allow me to say goodbye to him? I want to see him one last time, to know his touch, his intimacy..." I blushed a little,"...to share myself with him..."

"That I cannot allow," he said darkly. "Have you not understood why I have safeguarded your virtue, girl? As your ancestor was already a mother upon her sacrifice, I need you to be a virgin; for only the blood of a virgin girl descended from she who imprisoned Ragnarok and his brethren in her twenty-first year of life, may awaken them from their eternal slumber. Ironic, had you embraced such carnal pleasures with your beloved while with him, you would be of no use to me."

Now, I wished I had made love with Carden that night. If I had known that sex would have saved my life, I would have gladly had it to do so. I shook hard, feeling so distraught knowing that this was my fate and hating that such a simple act of physical love could have spared me this horror now.

Lord Morod stood again as I tensed my wrists against my restraints, my elbows aching at being pulled so tight. I looked up at him, my tears cold, my spine numb, and my stomach pressured with sickness at knowing all that he had told me.

"I will offer you this consolation, Princess," he said, turning towards the door, pausing there and looking over his shoulder back to me. "It will take three days for the mages I have taken from the college to open the first of the three vault doors to the tomb of Ragnarok and the ritual chamber itself. That is all the time you have left to make what peace you must with the world, for at the stroke of midnight on that day, the three moons will reach their alignment and open the way to free Lord Ragnarok and the Fallen Ones."

I shook so hard, feeling my tears bleed down my cheeks, my throat and chest tight with quiet panic.

Please, no. This can't be real. Don't let it be. Please...

"This is your fate, girl," he declared finitely with a wave of his thin hand. "Accept it or die screaming. The choice is yours, though, I believe I know which you will choose."

With that, he turned and left in a sweeping of black robes, vanishing from the doorway into the halls of the dark, ancient, musty aired redoubt. Only the two Shadow Knights remained, their white eyes shining from beneath their leering, sinister masked helms.

I slumped back, then looked over my shoulder at my wrists and fought so hard to break free, screaming at the air. I cried desperately, my screams of terror just another echo of innocent pain in the redoubt's black halls.

After hours of howling and pleading through my panicked cries, I had screamed myself hoarse. My throat was scratchy, and I was so thirsty, but my requests for food and water were utterly ignored by the Shadow Knights that stood watch over me.

It was when I was finally fed that I faced Carden's mother, Adriana. She had been assigned to care for me by the Shadow Lord, but her care was hardly anything kind. She permitted me to be freed only to relieve the needs of my body, the Shadow Knights retying me once I was done. The wicked woman - who could never be believed to have birthed my beloved soul mate - seemed to enjoy my suffering. My request to be restrained in a more comfortable position drew her jeering and taunting, the two men who worked with her and had the same strange pallor and eyes joining in.

I slept however little I could manage, the position I was in agonising and not allowing for any comfort. And when I could sleep, this place disturbed me, the screams that echoed from the depths of the redoubt terrifying me awake. I couldn't even escape into my dreams to be with Carden before my death.

I grew to be hopeless, my body feeling the grime of sitting there for so long, the room lit only by torches giving me no means to tell the time. I couldn't even see the sun, to know when day became night and turned back again. My imprisonment in that place was worse than in the tower of Castle Ortagaad, or the dungeons of Aneuran in Fane's grasp. Though my life had been reduced to three days remaining, it was an eternity of agony and complete and utter fear.

My time was spent either trying to free myself with no success or sobbing hopelessly. I started fantasying, imagining the others coming for me. I saw Joran tearing through the Shadow Lord's forces as the Dwarves flanked him, Ellora and Tallinn downing every enemy they could with their bows. Then Fawkner and Carden would slay every monster and carve down the two Shadow Knights guarding me as Ranzel blocked Morod with his magic.

Carden would kiss me, free me, and carry me bridal style in his arms, taking me away from this nightmare. He would be my hero as he always had been, and we would never feel anger or resentment towards one another again. I would confess to him what the Shadow Lord had done to me, tell him of the curse and find a way to live with him happily ever after...

The sound of footsteps woke me, my body jumping as I came to realise that I didn't even know I had fallen asleep. I blinked the tiredness from my eyes and watched as Adriana and her two sinister pale-skinned companions strode into the room.

She smirked down at me, her hands on her corseted waist. "It is time, Princess."

"Time for what?" I asked uneasily as she crouched down and freed my throat.

She met my gaze, still smirking. "Lord Morod has requested your presence. We have but *one* door left to open, girl."

"You're Carden's mother," I said, my voice shaking, tears trying to well up from my now dry eyes. "He loves me. I love him. Don't do this. Please, think of your son..."

She smiled, touching my chin with her thumb and forefinger. "Oh, if only I had such cares for that boy, I might actually have tried to spare you. But my loyalties are to my Master and he has commanded your death."

I shook, looking down at my knees as she worked on the rope tied to the loop in the stone behind me.

Adriana took the rope and dragged me to my feet, shoving me into the waiting grasps of the two men with her. They held me tight as she moved towards me, staring down at me with her frightening red eyes.

"Let's not keep Lord Morod waiting, gentlemen," she said, smirking down at me. "Bring her."

She strode past us, the two men dragging me with them, my wrists still tied tight behind me. With the flapping of black cloaks and the clanking of ebony armour, the two Shadow Knights followed on behind us, impressive and imposing.

I closed my eyes and drew in a shaking breath. Now I was going to meet the terrible fate designed for me and I had no way to escape it...

Chapter Twenty-Five
The Shadow in the Flames

*P*lease, *just give me something, just some way I can get out of this...* These thoughts were repeating, screaming in my head all the time. I was scared, more scared than I had ever been in my entire life. My mind was racing with terrifying images of what the Shadow Lord was going to do to me, flicking back to the visions Danika had shown me.

Oh please! Please don't let that come true! Don't let him kill me! Please!

The disciples dragged me into the main chambers, turning me to face the round ancient door I had seen the day I arrived. I frowned at the door, stunned to see it open.

The Mages. They've succeeded. Gods, what's become of them?

As we passed through that door and along the long corridor beyond, I soon came to regret that silent question. The second of the great doors lay open, blood strong in the air as I was brought towards it. I cringed and looked away, trying not to remember the horrible scene of the murdered mages laying there in their own blood. They hadn't simply been slain; they had been torn apart, what remained only a semblance of human beings.

"Such a waste of good blood," one of the men remarked as he and his companion led me by my arms over the mess of limbs and bodies. "Not a drop worth drinking now."

"A shame we can't taste her," the other man looked at me with a predatory sneer. "Virgin girls are always the best."

"Oh, I agree," the first man chuckled.

"The Mages," I murmured, shaking hard. "You murdered them."

"To open the second door," Adriana replied, glancing at me over her shoulder with a casual shrug. "They were needed to use their magicks to release the locks on the first door, but their deaths was the key to the second."

"And the third?" I asked before I thought about it, suddenly thinking that I didn't want to know.

"Oh, you'll see soon enough, Princess," she smirked, stepping over a dead mage and continuing on.

They led me along the next corridor, the three doors actually dividing this one great hall into three sections. It was dark, cold, foreboding, only the torchlight from ahead giving me anything to see by.

As we drew near the last door, I came to see the large gathering that had amassed before its ornate runes and carvings. Shadow Knights, Undead, Scourge, Gorven soldiers, black robed disciples, they had all come to bear witness. And at the very front before the door stood Keilantra, Manth, Ulric, the Revenant and Lord Morod himself. The Shadow Lord's eyes were studying the markings on the final door as his loyalists held torches to give him light.

I was led through the crowd and brought to stand before the Shadow Lord, trembling under the many evil and unfriendly gazes that were set upon me.

"Lord Morod," Adriana bowed her head to him.

"Ah," Morod turned his hooded head to look at me as I cringed in his followers' grasps. "At last, Princess, we come to your purpose and it begins simply with you opening this final door."

"I... I won't do it," I tried to be defiant, but I had no strength, no conviction that could be believed. "I won't help you..."

"Your consent is no longer required," he said simply, smirking a little with amusement at my attempts to refuse. "All I require for this door is your touch."

I shook my head. "I won't..."

He held out a hand, Manth handing him a sinister blade with an equally diabolical smile as she eyed me down. He started towards me, my immediate response to pull away hampered by the two men holding me by my arms.

"Please, don't!" I begged, but it was useless.

The Shadow Lord snared my bound wrists with one hand and cut my bindings with the blade. I relaxed at first, but then he took my left hand in his and I struggled in panic as he held up the blade, the men securing me so I couldn't escape.

Frantic, terrified thoughts ran like wild horses through my head, my struggles and whimpers growing in intensity as I feared he would take my hand. But he didn't. He turned my hand palm up, then pressed the sharp edge of the knife into my skin. He sliced with one slow, purposeful movement from the base of my palm to just below my middle finger, blood seeping from the agonising wound as whimpers and cries fell from my lips.

He handed the dagger off again, then stepped behind me, reaching with his hands to grasp both of my wrists. He held my right to my chest as I fought and struggled, thrashing against him.

"What are you doing?!" I cried out, struggling as he brought me to the door with so little effort.

He extended my arm forcefully towards the door, pressing my palm to the centre circle of stone, my slender fingers spreading out. The pressure on my palm hurt as the wound was stretched, my blood touching the stone. The door suddenly began to light up with an eerie supernatural golden glow from all of its runes and carvings. I squinted against the light, watching as the sections of the door began clicking and dropping back, moving like some gigantic puzzle in the wall.

I squirmed in the Shadow Lord's grasp, but he was so strong, keeping my hand on the door as it unlocked. It came apart and rolled into all parts of the frame, the scent of ancient, stale air hitting me as it relented and gave access to the main chamber.

"At last," Morod breathed in low excitement, staring over my shoulder at the chamber.

He pushed me into Ulric's waiting hands, the Knight grabbing my arms and holding me firm as the Shadow Lord moved like a graceful darkness into the opening. Slowly, one by one, his followers entered behind him, moving with purpose into the darkened chamber.

Ulric forced me to follow, my struggles useless, my hand hurting so badly. I breathed heavily, my hair flicking in front of my face, my arms aching with the strain he was putting on them.

Morod lit green flames in his hands and began casting them around the room in fireballs that exploded in braziers. The braziers came to life, illuminating the chamber's cold stone facade, letting me see the place where he intended for me to die.

It was a gigantic room; circular with a high domed ceiling that was left open to the air, the night sky clear with stars twinkling and the three full moons getting close to their alignment. Their pale light shone down over the main floor where a stone altar was laid out, its side facing the door. Opposite the door stood five gigantic and fearsome looking dragon statues, the most monstrous seated in the centre right before the altar. The Dragons were carved to be in chains, shackled in place to the five great arched alcoves that had been chiselled into that side of the room.

"After all these millennia," Morod mused, moving to stand by the altar with Manth, Keilantra and the Revenant, Ulric and I right behind him, "at long last I have succeeded where all other Shadow Lords have failed," he turned to me and smirked, then looked up at the centre dragon."Ragnarok, Lord of Destruction," he laughed victoriously. "I finally stand before his greatness and will be rewarded. And his disciples, the Fallen Ones, remain at his side: Amrit, Dragon of Death, Thorgeirr, Dragon of War, Ragnar, Dragon of Pestilence, and Lothair, Dragon of Famine. Once released, these five will devour this world and allow me to reshape it anew."

I trembled at the sight of the five monsters. Though they were stone, I could only imagine that once the ritual to free them was completed that they would either come from another world into ours, or that these statues would become them.

"Magnificent," the Shadow Lord smiled, admiring them.

"My Lord," Manth came to his side, speaking gently. "The moons are reaching their alignment. The time is almost at hand."

"Yes. Yes, you are right, my dear Manth," he nodded, meeting her gaze. "The time has come to make our final preparations. Have the altar set and sanctified, and have the girl prepared."

"Yes, Lord Morod," she bowed her head.

I squirmed and fought against Ulric as the Witch strode past me and back up through the doorway. I tried to fight, planting my feet and screaming against the man as he took me after her.

"There is no use in fighting this, Princess," Morod called after me. "Your fate is decided."

I was taken to a chamber off to the side before the doorway, the Witch leading a small group of black robed disciples in setting up. They began filling the black stone bath set into the floor as Manth prepared oils and soaps. I was forced out of my clothes, stripped of everything I had. I blushed as I tried desperately to cover myself, but to no avail, the men around me seeing everything to my humiliation.

They forced me into the water, the only mercy being that it was heated, steam rising into the chilled air. I was dunked, gasping as I scrambled to keep my head up, the disciples very roughly scrubbing me with hard brushes that hurt my skin. I cried out, thrashing to get away from them as they washed me with no care for my privacy or personal space. They laid their hands on my naked, soft skin, grabbing me, hurting me with every move they made. I screamed for them to stop, but was ignored, their focus clear.

When they were done, I was just dumped on the floor with nowhere to go and nothing to shield my nudity. I curled up, huddled in a corner of the room, holding my knees to my chest and my arms crossed with my hands on my shoulders.

This isn't happening. This isn't happening...

I cried, tears flowing harder than before, my cheeks hot and flushed from embarrassment. I shivered at the chill of the stone room that I was just abandoned in, my lack of clothing and the two Shadow Knights that stood at the doorway now all that was needed to hold me prisoner. My chest heaved and my body wretched with my hard sobs, my hair slowly drying. They had brushed it once they took me from the bath, tearing out strands with their rough work. But this was nothing compared to the pain in my heart or the fear I felt facing my dark fate.

Manth entered the room, carrying a white garment folded in her black nailed hands, her coal-like eyes locking on my shuddering, sobbing, naked form.

"Put this on, girl," she hissed, throwing it at me without caring.

I looked up at her, clutching the dress to my chest as she turned and swept from the room once again. I didn't argue with wearing this, gladly pulling on the clothing to shield my body from sight and at least regain my modesty, if nothing else.

The dress was simple, long sleeved and split at the wrists, the hem sitting just on my ankles. The neckline was scooped, the fabric light and not enough to guard against the cold. I still shivered all the same.

I sat down and hugged my knees, sobbing as I lay my head on them, my fingers curling tight to my ankles. I hid under my dark auburn hair, letting my tears flow as I came to realise that I would be dead very, very soon.

It was then that I felt a familiar presence in the room, though I hadn't felt it for more than two years. Not since my last day in the City of Eilath.

"You are not alone, child," that soft, feminine voice spoke, drawing me out of my fearful sobs. "You have more to hope for than you might believe."

I looked up, seeing her, though I couldn't believe it. Her long dark hair flowed around her waist, her porcelain skin only helping to highlight her turquoise eyes, her pointed ears visible beneath her dark strands. Her dress of gold and emerald seemed to glow and she smiled the most beautiful smile I could have wished to see in that moment.

"It is all right, Princess," Enchantress Illuminil smiled softly, reaching out to brush my tears away. "I am here."

"Enchantress Illuminil?" I gasped, still struggling to believe my eyes. "Am I... am I dreaming?"

"No, child, you are not. I am indeed here with you," she replied in her misty way.

"Then you can help me," I said in a desperate, quiet voice. "Please, before it's too late..."

"I am not with you in body, Princess," she clarified, my heart sinking at that fact. "I come to you across the astral worlds to offer you solace at this moment of greatest trial."

"They're going to kill me..." I wept.

"Yes. That is Lord Morod's intention. He will slay you slowly, painfully, all to release the greatest monsters the world has ever known. But know, child, that there is yet hope."

"Hope?" I shook my head, looking up through my tears at her. "What hope could there be? Why do you come to me if you can't help me?"

"I come to deliver a message," she said, brushing my hair from my face gently. "As I speak to you, the Guardians are mounting a rescue."

"What?" I couldn't believe it.

She nodded. "Tallinn, Fawkner and Carden, with the help of Ranzel and your companions, are coming to free you from Lord Morod. They are climbing the hills to Ragnarok's Redoubt even now."

"They are?" I asked, feeling my tears continue down my cheeks. "Can... can they save me?"

She nodded lightly. "As in all things, they have a chance to rescue you and they will fight to free you. You have inspired such loyalty among them, Princess.

And Carden will never relent when it comes to you, for Love is a power beyond all else."

"They're coming," I closed my eyes and cried with relief. "They're coming for me..."

"I am sorry that I can do no more, Leander," Illuminil said with regret. "Xzharn the White asked that I inform you of what is happening so that you might remain hopeful long enough for our success. Such is the power I possess, but now I must depart."

"Please, Enchantress Illuminil. Don't leave me," I pleaded fearfully.

She smiled down at me. "Do not fear, for they are coming, child. And you and I shall meet again. Farewell."

"No... Wait..." but she was gone, the room darkening from the light that had come with the Enchantress' presence.

I looked down at the floor, thinking on what she had told me. *My friends are coming for me. They're on the island right now. They're going to stop this...*

I closed my eyes and rested my head on my arms on top of my knees, feeling the first little bit of true relief that had come to me in days. My tiredness was clear and all I wanted was to go to sleep, but I needed to be strong, to hold on long enough for my friends to reach me. I had to delay this as much as I could to give them time.

It's almost over. They're coming for me. I knew they wouldn't abandon me...

I heard footsteps, my blood instantly running cold in my veins. I looked up, my tears slipping down my cheeks softly as *she* returned.

"It is time, child," Manth hissed, glaring down at me with a sinister smile.

I shook my head in fear, pulling further back into the wall that I sat against.

The Witch gestured to the Shadow Knights: "Bring her to the ritual chamber."

The two Shadow Knights stomped towards me, their armour clanking and their black cloaks sweeping. They reached for me with their cold, gauntleted hands as I struggled and jerked away from them.

"No! NO, DON'T! DON'T!" I screamed as they took hold of my arms and pulled me to my bare feet. "PLEASE, NO!"

Manth turned and started to lead the way as the two knights dragged me struggling and thrashing between them. I fought and kicked, trying to get free of their hands, screaming in panic. My feet planted, but I couldn't hold there as they forced me forward behind the Witch, turning now towards the door I had been made to open and the ritual chamber beyond.

They brought me down the stairs into the room, my eyes frantically taking in every detail through my tears. Shadow Knights had flanked the room all around, dozens of them to guard the ceremony, their swords at their hips and their shields on their arms. With them stood Undead soldiers in their armoured cowls, standing with their deathly faces watching everything before them, ready to take the Revenant's command at a moment's notice.

The black hooded followers of the Shadow Lord were gathered there, watching on in awe of their terrible Master, a few stepping aside to let Manth and the two Shadow Knights lead me towards the altar. Each of the eight main disciples stood around the altar watching us approach as well, the Revenant and Keilantra waiting with them.

As Manth drew her own hood, my eyes stared past her to see *Him* standing there with his back to the great Dragon statues. Morod smirked as he saw me, beckoning with his green eyes, his longing for my end beyond my imagining or comprehension.

Death had haunted me for *three* long, agonizing years, following me at every turn, prowling at my back like some great and terrible predator. Knowing what fate lay before me, I should have resigned myself to it, found the peace needed to face this horror and grief with the calm of a girl of my standing. But I couldn't.

Every fibre of my being fought to escape this terrible dark reality, to find a way to stop this from being truth. I had lost too many people I loved to Death's cold embrace, had prayed to Azmerath to guide them safely into the Beyond far too frequently of late.

But *this* promised death... *this* one I fought the hardest against, hoping that there was still time enough left to prevent another, worse tragedy.

I can't let this happen! I cried out in my tremulous and frantic thoughts. *I have to stop this! I have to stop Him! This can't become reality! It just can't!*

His dark smile beckoned to me, his cold, coarse, grey fingers curling to draw me forward. The gleam of those green eyes glowing beneath his shadowed cowl only strengthened my fear; his very presence trying to crush back my fighting spirit.

No! I decided as I met his cold, glowing gaze, my eyes darting to the sinister blade in his hand. *I will not let this happen! I will fight this! This will not be the end of all things!*

I struggled relentlessly, trying against all hope to break the Shadow Knights' hold on me and run. There was no way I could succeed, the two black armoured monsters bringing me to the altar, my eyes falling to the restraints at both ends. My heart sank and I trembled in terror as I stared down at it.

"Restrain her," Morod commanded softly.

"NO, NO!" I screamed, struggling harder again that I was to the point that I felt as if my arms would tear from my shoulders.

The Shadow Knights forced me down onto the altar, one grasping my wrists as the other held my ankles. I squirmed and thrashed, trying to slip free of their steel cold holds, but I soon felt the restraints closing over my wrists and ankles. They backed away and I lay there on that hard altar, looking up at my wrists held by the old shackles, my arms pulled firm above me.

The Witches moved to stand at either end of the altar, Manth anointing my forehead with oils. My writhing irritated her, but she did nothing to stop me, just continuing her task.

I looked up as Morod leaned over me, my body shaking from fear and cold, my chest hurting with my frightened heartbeat and hard breaths as my tears burned my eyes.

"Please... please, Morod, don't do this," I pleaded one last time, my tears the only warmth I had left to feel.

"This is your purpose, Princess," he smiled softly and stroked my face with the back of his hand.

He turned from me, moving to stand on the other side of the altar facing the Dragons.

I lay my head back, closing my eyes as they began their ritual, my sobs unstoppable now. I looked up at the ceiling's great opening, the three moons nearly fully aligned with each other. This was it.

Morod held his hands out to the side, looking up to the Dragons as he spoke clearly to the room: "With the aligning of the moons this night, we undo what was done by the powers of Light four thousand years past. Lord Ragnarok, I offer this virgin girl, descendant of the one who died upon this altar to seal you away, as the sacrifice that will set you and your brothers free upon the world."

He gestured to his left, Keilantra handing him something silver as Manth continued anointing me. I squirmed and thrashed my head, trying to make her stop.

"We anoint her in the oils of offering to let it be known that she is the one who's life force will free you," he leaned over me.

He held up a sinister looking silver necklace with a simple pendant hanging from the chain. At the heart of the pendant was a dark magenta stone that shimmered with a strange power.

That can't be a Dragon Pendant... Can it?

He set it around my neck, laying it against my collarbones as I shuddered and whimpered.

He went on: "I hang the fourteenth Dragon Pendant around her neck; the Dragon's Key Pendant, which has held you here in this prison for four millennia. May it bind with the light of the moons aligned and her blood to break the magical barriers that hold you here."

I wriggled against the restraints again, the chains rattling as I fought to get free. This Pendant was horrible to wear, heavy and choking, weighing me down as if it were some kind of evil anchor.

Morod tilted his head back, closing his eyes, his arms held out wide as he went on: "Powers of Shadows and of Evil, hear my pleas! Open the doorways and bring forth the Fallen Ones! Accept this girl as offering upon the aligning of the moons themselves in this, her twenty-first year! Undo what was done and set free the Devourer upon the world under my command!"

He reached out and took the sinister dagger from Keilantra, glaring down at me. I trembled in fear, staring at the gleaming ebony blade in terror, my heart racing and my stomach churning.

"With her blood, the doorway shall open," he recited darkly, hissing as he edged the blade towards my side, "with her death, the Fallen Ones shall be..."

Violence sounded behind him and he was interrupted. He turned around as I looked up, my heart soaring with relief.

"This dark ritual shall not be allowed to continue!" Ranzel bellowed, stamping his staff on the floor and calling green energy to explode from its crystal, knocking down all enemies that stood near him.

My friends rushed through the doorway behind him, all of them with their weapons at the ready; the Dwarves downing any who came too close. Ellora and Tallinn were stringing their bows in preparation to fire as Joran, Fawkner, Tristan and Carden rushed forward with their swords in hand.

Morod scowled and reached for his Pendant, the black stone glowing red.

Cathal appeared on the roof, peering down into the great gap with his sneering black face. As he went to breathe fire, there was another roar, Amethyst slamming into him and fiercely drawing him into the air. The two dragons began sweeping and fighting as Kuldar's golden form swept up from nowhere to attack. Gaspeite appeared and collided with him, drawing the golden dragon into a separate battle.

"CARDEN!" I screamed, struggling relentlessly against the chains on my wrists.

"LEANDER! HOLD ON!" Carden rushed forward with Fawkner and Joran at his back.

"You cannot stop us, Wizard," Morod seethed at Ranzel. "You and your companions are outnumbered."

Ranzel smirked knowingly. "No. We are not."

At that moment, armour clattered, and the Dragon Knights charged through the door, passing amidst my friends with their swords at the ready and their shields before them. Ser Callenhad led them, swinging his blade as they rushed the room, the golden knights running in to battle our enemies.

"Slay them!" Morod commanded. "Slay the Dragon Knights! Slay them all!"

The Shadow Knights and Undead Legions all drew their weapons and swarmed from their positions in the chamber. They howled as they clashed with the Dragon Knights, but our allies were not done yet.

Warden Alessa rushed the chamber door with a force of black and silver armoured Guardians at her back, relief and joy filling me as I watched them sweep into the room. As they began engaging the Shadow Lord's forces, my friends dived into the fray, striking with their weapons and a furious passion unlike any other.

Morod glared down at me as I briefly glanced at him nervously. He scowled and turned his fierce glowing eyes back to the scene.

"Cover me!" Carden shouted, downing an Undead with his sword. "I need to reach Leander!"

"I'm at your side!" Fawkner declared, spinning with a sweep of his cloak and slicing an Undead's head from its shoulders, Joran and Ellora staying at his back.

Tallinn was striking with her bow, downing soldier after soldier before suddenly casting it away and snatching up her sword. She engaged a Gorvennan soldier who tried to defeat her, easily besting him.

"Ulric!" Keilantra bellowed. "Stop them! The Master must not be reached!"

Ulric drew his sword and ran forward with Keilantra's knights, joining the battle.

A green energy blast struck Morod, the Shadow Lord staggering into the altar, pressing against me as I squinted. He scowled as he was hit again and again, Ranzel striding towards him with his staff throwing magic as the Dragons battled fiercely above us.

Manth and Keilantra looked at each other, then stepped in front of Morod, using their dark powers to lash lightning at the Wizard. Ranzel began defending, fighting them back, the flashes of magenta and green energy almost blinding as they drew him away. His Dragon Pendant was protecting him with a shield of green light just as mine would with purple energy.

The Revenant suddenly drew his sword and turned his attention towards my friends, Tallinn now his focus.

"Tallinn, watch out!" I shouted.

She heard me, looking up with wide eyes as the Revenant stalked towards her. He raised his weapon and swung, the Guardian girl managing to block his strike with her own sword as panic flooded her face. She began desperately defending herself, backing away with each of the Revenant's strikes.

"Hold on, lass!" Tristan shouted, slaying a disciple and downing a Gorvennan soldier before rushing to her.

The Wanderer called bright blue magic to his left hand and struck, the shimmering energy smashing into the Revenant's face. The Revenant shrieked and turned to engage him, now fighting both Tristan and Tallinn at once.

"Your friends cannot save you, Princess," Morod drew my attention with his hissing remark. "You shall watch them die before you meet your own death."

I squirmed and writhed under his glare, turning my gaze back to Carden, Fawkner, Joran, Ellora and the Dwarves. They were desperately trying to reach me, the Shadow Knights blocking them. They were being backed towards the doorway now, their weapons slashing and beating down any who came near them.

Then, there came roars and they turned, their eyes wide and their mouths dropping as they saw the force of Gathlorks that filled the doorway. The beasts carried black crossbows, pointing them directly at my friends. Carden held his sword up, glanced back at me, then faced the monsters, readying himself.

No, don't let them die! I pleaded mentally.

Suddenly, there were flashes of silver behind the Gathlorks, each of the beasts howling in agony as elegantly curved blades cleaved their spines. They fell forward in dead heaps, a force of silver armoured High Elves standing as their slayers with Lord Selwyn leading the way.

The Elven Lord was dressed in his own silver armour, his long dark hair pulled back from his face, his curved blade in hand. He turned his turquoise eyes from my friends, then locked his gaze on Morod and I.

"Larantil!" he shouted to his soldiers. "Slavori tis Sharvoran Lathar! Franoir alingil! Taanari scornavar!"

Immediately, the High Elves began to charge, their swords in both hands and pointed forward as if they were spears. The High Elves stepped over the corpses of the Gathlorks, charging across the room as Lord Selwyn led them fiercely, their blades cleaving through their enemies. My friends stepped aside and turned into the battle as the silver clad High Elves swept into the fray, their silvery weapons slashing swiftly, almost singing as they passed through the air.

At the door, the remaining Wizards appeared with yet more High Elves charging around them to join the fight. Lucilius, Ragdobar and Samhir turned their attentions to the Witches and the Revenant, joining Ranzel, Tallinn and Tristan in their desperate battle as Xzharn turned his eyes towards the Shadow Lord.

The White Wizard strode forward with his staff in hand, his dark eyes locked on Morod's sinister visage.

"Lord Selwyn, Ser Callenhad, Warden Alessa!" he called out, passing through the fight towards us. "This Shadow Lord needs to be dealt with!"

Ser Callenhad swept in with Warden Alessa from Xzharn's left, Lord Selwyn dispatching a Shadow Knight and joining them on his right.

"If you'll excuse me, Princess," Morod looked down at me, "I will be but a few moments," he turned and strode down the steps of the altar, his black form moving towards the four defenders.

I struggled and tried to get free, desperate to escape, but with no way of doing that I could only lay there and watch him face them.

"Your reign of terror ends here, Shadow Lord," Xzharn declared, his staff's crystal glowing bright white. "You shall not end the world with your violent means."

"And you four mean to stop me," Morod scanned them with his eyes and bowed his head. "So be it."

Their battle erupted violently within moments, the Shadow Lord a black swirling figure striking with incredible speed amidst the four fighters.

Xzharn twirled his staff, his magic flashing as it met the Shadow Lord's own dark flames, Lord Selwyn striking with blade and limb only to be deflected. Alessa and Callenhad swept their weapons into the fight, the Shadow Lord seeming able to defend himself with his magic alone, no weapon visible. It was like he was fast enough to sidestep every strike they tried to lay on him.

A Shadow Knight fell and suddenly the most welcome face came to my eyes.

"Leander, are you alright?" Carden looked so panicked as he reached me.

"Carden," I cried as he kissed me. "I knew you'd come for me."

"Hold on, I'm getting you out of this," he started trying to free my wrists, taking a lock pick from his belt and working on the shackles.

"Please, Carden, hurry," I pleaded, turning my eyes past him to the Shadow Lord's battle.

The Shadow Lord sidestepped Alessa's strike, then seized her by the back of the neck.

"I grow tired of this battle. I will not be delayed any longer in my task," he hissed, then took her sword and ran it through her chest, dropping her to the floor.

Selwyn and Callenhad saw her fall and swung their weapons with shouts of anguish, Morod catching their blades in each hand and glaring at them coldly. He melted the weapons with his dark magicks, the force knocking the two men to the floor. He turned then to Xzharn, holding his hand up and blocking the white energy strikes the Wizard cast at him as if he had an invisible shield. His pendant was protecting him with a shadowy energy. He then shoved his hand forward, the White Wizard crying out and hitting the floor hard as his staff exploded into shards.

Morod turned away from the men, his sweeping black robed form heading up the steps of the altar's dais again.

"Carden! Behind you!" I cried out in panic, fighting my restraints as I stared at the monster.

Carden turned around, scowling and drawing his sword, standing ready between me and the Shadow Lord.

"You won't touch her again!" he snarled, ready to fight and defend me.

"You think you can stop me, boy?" Morod scathed, striding towards him callously.

"I *won't* let you hurt her again!" Carden was determined, swinging his sword fast and hard.

I screamed as Morod took the blade in his grasp and swung Carden down to the floor. Carden got to his feet, crouching as he readied himself to leap at the monster. Morod turned his power towards him and suddenly Carden looked as if he were weighed down, his limbs straining, his right knee stuck to the ground and his sword hand trembling.

"I have no need to kill you, Guardian," Morod told him with a menacing glare. "Since you love her so very much, you shall have the honour of seeing her die."

Carden's eyes widened with terror. "No! No, don't! Get away from her!"

Morod moved to stand over me, taking up the dagger again. He pressed his hand to my throat as I thrashed, pinning me down and staring into my frightened, tear-filled eyes.

He repeated his previous incantation: "With her blood, the doorway shall open. With her death, the Fallen Ones shall be freed. With this dagger shall I loose her life's blood upon this altar..."

He carved into my ribs, the pain unbearable as I screamed, more tears burning my eyes. He was making shallow cuts in the dress and my skin, the white fabric of my clothing staining red as my blood began to drizzle into the troughs that edged the top of the altar.

"Leander!" Fawkner shouted, charging forward.

"Get away from her, vile monster!" Ellora shrieked, turning her twin elven blades to fight. She, Joran and Fawkner ran towards the altar, their weapons ready to strike.

Morod simply held out his hand towards them as he continued to cut me, turning now to my thighs. The same flickering of magic hit them and the three were frozen on the spot, struggling to move just as Carden was.

Morod lifted the blood coated dagger over me, hovering it above my neckline. My trembling was so hard and the pain of my fresh wounds so bad that I could barely see straight, my eyes locking on the blade.

"The Dragon's Key Pendant shall be charged with her blood, her life force the very power which frees the Fallen Ones," he recited, smirking down at me.

I watched as my blood dripped from the dagger, trembling in panic. I felt the hot droplets hit my skin and soak into my dress, my blood dripping onto the Pendant's stone. Then, with some terrible pain that filled me as the moons reached their alignment, the Pendant began to glow brightly, and the room began to shake. The moons above us turned blood red as they aligned, the room now being bathed in that terrible, murderous light.

Morod stepped back, looking up at the dragon statues as they began to crack and fracture. Their stone facades gave way, the five beasts' coming to life as their eyes flared and started to glow.

The Dragon of Death shrieked and shook off the stone from his black, skeletal looking form, his scales like bones. The Dragon of War roared violently, his eyes yearning blood as his scales appeared to be like great steel plates. The Dragon of Pestilence looked to be a sickly green and brown, vile clouds of yellow dust exuding from his great jaws, while the Dragon of Famine looked skinny and underfed, his flesh tight and his scales pale as he let out a mournful moan.

The centremost dragon shattered his stone prison, the chains binding him rattling as he seethed at the air. His eyes glowed with blue flames as his black armoured form twisted and writhed as if to release aches and pains that had gone unattended forever. From beneath his scales, dark flames of blue and black licked and lapped at him but were dull and struggling in their light.

I looked to my friends; their expressions darkened. Dolin and Holger ran up the steps where Carden, Ellora, Fawkner and Joran were stuck in place, bellowing as they charged to help me. Morod waved an abrupt hand, and the two Dwarves were hurled backwards, hitting the floor hard below the dais, his focus now on the great dragons alone.

I could only watch on fearfully, shaking in panic and pain, my head starting to swim with my blood draining from my body.

"Who is the one who awakens us?" the centre dragon demanded in a deep, fiery, booming voice, his glowing blue, flame-filled eyes focusing on the dais.

"My Lord Ragnarok," Morod bowed his head, his hand to his chest. "I am Shadow Lord Morod, he who has summoned you back to this world."

"What is it that you would ask of me, Shadow Lord?" Ragnarok hissed, his tongue flicking through his great teeth.

"Only that you fulfil your original intent and devour this world that I might rebuild it in my image," Morod replied evenly. "I beseech you to align yourself with me."

"I am destruction itself!" Ragnarok declared, his bellowing voice tearing at the sky. "I am the devourer of worlds, the shadow in the flames! I would relish the chance to destroy what my sister, Ankorect, has created here!"

"Then, you will side with me?" Morod asked, smirking.

Ragnarok nodded, glaring at me. "Kill her! Kill the girl you offer as sacrifice and drain her life force into the Pendant around her neck! Kill her and I shall wreak the greatest devastation at your command, Shadow Lord! Kill her and set me free!"

"As you command," Morod bowed his head, taking the dagger up again as he turned to me.

I shook my head, tears streaking my face as he came to stand over me.

"No! NO, DON'T!" Carden's desperate screams were frightening, drawing my glance to see him where he knelt, still struggling.

I wanted him to reach me, needed him to save me, but I couldn't see how. I looked back to Morod, trembling helplessly.

"Please, don't! Don't do this!" I begged through my sobs. "Please!"

Morod placed his hand over my throat and held me down, his right arm lifted high with the dagger in his grasp. I heard screams and shouts, everything else around me forgotten aside from the blade that now angled down towards me.

"Goodbye, Princess," he mewed and struck...

Epilogue
Love's Vow

I t was as if time suddenly slowed down, my perceptions of the world becoming like a dream, as if I were watching these terrible events being drawn by the hand of an artist. There was no escape, no hope, and I saw my death coming for me. This was it. The end of my life. And there was nothing I could do, no final plea I could make that would spare me from this terrible fate.

I felt a horrific, bone splintering, crushing, cracking pain in my breast, crying out as some impossible to describe sensation of agony overwhelmed me. I screamed, closing my eyes tight as I felt the blade pierce my beating heart through my broken sternum. Tears bled from my eyes to stain my cheeks, the shards of lightning that radiated up from my chest unbearable.

I heard the screams of my friends amidst the snapping of my bone and flesh, struggling now to keep myself aware while silently thinking that I should already be dead. But I wasn't. My eyes opened and I watched as the dark pendant around my neck glowed ever brighter, the horror of seeing a blade in own chest beyond my description.

I looked up at Morod, trembling with pain and shock, my body lurching involuntarily where I lay. I could feel my life's blood choking me as it left my body, my energy fading, and all of my strength now used to stay awake in the hope that I might survive this.

"NO! NO, LEANDER, NO!" that howl was Carden's, so terribly haunting that I couldn't even begin to comprehend it.

I felt the Shadow Lord applying pressure to the dagger in my chest, whimpering and shaking my head against what I knew he was about to do. He seemed to sneer at me, like he was enjoying my pain and misery, like the fear that I felt was an aphrodisiac to him. With one terrible, agonizing movement, he withdrew the blade from my heart, the sound of it hauntingly gruesome to my ears. I gasped in agony, watching as my blood tainted my white dress crimson, the stain deepening ever more. And yet, somehow, I still breathed.

He leaned forward slowly, his cold, spidery fingers caressing the pendant at my neck. He stared deep into my steel blue eyes with his glowing eerie green ones, studying me as an explorer would a strange find. I felt his hand curl around the necklace, my heart ripped apart, but still beating as I faced him.

"STOP HIM!" Ranzel's voice rang through the chamber as he continued battling the Witches with flashes of green and magenta light. "HE MUST NOT TAKE THE PENDANT FROM HER NECK!"

I heard the scraping of boots against stone suddenly, footsteps rushing, but I didn't look up to see their source. My eyes were locked on the Shadow Lord's face, my pain worsening as he began to tug at the pendant around my neck. As he did, I felt the beat of my torn-apart heart beginning to weaken, realising that my life force was no longer inside me, but within that dark pendant. It was all that was keeping me alive, and he meant to take it from me.

Morod turned his gaze to the footsteps rushing towards us, his glowing eyes hard and stern as he lifted up his right hand. There came a terrible, thunderous cracking from his greying palm as an invisible force was cast from it at the figures rushing the altar.

I looked up to see his target, watching on helplessly as Fawkner, Ellora, Joran and Carden - who had somehow overcome the effects of his magic - were lifted from their feet. They were cast like ragdolls into the air by the Shadow Lord's dark power and slammed hard into the floor with the heavy sound of bodies hitting stone.

Morod turned from them to face me again, looking down at me as he began to once more take the pendant from my neck. He was literally stealing my life from me as he sneered coldly. I tried to shake my head in protest, but I was weak, all of my strength now being used just to breathe and stay awake.

All I could do was gasp out pathetically: "No... don't..."

The monster who murdered me took the pendant from my neck with the clinking of its chain as it broke free, gazing down at it as its stone began to glow with a terrible blood coloured energy in his grasp. He gave me no final words, no last taunt, simply robbing me of my one chance to survive this.

Ellora had recovered, now in a crouch with her bow ready and lacing an arrow to the string. She fired two arrows in quick succession, both of them certain to hit their mark, but they didn't. The arrows passed through the Shadow Lord as if he were a misty illusion of shadow and smoke, clattering harmlessly to splinter on the stone wall behind him.

There came the snapping of great ancient chains as the five dreaded dragons roared and spread their enormous wings, launching their howls of flame into the air as they were freed. The flash of nightmarish blue and black flame erupted from Ragnarok as his fires engulfed his body, granting him his most terrifying appearance. He roared once again and leaped into the air with the beating of his mammoth wings. He flew up through the great opening in the domed ceiling, his four brothers close behind him, their roars rocking the foundations of that place.

As the violence that had engulfed the room vanished, my eyes lingered on the victorious Shadow Lord as he laughed wickedly. He became a great fog bank of shadow, disappearing as his laughter began to fade into silence.

Then all I felt was pain, struggling to stay alive. Every breath I drew was an agony on its own, my body weakening fast. I could barely concentrate now, my chest shuddering with each wheezing intake of breath.

"Leander..." I heard my name spoken by the voice that I most adored, suddenly aware that he was at my side, tugging at my restraints. "Help me! Someone, help me!"

As Ellora suddenly appeared, I looked to Carden, watching him fumble for a lock pick, panic in his green eyes as he fought the shackles holding my wrists. He freed me, the two of them lifting me from the altar to the ground where Carden cradled me as he slumped to sit, my head in the crook of his arm.

"C...Carden?" I managed to gasp, the pain worse with every attempt I made to move or breathe.

"It's me, Leander," he nodded as he stroked my hair to comfort me, fighting back tears. "I'm here. I've got you."

I choked out: "I... I can't... breathe..."

As Ellora held his shoulder, he looked to the green and brown clad wizard who had come to join us. I glanced up weakly, seeing all of my friends gathered there around me, the room behind them filled only with our allies now.

"Ranzel," Carden implored him. "Help her. Please, help her..."

Ranzel shook his head grievously. "If only I could. Sadly, there is no magic, nor medicine in this world that can save her. Only the Pendant that took her life force gave us any chance of bringing her back from the brink of Azmerath's realm... and Lord Morod has taken it."

Carden turned his eyes back to me, shaking his head as grief took over him. "No... I'm... I'm not letting you go. I won't," he promised me.

"Carden," I managed weakly, struggling to see him clearly. "I... I'm so happy I get to... to see you... again..."

He tried to force a smile. "As am I to see you, my beautiful girl."

I began to sob. "Please... forgive me..."

"Why?" he frowned, confused.

I didn't know how much longer I had left, and I needed to tell him the truth:"I... I was afraid. I was so scared that... that you would not want me... anymore because I was... cursed..."

He frowned even deeper. "Cursed?"

I struggled to nod, falling weaker in his arms, even that small gesture taking all of my effort: "The Shadow Lord... m-made me immortal. When he... he used me to regain... his powers... he took my changing. I couldn't... I couldn't grow old with you..."

He smiled softly at me. "That doesn't matter now. None of it does. I just want to be with you, my beautiful girl. Just you."

I smiled in return, feeling my cooling tears slipping down my cheeks. "I... I love you, Carden."

"I love you, Leander," he pledged in deepest truth. "I will *always* love you."

The pain grew worse, the struggle to breathe harder. I winced and gasped, clutching at his shirt if only to hold onto him and stay in his embrace. My eyes focused behind him, my tears coming faster as I saw the black shape of Death himself appear, beckoning to me with one gauntleted hand. I became afraid, trembling as I finally faced him.

"Carden..." I whimpered through my soft sobs.

"Yes, my love?" he whispered, tears falling from his cheeks.

"I... I can see him," I said softly, shaking as my tears fell fast. "He's frightening... I never knew he would be so frightening..."

"Who? Who scares you?" he asked, clutching me tighter.

I looked into his eyes. "Azmerath..." I began to cry. "I don't... I don't want to go with him. Please, Carden, don't let me go..."

"No..." Carden shook his head, clutching me tighter to him. "No, Leander, stay with me. Stay with me, sweetheart, please."

I couldn't hold on anymore, my breaths falling still, my heart bled dry. I tried to keep my eyes open, but they closed on their own and I felt the last of my life force being drawn away. I couldn't see now, but I felt him holding me.

"No... Leander, no..." he was crying, his words and sobs starting to fade from me.

I wanted to go back, to reach him and stay with him, but I couldn't.

"We have failed her..." Ranzel's voice spoke in the distance, grief stricken as the sobs of my companions came to me in the shadows of death. "Gods... we have failed her..."

I felt everything leaving me, all of my life gone. I was dead, lost to the ones I loved... Lost to Carden... Death was no release. I felt damned as the cold grasp of Azmerath took me from the world.

Then, in the dark I heard Carden speak, but it was different, like it was his thoughts rather than his spoken voice. These were his final words to me, or at least the last words I would hear from him: "*I will find a way to get you back, Leander... I will find a way to save you. This vow I swear...*"

His vow of love was all I had left to hold onto, the last thing I managed to clutch to me as everything else faded into darkness. I began to feel numb, my mind fading, though I tried to fight my way back. My last thought was of him, his words echoing in my head as I began to lose myself to the Beyond.

"*I will find a way to get you back, Leander... I will find a way to save you. This vow I swear...*"

The Story Continues in Book 4...

Pendant of Dragons
The Uncertain Road

Excerpt from The Uncertain Road

~ CARDEN ~

"What do we do?" Tallinn wondered, the look of a frightened woman masking her normally stoic exterior.

"Assemble what forces we can of our Orders," Lord Selwyn stated simply, "and attempt to form some sort of resistance to defend against the Shadow Lord and his Dominion."

"Defend?" Fawkner scoffed incredulously, leaning forward to gain the eyes of all those before him, his expression soured. "There is *no* defence. You speak as if we are a band of rebels seeking to strike against a corrupt king, not the formidable forces we are meant to be."

"Our forces are greatly diminished, Lord Caradoc," Lord Selwyn stated factually, meeting the man's steel coloured gaze. "What Dragon Knights remain are scattered far too few, and what Guardians are seemingly trapped between here and Balganis. The magic circles are all but obliterated and we High Elves cannot stand alone against this threat, even if we could call to the Blackfelds for reinforcement from our Queen. With what forces we yet have, defence is all we can muster without the aid of the Kingdoms of High-Realm."

"What of your kind, Eamnonn?" Fawkner looked to the great Aquari Dragon for hope. "Surely the Dragons can intervene and stop Ragnarok and his brethren. They *are* dragons after all."

Eamnonn shook his head, his fire-coloured eyes dulled by his emotions. "No. I am the only Dragon willing to stand with you beyond Gaspeite and young Amethyst. The others are all cloistered away, hiding from this realm in another we call the Valley. They cannot be counted on to assist."

"Truly," Ellora looked to the great dragon, "are all of your kind hidden away there?"

Eamnonn nodded, sighing a breath that sounded like a deep rumble from his brown and aqua scaled body: "All but one other are in the Valley, but he will not stand with us."

"Of whom do you speak, Eamnonn?" Ranzel asked, leaning on his staff as he looked into the Dragon's eyes.

"Kelapas, the Ice Dragon," Eamnonn replied, turning his face to the Wizard. "You know him well, Ranzel."

"Oh yes," Ranzel nodded with the look of a man who had just heard the name of someone he knew to be of poor reputation. "You're right. Kelapas will not aid us."

"He is too absorbed in his dominion over the Lorgath Pass and the Nartarn'lath Mountains," Eamnonn snarled, shaking his head. "Such possessiveness over a place is unbecoming of one of Dragon Blood."

"Then there is no way to stop Morod and Ragnarok?" I asked, feeling a deep feeling of defeat in my heart.

Xzharn sat back, sighing and shaking his head, his hands together on the table in front of him: "Not now, there isn't. Our only option to defeat Lord Morod was to do so before he could enact his plans on Safferan."

I felt a scowl rising as he spoke, dreading what I knew he was going to say.

Fawkner frowned. "There is nothing then?"

Xzharn looked around at each of us, speaking in his harsh, deep voice: "Keeping the Princess alive past the Lunar Joining was our *only* chance at defeating the Shadow Lord's plans and giving us the way to fight him head on. But we failed. We failed, and now Safferan is but smoke and magma bubbling from the ocean, Ragnarok and his brothers lay waste to our outposts and have weakened us tenfold in less than a week, and Princess Leander, descendent of High-Realm's last great champion, lies dead. All we can hope to do now is stave off utter destruction and find a way to convince others to aid us in this insurmountable fight for the fate of Therras itself."

I glared at him, feeling my hands shaking as I let my arms drop to my sides, my fingers clenching angrily. He sounded accusing and I felt that his gaze was directed at us, the Guardians who had defended her.

Because we were Leander's protectors... Of course he blames us...

"We tried to save her," I defended, thinking more of Tallinn and Fawkner than myself.

"If *you*, young Guardian, had kept your feelings for her *unknown* and remained her protector," Xzharn accused me with a hard, black stare, "then perhaps she would not have been so trusting of the Lost masquerading as you after your little quarrel. Perhaps she would not have been slain if she had not been seeking your attentions so ardently..."

"You accuse my relationship with her as being the reason she was murdered?!" I raged, glaring at him, feeling that side of me I tried to keep hidden deep down in the dark of my soul starting to snap and bay for blood.

"Carden, be calm," Ellora was at my side, trying to ease my anger with her gentle touch as Fawkner and Tallinn both stood from their seats.

"You dare to condemn our love as the reason Morod now wreaks havoc against this world?!" I was close to screaming at the old wizard now, held back only by Fawkner and Ellora.

"My Lord Xzharn," Lord Selwyn spoke up, looking to the Wizard and gesturing to me, "it is not fair to condemn this young man and his love for the girl as the cause of all that we now face. After all, we rested on our laurels in the wake of Aldwyn Draken's passing and did not bolster the city guard around the

Princess' rooms. Even if we had, could we have detected the Lost coming for her with its shape changing powers? I think not."

"Lord Selwyn is right," Ranzel chimed in, standing over the White Wizard. "The Princess is dead not because of her love for this young man, but due to the actions of vile monsters whose very goal was to achieve the destruction of our world. Whether she and Carden shared this bond or not, Morod would still have found a way to reach her and enact his dark plans."

"Perhaps," Xzharn nodded darkly, gazing back at me. "However, this does not excuse the fact that such emotional bonds are dangerous for protectors to have with their charges. It is the very reason the ancient Guardians took vows of celibacy; to prevent this very incident from occurring. It is a rule modern Guardians would do well to endorse."

Tallinn threw him a glare. "Enough! This is making things worse!"

"This infighting serves no one!" Fawkner added, holding me back as I felt the urge to tear the old man's head from his spine.

"Perhaps if such ideals had been maintained to this day," Xzharn continued, clearly pushing further with this subject, "then we would not be facing the dire circumstances we now are."

I shoved away from my companions, slamming my hands so hard down on the table that the section I hit bowed and splintered. I could feel the impulses of my predator deep inside me clawing to reach the surface, making it clear that I was starting to lose my control.

I need my medicine. I'm on the edge of losing myself to it...

I narrowed my eyes at Xzharn, gritting my teeth as I felt the familiar stinging of my gums that came with the changes my body had battled most of my life.

"You are a cold and heartless old man who will never know the touch of a woman's love," I hissed viciously, but quietly at him. "And you are not deserving of it. Do *not* dishonour her like that in front of me again, for it will be the last thing you do."

There was no need to wait for a response from him or any of the others in the room. I shoved away from the table, accidentally shifting the entire thing several inches towards the Wizard as I moved.

I slipped past Fawkner, Ellora and Tallinn, storming from the chamber and rushing down the staircase towards the ground floor of the Broken Towers. As I strode past High Elf guards, Dragon Knights and Guardians, I felt my rage starting to overwhelm me and I had to just keep moving or else risk exploding.

Suddenly, there came two sets of running footfalls from behind me, but I didn't turn.

"Carden!" Tallinn called out to me. "Carden, wait!"

I stopped, turning slowly to gaze back at her and Fawkner as they jogged up to me. The two of them slowed to a walk as they travelled the last few feet, concern on their faces.

"Carden, are you alright?" she asked, her blonde hair falling around her shoulders as she came to a stop.

"That musty old bastard had no right to talk about her like that!" I erupted, fighting the angry tears that I felt. "He had no right to tarnish what we shared in such a malicious way!"

"No, you're right, he didn't," Fawkner agreed, speaking with a calmness I couldn't muster. "He's scared, Carden. They all are."

"And can you truly blame them?" Tallinn looked to me with soft eyes. "Gods, we're all scared, and we all miss her."

"No one as much as me," I growled, looking down at their feet.

"You are her lover," Fawkner granted, touching my shoulder gently. "And you were together after two years apart for only the briefest of times. Not one of us believes that to be fair. But you cannot allow what was said back there to colour your actions now."

I looked up at him sadly. "I'd say that's too late, but for the fact that I had already decided what I'm going to do back at Safferan as she died in my arms."

"What do you mean when you say what you're going to do?" Tallinn looked uneasy at my words.

I took a deep breath, closing my eyes. I plunged my hand into my shirt and wrenched my Guardian medallion from my neck, the chain snapping at the force of my pull. I glared down at the emblem of the shield and two swords with disdain, then looked to my two friends coldly.

"I'm done," I said icily, clutching it in my hand, squeezing it as if to break it. "I am done being a Guardian!"

Tallinn shook her head. "No, brother, you're just upset..."

"I am not your brother, Tallinn," I said firmly, staring down at her. "I am and will always be your friend, but I am no longer your fellow Guardian."

I took my sword from my belt, casting it to the floor and slid out of my black and silver Guardian over tunic and cloak. I threw it down unceremoniously, left only with my shirt, pants and belt.

"I rescind my oath and make a new one," I said firmly, still holding the medallion. "I am a Guardian of High-Realm no longer, the oath I made when I joined the Order no longer in my heart as truth. I have but one truth: I love her, and I will do anything to get her back," with that said, I threw the medallion, hearing it clatter to the black stone floor with several resounding thuds before laying still.

"Carden..." Tallinn tried.

"I am sorry, Tallinn," I said sternly, throwing off my Guardian bracers to join my other Order apparel, "but there is no convincing me otherwise. I am through with the Guardian Order."

It hurt me to see Tallinn - my sister in oath - so wounded by my actions and decision, but my mind was made up. Being a Guardian no longer had any meaning for me.

"Why?" she asked, desperate to understand. "Why are you doing this?"

I looked back to her sadly, shrugging widely. "She's dead. It was my duty to protect her. I failed. It's as simple as that."

I turned and walked away, once again traversing the great staircase from the towers down towards Silvervale proper as the unending supernatural storm continued to rage on above. The sky seemed like a mirror for the storms that swirled and battered within my broken heart, a physical commentary on my position and emotion now. My soul was in turmoil and I had no way to calm it without Leander, so I didn't even deem it worthy to try...

Other titles by **K. Isabella Frost**

Pendant of Dragons: The Aldrich Legacy (Book 1)
Pendant of Dragons: Custodians of the Past (Book 2)

Visit whitelightshop.com

White Light PUBLISHING